The Gernsback Awards 1926

Volume I

Introduction by Forrest J Ackerman
Illustrations by Frank R. Paul

WILDSIDE PRESS

The Gernsback Awards Vol. 1, 1926

Published by

Wildside Press, LLC

P.O. Box 301

Holicong, PA 18928-0301 USA

www.wildsidepress.com

Wildside Press Edition: MMIII

Dedication

This First Volume in
the Gernsback Awards Series
is gratefully dedicated
to the memories of
those Sense-of-Wonderful Pioneers
Hugo Gernsback
and
Frank R. Paul
and to that
Foresighted Triangle
Tom Woods
Sylvia Woods
Mary Gernsback
who,
implemented by
First Fandom,
have brought forth This Book
from The Realm of Unwrought Things
— Forrest J Ackerman

Hugo Gernsback

Frank R. Paul

Table of Contents

All illustrations by Frank R. Paul
except "The Metal Giants"
by Joseph Dustin

"Retroactive Hugos"
by
Forrest J Ackerman

FOR YEARS both readers of science fiction and professionals in the field have expressed regret that it took so long to get around to honoring the movers and shakers, the leaders and trendmakers, the stellar creative talents of the genre.

No trophies, plaques or even scrolls for the scriveners, editors, artists and periodicals of the seminal decades.

"What a shame that the Achievement Awards [Hugos] weren't inaugurated before 1953 so that the pioneers and Golden Years authors et al could have been recognized and rewarded."

Like the weather, "retroactive Hugos" were frequently discussed but nothing was done to materialize them out of the Cummings-Wright Realm of Unwrought Things.

Finally, 4 years ago, I took the unicorn by the horn and contacted Hugo Gernsback's widow with the proposition that she permit me to rectify this egregious (I learned the word from an early bird in scientifiction, Bob Olsen) oversight. "I have no intention," I informed her, "of putting myself on a pedestal, of capitalizing on my calling card as Mr. Science Fiction to declare winners by fiat or ukase; the organization exists uniquely qualified to judge the values of the early works and workers, and it is the members of this group whose judgment I shall solicit and abide by."

Mary Gernsback (bless her) responded enthusiastically with her approval for the project--and put the cherry on the whipcream by gifting me with Hugo Gernsback's personal Hugo for my Science Fiction Museum. In June 1982 I was able to show it to millions on the *Merv Griffin* TV show.

So why (I telepath your mind) haven't you held this volume in your hands several years earlier? I won't enumerate the publishers who *could* have brought you the series as far back as 1979 but were negative in their reactions to my proposal. They lacked vision, business acumen, sense of wonder, spirit of history, call it what you will, but I am not here to criticize or embarras them; instead, I invite you to join me in expressing gratitude at this point to an amiable android, Tom 124C4U (One To ForeSee For You) [son of Ralph 124C41], his last name being Woods, constituting the publishing company known as Triton Books.

The people (I call them people purposely, not persons, for they are of the race of slans)--the people who voted for the stories are members of what is called First Fandom. To be a member of FF you must offer palpable proof that you were active in the science fiction field prior to the first World Science Fiction Convention (Nycon) in 1939. Among the members of First Fandom are such distinguished individuals as Isaac Asimov, Robert Bloch, L. Sprague de Camp, A.E. van Vogt, Philip José Farmer, Raymond Z. Gallun, H.L. Gold, Sam Moskowitz, Lester del Rey, Frederik Pohl, David A. Kyle, Lloyd Arthur Eshbach, Bob (Wilson) Tucker, Walt Liebscher, William

i

Crawford, Gerry de la Ree, Julius Schwartz, Jack Speer, Robert A.W. Lowndes, Kenneth F. Slater (England's inheritor of the First Hugo), Aubrey MacDermott ("the first fan"), Robert A. Madle, Donald A. Wollheim and others, most of whom will very likely be represented in future volumes with Introductions and--very possibly!--winning works.

On 19 February 1982 (it would have been the 59th birthday of my only brother, Alden Lorraine Ackerman, had he, not yet quite 21, not been killed New Years Day 1945 in World War 2's Battle of the Bulge in Belgium)--on 19 Feb 82, I addressed xopies (Xeroxed copies) of a letter to my "Dear Fellow Dinosaurs". A 2-page letter, the gist of which was this:

From 1953 futureward the Science Fiction Achievement Awards continue to be known as the HUGOS; from 1926 till the final volume covering the missing years, they're THE GERNSBACK AWARDS. "I have been appalled by the chutzpah of one writer who has had the nerve to tell all the voters where they went wrong in previous years and what works *should* have won the Hugos--in his opinion. Were it possible to assemble a Blue Ribbon Committee of Asimov, Boucher, Carr, Conklin, del Rey, Derleth, Greenberg, Knight, Miller, Moskowitz, Saha, Wollheim and Yours Sciencerely, *such* a clutch of critics might be considered to turn back the clock and rewrite Hugo history. But one man--?! Not even Hugo Gernsback!"

In 3 respects I have chosen to be arbitrary, not, I feel, as an intransigent tyrant but as a benevolent Dictator. I have opted to establish the Categories as Best Short Story (up to 7500 words), Medium Length 7500 to 15000, and Long from 15000 to 35000. I have elected, as anthologist, to present not only the Award Winner but the 2 runnersup. And, lastly, rather than follow strict chronological order--1926, 1927, 1928, etc.--I have deemed it more desirable to produce volumes with 10 year intervals between them: 1926, 1936, 1946; 1927, 1937, 1947; etc. None of the voters expressed dissatisfaction with my arbitrary, well-meant decisions.

To bring you the best "scientifiction" stories of 1926 (the ubiquitous term "science fiction" did not exist till Hugo Gernsback himself first expressed it in print in 1929), I considered tales in *Adventure, Amazing Stories, Argosy, Blue Book, Canadian Magazine, Complete Stories, Everybody's, Flynn's, Ghost Stories, Munsey's, Popular, Saturday Evening Post, Science & Invention* and *Weird Tales.* I'll need the shades of Gernsback, Boucher, Campbell, Conklin, Gnaedinger, Miller, "Doc" Smith, Verne, Wells, Shelley, Poe et al to assist me when we hit the late 40s or early 50s, for I seem to recall that around that fecund period there was one mad month when there were a humungous 49 *fantasy magazines* on the market!

The way the voting works is that I go to my archives and pore over the pages of all the periodicals of the year involved, refreshing my memory, and then I list all the stories, magazines, editors and artists I feel any reasonable individual would consider worth considering. Out of all the reminder stories I listed, there was only one that garnered no votes, and, although they were encouraged, there were very few write-ins for personal favorites.

In the course of creating the Awards some interesting correspondence was received, some of which I will quote.

"I hope you get enough response to make the choices reasonably close to the consensus of opinion. ('Consensus of opinion' is usually redundant; but not, I think, when it's contrasted with votes actually cast.) When the field for choice is as manageably small as it was in the early days, the results ought to be better informed than those for current Hugos.

"A point that occurs to me is that the best editor and best magazine are duplications of the same decision. Unless one wants to say that, like Robert E. Lee, the editor who did the best with what he had to work with (e.g., Hornig) deserves the Gernsback even if his magazine doesn't."—Jack F Speer. [It was no contest in '26, of course, for Gernsback & *Amazing*, but, jumping ahead a couple lustrums, there were 50 votes for Best Editor and 53 for the magazine he edited, which would seem to prove your point, although given another decade, 1946, Best Editor has received 60 votes but the magazine he edited only 45 (nevertheless the winner). Guess it can't hurt to let the voters vote on both.]

"Your Gernsback Award selections present a difficult task, indeed! It is a monumental task for you and a somewhat lesser task for those members of First Fandom who are sending in their selections. I know that many of us will be influenced by nostalgia, remembering the sheer enjoyment we received in first reading a story—which may or may not be as it should.

"In the last couple of decades my tastes have swung a bit away from the 'off this world' to material which is, perhaps, less science-oriented—though nonetheless fantasy. Therefore, I have gone to particular steps, especially in that 1926 period (the nostalgia slips through just a bit in 1946—I confess to not having read 'Pattern for Conquest' or 'The Toymaker' for some 20 years) to avoid nostalgia at least in part. Those 1926 stories are great favorites of mine today. This may be a bit blasphemous, since the awards are called the 'Gernsback Awards'; but you did state that *Adventure, Argosy, Blue Book* and others had been considered by you. I have done likewise."-- Donald M. Grant, publisher of handsome bound volumes by Robert E. Howard, Catherine L. Moore and many more. Don Grant's list for 1926 is worth noting in this preface because it was totally different from the rest. Basically, in my analysis, it differed because of a misinterpretation in the intent of the "Gernsbacks". They do *not* include fantasyarns. Hence, the Merrittale "The Woman of the Wood" (legend has it, the most popular piece of fiction ever published during *Weird Tales'* long run of 31 years), was not acceptable as a contender because it was not science fiction. *There is a very strong possibility*, if the reception accorded the Gernsback volumes warrants it, that the publishers will contract for my companion project, starting in 1923 with the first *Weird Tales*, notably the Merritt Awards (Awards of Merit!) for the fantasy field, patterned after the Gernsbacks.

In the Medium length Donald Grant chose "Durandal" by Harold Lamb from *Adventure*, mentioning: "Last week I had a young editor write me: 'Simply brilliant! First time I've read the story—*it is the foundation of modern heroic fantasy!*'" LONG: "The Messenger of Destiny" by Talbot Mundy, one of the Tros series, again from *Adventure*. "Mystic, however historic, and within the bounds of fantasy." NOVEL: "The Devil's Guard" (book version) by Talbot Mundy. "This appeared in *Adventure* as 'Ramsden' in 1926." EDITOR: "Blasphemy, but how can I consider anyone other than

ARTHUR SULLIVANT HOFFMAN after picking 4 tales from *Adventure*—shutting out all other magazines? Damn; I'm not trying to be confusing, and I'm not trying to underrate Hugo Gernsback. Simply, I consider ASH the greatest magazine editor; ever."

Voter Samuel A. Peeples, a very knowledgable man when it came to dates, would not accept 6 stories as viable choices because he argued (and rightly so) they were not vintage 1926. The proper dates, he pointed out, were "The Diamond Lens", 1860s; "The Moon Metal" (1900—*Argosy*); "A Columbus of Space" (1911); "The Island of Dr. Moreau" (1896); Off on a Comet (1878—"right title, 'Hector Servadac'"); and "A Trip to the Center of the Earth" ("'Journey'—not 'Trip'—1874"). I overruled him, arguing that for the majority of the voters, most of whom were teenagers if not preteens in 1926, all those stories were being seen and read for the *firstime*. Most of the earliest stories were reprints and if we were too much purists we wouldn't have anything left to vote on. Peeples was another of those persons who considered "Woman of the Wood" the best short story of 1926 (but it was fantasy, not scientifiction), and "The Ship of Ishtar" a tie with Burroughs' "Moon Maid" for the best sf novel (but again, fantasy—a sure contender for a Merritt Award).

Finally, oldtime fan John H. Hull wrote, along with his vote tally: "I am sure all Fellow Dinosaurs thank you. I know I do. I am pleased by the "Retroactive Hugos" project. I know it will be a work of Love for you and all who help you on it. I would not like to try to pick the best stories from the years of '26 to '46 for as I reread them all over I find no reason to be too critical on any. There are always the best favorites and the worst story in any group of stories printed. Different Strokes for Different Folks. Best of Luck. I am sure the best of stories will be picked."

THE FIRST FANDOM MEMBERS
WHO VOTED ON THE NOMINATIONS WERE

CLIFTON AMSBURY	JEAN ENGEL
LESTER ANDERSON	THEODORE H. ENGEL
F. LEE BALDWIN	LLOYD ARTHUR ESHBACH
JOHN V. BALTADONIS	PHILIP JOSE FARMER
ALLEN BARTLETT	JOHN A. FLORY
SAM J. BASHAM, JR.	MIKE FOGARIS
RAY E. BEAM	RICHARD A. FRANK
CLAIRE BECK	DONALD FRANSON
ARDEN R. BENSON	RAYMOND Z. GALLUN
ROBERT BLOCH	DONALD M. GRANT
REDD BOGGS	PAUL G. HERKART
PHILIP N. BRIDGES	ROSEMARY HICKEY
JOHN BRISTON	LYNN A. HICKMAN
JOHN BRUDY	RUSSELL J. HODGKINS
BILL CRAWFORD	ALLAN HOWARD
R. CREIGHTON BUCK	JOHN H. HULL
GERRY DE LA REE	CLARENCE HYDE
MORRIS DOLLENS	BEN P. INDICK
J.C. DUNCAN JR.	TERRY JEEVES

VIRGINIA KIDD
WALT LIEBSCHER
ROBERT A.W. LOWNDES
ROY LAVENDER
AUBREY M. MACDERMOTT
ROBERT A. MADLE
MARY M. MARTIN MD
RICHARD H. MINTER
SAMUEL A. PEEPLES
ROBERT C. PETERSEN
FREDERIK POHL
GENE RAYMER
NICHOLAS RINGELBERG
JACK ROBINS
AL ROGERS

JOHN FLINT ROY
ARTHUR W. SAHA
JULIUS SCHWARTZ
LARRY T. SHAW
KENNETH SLATER
JACK F. SPEER
ROY TACKETT
DALE TARR
VERNA SMITH TRESTRAIL
BOB TUCKER
A.E. VAN VOGT
ART WIDNER
EDWARD WOOD
and
FORREST J ACKERMAN

The Best Magazine was:
AMAZING STORIES
The Best Editor was:
HUGO GERNSBACK
The Best Artist was:
FRANK R. PAUL
The Best Novel was:
THE MOON MAID
By Edgar Rice Burroughs

Stop Press! It is rare that linotypists and proofreaders become excited over a manuscript they are processing and the phenomenon is doubly significant because the individuals involved are not science fiction buffs. It is amazing and gratifying to report the enthusiasm generated for this volume by the "mundanes" working on it. Proof that the imaginations of the early authors still command the attention today of generations unborn when the pioneers literally *penned* many of their thrilling wonder stories before the universal auctorial use of typewriters and wordprocessors. Wells of wonder still well up from the short stories of H.G. Wells; names little-known today like Wertenbaker, Serviss, Verrill, O'Brien demonstrate they still have "it".

Here is a volume, selected by a blue ribbon panel of experts, destined to become a cornerstone in libraries and colleges, a milestone in readers' and fans' collections.

That Old (Gerns)Back Magic Lives!

What I wish for myself now is that I live till at least 74, retain my faculties and my energy and complete the job of presenting posterity with the complete Gernsback Awards. If, before that time, I should go to my reward (if any), I have prepared for the Publisher a recommended list of "dinosaurs" to carry on anthologizing for this Ackersaurus.

I commend you now to the shades of the Great Departed to entertain you.

—FJA: 124E41

v

SHORT

First Place: **The Coming of the Ice**   G. Peyton Wertenbaker

This powerful and tragic story by the author of "The Man from the Atom" tells of a man who acquired terrestial immortality—tells of a world many centuries hence—a time when everything is changed. This one man remains as a relic of the 20th century. He is alone with strangely developed human beings, the product of ages of evolution. Climatic changes are taking place. The world begins to grow cold. New York is almost in the Artic region and Italy is covered with snow all the year around. In spite of their enormous intellectual development, all human beings must perish. Our hero alone can withstand the intense cold. He wanted eternal life and he got it—eternal life, purely intellectual. What does he do with all his years? And how does he enjoy them? Read this powerful story.   Hugo Gernsback—1926

Second Place: **The Empire of the Ants**   H.G. Wells

A well-known entomologist once made the remark that if the insect world, instead of fighting each other, should suddenly decide to fight the human race, we should all soon be annihilated. We know the tremendous power for organization among the ants, and we also know that they have reached a pretty high stage of civilization. For one thing, they seem to be able to govern themselves much better than we can ourselves. In the tropical countries there are many species of giant and poisonous ants existing even now, and they are well known for their ravages and for their destructive power. We can only wish that the brilliant story penned here by our famous author will never come true.   Hugo Gernsback—1926

Third Place: **The Crystal Egg**   H.G. Wells

Here is a tremendous story by one of the greatest living scientifiction writers. Here is a story that will keep you guessing to the end—a story which will recur to your mind many years hence. Mr. Wells' imagination is not running loose—he knows his science—and while the story at first glance may seem entirely too fantastic, no one knows but that it may, 5,000 years from now be quite tame and of every day occurrence.

If a civilization on another world were sometime to communicate with us, there might be thousands of methods, to us undreamt of, by which this could be achieved. The crystal egg method which Mr. Wells uses in this story may be one of them. We who are accustomed to radio and who can bring voices out of the thin air with a pocket radio receptor, will not think that the crystal egg is impossible of fulfillment at some future date.

We recommmend this amazing story to you.   Hugo Gernsback—1926

Special Pioneer Award: **The Eggs from**

Lake Tanganyika   **Curt Siodmak**

We consider this extraordinary story a classic, and certainly the best scientificion story so far for 1926.

How large can insects grow? Is there any limit to their size? Frankly, no one knows. We have almost microscopically small flies, and in some of the tropical countries we have some almost as large as the fist. Is it possible to have still larger flies, and could monstrous flies such as are depicted in this story, be bred at some future date? The author of this brilliant tale evidently thinks so.

Anyway, we trust he is mistaken, as we should not like to meet such monsters. The science of entomology presented in this story is excellent, and will arouse your imagination.   Hugo Gernsback—1926

1

The COMING of the ICE
~ By G. Peyton Wertenbaker ~

t is strange to be alone, and so cold. To be the last man on earth ....

The snow drives silently about me, ceaselessly, drearily. And I am isolated in this tiny white, indistinguishable corner of a blurred world, surely the loneliest creature in the universe. How many thousands of years is it since I last knew the true companionship? For a long time I have been lonely, but there were people, creatures of flesh and blood. Now they are gone. Now I have not even the stars to keep me company, for they are all lost in an infinity of snow and twilight above, as the earth is lost in its grey infinity here below.

If only I could know how long it has been since first I was imprisoned upon the earth. It cannot matter now. And yet some vague dissatisfaction, some faint instinct, asks over and over in my throbbing ears: What year? What year?

It was in the year 1930 that the great thing began in my life. There was then a very great man who performed operations upon his fellows to compose their vitals—we called such men surgeons. John Granden wore the title "Sir" before his name, in indication of nobility by birth according to the prevailing standards in England. But surgery was only a hobby of Sir John's, if I must be precise, for, while he had achieved an enormous reputation as a surgeon, he always felt that his real work lay in the experimental end of his profession. He was, in a way, a dreamer, but a dreamer who could make his dreams come true.

I was a very close friend of Sir John's. In fact, we shared the same apartments in London. I have never forgotten that day when he first mentioned to me his momentous discovery. I had just come in from a long sleigh-ride in the country with Alice, and I was seated drowsily in the window-seat, writing idly in my mind a description of the wind and the snow and the gray twilight of the evening. It is strange, is it not, that my tale should begin and end with the snow and the twilight.

Sir John opened suddenly a door at one end of the room and came hurrying across to another door. He looked at me, grinning rather like a triumphant maniac.

"It's coming!" he cried, without pausing, "I've almost got it!" I smiled at him: he looked very ludicrous at that moment.

"What have you got?" I asked.

"Good Lord, man, the Secret—the Secret!" And then he was gone again, the door closing upon his victorious cry, "The Secret!"

I was, of course, amused. But I was also very much interested. I knew Sir John well enough to realize that, however amazing his appearance might be, there would be nothing absurd about his "Secret"—whatever it was. But it was useless to speculate. I could only hope for enlightenment at dinner. So I immersed myself in one of the surgeons' volumes from his fine Library of Imagination, and waited.

I think the book was one of Mr. H. G. Wells', probably "The Sleeper Awakes," or some other of his brilliant fantasies and predictions, for I was in a mood conducive to belief in almost anything when, later, we sat down together across the table. I only wish I could give some idea of the atmosphere that permeated our apartments, the reality it lent to whatever was vast and amazing and strange. You could then, whoever you are, understand a little the ease with which I accepted Sir John's new discovery.

He began to explain it to me at once, as though he could keep it to himself no longer.

"Did you think I had gone mad, Dennell?" he asked. "I quite wonder that I haven't. Why, I have been studying for many years—for most of my life—on this problem. And, suddenly, I have solved it! Or, rather, I am afraid I have solved another one much greater."

"Tell me about it," I suggested. "But for God's sake don't be technical." He smiled.

"Right," he said. Then he paused. "Dennell, it's *magnificent!* It will change the whole social order of the world. It will change everything that is in the world". His eyes held mine suddenly with the fatality of an hypnotist's. "Dennell, it is the Secret of Eternal Life," he said.

"Good Lord, Sir John!" I cried, half inclined to laugh.

"I mean it," he said. "You know I have spent most of my life studying the processes of birth, trying to find out precisely what went on in the whole history of conception."

"You have found out?"

"No, that is just what amuses me. I have discovered something else without knowing yet what causes either process.

"I don't want to be technical, and I know very little of what actually takes place myself. But I can try to give you some idea of it."

.. It is thousands, perhaps millions of years since Sir John explained to me. What little I understood at the time I may have forgotten since. Yet I try to reproduce what I can of his theory.

"In my study of the processes of birth," he began, "I discovered the rudiments of an action which takes place in the bodies of both men and women. There are certain properties in the foods we eat that remain in the body for the reproduction of life, two distinct Essences, so to speak, of which one is retained by the woman, another by the man. It is the union of these two properties that, of course, creates the child.

"Now, I made a slight mistake one day in experimenting with a guinea-pig, and I re-arranged certain organs which I need not describe so that I thought I had completely messed up the poor creatures abdomen. It lived, however, and I laid it aside. It was some years later that I happened to notice it again. It had not given birth to any young, but I was amazed to note that it had apparently grown no older: it seemed precisely in the same state of growth in which I had left it.

"From that I built up. I re-examined the guinea-pig, and observed it carefully. I need not detail my studies. But in the end I found that my 'mistake' had in reality been a momentous discovery. I found that I had only to close certain organs, to re-arrange certain ducts, and to open certain dormant organs, and, *mirabile dictu*, the whole process of reproduction was changed.

"You have heard, of course, that our bodies are continually changing, hour by hour, minute by minute, so that every few years we have been literally reborn. Some such principle as this seems to operate in reproduction, except that, instead of the old body being replaced by the new, and in its form, approximately, the new body is created apart from it. It is the creation of children that causes us to die, it would seem, because if this activity is, so to speak, dammed up or turned aside into new channels, the reproduction operates on the old body, renewing it continually. It is very obscure and very absurd, is it not? But the most absurd part of it is that it is true. Whatever the true explanation may be, the fact remains that the operation can be done, that it actually prolongs life indefinitely, and that I alone know the secret."

Sir John told me a very great deal more, but, after all, I think it amounted to little more than this. It would be impossible for me to express the great hold his discovery took upon my mind the moment he recounted it. From the very first, under the spell of his personality, I believed, and I knew he was speaking the truth. And it opened up before me new vistas. I began to see myself become suddenly eternal, never again to know the fear of death. I could see myself storing up, century after century, an amplitude of wisdom and experience that would make me truly a god.

"Sir John!" I cried, long before he was finished, "You must perform that operation on me!"

"But, Dennell, you are too hasty. You must not put yourself so rashly into my hands."

"You have perfected the operation, haven't you?"

"That is true," he said.

"You must try it out on somebody, must you not?"

"Yes, of course. And yet—somehow, Dennell, I am afraid. I cannot help feeling that man is not yet prepared for such a vast thing. There are sacrifices. One must give up love and all sensual pleasure. This operation not only takes away the mere fact of reproduction, but it deprives one of all the things that go with sex, all love, all sense of beauty, all feeling for poetry and the arts. It leaves only the few emotions, selfish emotions, that are necessary to self-preservation. Do you not see? One becomes an intellect, nothing more—a cold apotheosis of reason. And I, for one, cannot face such a thing calmly."

"But, Sir John, like many fears, it is largely horrible in the foresight. After you have changed your nature you cannot regret it. What you are would be as horrible an idea to you afterwards as the thought of what you will be seems now."

"True, true. I know it. But it is hard to face, nevertheless."

"I am not afraid to face it," I said, a little boastfully.

"You do not understand it, Dennell, I am afraid. And I wonder whether you or I or any of us on this earth are ready for such a step. After all, to make a race deathless, one should be sure it is a perfect race."

"Sir John," I said, "it is not you who have to face this, nor any one else in the world till you are ready. But I am firmly resolved, and I demand it of you as my friend."

Well, we argued much further, but in the end I won. Sir John promised to perform the operation three days later.

... But do you perceive now what I had forgotten during all that discussion, the one thing I had thought I could never forget so long as I lived, not even for an instant? It was my love for Alice—I had forgotten that!

I cannot write here all the infinity of emotions I experienced later, when, with Alice in my arms, it suddenly came upon me what I had done. Ages ago—I have forgotten how to feel. I could name now a thousand feelings I used to have, but I can no longer even understand them. For only the heart can understand the heart, and the intellect only the intellect.

With Alice in my arms, I told the whole story. It was she who, with her quick instinct, grasped what I had never noticed.

6

"But Carl!" she cried, "Don't you see?—It will mean that we can never be married!" And, for the first time, I understood. If only I could re-capture some conception of that love! I have always known, since the last shred of comprehension slipped from me, that I lost something very wonderful when I lost love. But what does it matter? I lost Alice too, and I suppose I could not have known love again without her.

We were very sad and very tragic that night. For hours and hours we argued the question over. But I felt somewhat that I was inextricably caught in my fate, that I could not retreat now from my resolve. I was, perhaps, very school-boyish, but I felt that it would be cowardice to back out now. But it was Alice again who perceived a final aspect of the matter.

"Carl," she said to me, her lips very close to mine, "it need not come between our love. After all, ours would be a poor sort of love if it were not more of the mind than of the flesh. We shall remain lovers, but we shall forget mere carnal desire. I shall submit to that operation too!"

And I could not shake her from her resolve. I would speak of danger that I could not let her face. But, after the fashion of women, she disarmed me with the accusation that I did not love her, that I did not want her love, that I was trying to escape from love. What answer had I for that, but that I loved her and would do anything in the world not to lose her?

I have wondered sometimes since whether we might have known the love of the mind. Is love something entirely of the flesh, something created by an ironic God merely to propagate His race? Or can there be love without emotion, love without passion—love between two cold intellects? I do not know. I did not ask then. I accepted anything that would make our way more easy.

There is no need to draw out the tale. Already my hand wavers, and my time grows short. Soon there will be no more of me, no more of my tale—no more of Mankind. There will be only the snow, and the ice, and the cold ....

Three days later I entered Sir John's Hospital, with Alice on my arm. All my affairs—and they were few enough—were in order. I had insisted that Alice wait until I had come safely through the operation, before she submitted to it. I had been carefully starved for two days, and I was lost in an unreal world of white walls and white clothes and white lights, drunk with my dreams of the future. When I was wheeled into the operating room on the long, hard table, for a moment it shown with brilliant distinctness, a neat, methodical white chamber, tall and more or less circular. Then I was beneath

7

the glare of soft white lights, and the room faded into a misty vagueness from which little steel rays flashed and quivered from silvery cold instruments. For a moment our hands, Sir John's and mine, gripped, and we were saying good-bye—for a little while—in the way men say these things. Then I felt the warm touch of Alice's lips upon mine, and I felt sudden painful things that I cannot describe, that I could not have described then. For a moment I felt that I must rise and cry out that I could not do it. But the feeling passed, and I was passive.

Something was pressed about my mouth and nose, something with an etherial smell. Staring eyes swam about me from behind their white masks. I struggled instinctively, but in vain—I was held securely. Infinitesimal points of light began to wave back and forth on a pitch-black background; a great hollow buzzing echoed in my head. My head seemed suddenly to have become all throat, a great, cavernous, empty throat in which sounds and lights were mingled together, in a swift rhythm, approaching, receding eternally. Then, I think, there were dreams. But I have forgotten them ....

I began to emerge from the effect of the ether. Everything was dim, but I could perceive Alice beside me, and Sir John.

"Bravely done!" Sir John was saying, and Alice, too, was saying something, but I cannot remember what. For a long while we talked, I speaking the nonsense of those who are coming out from under ether, they teasing me a little solemnly. But after a little while I became aware of the fact that they were about to leave. Suddenly, God knows why, I knew that they must not leave. Something cried in the back of my head that they *must* stay—one cannot explain these things, except by after events. I began to press them to remain, but they smiled and said they must get their dinner. I commanded them not to go; but they spoke kindly and said they would be back before long. I think I even wept a little, like a child, but Sir John said something to the nurse, who began to reason with me firmly. And then they were gone, and somehow I was asleep ...

When I awoke again, my head was fairly clear, but there was an abominable reek of ether all about me. The moment I opened my eyes, I felt that something had happened. I asked for Sir John and for Alice. I saw a swift, curious look that I could not interpret come over the face of the nurse, then she was calm again, her countenance impassive. She reassured me in quick meaningless phrases, and told me to sleep. But I could not sleep: I was absolutely sure that something had happened to them, to my friend and to the woman I loved. Yet all my insistence profited me nothing, for the nurses were a silent lot. Finally, I think, they must have given me a sleeping potion of some sort, for I fell asleep again.

For two days, two endless, chaotic days, I saw nothing of either of them, Alice or Sir John. I became more and more agitated, the nurse more and more taciturn. She would only say that they had gone away for a day or two.

And then, on the third day, I found out. They thought I was asleep. The night nurse had just come in to relieve the other.

"Has he been asking about them again?" she asked.

"Yes, poor fellow. I have hardly managed to keep him quiet."

"It is going to be very hard to tell him."

"We will have to keep it from him until he is recovered fully." There was a long pause, and I could hardly control my labored breathing.

"How sudden it was!" one of them said. "To be killed like that—" I heard no more, for I lept suddenly up in bed, crying out.

"Quick! For God's sake, tell me what has happened!" I jumped to the floor and seized one of them by the collar. She was horrified. I shook her with a superhuman strength.

"Tell me!" I shouted, "Tell me—Or I'll—!" She told me—what else could she do.

"They were killed in an accident," she gasped, "in a taxi—a collision—the Strand—!" And at that moment a crowd of nurses and attendants arrived, called by the other frantic woman, and they put me to bed again.

I have no memory of the next few days. I was in delirium, and I was never told what I said during my ravings. Nor can I express the feelings I was saturated with when at last I regained my mind again. Between my old emotions and any attempt to put them into words, or even to remember them, lies always that insurmountable wall of my Change. I cannot understand what I must have felt, I cannot express it.

I only know that for weeks I was sunk in a misery beyond any misery I had ever imagined before. The two only friends I had on earth were gone to me. I was left alone. And, for the first time, I began to see before me all these endless years that would be the same, dull, lonely.

Yet I recovered. I could feel each day the growth of a strange new vigour in my limbs, a vast force that was something tangibly expressive of eternal life. Slowly my anguish began to die. After a week more, I began to understand how my emotions were leaving me, how love and beauty and everything of which poetry was made—how all this was going. I could not bear the thought at first. I would look at the golden sunlight and the blue shadow of the wind, and I would say,

"God! How beautiful!" And the words would echo meaninglessly in my ears. Or I would remember Alice's face, that face I had once loved so inextinguishably, and I would weep and clutch my forehead, and clench my fists, crying,

"Oh God, how can I live without her!" Yet there would be a little strange fancy in my head at the same moment, saying,

"Who is this Alice? You know no such person." And truly I would wonder whether she had ever existed.

So, slowly, the old emotions were shed away from me, and I began to joy in a corresponding growth of my mental perceptions. I began to toy idly with mathematical formulae I had forgotten years ago, in the same fashion that a poet toys with a word and its shades of meaning. I would look at everything with new, seeing eyes, new perception, and I would understand things I had never understood before, because formerly my emotions had always occupied me more than my thoughts.

And so the weeks went by, until, one day, I was well.

... What, after all, is the use of this chronicle? Surely there will never be men to read it. I have heard them say that the snow will never go. I will be buried, it will be buried with me; and it will be the end of us both. Yet, somehow, it eases my weary soul a little to write ....

Need I say that I lived, thereafter, many thousands of thousands of years, until this day? I cannot detail that life. It is a long round of new, fantastic impressions, coming dream-like, one after another, melting into each other. In looking back, as in looking back upon dreams, I seem to recall only a few isolated periods clearly; and it seems that my imagination must have filled in the swift movement between episodes. I think now, of necessity, in terms of centuries and milleniums, rather than days and months .... The snow blows terribly about my little fire, and I know it will soon gather courage to quench us both ....

Years passed, at first with a sort of clear wonder. I watched things that took place everywhere in the world. I studied. The other students were much amazed to see me, a man of thirty odd, coming back to college.

"But Judas, Dennel, you've already got your Ph.D! What more do you want?" So they would all ask me. And I would reply;

"I want an M.D. and an F.R.C.S." I didn't tell them that I wanted degrees in Law, too, and in Biology and Chemistry, in Architecture and Engineering, in Psychology and Philosophy. Even so, I believe they thought me mad. But poor fools! I would think. They can hardly realize that I have all of eternity before me for study.

I went to school for many decades. I would pass from University to University, leisurely gathering all the fruits of every subject I took up, revelling in study as no student revelled ever before. There was no need of hurry in my life, no fear of death too soon. There was a magnificence of vigour in my body, and a magnificence of vision and clarity in my brain. I felt myself a super-man. I had only to go on storing up wisdom until the day should come when all knowledge of the world was mine, and then I could command the world. I had no need for hurry. O vast life! How I gloried in my eternity! And how little good it has ever done me, by the irony of God.

For several centuries, changing my name and passing from place to place, I continued my studies. I had no consciousness of monotony, for, to the intellect, monotony cannot exist: it was one of those emotions I had left behind. One day, however, in the year 2132, a great discovery was made by a man called Zarentzov. It had to do with the curvature of space, quite changing the conceptions that we had all followed since Einstein. I had long ago mastered the last detail of Einstein's theory, as had, in time, the rest of the world. I threw myself immediately into the study of this new, epoch-making conception.

To my amazement, it all seemed to me curiously dim and elusive. I could not quite grasp what Zarentzov was trying to formulate.

"Why," I cried, "the thing is a monstrous fraud!" I went to the professor of Physics in the University I then attended, and I told him it was a fraud, a huge book of mere nonsense. He looked at me rather pityingly.

"I am afraid, Modevski," he said, addressing me by the name I was at the time using, "I am afraid you do not understand it, that is all. When your mind has broadened, you will. You should apply yourself more carefully to your Physics." But that angered me, for I had mastered my Physics before he was ever born. I challenged him to explain the theory. And he did! He put it, obviously, in the clearest language he could. Yet I understood nothing. I stared at him dumbly, until he shook his head impatiently, saying that it was useless, that if I could not grasp it I would simply have to keep on studying. I was stunned. I wandered away in a daze.

For do you see what had happened? During all those years I had studied ceaselessly, and my mind had been clear and quick as the day I first had left the hospital. But all that time I had been able only to remain what I was—an extraordinarily intelligent man of the twentieth century. And the rest of the race had been progressing! It had been swiftly gathering knowledge and power and ability all that

11

time, faster and faster, while I had been only remaining still. And now here was Zarentzov and the teachers of the Universities, and, probably, a hundred intelligent men, who had all outstripped me! I was being left behind.

And that is what happened. I need not dilate further upon it. By the end of that century I had been left behind by all the students of the world, and I never did understand Zarentzov. Other men came with other theories, and these theories were accepted by the world. But I could not understand them. My intellectual life was at an end. I had nothing more to understand. I knew everything I was capable of knowing, and, thenceforth, I could only play wearily with the old ideas.

Many things happened in the world. A time came when the East and West, two mighty unified hemispheres, rose up in arms: the civil war of a planet. I recall only chaotic visions of fire and thunder and hell. It was all incomprehensible to me: like a bizarre dream, things happened, people rushed about, but I never knew what they were doing. I lurked during all that time in a tiny shuddering hole under the city of Yokohama, and by a miracle I survived. And the East won. But it seems to have mattered little who did win, for all the world had become, in all except its few remaining prejudices, a single race, and nothing was changed when it was all rebuilt again, under a single government.

I saw the first of the strange creatures who appeared among us in the year 6371, men who were later known to be from the planet Venus. But they were repulsed, for they were savages compared with the Earthmen, although they were about equal to the people of my own century, 1900. Those of them who did not perish of the cold after the intense warmth of their world, and those who were not killed by our hands, those few returned silently home again. And I have always regretted that I had not the courage to go with them.

I watched a time when the world reached perfection in mechanics, when men could accomplish anything with a touch of the finger. Strange men, these creatures of the hundredth century, men with huge brains and tiny, shriveled bodies, atrophied limbs, and slow, ponderous movements on their little conveyances. It was I, with my ancient compunctions, who shuddered when at last they put to death all the perverts, the criminals, and the insane, ridding the world of the scum for which they had no more need. It was then that I was forced to produce my tattered old papers, proving my identity and my story. They knew it was true, in some strange fashion of theirs, and, thereafter, I was kept on exhibition as an archaic survival.

I saw the world made immortal through the new invention of a man called Kathol, who used somewhat the same method "legend" decreed had been used upon me. I observed the end of speech, of all perceptions except one, when men learned to communicate directly by thought, and to receive directly into the brain all the myriad vibrations of the universe.

All these things I saw, and more, until that time when there was no more discovery, but a Perfect World in which there was no need for anything but memory. Men ceased to count time at last. Several hundred years after the 154th Dynasty from the Last War, or, as we would have counted in my time, about 200,000 A.D., official records of time were no longer kept carefully. They fell into disuse. Men began to forget years, to forget time at all. Of what significance was time when one was immortal?

After long, long uncounted centuries, a time came when the days grew noticeably colder. Slowly the winters became longer, and the summers diminished to but a month or two. Fierce storms raged endlessly in winter, and in summer sometimes there was severe frost, sometimes there was only frost. In the high places and in the north and the subequatorial south, the snow came and would not go.

Men died by the thousands in the higher latitudes. New York became, after awhile, the furthest habitable city north, an arctic city, where warmth seldom penetrated. And great fields of ice began to make their way southward, grinding before them the brittle remains of civilizations, covering over relentlessly all of man's proud work.

Snow appeared in Florida and Italy one summer. In the end, snow was there always. Men left New York, Chicago, Paris, Yokohama, and everywhere they traveled by the millions southward, perishing as they went, pursued by the snow and the cold, and that inevitable field of ice. They were feeble creatures when the Cold first came upon them, but I speak in terms of thousands of years; and they turned every weapon of science to the recovery of their physical power, for they foresaw that the only chance for survival lay in a hard, strong body. As for me, at last I had found a use for my few powers, for my physique was the finest in that world. It was but little comfort, however, for we were all united in our awful fear of that Cold and that grinding field of Ice. All the great cities were deserted. We would catch silent, fearful glimpses of them as we sped on in our machines over the snow—great hungry, haggard skeletons of cities, shrouded in banks of snow, snow that the wind rustled through desolate streets where the cream of human life once had passed in calm security. Yet still the Ice pursued. For men had forgotten about that Last Ice Age when they ceased to reckon time, when they lost sight of the future and steeped themselves in memories. They had

13

not remembered that a time must come when Ice would lie white and smooth over all the earth, when the sun would shine bleakly between unending intervals of dim, twilit snow and sleet.

Slowly the Ice pursued us down the earth, until all the feeble remains of civilization were gathered in Egypt and India and South America. The deserts flowered again, but the frost would come always to bite the tiny crops. For still the Ice came. All the world now, but for a narrow strip about the equator, was one great silent desolate vista of stark ice-plains, ice that brooded above the hidden ruins of cities that had endured for hundreds of thousands of years. It was terrible to imagine the awful solitude and the endless twilight that lay on these places, and the grim snow, sailing in silence over all ....

And so we existed, hoping still that the Ice might go again, until at last it closed in upon us. From north and south it came, from every side, and the boundaries of east and west were the frozen oceans, fathoms deep in Ice. It closed about us ....

It surrounded us on all sides, until life remained only in a few scattered clearings all about that equator of the globe, with an eternal fire going to hold away the hungry Ice. Perpetual winter reigned now; and we were becoming terror-stricken beasts that preyed on each other for a life already doomed. Ah, but I, I the archaic survival, I had my revenge then, with my great physique and strong jaws—God! Let me think of something else. Those men who lived upon each other—it was horrible. And I was one.

So inevitably the Ice closed in .... One day the men of our tiny clearing were but a score. We huddled about our dying fire of bones and stray logs. We said nothing. We just sat, in deep, wordless, thoughtless silence. We were the last outpost of Mankind.

I think suddenly something very noble must have transformed these creatures to a semblance of what they had been of old. I saw, in their eyes, the question they sent from one to another, and in every eye I saw that the answer was, Yes. With one accord they rose before my eyes and, ignoring me as a baser creature, they stripped away their load of tattered rags and, one by one, they stalked with their tiny shriveled limbs into the shivering gail of swirling, gusting snow, and disappeared. And I was alone ....

So am I alone now. I have written this last fantastic history of myself and of Mankind upon a substance that will, I know, outlast even the snow and the Ice—as it has outlasted Mankind that made it. It is the only thing with which I have never parted. For is it not irony that I should be the historian of this race—I, a savage, an "archaic survival?" Why do I write? God knows, but some instinct

14

prompts me, although there will never be men to read.

I have been sitting here, waiting, and I have thought often of Sir John and Alice, whom I loved. Can it be that I am feeling again, after all these ages, some tiny portion of that emotion, that great passion I once knew? I see her face before me, the face I have lost from my thoughts for eons, and something is in it that stirs my blood again. Her eyes are half-closed and deep, her lips are parted as though I could crush them with an infinity of wonder and discovery. O God! It is love again, love that I thought was lost! They have often smiled upon me when I spoke of God, and muttered about my foolish, primitive superstitions. But they are gone, and I am left who believe in God, and surely there is purpose in it.

I am cold, I have written. Ah, I am frozen. My breath freezes as it mingles with the air, and I can hardly move my numbed fingers. The Ice is closing over me, and I cannot break it any longer. The storm cries weirdly all about me in the twilight, and I know this is the end. The end of the world. And I—I, the last man ....

The last man ....

... I am cold—cold ....

But is it you, Alice, Is it you?

THE END

The EMPIRE of the ANTS
~ By H. G. Wells ~

Chapter I

The Great River

hen Captain Gerilleau received instructions to take his new gunboat, the *Benjamin Constant*, to Badama on the Batemo arm of the Guaramadema and there assist the inhabitants against a plague of ants, he suspected the authorities of mockery. His promotion had been romantic and irregular, the affections of a prominent Brazilian lady and the captain's liquid eyes had played a part in the process, and the *Diario* and *O Futuro* had been lamentably disrespectful in their comments. He felt he was to give further occasion for disrespect.

He was a Creole, his conceptions of etiquette and discipline were pure-blooded Portuguese, and it was only to Holroyd, the Lancashire engineer who had come over with the boat, and as an exercise in the use of English—his "th" sounds were very uncertain—that he opened his heart.

"It is in effect," he said, "to make me absurd! What can a man do against ants? Dey come, dey go."

"They say," said Holroyd, "that these don't go. That chap you said was a Sambo——"

"Zambo;—it is a sort of mixture of blood."

"Sambo. He said the people are going!"

The captain smoked fretfully for a time. "Dese tings 'ave to happen," he said at last. "What is it? Plagues of ants and suchlike as God wills. Dere was a plague in Trinidad—the little ants that carry leaves. All der orange-trees, all der mangoes! What does it matter? Sometimes ant armies come into your houses—fighting ants; a different sort. You go and they clean the house. Then you come back again;—the house is clean, like new! No cockroaches, no fleas, no jiggers in the floor."

"That Sambo chap," said Holroyd, "says these are a different sort of ant."

The captain shrugged his shoulders, fumed, and gave his attention to a cigarette.

Afterwards he reopened the subject. "My dear 'Olroyd, what am I to do about dese infernal ants?"

Six Days Up the Amazon

The captain reflected. "It is ridiculous," he said. But in the afternoon he put on his full uniform and went ashore, and jars and boxes came back to the ship and subsequently he did. And Holyroyd sat on deck in the evening coolness and smoked profoundly and marvelled at Brazil. They were six days up the Amazon, some hundreds of miles from the ocean, and east and west of him there was a horizon like the sea, and to the south nothing but a sand-bank island with some tufts of scrub. The water was always running like a sluice, thick with dirt, animated with crocodiles and hovering birds, and few by some inexhaustible source of tree trunks; and the waste of it, the headlong waste of it, filled his soul. The town of Alemquer, with its meagre church, its thatched sheds for houses, its discolored ruins of ampler days, seemed a little thing lost in this wilderness of Nature, a sixpence dropped on Sahara. He was a young man, this was his first sight of the tropics, he came straight from England, where Nature is hedged, ditched, and drained into the perfection of submission, and he had suddenly discovered the insignificance of man. For six days they had been steaming up from the sea by unfrequented channels, and man had been as rare as a rare butterfly. One saw one day a canoe, another day a distant station, the next no men at all. He began to perceive that man is indeed a rare animal, having but a precarious hold upon this land.

He perceived it more clearly as the days passed, and he made his devious way to the Batemo, in the company of this remarkable commander, who ruled over one big gun, and was forbidden to waste his ammunition. Holroyd was learning Spanish industriously, but he was still in the present tense and substantive stage of speech, and the only other person who had any words of English was a negro stoker, who had them all wrong. The second in command was a Portuguese, da Cunha, who spoke French, but it was a different sort of French from the French Holroyd had learnt in Southport, and their intercourse was confined to politenesses and simple propositions about the weather. And the weather, like everything else in this amazing new world, the weather had no human aspect, and was hot by night and hot by day, and the air was steam, even the wind was hot steam, smelling of vegetation in decay: and the alligators and the strange birds, the flies of many sorts and sizes, the beetles, the ants, the snakes, and monkeys seemed to wonder what man was doing in an atmosphere that had no gladness in its sunshine and no coolness in its night. To wear clothing was intolerable, but to cast it aside was to scorch by day, and expose an ampler area to the mosquitoes by night; to go on deck by day was to be blinded by glare and to stay below was to suffocate. And in the daytime came certain flies, extremely clever and noxious about one's wrist and ankle. Captain Gerilleau, who was Holroyd's sole distraction from these physical distresses, developed into a formidable bore, telling the simple story of his heart's affection day by day, a string of anonymous women, as if he were telling beads. Sometimes he suggested sport, and they shot at alligators, and at rare intervals they came to human aggregations in the waste of trees, and stayed for a day or so, and drank and sat about, and, one night, danced with Creole girls who found Holroyd's poor elements of Spanish, without either past tense or future, amply sufficient for their purposes. But these were mere luminous chinks in the long gray passage of the streaming river up which the throbbing engines beat. A certain liberal heathen deity, in the shape of a demi-john, held seductive court aft, and, it is probable, forward.

But Gerilleau learnt things about the ants, more things and more, at this stopping-place and that, and became interested in his mission.

"Dey are a new sort of ant," he said. "We have got to be—what do you call it?—entomologie? Big. Five centimetres!* Some bigger! It is ridiculous. We are like the monkeys—sent to pick insects .... But dey are eating up the country."

The Fatal Ants

He burst out indignantly. "Suppose—suddenly, there are complications with Europe. Here and I—soon we shall be above the Rio Negro—and my gun, useless!"

He nursed his knee and mused.

"Dose people who were dere at de dancing place, dey 'ave come down. Dey 'ave lost all they got. De ants come to deir house one afternoon. Every one run out. You know when de ants come one must—every one runs out and they go over the house. If you stayed they'd eat you. See? Well, presently dey go back; dey say, 'The ants 'ave gone.' ... De ants *aven't* gone. Dey try to go in—de son, 'e goes in. De ants fight."

"Swarm over him?"

"Bite 'im. Presently he comes out again—screaming and running. He runs past them to the river. See? He gets into de water and drowns de ants—yes." Gerilleau paused, brought his liquid eyes close to Holroyd's face, tapped Holroyd's knee with his knuckle. "That night he dies, just as if he was stung by a snake."

"Poisoned—by the ants?"

"Who knows?" Gerilleau shrugged his shoulders. "Perhaps they bit him badly .... When I joined dis service I joined to fight men. Dese things, dese ants, dey come and go. It is no business for men."

After that he talked frequently of the ants to Holroyd, and whenever they chanced to drift against any speck of humanity in that waste of water and sunshine and distant trees, Holroyd's improving knowledge of the language enabled him to recognize the ascendant word *Saüba*, [1] more and more completely dominating the whole.

He perceived the ants were becoming interesting, and the nearer he drew to them the more interesting they became. Gerilleau abandoned his old themes almost suddenly, and the Portuguese lieutenant became a conversational figure; he knew something about the leaf-cutting ant, and expanded his knowledge. Gerilleau sometimes rendered what he had to tell to Holroyd. He told of the little workers that swarm and fight, and the big workers that command and rule, and how these latter always crawled to the neck and how their bites drew blood. He told how they cut leaves and made fungus beds, and how their nests in Caracas are sometimes a hundred yards across. Two days the three men spent disputing whether ants have eyes. The discussion grew dangerously heated on the second afternoon, and Holroyd saved the situation by going ashore in a boat to catch ants and see. He captured various specimens and returned, and some had eyes and some hadn't. Also, they argued, do ants bite or sting?

"Dese ants," said Gerilleau, after collecting information at a rancho, "have big eyes. They don't run about blind—not as most ants do. No! Dey get in corners and watch what you do."

"And they sting?" asked Holroyd.

"Yes. Dey sting. Dere is poison in the sting." He meditated. "I do not see what men can do against ants. Dey come and go."

"But these don't go."

"They will," said Gerilleau.

The Hopeless Wilderness

Past Tamandu there is a long low coast of eighty miles without any population, and then one comes to the confluence of the main river and the Batemo arm like a great lake, and then the forest came nearer, came at last intimately near. The character of the channel changes, snags abound, and the *Benjamin Constant* moored by a cable that night, under the very shadow of dark trees. For the first time for many days came a spell of coolness, and Holroyd and Gerilleau sat late, smoking cigars and enjoying this delicious sensation. Gerilleau's mind was full of ants and what they could do. He decided to sleep at last, and lay down on a mattress on deck, a man hopelessly perplexed, his last words, when he already seemed asleep, were to ask, with a flourish of despair, "What can one do with ants? ... De whole thing is absurd."

Holroyd was left to scratch his bitten wrists, and meditate alone.

He sat on the bulwark and listened to the little changes in Gerilleau's breathing until he was fast asleep, and then the ripple and lap of the stream took his mind, and brought back that sense of immensity that had been growing upon him since first he had left Para and come up the river. The monitor showed but one small light, and there was first a little talking forward and then stillness. His eyes went from the dim black outlines of the middle works of the gunboat towards the bank, to the black overwhelming mysteries of forest, lit now and then by a fire-fly and never still from the murmur of alien and mysterious activities ....

It was the inhuman immensity of this land that astonished and oppressed him. He knew the skies were empty of men, the stars were specks in an incredible vastness of space; he knew the ocean was enormous and untamable, but in England he had come to think of the land as man's. In England it is indeed man's, the wild things live by sufferance, grow on lease, everywhere the roads, the fences, and absolute security runs. In an atlas, too, the land is man's, and all coloured to show his claim to it—in vivid contrast to the universal independent blueness of the sea. He had taken it for granted that a day would come when everywhere about the earth, plough and culture, light tramways and good roads, an ordered security, would prevail. But now, he doubted.

The Ants the Real Masters of the Country

This forest was interminable, it had an air of being invincible, and Man seemed at best an infrequent precarious intruder. One traveled for miles, amidst the still, silent struggle of giant trees, of strangulating creepers, of assertive flowers, everywhere the alligator, the turtle, and endless varieties of birds and insects seemed at home, dwelt irreplaceably—but man, man at most held a footing upon resentful clearings, fought weeds, fought beasts and insects for the

†canoe

barest foothold, fell a prey to snake and beast, insect and fever, and was presently carried away. In many places down the river he had been manifestly driven back, this deserted creek or that preserved the name of a *casa,** and here and there ruinous white walls and a shattered tower enforced the lesson. The puma, the jaguar, were more the masters here ....

Who were the real masters?

In a few miles of this forest there must be more ants than there are men in the whole world! This seemed to Holroyd a perfectly new idea. In a few thousand years men had emerged from barbarism to a stage of civilization that made them feel lords of the future and masters of the earth! But what was to prevent the ants evolving also? Such ants as one knew lived in little communities of a few thousand individuals, made no concerted efforts against the greater world. But they had a language, they had an intelligence! Why should things stop at that any more than men had stopped at the barbaric stage? Suppose presently the ants began to store knowledge, just as men had done by means of books and records, use weapons, form great empires, sustain a planned and organized war?

Things came back to him that Gerilleau had gathered about these ants they were approaching. They used a poison like the poison of snakes. They obeyed greater leaders even as the leaf-cutting ants do. They were carnivorous, and where they came they stayed ...

The forest was very still. The water lapped incessantly against the side. About the lantern overhead there eddied a noiseless whirl of phantom moths.

Gerilleau stirred in the darkness and sighed. "What can one *do?*" he murmured, and turned over and was still again.

Holroyd was roused from meditations that were becoming sinister by the hum of a mosquito.

Chapter II
The Ants in Command of the Canoe

The next morning Holroyd learned they were within 40 kilometers of Badama, and his interest in the banks intensified. He came up whenever an opportunity offered to examine the surroundings. He could see no signs of human occupation whatever, save for a weedy ruin of a house and the green-stained facade of the long-deserted monastery at Moju, with a forest tree growing out of a vacant window space, and great creepers netted across its vacant portals.

*house

Several flights of strange yellow butterflies with semi-transparent wings crossed the river that morning, and many alighted on the monitor and were killed by the men. It was towards afternoon that they came upon the derelict *cuberta*.[2]

She did not at first appear to be derelict; both her sails were set and hanging slack in the afternoon calm, and there was the figure of a man sitting on the fore planking beside the shipped sweeps. Another man appeared to be sleeping face downwards on the sort of longitudinal bridge these big canoes have in the waist. But it was presently apparent, from the sway of her rudder and the way she drifted into the course of the gunboat, that something was out of order with her. Gerilleau surveyed her through a field-glass, and became interested in the queer darkness of the face of the sitting man, a red-faced man he seemed, without a nose—crouching he was rather than sitting, and the longer the captain looked the less he liked to look at him, and the less able he was to take his glasses away.

But he did so at last, and went a little way to call up Holroyd. Then he went back to hail the cuberta. He hailed her again, and so she drove past him. *Santa Rosa* stood out clearly as her name.

As she came by and into the wake of the monitor, she pitched a little, and suddenly the figure of the crouching man collapsed as though all its joints had given way. His hat fell off, his head was not nice to look at, and his body flopped lax and rolled out of sight behind the bulwarks.

"Caramba!" cried Gerilleau, and resorted to Holroyd forthwith.

Holroyd was half-way up the companion. "Did you see dat?" said the captain.

"Dead!" said Holroyd. "Yees. You'd better send a boat aboard. There's something wrong."

"Did you—by any chance—see his face?"

"What was it like?"

"It was—ugh!—I have no words," And the captain suddenly turned his back on Holroyd and became an active and strident commander.

The Dead Men on the Canoe

The gunboat came about, steamed parallel to the erratic course of the canoe, and dropped the boat with Lieutenant de Cunha and three sailors to board her. Then the curiosity of the captain made him draw up almost alongside as the lieutenant got aboard, so that the whole of the *Santa Rosa*, deck and hold, was visible to Holroyd.

He saw now clearly that the sole crew of the vessel was these two dead men, and though he could not see their faces, he saw by their outstretched hands, which were all of ragged flesh, that they had been subjected to some strange exceptional process of decay. For a moment his attention concentrated on those two enigmatical bundles of dirty clothes and laxly flung limbs, and then his eyes went forward to discover the open hold piled high with trunks and cases, and aft, to where the little cabin gaped inexplicably empty. Then he became aware that the planks of the middle decking were dotted with moving black specks.

His attention was riveted by these specks. They were all walking in directions radiating from the fallen man in a manner—the image came unsought to his mind—like the crowd dispersing from a bullfight.

He became aware of Gerilleau beside him.

"Capo," he said, "have you your glasses? Can you focus as closely as those planks there?"

Gerilleau made an effort, grunted, and handed him the glasses.

There followed a moment of scrutiny. "It's ants," said the Englishman, and handed the focused fieldglass back to Gerilleau.

His impression of them was of a crowd of large black ants, very like ordinary ants except for their size, and for the fact that some of the larger of them bore a sort of clothing of gray. But at the time his inspection was too brief for particulars. The head of Lieutenant da Cunha appeared over the side of the cuberta, and a brief colloquy ensued.

"You must go aboard," said Gerilleau.

The lieutenant objected that the boat was full of ants.

"You have your boots," said Gerilleau.

The lieutenant changed the subject. "How did these men die?" he asked.

Captain Gerilleau embarked upon speculations that Holroyd could not follow, and the two men disputed with a certain increasing vehemence. Holroyd took up the field-glass and resumed his scrutiny, first of the ants and then of the dead man amidships.

He has described these ants to me very particularly.

The Lieutenant Goes on Board the Canoe

He says they were as large as any ants he has ever seen, black and moving with a steady deliberation very different from the mechanical fussiness of the common ant. About one in twenty was much larger than its fellows, and with an exceptionally large head.

24

These reminded him at once of the master workers who are said to rule over the leaf-cutter ants; like them they seemed to be directing and co-ordinating the general movements. They tilted their bodies back in a manner altogether singular as if they made some use of the fore feet. And he had a curious fancy that he was too far off to verify, that most of these ants of both kinds were wearing accoutrements, had things strapped about their bodies by bright white bands like white metal threads ....

He put down the glasses abruptly, realizing that the question of discipline between the captain and his subordinate had become acute.

"It is your duty," said the captain, "to go aboard. It is my instructions."

The lieutenant seemed on the verge of refusing. The head of one of the mulatto sailors appeared beside him.

"I believe these men were killed by the ants," said Holroyd abruptly in English.

The captain burst into a rage. He made no answer to Holroyd. "I have commanded you to go aboard," he screamed to his subordinate in Portuguese. "If you do not go aboard forthwith it is mutiny—rank mutiny. Mutiny and cowardice! Where is the courage that should animate us? I will have you in irons, I will have you shot like a dog." He began a torrent of abuse and curses, he danced to and fro. He shook his fist, he behaved as if beside himself with rage, and the lieutenant, white and still, stood looking at him. The crew appeared forward, with amazed faces.

Suddenly, in a pause of this outbreak, the lieutenant came to some heroic decision, saluted, drew himself together and clambered upon the deck of the cuberta.

"Ah!" said Gerilleau, and his mouth shut like a trap. Holroyd saw the ants retreating before da Cunha's boots. The Portuguese walked slowly to the fallen man, stooped down, hesitated, clutched his coat and turned him over. A black swarm of ants rushed out of the clothes, and da Cunha stepped back very quickly and trod two or three times on the deck.

Holroyd put up the glasses. He saw the scattered ants about the invader's feet, and doing what he had never seen ants doing before. They had nothing of the blind movements of the common ant; they were looking at him—as a rallying crowd of men might look at some gigantic monster that had dispersed it.

"How did he die?" the captain shouted.

Holroyd understood the Portuguese to say the body was too much eaten to tell.

"What is there forward?" asked Gerilleau.

The Death of the Lieutenant

The lieutenant walked a few paces, and began his answer in Portuguese. He stopped abruptly and beat off something from his leg. He made some peculiar steps as if he was trying to stamp on something invisible, and went quickly towards the side. Then he controlled himself, turned about, walked deliberately forward to the hold, clambered up to the fore decking, from which the sweeps are worked, stooped for a time over the second man, groaned audibly, and made his way back and aft to the cabin, moving very rigidly. He turned and began a conversation with his captain, cold and respectful in tone on either side, contrasting vividly with the wrath and insult of a few moments before. Holroyd gathered only fragments of its purport.

He reverted to the field-glass, and was surprised to find the ants had vanished from all the exposed surfaces of the deck. He turned towards the shadows beneath the decking, and it seemed to him they were full of watching eyes.

The cuberta, it was agreed, was derelict, but too full of ants to put men aboard to sit and sleep; it must be towed. The lieutenant went forward to take in and adjust the cable, and the men in the boat stood up to be ready to help him. Holroyd's glasses searched the canoe.

He became more and more impressed by the fact that a great if minute and furtive activity was going on. He perceived that a number of gigantic ants—they seemed nearly a couple of inches in length—carrying oddly-shaped burthens for which he could imagine no use—were moving in rushes from one point of obscurity to another. They did not move in columns across the exposed places, but in open spaced-out lines, oddly suggestive of the rushes of modern infantry advancing under fire. A number were taking cover under the dead man's clothes, and a perfect swarm was gathering along the side over which da Cunha must presently go.

He did not see them actually rush for the lieutenant as he returned, but he has no doubt they did make a concerted rush. Suddenly the lieutenant was shouting and cursing and beating at his legs. "I'm stung!" he shouted, with a face of hate and accusation towards Gerilleau.

Then he vanished over the side, dropped into his boat, and plunged at once into the water. Holroyd heard the splash.

26

The three men in the boat pulled him out and brought him aboard, and that night he died.

Chapter III
The Sinister Canoe

Holroyd and the captain came out of the cabin in which the swollen and contorted body of the lieutenant lay and stood together at the stern of the monitor, staring at the sinister vessel they trailed behind them. It was a close, dark night that had only phantom flickerings of sheet lightning to illuminate it. The cuberta, a vague black triangle, rocked about in the steamer's wake, her sails bobbing and flapping, and the black smoke from the funnels, spark-lit ever and again, streamed over her swaying masts.

Gerilleau's mind was inclined to run on the unkind things the lieutenant had said in the heat of his last fever.

"He says I murdered 'im," he protested. "It is simply absurd. Some one 'ad to go aboard. Are we to run away from these confounded ants whenever they show up?"

Holroyd said nothing. He was thinking of a disciplined rush of little black shapes across bare sunlit planking.

"It was his place to go," harped Gerilleau. "He died in the execution of his duty. What has he to complain of? Murdered! ... But the poor fellow was—what is it?—demented. He was not in his right mind. The poison swelled him.... U'm."

They came to a long silence.

"We will sink that canoe—burn it."

"And then?"

The inquiry irritated Gerilleau. His shoulders went up, his hands flew out at right angles from his body. "What is one to *do*?" he said, his voice going up to an angry squeak.

"Anyhow," he broke out vindictively. "every ant in dat cuberta?—I will burn dem alive!"

Holroyd was not moved to conversation. A distant ululation of howling monkeys filled the sultry night with foreboding sounds, and as the gunboat drew near the black mysterious banks this was reinforced by a depressing clamour of frogs.

Burning the Canoe

27

"What is one to *do?*" the captain repeated after a vast interval, and suddenly becoming active and savage and blasphemous, decided to burn the *Santa Rosa* without further delay. Every one aboard was pleased by that idea, every one helped with zest; they pulled in the cable, cut it, and dropped the boat and fired her with tow and kerosene, and soon the cuberta was crackling and flaring merrily amidst the immensities of the tropical night. Holroyd watched the mounting yellow flare against the blackness, and the livid flashes of sheet lightning that came and went above the forest summits, throwing them into momentary silhouette, and his stoker stood behind him watching also.

The stoker was stirred to the depths of his linguistics. "*Saüba,* go pop, pop," he said, "Wahaw!" and laughed richly.

But Holroyd was thinking that these little creatures on the decked canoe had also eyes and brains.

The whole thing impressed him as incredibly foolish and wrong, but—what was one to *do?* This question came back enormously reinforced on the morrow, when at last the gunboat reached Badama.

The Deserted Village

This place, with its leaf-thatch-covered houses and sheds, its creeper-invaded sugar-mill, its little jetty of timber and canes, was very still in the morning heat, and showed never a sign of living men. Whatever ants there were at that distance were too small to see.

"All the people have gone," said Gerilleau, "but we will do one thing anyhow. We will 'oot and vissel."

So Holroyd hooted and whistled.

Then the captain fell into a doubting fit of the worst kind. "Dere is one thing we can do," he said presently.

"What's that? said Holroyd.

"'Oot and vissel again."

So they did.

The captain walked his deck and gesticulated to himself. He seemed to have many things on his mind. Fragments of speeches came from his lips. He appeared to be addressing some imaginary public tribunal either in Spanish or Portuguese. Holroyd's improving ear detected something about ammunition. He came out of these preoccupations suddenly into English. "My dear 'Olroyd!" he cried, and broke off with "But what *can* one do?"

They took the boat and the field-glasses, and went close in to examine the place. They made out a number of big ants, whose still postures had a certain effect of watching them, dotted about the edge of the rude embarkation jetty. Gerilleau tried ineffectual pistol shots at these. Holroyd thinks he distinguished curious earthworks running between the nearer houses, that may have been the work of the insect conquerors of those human habitations. The explorers pulled past the jetty, and became aware of a human skeleton wearing a loin cloth, and very bright and clean and shining, lying beyond. They came to a pause regarding this....

"I 'ave all dose lives to consider," said Gerilleau suddenly.

Holroyd turned and stared at the captain, realizing slowly that he referred to the unappetizing mixture of races that constituted his crew.

"To send a landing party—it is impossible—impossible. They will be poisoned, they will swell, they will swell up and abuse me and die. It is totally impossible.... if we land, I must land alone, in thick boot and with my life in my hand. Perhaps I should live. Or again—I might not land. I do not know. I do not know."

Holroyd thought he did, but he said nothing.

"De whole thing," said Gerilleau suddenly, "'as been got up to make me ridiculous. De whole thing!"

Bombarding the Ants—A Strange Decision

They paddled about and regarded the clean white skeleton from various points of view, and then they returned to the gunboat. Then Gerilleau's indecisions became terrible. Steam was got up, and in the afternoon the monitor went on up the river with an air of going to ask somebody something, and by sunset came back again and anchored. A thunderstorm gathered and broke furiously, and then the night became beautifully cool and quiet and every one slept on deck. Except Gerilleau, who tossed about and muttered. In the dawn he awakened Holroyd.

"Lord!" said Holroyd, "what now?"

"I have decided," said the captain.

"What—to land?" said Holroyd, sitting up brightly.

"No!" said the captain, and was for a time very reserved. "I have decided," he repeated, and Holroyd manifested symptoms of impatience.

"Well—yes," said the captain, "*I shall fire de big gun!*"

And he did! Heaven knows what the ants thought of it, but he did. He fired it twice with great sternness and ceremony. All the crew had wadding in their ears, and there was an effect of going into action about the whole affair, and first they hit and wrecked the old sugar-mill, and then they smashed the abandoned store behind the jetty. And then Gerilleau experienced the inevitable reaction.

"It is no good," he said to Holroyd; "no good at all. No sort of bally good. We must go back—for instructions. Dere will be de devil of a row about dis ammunition—oh! de *devil* of a row! You don't know, 'Olroyd. . . ."

He stood regarding the world in infinite perplexity for a space.

"But what else was there to *do?*" he cried.

In the afternoon the monitor started down-stream again, and in the evening a landing party took the body of the lieutenant and buried it on the bank upon which the new ants had so far not appeared . . . .

Chapter IV
The Conclusion

I heard this story in a fragmentary state from Holroyd not three weeks ago.

These new ants have got into his brain, and he has come back to England with the idea, as he says, of "exciting people" about them "before it is too late." He said they threaten British Guiana, which cannot be much over a trifle of a thousand miles from their present sphere of activity, and that the Colonial Office ought to get to work upon them at once. He declaims with great passion: "These are intelligent ants. Just think what that means!"

There can be no doubt they are a serious pest, and that the Brazilian Government is well advised in offering a prize of five hundred pounds for some effectual method of extirpation. It is certain too that since they first appeared in the hills beyond Badama, about three years ago, they have achieved extraordinary conquests. The whole of the south bank of the Batemo River, for nearly sixty miles, they have in their effectual occupation; they have driven men out completely, occupied plantations and settlements, and boarded and captured at least one ship. It is even said they have in some inexplicable way bridged the very considerable Capuarana arm and pushed many miles towards the Amazon itself. There can be little doubt that they are far more reasonable and with a far better social organization than any previously known ant species; instead of being in dispersed societies they are organized into what is in effect a single nation; but their peculiar and immediate formidableness lies not so much in this as in the intelligent use they make of poison against their larger enemies. It would seem this poison of theirs is closely akin to snake poison, and it is highly probable they actually manufacture it, and that the larger individuals among them carry the needle-like crystals of it in their attacks upon men.

What Will the Ants Do In The Future?

Of course, it is extremely difficult to get any detailed information about these new competitors for the sovereignty of the globe. No eye-witnesses of their activity, except for such glimpses as Holroyd's, have survived the encounter. The most extraordinary legends of their prowess and capacity are in circulation in the region of the Upper Amazon, and grow daily as the steady advance of the invader stimulates men's imaginations through their fears. These strange little creatures are credited not only with the use of implements and a knowledge of fire and metals and with organized feats of engineering that stagger our northern minds—unused as we are to such feats as that of the Saübas of Rio de Janeiro, who in 1841 drove a tunnel under the Parahyba where it is as wide as the Thames at Londan Bridge—but with an organized and detailed method of record and communication analogous to our books. So far their action has been a steady progressive settlement, involving the flight or slaughter of every human being in the new areas they invade. They are increasing rapidly in numbers, and Holroyd at least is firmly convinced that they will finally dispossess man over the whole of tropical South America.

And why should they stop at tropical South America?

Well, there they are, anyhow. By 1911 or thereabouts, if they go on as they are doing, they ought to strike the Capuarana Extension Railway, and force themselves upon the attention of the European capitalist.

By 1920 they will be half-way down the Amazon. I fix 1950 or '60 at the latest for their discovery of Europe.

THE END

31

The CRYSTAL EGG
By H. G. Wells

here was, until a year ago, a little and very grimy-looking shop near Seven Dials, over which, in weather-worn yellow lettering, the name of "C. Cave, Naturalist and Dealer in Antiquities," was inscribed. The contents of its window were curiously variegated. They comprised some elephant tusks and an imperfect set of chessmen, beads and weapons, a box of glass eyes, two skulls of tigers and one human, several moth-eaten stuffed monkeys (one holding a lamp), an old-fashioned cabinet, a fly-blown ostrich egg or so, some fishing-tackle, and an extraordinary dirty, empty glass fish-tank. There was also, at the moment the story begins, a mass of crystal, worked into the shape of an egg and brilliantly polished. And at that two people, who stood outside the window, were looking, one of them a tall, thin clergyman, the other a black-bearded young man of dusky complexion and unobtrusive costume. The dusky young man spoke with eager gesticulation, and seemed anxious for his companion to purchase the article.

While they were there, Mr. Cave came into his shop, his beard still wagging with the bread and butter of his tea. When he saw these men and the object of their regard, his countenance fell. He glanced guiltily over his shoulder, and softly shut the door. He was a little old man, with pale face and peculiar watery blue eyes; his hair was a dirty grey, and he wore a shabby blue frock-coat, an ancient silk hat, and carpet slippers very much down at the heel. He remained watching the two men as they talked. The clergyman went deep into his trouser pocket, examined a handful of money, and showed his teeth in an agreeable smile. Mr. Cave seemed still more depressed when they came into the shop.

The clergyman, without any ceremony, asked the price of the crystal egg. Mr. Cave glanced nervously towards the door leading into the parlor, and said five pounds. The clergyman protested to his companion as well as to Mr. Cave, that the price was high—it was, indeed, very much more than Mr. Cave had intended to ask, when he had stocked the article—and an attempt at bargaining ensued. Mr. Cave stepped to the shop-door, and held it open. "Five pounds is my price," he said, as though he wished to save himself the trouble of unprofitable discussion. As he did so, the upper portion of a woman's face appeared above the blind in the glass upper panel of the door leading into the parlor, and stared curiously at the two customers.

"Five pounds is my price," said Mr. Cave, with a quiver in his voice.

The swarthy young man had so far remained a spectator watching Cave keenly. Now he spoke. "Give him five pounds," he said. The clergyman glanced at him to see if he were in earnest, and, when he looked at Mr. Cave again, he saw that the latter's face was white. "It's a lot of money," said the clergyman, and diving into his pocket, began counting his resources. He had little more than thirty shillings, and he appealed to his companion, with whom he seemed to be on terms of considerable intimacy. This gave Mr. Cave an opportunity of collecting his thoughts, and he began to explain in an agitated manner that the crystal was not, as a matter of fact, entirely free for sale. His two customers were naturally surprised at this, and inquired why he had not thought of that before he began to bargain. Mr. Cave became confused, but he stuck to his story, that the crystal was not in the market that afternoon, that a probable purchaser of it had already appeared. The two, treating this as an attempt to raise the price still further, made as if they would leave the shop. But at this point the parlor door opened, and the owner of the dark fringe and the little eyes appeared.

She was a coarse-featured, corpulent woman, younger and very much larger than Mr. Cave; she walked heavily, and her face was flushed. "That crystal *is* for sale," she said. "And five pounds is a good price for it. I can't think what you're about, Cave, not to take the gentleman's offer!"

Mr. Cave, greatly perturbed by the interruption, looked angrily at her over the rims of his spectacles, and, without excessive assurance, asserted his right to manage his business in his own way. An altercation began. The two customers watched the scene with interest and some amusement, occasionally assisting Mrs. Cave with suggestions. Mr. Cave, hard driven, persisted in a confused and impossible story of an inquiry for the crystal that morning, and his agitation became painful. But he stuck to his point with extraordinary persistence. It was the young Oriental who ended this curious controversy. He proposed that they should call again in the course of two days—so as to give the alleged enquirer a fair chance. "And then we must insist," said the clergyman. "Five pounds." Mrs. Cave took it on herself to apologize for her husband, explaining that he was sometimes "a little odd," and as the two customers left, the couple prepared for a free discussion of the incident in all its bearings.

Mrs. Cave talked to her husband with singular directness. The poor little man, quivering with emotion, muddled himself between his stories, maintaining on the one hand that he had another customer in view, and on the other asserting that the crystal was honestly worth ten guineas. "Why did you ask five pounds?" said his wife. *"Do let me manage my business my own way!"* said Mr. Cave.

Mr. Cave had living with him a step-daughter and a step-son, and at supper that night the transaction was rediscussed. None of them had a very high opinion of Mr. Cave's business methods, and this action seemed a culminating folly.

"It's my opinion he's refused that crystal before," said the step-son, a loose-limbed lout of eighteen.

"But *Five Pounds!*" said the step-daughter, an argumentative young woman of six-and-twenty.

Mr. Cave's answers were wretched; he could only mumble weak assertions that he knew his own business best. They drove him from his half-eaten supper into the shop, to close it for the night, his ears aflame and tears of vexation behind his spectacles. "Why had he left the crystal in the window so long? The folly of it!" That was the trouble closest to his mind. For a time he could see no way of evading the sale.

After supper his step-daughter and step-son smartened themselves up and went out. His wife retired upstairs and over a little sugar and lemon and so forth, in hot water, reflected upon the business aspects of the crystal. Mr. Cave went into the shop, and stayed there until late, ostensibly to make ornamental rockeries for gold-fish globes but really for a private purpose that will be better explained later. The next day Mrs. Cave found that the crystal had been removed from the window, and was lying behind some second-hand books on angling. She replaced it in a conspicuous position. But she did not argue further about it, as a nervous headache disinclined her from debate. Mr. Cave was always disinclined. The day passed disagreeably. Mr. Cave was, if anything, more absent-minded than usual, and uncommonly irritable withal. In the afternoon, when his wife was taking her customary sleep, he removed the crystal from the window again.

The next day Mr. Cave had to deliver a consignment of dog-fish at one of the hospital schools, where they were needed for dissection. In his absence, Mrs. Cave's mind reverted to the topic of the crystal, and the methods of expenditure suitable to a windfall of five pounds. She had already devised some very agreeable expedients, among others, a dress of green silk for herself and a trip to Richmond, when a jangling of the front door bell summoned her into the shop. The customer was an examination coach, who came to complain of the non-delivery of certain frogs asked for on the previous day. Mrs. Cave did not approve of this particular branch of

Mr. Cave's business, and the gentleman, who had called in a somewhat aggressive mood, retired after a brief exchange of words—entirely civil so far as he was concerned. Mrs. Cave's eye then naturally turned to the window; for the sight of the crystal was an assurance of five pounds and of her dreams. What was her surprise to find it gone!

She went to the place behind the locker on the counter, where she had discovered it the day before. It was not there; and she immediately began an eager search about the shop.

When Mr. Cave returned from his business about the dog-fish, about a quarter to two in the afternoon, he found the shop in some confusion, and his wife, extremely exasperated and on her knees behind the counter, routing among his taxidermic material. Her face came up hot and angry over the counter, as the jangling bell announced his return, and she fortwith accused him of "hiding it."

"Hid *what?*" asked Mr. Cave.

"The crystal! Where did you hide the crystal?"

At that Mr. Cave, apparently much surprised, rushed to the window. "Isn't it here?" he said. "Great Heavens! what has become of it?"

Just then, Mr. Cave's step-son re-entered the shop from the inner room—he had come home a minute or so before Mr. Cave—and he was blaspheming freely. He was apprenticed to a second-hand furniture dealer down the road, but he had his meals at home, and he was naturally annoyed to find no dinner ready.

But, when he heard of the loss of the crystal, he forgot his meal, and his anger was diverted from his mother to his step-father. Their first idea, of course, was that he had hidden it. But Mr. Cave stoutly denied all knowledge of its fate—freely offering his bedabbled affadavit in the matter—and at last was worked up to the point of accusing, first, his wife and then his step-son of having taken it with a view to a private sale. So began an exceedingly acrimonious and emotional discussion, which ended for Mrs. Cave in a peculiar nervous condition midway between hysterics and amuck, and caused the step-son to be half-an-hour late at the furniture establishment in the afternoon. Mr. Cave took refuge from his wife's emotions in the shop.

In the evening the topic was resumed, with less passion and in a more judicial spirit, under the presidency of the step-daughter. The supper passed unhappily and ended in a painful scene. Mr. Cave gave way at last to extreme exasperation, and went out banging the front door violently. The rest of the family, having discussed him with the freedom which his absence warranted, hunted the house from garret to cellar, hoping to light upon the crystal.

The next day the two customers called again. They were received by Mrs. Cave almost in tears. It transpired that no one *could* imagine all that she had stood from Cave at various times in her married pilgrimage.... She also gave a garbled account of the disappearance. The clergyman and the Oriental laughed silently at one another, and said it was extraordinary. As Mrs. Cave seemed disposed to give them the complete history of her life they made to leave the shop. Thereupon Mrs. Cave, still clinging to hope, asked for the clergyman's address, so that, if she could get anything out of Cave, she might communicate it. The address was duly given, but apparently was afterwards mislaid. Mrs. Cave can remember nothing about it.

By the evening of that day, the Caves seem to have exhausted their emotions, and Mr. Cave, who had been out in the afternoon, supped in a gloomy isolation that contrasted pleasantly with the impassioned controversy of the previous days. For some time matters were very badly strained in the Cave household, but neither crystal nor customer reappeared.

Now, without mincing the matter, we must admit that Mr. Cave was a liar. He knew perfectly well where the crystal was. It was in the rooms of Mr. Jacoby Wace, Assistant Demonstrator at St. Catherine's Hospital, Westbourne Street. It stood on the sideboard partially covered by a black velvet cloth, beside a decanter of American whiskey. It is from Mr. Wace, indeed, that the particulars upon which this narrative is based were derived. Cave had taken the thing off to the hospital hidden in the dog-fish sack, and there had pressed the young investigator to keep it for him. Mr. Wace was a little dubious at first. His relationship to Cave was peculiar. He had a taste for singular characters, and he had more than once invited the old man to smoke and drink in his rooms, and to unfold his rather amusing views of life in general and of his wife in particular. Mr. Wace had encountered Mrs. Cave, too, on occasions when Mr. Cave was not at home to attend to him. He knew the constant interference to which Cave was subjected, and having weighed the story judicially, he decided to give the crystal a refuge. Mr. Cave promised to explain the reasons for his remarkable affection for the crystal more fully on a later occasion, but he spoke distinctly of seeing visions therein. He called on Mr. Wace the same evening.

He told a complicated story. The crystal he said had come into his possession with other oddments at the forced sale of another curiosity dealer's effects, and not knowing what its value might be, he had ticketed it at ten shillings. It had hung upon his hands at that price for some months, and he was thinking of "reducing the figure," when he made a singular discovery.

At that time his health was very bad—and it must be borne in mind that, throughout all this experience, his physical condition was one of ebb—and he was in considerable distress by reason of the negligence, the positive ill-treatment even, he received from his wife and step-children. His wife was vain, extravagant, unfeeling, and had a growing taste for private drinking; his step-daughter was mean and over-reaching; and his step-son had conceived a violent dislike for him, and lost no opportunity of showing it. The requirements of his business pressed heavily upon him, and Mr. Wace does not think that he was altogether free from occasional intemperance. He had begun life in a comfortable position, he was a man of fair education, and he suffered, for weeks at a stretch, from melancholia and insomnia. Afraid to disturb his family, he would slip quietly from his wife's side, when his thoughts become intolerable, and wander about the house. And about three o'clock one morning, late in August, chance directed him into the shop.

The dirty little place was impenetrably black except in one spot, where he perceived an unusual glow of light. Approaching this, he discovered it to be the crystal egg, which was standing on the corner of the counter towards the window. A thin ray shot through a crack in the shutters, impinged upon the object, and seemed as it were to fill its entire interior.

It occurred to Mr. Cave that this was not in accordance with the laws of optics as he had known them in his younger days. He could understand the rays being reflected by the crystal and coming to a focus in its interior, but this diffusion jarred with his physical conceptions. He approached the crystal more nearly, peering into it and around it, with a transient revival of the scientific curiosity that in his youth had determined his choice of a calling. He was surprised to find the light not steady, but writhing within the substance of the egg, as though that object was a hollow sphere of some luminous vapor. In moving about to get different points of view, he suddenly found that he had come between it and the ray, and that the crystal none the less remained luminous. Greatly astonished, he lifted it out of the light ray and carried it to the darkest part of the shop. It remained bright for some four or five minutes, then it slowly faded and went out. He placed it in the thin streak of daylight, and its luminousness was almost immediately restored.

So far, at least, Mr. Wace was able to verify the remarkable story of Mr. Cave. He had himself repeatedly held this crystal in a ray of light (which had to be of a smaller diameter than one milimetre). And in a perfect darkness, such as could be produced by velvet wrapping, the crystal did undoubtedly appear very faintly phosphorescent. It would seem, however, that the luminousness was of some exceptional sort, and not equally visible to all eyes; for Mr. Harbinger—whose name will be familiar to the scientific reader in connection with the Pasteur Institute—was quite unable to see any light whatever. And Mr. Wace's own capacity for its appreciation was out of comparison inferior to that of Mr. Cave's. Even with Mr. Cave the power varied very considerably; his vision was most vivid during states of extreme weakness and fatigue.

Now, from the outset this light in the crystal exercised a curious fascination upon Mr. Cave. And it says more for his loneliness of soul than a volume of pathetic writing could do, that he told no human being of his curious observations. He seems to have been living in such an atmosphere of petty spite that to admit the existence of a pleasure would have been to risk the loss of it. He found that as the dawn advanced, and the amount of diffused light increased, the crystal became to all appearance non-luminous. And for some time he was unable to see anything in it, except at night-time, in dark corners of the shop.

But the use of an old velvet cloth, which he used as a background for a collection of minerals, occurred to him, and by doubling this, and putting it over his head and hands, he was able to get a slight luminous movement within the crystal even in the day-time. He was very cautious lest he should be thus discovered by his wife, and he practiced this occupation only in the afternoons, while she was asleep upstairs, and then circumspectly in a hollow under the counter. And one day, turning the crystal about in his hands, he saw something. It came and went like a flash, but it gave him the impression that the object had for a moment opened to him the view of a wide and spacious and strange country; and, turning it about, he did, just as the light faded, see the same vision again.

Now, it would be tedious and unnecessary to state all the phases of Mr. Cave's discovery from this point. Suffice that the effect was this: the crystal, being peered into at an angle of about 137 degrees from the direction of the illuminating ray, gave a clear and consistent picture of a wide and peculiar country-side. It was not dream-like at all: it produced a definite impression of reality, and the better the light the more real and solid it seemed. It was a moving picture: that is to say, certain objects moved in it, but slowly in an orderly manner like real things, and, according as the direction of the lighting and vision changed, the picture changed also. It must, indeed, have been like looking through an oval glass at a view, and turning the glass about to get at different aspects.

Mr. Cave's statements, Mr. Wace assures me, were extremely circumstantial, and entirely free from any of that emotional quality that taints hallucinatory impressions. But it must be remembered that all the efforts of Mr. Wace to see with any similar clarity in the faint opalescence of the crystal were wholly unsuccessful, try as he would. The difference in intensity of the impressions received by the two men was very great, and it is quite conceivable that what was a view to Mr. Cave was a mere blurred nebulosity to Mr. Wace.

The view, as Mr. Cave described it, was invariably of an extensive plain, and he seemed always to be looking at it from a considerable height, as if from a tower or a mast. To the east and to the west the plain was bounded at a remote distance by vast reddish cliffs, which reminded him of those he had seen in some picture; but what the picture was Mr. Wace was unable to ascertain. These cliffs passed north and south—he could tell the points of the compass by the stars that were visible of a night—receding in an almost illimitable perspective and fading into the mists of the distance before they met. He was nearer the eastern set of cliffs, on the occasion of his first vision the sun was rising over them, and black against the sunlight and pale against their shadow appeared a multitude of soaring forms that Mr. Cave regarded as birds. A vast range of buildings spread below him; he seemed to be looking down upon them; and, as they approached the blurred and refracted edge of the picture, they became indistinct. There were also trees curious in shape, and in coloring, a deep mossy green and an exquisite grey, beside a wide and shining canal. And something great and brilliantly colored flew across the picture. But the first time Mr. Cave saw these pictures he saw only in flashes, his hands shook, his head moved, the vision came and went, and grew foggy and indistinct. And at first he had the greatest difficulty in finding the picture again once the direction of it was lost.

His next clear vision, which came about a week after the first, the interval having yielded nothing but tantalizing glimpses and some useful experience, showed him the view down the length of the valley. The view was different but he had a curious persuasion, which his subsequent observations abundantly confirmed, that he was regarding this strange world from exactly the same spot, although he was looking in a different direction. The long facade of the great building, whose roof he had looked down upon before, was now receding in perspective. He recognized the roof. In the front of the facade was a terrace of massive proportions and extraordinary length, and down the middle of the terrace, at certain intervals, stood

40

huge but very graceful masts, bearing small shiny objects which reflected the setting sun. The import of these small objects did not occur to Mr. Cave until some time after, as he was describing the scene to Mr. Wace. The terrace overhung a thicket of the most luxuriant and graceful vegetation, and beyond this was a wide grassy lawn on which certain broad creatures, in form like beetles but enormously larger, reposed. Beyond this again was a richly decorated causeway of pinkish stone; and beyond that, and lined with dense *red* weeds, and passing up the valley exactly parallel with the distant cliffs, was a broad and mirror-like expanse of water. The air seemed full of squadrons of great birds, manuevering in stately curves; and across the river was a multitude of spendid buildings, richly coloured and glittering with metallic tracery and facets, among a forest of moss-like and lichenous trees. And suddenly something flapped repeatedly across the vision, like the fluttering of a jewelled fan or the beating of a wing, and a face, or rather the upper part of a face with very large eyes, came as it were close to his own and as if on the other side of the crystal. Mr. Cave was so startled and so impressed by the absolute reality of these eyes, that he drew his head back from the crystal to look behind it. He had become so absorbed in watching that he was quite surprised to find himself in the cool darkness of his little shop, with its familiar odor of methyl alcohol, mustiness, and decay. And, as he blinked about him, the glowing crystal faded, and went out.

Such were the first general impressions of Mr. Cave. The story is curiously direct and circumstantial. From the outset, when the valley first flashed momentarily on his senses, his imagination was strangely affected, and, as he began to appreciate the details of the scene he saw, his wonder rose to the point of a passion. He went about his business listless and distraught, thinking only of the time when he should be able to return to his watching. And then a few weeks after his first sight of the valley came the two customers, the stress and excitement of their offer, and the narrow escape of the crystal from sale, as I have already told.

Now, while the thing was Mr. Cave's secret, it remained a mere wonder, a thing to creep to covertly and a peep at, as a child might peep upon a forbidden garden. But Mr. Wace has, for a young scientific investigator, a particularly lucid and consecutive habit of mind. Directly the crystal and its story came to him, and he had satisfied himself, by seeing the phosphorescence with his own eyes, that there really was a certain evidence for Mr. Cave's statements, he proceeded to develop the matter systematically. Mr. Cave was only too eager to come and feast his eyes on this wonderland he

41

saw, and he came every night from half-past eight until half-past ten, and sometimes in Mr. Wace's absence, during the day. On Sunday afternoons also, he came. From the outset Mr. Wace made copious notes, and it was due to his scientific method that the relation between the direction from which the initiating ray entered the crystal and the orientation of the picture were proved. And, by covering the crystal in a box perforated only with a small aperture to admit the exciting ray, and by substituting black holland for his buff blinds, he greatly improved the conditions of the observations; so that in a little while they were able to survey the valley in any direction they desired.

So, having cleared the way, we may give a brief account of this visionary world within the crystal. The things were in all cases seen by Mr. Cave, and his method of working was invariably to watch the crystal and report what he saw, while Mr. Wace (who as a science student had learned the trick of writing in the dark) wrote a brief note of his report. When the crystal faded, it was put into its box in the proper position and the electric light turned on. Mr. Wace asked questions, and suggested observations to clear up difficult points. Nothing, indeed, could have been less visionary and more matter-of-fact.

The attention of Mr. Cave had been speedily directed to the bird-like creatures he had seen so abundantly present in each of his earlier visions. His first impression was soon corrected, and he considered for a time that they might represent a diurnal species of bat. Then he thought, grotesquely enough, that they might be cherubs. Their heads were round, and curiously human, and it was the eyes of one of them that had so startled him on his second observation. They had broad, silvery wings, not feathered, but glistening almost as brilliantly as a new-killed fish and with the same subtle play of color, and these wings were not built on the plan of bird-wing or bat, Mr. Wace learned, but supported by curved ribs radiating from the body. (A sort of butterfly wing with curved ribs seems best to express their appearance.) The body was small, but fitted with two bunches of prehensile organs, like long tentacles, immediately under the mouth. Incredible as it appeared to Mr. Wace, the persuasion at last became irresistible, that it was these creatures who owned the great quasi-human buildings and the magnificent garden that made the broad valley so spendid. And Mr. Cave perceived that the buildings, with other peculiarities, had no doors, but that the great circular windows, which opened freely, gave the creatures egress and entrance. They would alight upon their tentacles, fold their wings to a smallness almost rod-like, and hop into the interior. But among them was a multitude of smaller-winged creatures, like great dragon-flies and moths and flying beetles, and across the greensward brilliantly-colored gigantic ground-beetles crawled lazily to and fro. Moreover, on the causeways and terraces, large-headed creatures similar to the greater winged flies, but wingless, were visible, hopping busily upon their hand-like tangle of tentacles.

Allusion has already been made to the glittering objects upon masts that stood upon the terrace of the nearer building. It dawned upon Mr. Cave, after regarding one of these masts very fixedly on one particularly vivid day, that the glittering object there was a crystal exactly like that into which he peered. And a still more careful scrutiny convinced him that each mast in a vista of nearly twenty carried a similar object.

Occasionally one of the large flying creatures would flutter up to one, and, folding its wings and coiling a number of its tentacles about the mast, would regard the crystal fixedly for a space,—sometimes for as long as 15 minutes. And a series of observations, made at the suggestion of Mr. Wace, convinced both watchers that, so far as this visionary world was concerned, the crystal into which they peered actually stood at the summit of the endmost mast on the terrace, and that on one occasion at least one of these inhabitants of this other world had looked into Mr. Cave's face while he was making these observations.

So much for the essential facts of this very singular story. Unless we dismiss it all as the ingenious fabrication of Mr. Wace, we have to believe one of two things; either that Mr. Cave's crystal was in two worlds at once, and that, while it was carried about in one, it remained stationary in the other, which seems altogether absurd; or else that it had some peculiar relation of sympathy with another and exactly similar crystal in this other world, so that what was seen in the interior of the one in this world was, under suitable conditions, visible to an observer in the corresponding crystal in the other world; and *vice versa*. At present, indeed, we do not know of any way in which two crystals could so come *en rapport*, but nowadays we know enough to understand that the thing is not altogether impossible. This view of the crystals as *en rapport* was the supposition that occurred to Mr. Wace, and to me at least it seems extremely plausible ...

And where was this other world? On this, also, the alert intelligence of Mr. Wace speedily threw light. After sunset, the sky darkened rapidly—there was a very brief twilight interval indeed—and the stars shown out. They were recognizably the same as those we see, arranged in the same constellations. Mr. Cave recognized the Bear, the Pleiades, Aldebaran, and Sirius; so that the other world must be somewhere in the solar system, and, at the utmost only a few hundreds of millions of miles from our own. Following up this clue, Mr. Wace learned that the midnight sky was a darker blue even than our midwinter sky, and that the sun seemed a little smaller. *And there were two small moons!* —"like our moon but smaller, and quite differently marked"—one of which moved so rapidly that its motion was clearly visible as one regarded it. These moons were never high in the sky, but vanished as they rose; that is, every time they revolved they were eclipsed because they were so near their primary planet. And all this answers quite completely, although Mr. Cave did not know it, to what must be the condition of things on Mars.

Indeed, it seems an exceedingly plausible conclusion that peering into this crystal, Mr. Cave did actually see the planet Mars and its inhabitants. And, if that be the case, then the evening star that shown so brilliantly in the sky of that distant vision, was neither more nor less than our own familiar earth.

For a time the Martians—if they were Martians—do not seem to have known of Mr. Cave's inspection. Once or twice one would come to peer, and go away very shortly to some other mast, as though the vision was unsatisfactory. During this time Mr. Cave was able to watch the proceedings of these winged people without being disturbed by their attentions, and, although his report is necessarily vague and fragmentary, it is nevertheless very suggestive. Imagine the impression of humanity a Martian observer would get who, after a difficult process of preparation and with considerable fatigue to the eyes, was able to peer at London from the steeple of St. Martin's Church for stretches, at longest, of four minutes at a time. Mr. Cave was unable to ascertain if the winged Martians were the same as the Martians who hopped about the causeways and terraces, and if the latter could put on wings at will. He several times saw certain clumsy bipeds, dimly suggestive of apes, white and partially translucent, feeding among certain of the lichenous trees, and once some of these fled before one of the hopping, round-headed Martians. The latter caught one in its tentacles, and then the picture faded suddenly and left Mr. Cave most tantalizingly in the dark. On another occasion a vast thing, that Mr. Cave thought at first was some gigantic insect, appeared advancing along the causeway beside the canal with extraordinary rapidity. As this drew nearer Mr. Cave perceived that it was a mechanism of shining metals and of extraordinary complexity. And when he looked again, it had disappeared.

44

After a time Mr. Wace aspired to attract the attention of the Martians, and the next time that the strange eyes of one of them appeared close to the crystal Mr. Cave cried out and sprang away, and they immediately turned on the light and began to gesticulate in a manner suggestive of signalling. But when at last Mr. Cave examined the crystal again the Martian had departed.

These observations had progressed thus far in early November, and then Mr. Cave, feeling that the suspicions of his family about the crystal were allayed, began to take it to and fro with him in order that, as occasion arose in the daytime or night, he might comfort himself with what was fast becoming the most real thing in his existence.

In December Mr. Wace's work in connection with a forthcoming examination became heavy, the sittings were reluctantly suspended for a week, and for ten or eleven days—he is not quite sure which— he saw nothing of Cave. He then grew anxious to resume these investigations, and, the stress of his seasonal labors being abated, he went down to Seven Dials. At the corner he noticed a shutter before a bird fancier's window, and then another at a cobbler's. Mr. Cave's shop was closed.

He rapped and the door was opened by the step-son in black. He at once called Mrs. Cave, who was, Mr. Wace could not but observe, in cheap but ample widow's weeds of the most imposing pattern. Without any very great surprise Mr. Wace learned that Cave was dead and already buried. She was in tears, and her voice was a little thick. She had just returned from Highgate. Her mind seemed occupied with her own prospects and the honorable details of the obsequies, but Mr. Wace was at last able to learn the particulars of Mr. Cave's death. He had been found dead in his shop in the early morning, the day after his last visit to Mr. Wace, and the crystal had been clasped in his stone-cold hands. His face was smiling, said Mrs. Cave, and the velvet cloth from the minerals lay on the floor at his feet. He must have been dead five or six hours when he was found.

This came as a great shock to Wace, and he began to reproach himself bitterly for having neglected the plain symptoms of the old man's ill-health. But his chief thought was of the crystal. He approached that topic in a gingerly manner, because he knew Mrs. Cave's peculiarities. He was dumbfounded to learn that it was sold.

Mrs. Cave's first impulse, directly Cave's body had been taken upstairs, had been to write to the mad clergyman who had offered five pounds for the crystal, informing him of its recovery; but after a violent hunt in which her daughter joined her, they were convinced of the loss of his address. As they were without the means required to mourn and bury Cave in the elaborate style the dignitiy of an old Seven Dials inhabitant demands, they had appealed to a friendly fellow-tradesman in Great Portland Street. He had very kindly taken over a portion of the stock at a valuation. The valuation was his own and the crystal egg was included in one of the lots. Mr. Wace, after a few suitable consolatory observations, a little off-handedly proffered perhaps, hurried at once to Great Portland Street. But there he learned that the crystal egg had already been sold to a tall, dark man in grey. And there the material facts in this curious, and to me at least very suggestive, story came abruptly to an end. For a time Mr. Wace remained in the shop, trying the dealer's patience with hopeless questions, venting his own exasperation. And at last, realizing abruptly that the whole thing had passed out of his hands, had vanished like a vision of the night, he returned to his own rooms, a little astonished to find the notes he had made still tangible and visible upon his untidy table.

His annoyance and disappointment were naturally very great. He made a second call (equally ineffectual) upon the Great Portland Street dealer, and he resorted to advertisements in such periodicals as were likely to come into the hands of a brick-a-brack collector. He also wrote letters to *The Daily Chronicle* and *Nature*, but both these periodicals, suspecting a hoax, asked him to reconsider his action before they printed, and he was advised that such a strange story, unfortunately so bare of supporting evidence, might imperil his reputation as an investigator. Moreover, the calls of his proper work were urgent. So that after a month or so, save for an occasional reminder to certain dealers, he had reluctantly to abandon the quest for the crystal egg, and from that day to this it remains undiscovered. Occasionally, however, he tells me, and I can quite believe him, he has bursts of zeal, in which he abandons his more urgent occupation and resumes the search.

Whether or not it will remain lost for ever, with the material and origin of it, are things equally speculative at the present time. If the present purchaser is a collector, one would have expected the enquiries of Mr. Wace to have reached him through the dealers. He has been able to discover Mr. Cave's clergyman and "Oriental"—no other than the Rev. James Parker and the young Prince of Bosso-Kuni in Java. I am obliged to them for certain particulars. The object of the Prince was simply curiosity—and extravagance. He was so eager to buy, because Cave was so oddly reluctant to sell. It is just possible that the buyer in the second instance was simply a casual purchaser and not a collector at all, and the crystal egg, for all I know, may at the present moment be within a mile of me, decorating a drawing room or serving as a paper-weight—its remarkable functions all unknown. Indeed, it is partly with the idea of such a possibility that I have thrown this narrative into a form that will give it a chance of being read by the ordinary consumer of fiction.

My own ideas in the matter are practically identical with those of Mr. Wace. I believe the crystal on the mast in Mars and the crystal egg of Mr. Cave's to be in some physical, but at present quite inexplicable, way *en rapport,* and we both believed further that the terrestrial crystal must have been—possibly at some remote date— sent hither from that planet, in order to give the Martians a near view of our affairs. Possibly the fellows to the crystals in the other masts are also on our globe. No theory of hallucination suffices for the facts.

THE END

The EGGS from LAKE TANGANYIKA
» By Curt Siodmak «

**P**rofessor Meyer-Maier drew a sharp needle out of the cushion, carefully picked up with the pincers the fly lying in front of him and stuck it carefully upon a piece of white paper. He looked over the rim of his glasses, dipped his pen in the ink and wrote under the specimen:

"*Glossina palpalis,* specimen from Tsetsefly River. In the aboriginal language termed *nsi-nsi.* Usually found on river courses and lakes in West Africa. Bearer of the malady Negana (Tse-tse sickness—sleeping sickness.)"

He laid down the pen and took up a powerful magnifying glass for a closer examination. "A horrible creature," he murmered, and shivered involuntarily. On each side of the head of the flying horror, there was a monstrous eye surrounded by many sharp lashes and divided up into a hundred thousand flashing facets. An ugly proboscis thickly studded with curved barbs or hooks grew out of the lower side of the head. The wings were small and pointed, the legs armed with thorns, spines and claws. The thorax was muscular, like that of a prize fighter. The abdomen was thin and looked like India rubber. It could take in a great quantity of blood and expand like a balloon. On the whole, the flying horror, resembling a pre-historic flying dragon, was not very pleasant looking—Prof. Meyer-Maier took a pin and transfixed the body of the fly. It seemed to him that a vicious sheen of light eminated from the eyes and that the proboscis rolled up. Quickly he picked up the magnifying glass, but it was an optical illusion—the thing was dead, with all its poison still within its body.

Memories of the Expedition to Africa

With a deep sigh he laid aside pincers and magnifying glass and sank into a deep revery. The clock struck 12, 1-2-3-4-5, counted Professor Meyer-Maier.

In Udjidji, a village on lake Tanganyika, the natives had told him of gigantic flies inhabiting the interior further north. These monsters were three times as big as the giants composing the giant bodyguard of the Prince of Ssuggi, who all had to be of at least standard height. Meyer-Maier laughed over this negro fable, but the negroes were obstinate. They refused to follow him to the northern part of Lake Tanganyika. Even Msu-uru, his black servant, who otherwise made an intelligent impression, trembled with excitement and begged to be left out of the expedition—because there enormous flies and bees were to be found,—that let no man approach. They drank the river dry and guarded the valley of the elephants. "The Valley of the Elephants" was a fabled place where the old pachyderms withdrew to die. "It is inexplicable," soliloquized Meyer-Maier, "that no one ever found a dead elephant."

The clock struck 6-7-8.

The natives had come along on the expedition much against their will. Meyer-Maier had trouble to keep the caravan moving up to the day when he found four great, strange looking eggs, larger than ostrich eggs. The negroes were seized with a panic, half of them deserting in the night, in spite of the great distance from the coast. The other half could only be kept there by tremendous efforts. He had to make up his mind finally, to go back, but he secretly put the eggs he had found into his camping chest to solve their riddle.

Now they were here in his Berlin home, in his work-room. He had not found time as yet to examine them, for he had brought much material home to be worked over.

The clock struck 9-10.

Meyer-Maier kept thinking of the ugly head of the tse-tse fly that he had seen through the magnifying glass. A strange thought occurred to him and made him smile. Suppose the stories of the negroes were true and the giant flies—butterflies and beetles as big as elephants did exist! And suppose that they propagated as flies do!—each one laying eighty million eggs a year! He laughed aloud and pictured to himself how such a creature would stalk through the streets.

A Strange Sound and the Hatching of An Egg

He broke off suddenly, in the midst of his laughter. A sound reached his ear, an earsplitting buzzing like that of a thousand flies, a deafening hum, as if a swarm of bees were entering the room; it burst out like a blast of wind through the room and then stopped. Meyer-Maier jerked the door open. Nothing. All was quiet.

"I must relax for a while," said he, and opened the window. He turned on the light and threw back the lid of the big chest, which contained the giant eggs. Suddenly he grew pale as death and staggered back. A creature was crawling out, a creature as big as a police dog—a frightful creature, with wings—a muscular body, and six hairy legs with claws. It crept slowly, raised its incandescent head to the light and polished its wings with its hind legs. Faint with fright, Meyer-Maier pressed against the wall with outspread arms. A loud buzzing,—the creature swept across the room, climbed up on the windowsill and was gone.

Meyer-Maier came slowly to himself. "My nerves are deceiving me. Did I dream?" he whispered, and dragged himself to the camp-chest. But he became frozen with horror. One egg was broken open. "It breaks out of its shell like a chicken, it does not change into a chrysalis," he thought mechanically. At last his mind cleared and he awoke to the emergency. He sprang to the desk, snatched up his revolver, ran downstairs and out into the street. He saw no trace of the escaped giant insect. Meyer-Maier looked up at the lighted windows of his home. Suddenly the light became dim. "The other eggs"—like a blow came the thought—"the other eggs too have broken." He raced back up the stairs. A deafening buzzing filled the room. He jerked his door open and fired—once, twice, until the magazine was empty—the room was silent. Through the window he saw three silhouettes sweeping high across the night-sky and disappearing in the direction of the great woods in the West. In the chest there lay the four broken giant eggs .....

A Call for His Colleague

MEYER-MAIER sank upon a chair. "It's against all logic," he thought, and glanced at the empty revolver in his hand. "My delirium has taken wings and crawled out of the egg. What should I do? Shall I call the police? They will send me to an alienist! Keep quiet about it? Look for the creatures? I'll call up my colleague, Schmidt-Schmitt!" He dragged himself to the telephone and got a connection. Schmidt-Schmitt was at home! "This is Meyer-Maier," sounded a tired voice. "Come over at once!"

"What's the trouble?" asked Schmidt-Schmitt.

"My African giant eggs have burst," lisped Meyer-Maier with a failing voice. "You must come at once!"

"Your nerves are out of order," answered Schmidt-Schmitt. Have you still got the creatures?"

"They've gone," whispered Meyer-Maier,—he thought he would collapse,—"flew out of the window."

"There, there," laughed Schmidt-Schmitt. "Now, we are getting to the truth—of course they aren't there. Anyhow, I'll come over.

Meanwhile take a cognac and put on a cold pack."

"Take your car, and say nothing about what I told you."

Professor Meyer-Maier hung up the receiver.

It was incredible. He pressed his hand to his forehead. If the empty shells were not irrefutable evidence, he would have been inclined to think of hallucinations.

He helped himself to some brandy and after the second glass he felt better. "I wish Professor Schmidt-Schmitt would come. He ought to be here by now. He will have an explanation and will help me to get myself in hand again. The day of ghosts and miracles is long past. But why isn't he here? He ought to have come by this time."

Meyer-Maier looked out of the window. A car came tearing through the dark street and stopped with squeaking brakes in front of Meyer-Maier's residence. A form jumped out like an India rubber ball, ran up the steps, burst into Meyer-Maier's study, and collapsed into a chair.

"How awful," he gasped.

"It seems to me, you are even more excited over it than I," said Professor Meyer-Maier dispiritedly while he watched his shaking friend.

"Absolutely terrible," Professor Schmidt-Schmitt wiped his forehead with a silk handkerchief. "You were not suffering from nerves, you had no hallucinations. Just now I saw a fly-creature as large as a heifer falling upon a horse. The monster grew big and heavy, while the horse collapsed and the fly flew away. I examined the horse. Its veins and arteries were empty. Not a drop of blood was left in its body. The driver fainted with fright and has not come to yet. It is a world catastrophy."

Notifying the Police

"We must notify the police at once."

A quick telephone connection was obtained. The police Lieutenant in charge himself answered.

"This is Professor Meyer-Maier talking! Please believe what I am going to tell you. I am neither drunk nor crazy. Four poisonous gigantic flies, as large as horses, are at large in the city. They must be destroyed at all costs."

"What are you trying to do? Kid me?" the Lieutenant came back in an angry voice.

"Believe me—for God's sake," yelled Meyer-Maier, reaching the end of his nervous strength.

"Hold the wire." The Lieutenant turned to the desk of the sergeant. "What is up now?"

"A cab driver has been here who says that his horse was killed by a gigantic bird on Karlstrasse."

"Get the men of the second platoon ready for immediate action," he ordered the sergeant, and turned back to the telephone. "Hello Professor! Are you still there? Please come over as quickly as possible. What you told me is true. One of these giant insects has been seen."

Professor Meyer-Maier hung up. He loaded his revolver and put a Browning pistol into his colleague's hand. "Is your car still downstairs?"

"Yes I took the little limosine."

"Excellent—then the monster cannot attack us." They rushed on through the night.

"What can happen now?" inquired Professor Schmidt-Schmitt.

"These giant flies may propagate and multiply in the manner of the housefly. And in that case, due to their strength and poisonous qualities," continued Professor Meyer-Maier, "the whole human race will perish in a few weeks. When they crept from the shell they were as large as dogs. They grew to the size of a horse within an hour. God knows what will happen next. Let us hope and pray that we will be able to find and kill the four flies and destroy the eggs which they have laid in the meantime, within fourteen days."

The car came to a stop in front of the Police Station. A policeman armed with steel hemet and hand trench bombs swinging from his belt tore open the limousine door. The Lieutenant hastened out and conducted the scientists into the station house.

"Any more news?" inquired Meyer-Maier.

"The West Precinct station just called up. One of their patrolmen saw a giant animal fly over the Teutoburger Forest. Luckily we had war tanks near there which immediately set out in search of the creature."

The telephone-bell rang. The Lieutenant rushed to the phone.

"Central Police Station."

"East Station talking. Report comes from Lake Wieler, that a gigantic fly has attacked two motor boats."

"Put small trench mortars on the police-boat and go out on the lake. Shoot when the beast gets near you."

The door of the Station-House opened and the city commissioner entered. "I have just heard some fabulous stories," he said, and approached the visitors. "Professor Meyer-Maier? Major Pritzel-Wilzell ! Can you explain all this?"

"I brought home with me four large eggs from my African expedition, for examination. Tonight these eggs broke open. Four great flies came out—a sort of tse-tse fly, such as is found on Lake Tangangika. The creatures escaped through the window and we must make every endeavor to kill them at once."

The telephone bell rang as if possessed.

"This is the Central Broadcasting Station. A giant bird has been caught in the high voltage lines. It has fallen down and lies on the street."

"Close the street at once." The Major took up the instrument. "Call up the Second Company. Let all four flying companies go off with munition and gasoline for three days. Come with me my friends, we will get at least one of them!"

An armored automobile came tearing along at a frightful speed. We appreciate your foresight, Major," said Meyer-Maier, as they stepped into the steel-armored machine.

One of the Giant Flies Is Electrocuted

Although it was five o'clock in the morning, the square in front of the broadcasting station was black with people. The police kept a space clear in the center, where monstrously large and ugly, lay the dead giant fly. Its wings were burnt, its proboscis extended, while the legs, with their claws, were drawn up against the body. The abdomen was a great ball, full of bright red liquid. "That is certainly the creature that killed the horse," said Schmidt-Schmitt, and pointed at the thick abdomen. He then walked around the creature. "*Glossina palpalis*. A monstrous tse-tse fly."

"Will you please send the monster to the zoological laboratory?" The Major nodded assent. The firemen, prepared for service, pushed poles under the insect and tried to lift it up from the ground. Out of the air came a droning sound. An airplane squadron dropped out of the clouds and again disappeared. A bright body with vibrating wings flew across the sky. The airplanes dropped on it. The noise of the machine-guns started. The bright body fell in a spiral course to the ground. Crying and screaming, the people fled from the street and crowded into the houses. They couldn't tell where the insect would fall and they were afraid of their heads. The street was empty in an instant. The body of the monster fell directly in front of the armored car and lay there, stiff. In its fall it carried away a lot of aerial cable and now it lay on the pavement as if caught in a net, the head torn by the machine gun bullets. It looked like a strange gleaming cactus.

"Take me to my home, Major," groaned Meyer-Maier. "I can't stand it any longer. The excitement is too much for me."

In the Hospital

The armored car started noisily into motion. Meyer-Maier fell from the seat, senseless, upon the floor of the tonneau. When he came to himself, he lay in a strange bed. His gaze fell upon a bell which swung to and fro above his face. In his head there was a humming like an airplane motor. He made no attempt, even to think. His finger pressed the push-button and he never released it until half-a-dozen attendants came rushing into the room. One figure stood out in dark colors, in the group of white-clad interns. It was his colleague, Schmidt-Schmitt.

"You're awake?" said he, and stepped to his bed. "How are you feeling?"

"My head is buzzing as if there were a swarm of hornets living in it. How many hours have I lain here?"

"Hours?" Schmidt-Schmitt dwelt upon the word. "Today is the fifteenth day that you are lying in Professor Stiebling's sanitorium. It was a difficult case. You always woke up at meal-time and without saying a word, went to sleep again."

"Fifteen days!" cried Meyer-Maier excitely. And the insects? Have they been killed?"

"I'll tell you the whole story when you are well again," said Schmidt-Schmitt, quieting him. "Lie as you are, quietly—any excitement may hurt you."

"They must not come into the room!" he screamed out to an excited messenger, who breathlessly pulled the door open.

"Professor! ——" the man was in deadly fear ——"the Central Police station has given out the news that a swarm of giant flies are descending upon the city."

Barricade all windows at once!"

"You wasted precious time," screamed Meyer-Maier, and jumped out of the bed. "Let me go to my house. I must solve the riddle as to how to get at the insects. Don't touch me," he raved. He snatched a coat from the rack, ran out of the house, and jumped into Schmidt-Schmitt's automobile which stood at the gate, and went like the wind, to his home. The door of his house was ajar. He rushed up four flights and in delirious haste rushed into his workroom. The telephone bell rang.

55

The Danger Is Over

Meyer-Maier snatched up the receiver. He got the consoling message from the city police-commissioner: "The danger is over, Professor. Our air-squadron has destroyed the swarm with a cloud of poison-gas. Only two of the insects escaped death. These we have caught in a net and are taking them to the zoological gardens."

"And if they have left eggs behind them?"

"We are going to search the woods systematically and will inject Lysol into any eggs we find. I think that will help," laughed the Major. "Shall I send some of them to you for examination?"

"No," cried Meyer-Maier in fright. "Keep them off my neck."

He sat down at his work-table. There seemed a vicious smile on the face of the transfixed dead tse-tse fly. "You frightful ghost," murmured the professor with palid lips, and threw a book on the insect. His head was in a daze. He tried his best to think clearly. An axiom of science came to him: if the flies are as large as elephants, they can only propagate as fast as elephants do. They can't have a million young ones, but only a few. "I can't be wrong," he murmured. "I'll look up the confirmation."

He took up the telephone and called the city Commissioner. "Major, how many insects were in the swarm?"

"Thirteen. Eleven are dead. The other two will never escape alive. They are fed up with the poison-gas."

"Thank you." Meyer-Maier hung up the receiver. "Very well," he murmured, "now there can be no question of any danger, for each fly can only lay three or four eggs at once,—not a million."

An immense weariness overcame him. He went into his bed-room and fell exhausted on his bed. "It is well that there is a supreme wisdom which controls the laws of nature. Otherwise the world would be subject to the strangest surprises" he thought of the monsters and crept anxiously under the bed-clothes. "I'll entrust Schmidt-Schmitt with the investigation of the creature phenomenon, I simply can't stand further excitement."

And sleep spread the mantle of well-deserved quiet over him.

THE END

Medium

First Place: **The Metal Giants**   **Edmond Hamilton**

[Ed. Note: Not edited by Gernsback]

Second Place: **The Diamond Lens**   **Fitz-James O'Brien**

This classic, by the famous author, is not as widely known as it deserves to be. The story is a masterpiece from every angle, although it was written over fifty years ago. There is no question that Mr. O'Brien must have been an expert on microscopy, because only a master could go into the details as he does in this story.

The theme, while fantastic, is beautiful in its extreme, and the advent of the ultra-microscope, invented long after O'Brien had died, lends new color to this story, which can be read and re-read many times—a story that will stand out from many others for generations to come.   *Hugo Gernsback—1926*

Third Place: **The Thing from—"Outside"**   **George Allan England**

Here is an extraordinary story by the well-known magazine writer, George Allan England. This story should be read quite carefully, and it is necessary to use one's imagination in reading it.

The theme of Mr. England's story is unusual and extraordinary. If we can take insects and put them upon the dissecting table in order to study their anatomy, is there a good reason why some super-Intelligence cannot do the same thing with us humans?

It may be taken as a certainty that Intelligence, as we understand it, is not only of our earth. It is also not necessary to presume that Intelligence may have its setting only in a body of flesh and blood.

There is no reason for disbelieving that a Super-intelligence might not reside in gases or invisible structures, something which we of today cannot even imagine.   *Hugo Gernsback—1926*

Incorrect spelling of George Allan England on page 106 from original magazine.

The METAL GIANTS

BY
Edmond Hamilton

As to the beginning of the matter, there is information in plenty. Dusty files of yellowing newspapers yield columns about it, for it was a mild sensation at the time. And concerning the appalling climax of the business, when the machine-monsters burst upon an incredulous world, there are but few who need to be informed. But what of the four years between, when that monstrous menace to humanity lay hidden in the West Virginia hills, germinating, growing, reaching? Will anything more of that time ever be known than a few scrawled pages in a little diary? Shall we ever comprehend much of the story but the petty furor of its beginning and its flaming, tragic end? Well, to that beginning.

One starts with Detmold. A professor of electro-chemistry, a rather unusual professor, who was constantly advancing radical, astounding theories in almost every branch of science. A few of his theories he proved, but most of them were unprovable, wild, untrammeled speculations. Today his suggestions are genuinely interesting and stimulating, but at the time it seemed that his experiments, his statements, were becoming more and more fantastic, calling forth an ever-increasing flood of shocked protests from outraged scientists. And this was not at all to the liking of Juston University, where he taught. Juston is the third oldest college in the country, and has an ancient, scholarly tradition that it takes very seriously.

So when complaints began to come in from some of the more prosperous alumni, possible donors of buildings and the like, the middle-aged gentlemen who directed the university's policy met around a mahogany table and decided that Detmold must be removed from the institution at the first opportunity, as quietly as possible. And the next morning, as if to confirm the wisdom of their decision, Detmold announced the partial success of his latest experiment, which was the making of an artificial brain.

It was a supreme chance for the sensation-mongering Sunday supplements, for the gibing columnists, and they seized it at once. Detmold's brain, as it was called, was derided in the theaters, cartooned in the newspapers and jeered at by his fellow scientists. And yet, reading over the man's ideas now, it is hard for us to detect any flagrant absurdity.

No doubt it was a startling proposition, to construct an artificial brain that would possess consciousness, memory, reasoning power.

That mass of fiber inside our skulls by virtue of which we comprehend the world about us is a seemingly unsolvable mystery. Yet even such an idea as Detmold's, advanced by a man of his admitted intellect and achievements, should have been given a fair hearing, at least.

In fact, experimenters had already tried to reproduce the make-up of the brain. Several scientists, following up the work of Loeb and Kendler in their efforts to manufacture living protoplasm from chemicals, had tried to produce a mass of living cells, with which to form a living organ, a heart or a brain. All such efforts had been failures, and it was admitted that success seemed impossible.

But Detmold had attacked the problem from an entirely different standpoint. It was his theory that the sensations of the nervous system are flashed to the brain as electric currents, or vibrations, and that it was the action of these vibratory currents on the brain-stuff that caused consciousness and thought. Thus, instead of trying to make simple, living cells and from them work up the complicated structure of the brain, he had constructed an organ, a brain of metal, entirely inorganic and lifeless, yet whose atomic structure he claimed was analogous to the atomic structure of a living brain. He had then applied countless different electrical vibrations to this metallic brain-stuff, and finally announced that under vibrations of certain frequency the organ had shown faint signs of consciousness.

To the public of that time, such an assertion must have seemed quite insane. The usual comment on the subject was that if this were a sample of Detmold's ideas, he had best keep the first brain he manufactured for his own use. And Detmold's own attitude did not help his case, for he was an impatient, high-tempered type, prone to regard as fools and asses all those people who expressed any doubt concerning his work.

Three eminent scientists accepted his invitation to witness a demonstration of his experiment, and their comments later were caustic. It would seem that when the three illustrious gentlemen called at his laboratory at the appointed hour, Detmold had bruskly informed them that he was working out a sudden new idea concerning the experiment, and that they would have to call a few days later, by which time he hoped to have achieved complete success.

Naturally, that was the end of him at the university. It was plain to everyone that the man was a cheap faker who had warded off investigation and exposure at the last moment, and a cry went up that he should be removed from the institution he was disgracing. At the year's biggest football game the next afternoon, when Juston played Bannister College, ten enterprising students rushed onto the field between halfs and unrolled a large cloth banner, with the painted words, "Fire Detmold!" A wave of applause and laughter rippled across the stadium at sight of it.

And after the game, the football team, become heroes of the hour by their victory over Bannister, marched together to the home of the university's president and presented him with a petition demanding the summary dismissal of the professor whose charlatanry was smirching the name of Juston. The president smilingly accepted the document.

So the next morning, after an hour of nervous fidgeting and snapping of fingers, the president summoned Detmold and smoothly informed him that his resignation would be accepted.

There was a stormy scene in that office when Detmold learned that he was to be shunted out of the university. He was a tall, powerful man with a keen, relentless face, and in his rage he came near to laying violent hands on the president, and said a number of scathing things regarding that individual's stupidity and cowardice, winding up with a red-hot denunciation of the world at large. When he burst out of the office, he thrust rudely through the little knot of curious listeners at the door, and hurried over to his laboratory, to begin packing the experiment that had caused his dismissal.

It was there that he was found an hour later by Gilbert Lanier, the one instructor at Juston who understood and sympathized with the man. Also Lanier, a diffident young English teacher, was probably Detmold's only friend, for Detmold seemed to have no close relatives at all, and his testy, high-strung nature repelled most people. Sitting on a desk, moodily contemplating the little room that had been his private laboratory for years, he told Lanier of his dismissal, raging the while at the president and his disapproval of "impossible theories."

"Impossible theories!" he mocked. "My God, and I used to think that a great scientific discovery was welcomed with open arms! And these fools think I am crazy, to work on such a thing at all! Look at this, Lanier,—you haven't seen it since I made the improvements," and he turned to a table on which rested the artificial brain.

It was very simple in appearance, resembling an egg of black metal, some ten inches in length. Inset in its upper surface was a small lens of glass, and leading into each end of the thing were three wires, which were connected to a complicated tangle of electrical apparatus on the other side of the room.

As Lanier watched, Detmold made swift adjustments and snapped on several switches, and the low humming of a motor-generator filled the room. Turning eagerly, his smoldering resentment forgotten for the moment, he said, "The same basic principle. The T-wave, the vibratory current, is produced over there and led into the brain-case to act on the atomic organism inside. Right now that thing is conscious," and he gazed at it with mingled fondness and pride.

Lanier could not restrain an incredulous shrug of his shoulders, and Detmold took it up at once. "I repeat, conscious," he asserted. "It is consciousness of a crude, dim sort, but still consciousness, awareness, knowledge. And I can prove it now. Since you last saw it I've provided it with the sense of sight. See that inset lens? Well, it's like no lens you ever saw, for it's really an artificial eye, that I made myself. There is an artificial retina beneath and it is connected direct to the brain-stuff, and carries its sensations to it, as electric currents."

"An artificial retina?" asked Lanier. "Isn't that going a bit too far? An inorganic material sensitive to light?"

"Did you never hear of a substance called selenium?" asked Detmold with fine sarcasm, and as Lanier started, he added, "Ah, you begin to see! You remember that the electrical resistance of selenium varies enormously in light and in darkness, and you begin to perceive how the light striking that artificial retina could be translated into electricity and flashed to the brain. It is all so clear—now. But I was telling you about the eye. There's a shutter that closes across that lens, much like a high-speed camera shutter, but capable of being opened or closed by an inconceivably delicate force. I'm not going to tell you all about it, you or anyone, but watch it now," and taking a small flashlight from his pocket, he flashed its brilliant little beam directly on the inset lens.

Lanier watched intently. There was no change for a space of seconds, then, with a tiny click, the shutter closed across the lens. He drew a long breath as he straightened up.

"You saw?" asked Detmold, snapping off the switches. "The thing can see with that eye, just enough to differentiate between light and dark, and it hates bright light, so what? It closes the shutter, cutting off the light. Isn't that intelligence, mind, reason? Crude and feeble now, I grant you, but it will grow. I will develop it. I'll go farther yet." His voice dropped, and the brooding, sullen expression crept back over his face. "And yet those fools say, 'Impossible, impossible!' Damn them, this metal brain has more intelligence than they. Or it will have. It *will* have." As his friend remained silent he asked, "Do you think I am faking it, Lanier?"

"No," was the slow answer, "but I do think you're treading very near forbidden ground. That movement—that intelligence—have you considered, Detmold,.what an intelligence might be like, that had no controlling, directing power, a brain without a soul?"

"Theology, mysticism!" cried the other. "No, Lanier, I am going on with this, if only to show these fools the depth of their folly. I have a place where I can work in peace, thank God, and where the confounded newspapers won't pester me, for I'll tell no one where I'm going. No, not even you," he added, clapping his friend on the back affectionately, "for you might talk in your sleep. But when I finish it, you'll hear from me. And so will the world."

Lanier did not reply, and in silence they began the work of packing. And the next day, when they stood on the station platform in the last few minutes before the train's departure, there seemed little to say. The whistle of the locomotive, a last clasp of Detmold's hand and a muttered "Good-bye," and the train was receding swiftly down the track, and he was gone.

More than one person wondered where Detmold had gone. His name was prominent in the newspapers that night, was mentioned often in homes and clubs and restaurants, with a chuckle or a sneer. It was not mentioned so much the next night; a month afterward it was seldom heard; and in a year not one person in ten thousand remembered the man. None knew where he had gone, his name and personality and strange ideas had sunk into silence and forgetfulness; and laughing, toiling, hurrying, the world sped on.

Chapter 2

It was fully four years after Detmold's disappearance that the strange phenomena at Stockton began to attract attention. Stockton was a small steel town in northern West Virginia, set in a long valley between dark, thickly wooded hills, and from those hills came news of mysterious occurences.

The first thing to reach the newspapers was a small article printed early in July, telling of some very curious ground-markings that had been discovered several miles west of Stockton. These marks were circles some ten feet across in which trees, bushes and ground had evidently been stamped down by some tremendous force, forming circular pits in the ground some three feet in depth. A number of these strange pits had been found by farmers and no one seemed able to advance a plausible suggestion as to their cause.

The article was published throughout the country, but as no further news on the matter was immediately forthcoming, it was forgotten in a week, as stranger incidents have been forgotten.

Ten days passed before the second Stockton dispatch was printed, an article that caused a good many smiles. This dispatch told of a farmer named Morgan who lived in the hills north of the city, a wild lonely district, and who had suddenly appeared in Stockton with his family and few possessions packed into a ramshackle Ford, intent on departing from the vicinity as soon as possible. When questioned as to the cause of his sudden migration, he told a very strange story.

Two nights before, he said, he had been awakened shortly after midnight by a crashing, snapping sound outside. His small house was set on the steep side of a narrow, winding valley, and the noise seemed to come from the forests at its foot. His curiosity aroused, he had stepped out on his little porch and had dimly seen, in the moonlight, a gigantic shape that was moving along the valley.

He described it, very vaguely, as being a monstrous parody of a human figure, with two huge legs or supports, all of three hundred feet in height, and for body, a large, cylindrical mass. It gleamed in the moonlight, he said, as if it were made of *metal*. It was striding down the valley in a stiff, immense imitation of the human step, and he could see that its towering limbs or supports, which buckled and straightened midway, like a human knee, were crushing the forest beneath them like a forest of twigs. Only one hurried, misty glimpse of the thing he got, and it disappeared around a turn in the valley, but when he explored the next morning he found its tracks, shallow, circular pits, identical in appearance with the strange markings that had already been found.

There was a good deal of amusement in Stockton over this tale, though Morgan sullenly asserted its truth. When it was reprinted throughout the country, the story was generally accompanied by some humorous comment regarding the powers of West Virginia moonshine, and the progressiveness of the day, when tipplers now saw weird machines instead of the traditional serpents.

But the next day, after Morgan and his family had clattered out of Stockton in the rickety little car, it occurred to an inquisitive newspaper reporter to drive out to the valley and gather some information—not that he put any faith in Morgan's story, but in order to get the views of the man's former neighbors, the farmers of that section.

Early that evening the reporter returned, and the news he brought set Stockton buzzing with conjecture and argument. For he had not only found the markings Morgan had described, he had definitely ascertained that before the night in question no such marks had been seen in the little valley. And the few families who made their homes in that district were not laughing over the matter, but seemed considerably perturbed. All of them testified as to Morgan's sobriety and truthfulness, and one household added a corroberating occurence of a few days before, when an eight-year old son had returned from a ramble in the hills with a twisted, childish story of having seen "a big tin man" a long way off.

Such was the information the reporter brought back, and it caused excited discussion through all the town. Was such a thing possible? Could Morgan's story have been true? But if so, if such a thing had actually been seen, what was it? Machine, vehicle, what? No, it could not be true, there must be some mistake, some exaggeration. And yet—

The wires out of Stockton were humming that night, and in Boston and Duluth and Fort Worth, the next morning, people were to read and wonder. It was a new sensation, and they waited with interest for further news. Whatever happened, the reporters would get it and serve it up in their daily paper, with photographs made on the spot and a diagram to make it all clear.

Until late that night the city's principal streets were quite crowded and there was constant discussion and speculation. For the first time, Stockton was finding itself a center of national interest, and it was very proud of its sudden fame.

Once, an hour before midnight, a great light was seen above the northern hills, a brilliant shaft of purple light that swept across the sky like a gigantic, flaming finger, then faded into the darkness. The crowds in the streets saw and marveled. For some time they watched, but it was not seen again, and the blackness of the night seemed to close around the city like a giant hand.

From the steel mills, great tongues of red flame shot up, soaring, beautiful, conveying a warm quality of reassurance against the vast, brooding darkness. The mighty furnaces and towers, standing out black and austere against the glare of molten steel, held within them a calm, silent encouragement, as if proclaiming the greatness and power of their builder, man. But the flame-shot sky behind them, like blood ....

Chapter 3

Lanier arrived in Stockton early the next morning. His face was drawn and haggard, as it had been since he first read a certain humorous newspaper dispatch, and in his mind was an immense perplexity, a vague, chilling fear.

Until late in the afternoon he tramped wearily through the town, asking in all quarters the same question: "Do you know of anyone named Detmold who lives in or around Stockton? A tall, strong man—" And from all he questioned he got no trace, until he happened into the office of a small trucking and hauling company.

None there knew anything of Detmold, but they had done some work for a certain Foster, who corresponded exactly to Lanier's description. This man lived several miles from the city, in a northeastern direction, and had hired them to haul some boxes from the railroad to his home, an old farmhouse. A mighty bad road it was, too, and this Foster had been very particular about the moving of his stuff. Yes, they could direct him to the place. You went out such and such a concrete road, and turned up a rutty lane, very steep ....

By the time the sun hung poised above the western horizon, Lanier was already ascending that steep, twisted road. More than once he glanced back at the city below, a city bathed in the golden afternoon sunlight. Its streets were filled now with workers returning home from the mills, tired and blackened, calling out to the friends they met for the latest news on "that Morgan critter," as they termed it.

A quiet serenity, a dreamy, contented peace pervaded Stockton, contrasting with the tense excitement of the preceding night. In a thousand homes, the evening meal was being prepared and the day's gossip related, in the west the sun sank lower and lower, and all around, beyond the encircling hills, death marched toward the city with crashing, giant strides.

Chapter 4

The sun had slipped down very near the horizon when a sudden jangling of bells ran through Stockton, hurried, confused. The factory whistles blew frantically for a few minutes, then suddenly, unaccountably stopped. A cry, a shout was running over the city swift as spreading flame, and everywhere houses belched forth their inmates and people looked anxiously about for the cause of disturbance. And then they looked up to the hills and saw their doom.

For on the heights around Stockton, in a great circle, stood a score or more of gigantic shapes, silent, motionless. They seemed quite identical in appearance, towering metal giants cast in a roughly human form, each with two immense limbs, smooth columns of metal 10 feet across, looming up all of a hundred yards in height. And set on those two huge supports, the *body*, an upright cylinder of the same gleaming metal, 50 feet in diamter, quite smooth and unbroken of surface, and bearing on its smooth top something that flashed brilliantly in the sunlight, a small, triangular case in each side of which glittered a lens of glass. And from each cylinder projected two additional limbs, arms shining and flexible, hanging almost to the ground, tapering, twisting.

The bells had stopped ringing, and in thick stupefied silence the people in the streets gazed up at the metal giants, who surveyed them in equal immobility and silence. Then from one of their number sounded a weird call, a harsh, wailing sound that rose to a high-pitched scream. And at that signal all of the things began to stride swiftly down to the city, the mighty limbs whirling out and crashing down in steps of unbelievable length, buckling and straightening and whirling out in another step. Rapidly, inexorably, they closed in on Stockton, a diminishing, tightening circle.

That stunned moment of sheer astonishment fled, and a vast, hoarse bellow sounded, the mad shout of thousands of panic-stricken people. Down the streets raced careening autos, ripping through crowds of hapless pedestrians, driving into the mass of tangled wrecks that blocked every corner in a few minutes. Screaming, pushing, striking, the mobs flowed along the streets, striving always to win away from the city's central section and escape into the surrounding country. And all the while, with thundering, earth-shaking strides, the metal shapes marched on toward the city.

On and on they came, until they had reached the outer suburbs, looming up above the buildings like giants in a toy village. The long, flexible arms were whipping out now, with tremendous power. Smash!—and a small brick building toppled. Smash!—a giant limb crashed down through a bungalow. Smash! smash! smash!—on and on, slowly, deliberately, reducing the city to ruins.

They made but small effort to kill the screaming little figures that ran about beneath them, but they let few of these escape outside their circle, herding them always toward the center of the city, as they closed in on it.

Nearly an hour had passed before that ring of giants had contracted to a mile diameter. Inside of it the streets were solidly packed with people, and the buildings were full to bursting, the supposedly safer cellars being pools of suffocating, trampling humanity.

Around was ranged the circle of the metal shapes, and for a moment they seemed to be contemplating the tiny, frenzied throngs beneath them. Again sounded the wailing signal, and each of the things seemed to be fumbling behind itself with a flexible arm, an arm that reappeared grasping a small, black sphere. In unison, they thrust forward these globes from each of which a cloud of yellow gas instantly spurted, falling on the crowds beneath, flowing over and through them, a saffron flood that rolled on through the buildings and down into the packed cellars.

Wherever it touched, the people sank into death, slumping down like bags of sawdust, suddenly limp and inert. And the faces of the dead were dreadful to see, shrunken, collapsed, like shriveled masks of skin.

Swiftly the gas flowed away and sank into the ground, and the heaps of bodies were revealed, silent and unmoving, a strange contrast to the shouting and running of the moment before. Then smash! smash!—and the huge limbs were jerking out and crashing buildings down, kicking them over, pushing them aside, covering the mounds of dead with a tangled mass of broken bricks and twisted steel.

The metal giants strode away, here and there crushing a building, uprooting a track, moving toward the eastern end of the valley, whose inhabitants had seen and were fleeing in terror. And one man had seen who did not flee, a man whose face was stamped with horror. It was Lanier, and from his distant hill-top he looked down on a mass of broken ruins where an hour before had been a bustling city.

As he watched, darkness flowed down on the city, veiling its shattered remnants. He heard distant shouts snapping out, up the valley, where the metal shapes had gone. He could hear, too, a humming drone, as an airplane came and went and circled over the broken city, hovering for a time, then winging away toward the north. For some minutes he continued to peer into the deepening darkness, then rose stiffly from his crouched position and stumbled back into the forest, moving as a man in a daze. His brain held but one thought his lips uttered but one word: "Detmold!"

Chapter 5

And fear swept through the land.

In New York the first fragmentary reports of the annihilation of Stockton had been greeted with a good-natured laugh, but as more and more details came in, extras began to pour into the streets, and crowds gathered around the clamorous bulletins. In troubled silence they read the account of the few survivors, the story of that red hour of Stockton's death. There came, too, later, short dispatches relating the further advance of the metal giants, who were evidently proceeding leisurely northward, killing, destroying, uprooting all in their path.

Clicking out over the network of wires, flashing across the night in radio waves went the short, ominous sentences, sentences in which an epoch of comparative safety and peace was dissolving, crumbling, falling. There were reports of action at Washington, of hurried meetings and swift discussions, and finally, late in the morning, a proclamation of the Federal government was flashed to every section of the country

It was evident, declared this statement, that the country was being attacked from within by men possessing new types of fighting machines, with vast and unknown powers. These men, who were probably either anarchists or agents of some foreign power, were using as a weapon a new and very deadly poison gas, a gas that sank harmlessly through skin and flesh but which dissolved all kinds of bone like sugar in water, causing instant dissolution of the skeleton and skull of every human body it touched, resulting in instant collapse and death. Therefore, it was advisable for everyone living within a three hundred mile radius of Stockton to take refuge in flight. Troops and artillery were already on the way to meet and battle the new foe, and scientists were being consulted as to the best method of combating it. It was hoped that the people would give full co-operation to the government by following its orders carefully, refraining from spreading alarmist rumors and trying to carry on all essential business as usual.

Thus the proclamation, and its businesslike sound caused people to breathe easier for a time. There had been so many emergencies before that had been met and conquered. War and riot, flood and fire. And after all, these new war-machines could not be so very formidable, even though they had devastated a city. That story of their size, hundreds of feet and such, must be exaggerated. As for the deadly gas, well, there had been deadly gases before. Anarchists, foreign invaders, whoever they were, the soldiers would stop them. A few high-explosive shells would fix them.

Thus did the average citizen reassure his household when anyone in it expressed anxiety or fear. After that first panicky moment, the usual serenity of the country was again ascendant, and there was but little open worry concerning the enemy. An ignorant observer would scarcely have suspected the existence of the things, except for the newspapers.

It was definitely known that the metal giants, leaving four of their number at Stockton, were now advancing north toward Wheeling and Pittsburgh, eighteen in number. Airplanes and scouts reported their destruction of all towns and villages in their path, whose inhabitants had fled at the first alarm. The War Department had decided to concentrate its force a few miles south of Wheeling, and ten thousand soldiers, part of them hastily assembled militia, had been flung across the enemy's path at that spot, backed by a heavy force of artillery. There were vague rumors of ambushes prepared for the foe, pits and high-explosive mines and the like.

On the evening of the third day after Stockton's destruction, the fighting-machines were reported to be less than twenty miles south of the troops, and were already being shelled by a few heavy guns that were mounted on railway platforms. In every city, all waited tensely for news of the first clash. The hours dragged past, the crowds moved restlessly about, and still came no news.

It was well after 2 o'clock in the morning that word finally came, that short, fateful dispatch that loosed terror on the world. It emanated from the fast-crumbling Federal government, which had been transferred from Washington to Philadelphia:

> PHILADELPHIA, July 24.—*Word has been received by the War Department here that the troops defending Wheeling have been severly defeated by the enemy's fighting-machines, which, using some unknown device, projected a blanket of their deadly gas over the country for several miles ahead of them, nine-tenths of the troops have been killed without seeing the enemy. The remnant of the force has retreated toward Pittsburgh, and it is thought that the fighting-machines have already entered Wheeling. One is believed to have been destroyed by shell-fire early in the engagement, but aside from this they have proved to be quite unvulnerable. No word has yet been received concerning the smaller force of troops detailed to attack the four machines at Stockton, but it is doubtful, if such an attack has already been made, whether it was successful. No one has yet seen the men controlling and operating the fighting-machines, as they seem to stay closely hidden within the latter, but they have shown by their actions that they are quite merciless, so warning is conveyed to the people of the country that when any section of the country is invaded by the enemy in these machines, the only safety at present lies in flight. Offers of military aid have been tendered this government by several European powers, but until some new and effective weapon can be devised, it will be impossible to meet this unknown foe in battle with any chances of success.*

Chapter 6

When Lanier stumbled into Detmold's farmhouse, early in the second day after the massacre of Stockton, he could only half understand that he had finally found the object of his hours of searching. After that seeming eternity of wandering wildly through the forest, he was very near collapse. Even after his brain had cleared enough to recognize that this was the place that had been described to him, he took but little interest. In the kitchen of the house he found canned food, and after wolfing some of this he flung himself on the couch and slept heavily for all of that day and night, not waking until near noon of the third day.

But he woke with mind clear and alert and feeling immensely hungry. After another sketchy meal from tins he began to prowl about the house. And to his dismay, he found that there was no sign of Detmold's having occupied the place for weeks at least.

The furniture of the house was very simple, and it was in the condition to be expected when kept by a careless bachelor. A single large room had been converted into a laboratory, but even this was in great disorder and had evidently been stripped of most of its apparatus. There were many unmistakable signs of Detmold's residence in the place, but none that would indicate how long before he had deserted it.

But in the laboratory, by chance, he found Detmold's diary, a thick, canvas-covered book tossed to one side of a table. Lanier glanced into it idly, then with startled interest, and an hour later was still reading intently.

For in it he found explanation, and found too, greater fear. Now, for the first time he saw clearly the monstrous horror that had been loosed on the world, saw it in its most terrible aspect.

The diary began with the events immediately previous to Detmold's departure from Juston, and seemed to be kept as a record of his various experiments, references to many of which Lanier could not understand. On the day of his ousting from the university, he had made some very vitriolic comments in the little book concerning the officials of Juston, and, their general asininity. He also spoke of the place where he intended to carry on his experiments, an old farmhouse outside of Stockton, a half-forgotten inheritance. And when he had gone there, fitting the place up as a laboratory, he had done so under the name of Foster, in order to escape the unwelcome attention of prying reporters.

71

There were a number of gaps in the diary's entries, but on the whole, the story it told was quite continuous. He had found a place where he could work in peace, and had centered his time and effort on the metal brain, constantly striving to improve it. And as the months passed, he had made vast progress with the thing. Though the basic principle of it was the same, he had made it much larger, had made the ramifications of its atomic organism far more complex, with a corresponding increase in the thing's mental power. Instead of a crude, single lens, he had furnished it with two large, all-seeing eyes, one on each side of its oval case. He had added an ear for the perception of sound, a super-microphone that caught the smallest sounds and, translating them into electrical impulses, flashed them to the central, conscious brain. And after months of weary trials, he had been able to furnish the brain with arms or members, two small, hollow limbs of flexible metal that projected from each end of the brain-case, being actuated by a chain of electro-magnets inside, so that the brain, by sending the correct electrical current through these magnets, could twist the arms about at its pleasure.

There came a page where the diary was spotted and hard to understand, where Detmold's mind had out-leaped his pen in his exultation. Gradually Lanier made out that he had perfected a method which made it unnecessary to produce the actuating electric-vibrations outside the brain. Instead, he had found a way to produce these vibrations inside of the very brain-stuff itself, inside of its atomic structure, constantly and automatically. He had achieved this by a manipulation of electrons, a tampering with the innermost secrets of matter. How he had accomplished this stupendous feat was not explained, for he had confided but few technical secrets to the diary. But by virtue of this discovery, the metal brain became, for the first time, wholly independent of anything outside itself, quite self-sufficient and almost, one could say, living.

And from that point forward, the pages of the little book were records of wonder. Detmold wrote always of the brain's leaping intelligence, its growing power to differentiate between the sensations it received, its deft handling of objects and instruments. And later, of teaching it to read, of starting with children's picture-books and working on with models and printed words, until finally it could read books, and evidently understand them, at least partly. It was significant, he noted, that while it would read, with unvarying attention, any scientific work, it rejected completely all fiction, poetry, and other imaginative literature, preferring facts. It made him realize, he wrote, the limitations of the thing. It had intelligence, yes, but not human intelligence, for all it had been constructed by a

72

human. And it was for this reason that he gave up his efforts to communicate with the thing. Evidently it did not understand his spoken words, and when he wrote numberless messages and held them for it to see, it made no response. He began to understand that the thing had no point of contact, no common ground, with himself, except in the realm of science.

So he took another course and taught it to handle experiments, to duplicate the simple experiments he performed before it, which it did with ease. Apparently it showed astounding ability along these lines and could perform highly complex experiments in chemistry and physics without a single error, unhumanly perfect. And finally a day came when his triumph was complete, for the brain performed successfuly an experiment that had baffled Detmold himself, as well as all other experimenters. The creature was proving itself greater than its creator.

He wrote that as he watched the flexible, snakelike metal arms flashing about with beaker and test-tube and burner, unerringly, swiftly, he realized that he had constructed an intelligence that was more than human. A mind that was far greater than man's, aided as it was by cold, ruthless reasoning power, precise, perfect memory, and quite unswayed by the thousand and one emotions that affect human intelligence, untroubled by love and hate and fear and joy and sorrow.

Detmold's triumph was complete, and he could return to the mocking world with the metal brain, as he had planned. But the three years of strain and solitude and toil, and this sudden realization of his hopes, were too much for him, and he was stricken with sudden sickness, while he was making one of his infrequent visits to Stockton. For a short time he was cared for at the hospital there, then was taken to Pittsburgh for a necessary operation, which was neatly and successfully performed, but which kept him in a Pittsburgh hospital for more than a month. And back in the house in the hills, the metal brain, conscious, reasoning, planning ....

This much Lanier learned from entries farther on in the diary. But the first note after that gap of weeks is one of sudden dismay. Detmold had returned, eager to get back to his precious experiment, and had walked into his house to find the laboratory in confusion and the metal brain missing. There were signs of work there, sawed pieces of steel and smashed test-tubes, but no indication of the location of the brain.

From the disjointed entries in the diary, he seemed to have been almost mad with anxiety and rage, for if the thing had been stolen from him, he alone knew the imposibility of replacing it without years of work. So for days he ranged the forest in search, and on a morning early in June he stumbled on the thing he sought, hidden far back within the hills.

In a circle some hundreds of feet across, trees and shrubs and grass had been cleared away and the ground stamped down hard and smooth, forming a great clearing surrounded by a high embankment of earth. And in this circle there was extraordinary activity. Watching from the top of the embankment, he noted first a small, solid-looking machine directly beneath him, constructed of shining, unfamiliar metal. It looks very much like an old fashioned pump, without the handle, having a spout at its top from which powered a thin stream of molten, gleaming metal, falling into black molds beneath, and solidifying instantly. This small, pump-like structure seemed to be sunken into the earth for an unguessable distance, but the source of the molten metal was a mystery to the wondering Detmold, as also was the use it was intended to serve.

But as he looked about, that, at least, became clearer. For on the farther side of the circle, a half-dozen machines were busy with large lengths of shining metal, similar to those in the molds, fastening them together. And it was these latter busy mechanisms that were even greater mysteries to him for the moment.

They were simply shining globes of the omnipresent metal, perhaps five feet in diameter, provided with six long tentacles or arms, many yards in length, twisting, flexible, busy holding and fastening and tightening, accomplishing an incredible amount of work as he watched. They resembled large octopuses of shining metal, but except for the arms that projected from the globes, were entirely featureless. Those twisting, tapering arms held his attention. They were like—they were like the arms that he had provided the metal brain! As that thought flashed over him, he turned his gaze and saw the brain itself, near the right side of the circle.

The brain—but different. For it moved, possessed the power of motion in any direction, instead of being set on a table, as he had made it. Even as he stared, it seemed to glimpse him, and glided smoothly toward him, across the clearing, its great weight of metal being suspended above the ground six inches or more by some unknown, unguessed force.

Over it came until it stood motionless beneath that part of the embankment on which Detmold was standing. A black, oval case, more than a yard its greater length, eerily suspended above the ground, contemplating him with its dark lens.

And as Detmold stared back, the explanation of all flashed over

74

him and he cried aloud. He saw that the metal brain had never been stolen from him, that it had, in his absence, discovered a method by which it could move about in that unearthly fashion, and, using that method, and using the tools it had stolen from him, and its own vaulting intelligence, had come to this place and constructed those machines that were working its will. And it was doing—what? Constructing what? Those great lengths of metal on which the tentacle-machines worked, that device that sucked molten metal from the earth itself, all for what?

According to the broken account in the diary he must have stared at the thing for minutes, realizing at least what a monster he had created and set free. Then one of the brain's twisting arms dipped down behind it, and instantly he caught the suggestion of sudden peril, of nearing death, and leaped back behind the embankment. As he did so, he glimpsed the metal arm flashing up with a small globe in its grasp from which a cloud of yellow gas sprang toward him. He was already over the embankment and the gas touched only a small part of his left hand, but it stung intensely. When he stopped to inspect the hand, a mile away, he was amazed to see that where the gas had touched, the bones of the land were quite dissolved, without wound or break of skin, leaving two fingers partly boneless and hurting intensely.

And all of the time he stumbled homeward, one word beat through his dazed mind like the stroke of a mighty bell—a word that seemed to be written in letters of flame before his eyes: "Frankenstein."

Chapter 7

From that point onward, Lanier found the diary almost undecipherable, spotted and torn, with a broken scrawl here and there. There were entries that seemed to indicate that following his discovery of the metal brain's activities, he had not left the house for several days, brooding over what he had seen. There were wild speculations on his part—he constantly accused himself of having loosed a terror on the world, foresaw a metal horde that would sweep over the earth, destroying, conquering, perhaps swinging out to other planets in its irresistible march, a cosmic metal plague. And all his work!

There was a gap of two days in the entries, and the following notes showed that he had spent those two days crouching near the fortress of the metal brain, observing the activity there. He wrote of the tentacle-machines and claimed that they were merely machines, without any trace of brain or intelligence, simply complex, automatic, and self-powered mechanism that were controlled by the metal brain, perhaps by some intricate form of radio-control. But he wrote also of a thing he had not seen on his first glimpse of the clearing, and that was the existence of the cylinders, as he called them throughout. They were just that, gleaming cylinders of metal, some 50 feet in diameter and half again as much in height, provided with two flexible arms on the same principle as the arms of the metal brain and the tentacles of the working-machines, but much larger and longer. And he believed these cylinders to contain some artificial brain like the one he had built, though not so intelligent, he thought. To think of it! The metal brain was constructing intelligent, similar servants, in addition to the mindless tentacled slave-machines.

There is a note of bitterness in that entry, where he wrote that while the cylinders undoubtedly had been furnished some portion of intelligence by their master, the metal brain, that master had been careful, evidently, not to repeat his own mistake and make them powerful enough to revolt against it. He believed these cylinders to be dependent almost entirely on the metal brain's commands, though they had been furnished also with a triple, all-seeing eye, set in a small case on their upper surfaces.

And now it was that Detmold first glimpsed the purpose and plans of the brain. For the tentacle-machines had finished their work, strewn about the clearing lay a number of gigantic columns of metal, smooth and round, whose purpose he could not understand until he saw one of the cylinders, aided by the working-machines and directed by the metal brain, connect the ends of two of those huge columns to its lower surface and then scramble up to a towering height, erect, powerful! Aided by this giant, the other cylinders were soon in position also, and the clearing was filled by a score or more of towering metal giants, who strode about in humanlike steps, under the commands of the comparatively tiny brain beneath.

There was no speculation on his part as to why the metal brain had picked this form for its huge servants, why it had cast on a shape so nearly human. Was it unconscious imitation, mimicry?

For several days Detmold returned to the clearing and saw the metal giants walking about, testing, drilling. Once he narrowly escaped being stepped on by a great limb and thereafter was more careful. He could not understand the power of locomotion of the things, but set it down to some application of atomic force, discovered by the brain. Almost two weeks after his first discovery of the metal brain's fort, he returned to find it deserted, the tentacle-machines and the metal-pourer lying in a heap at one side. But after a period of beating through the hills on the tracks of the giant fighting-machines, he found the brain's new camp, a grassy basin in the hills, only a few miles from Stockton, where it sat like a spider in a gigantic web, guarded by the metal giants.

It was then that Detmold saw the immediate purpose of the brain, saw that Stockton was marked for annihilation. The writing at that point was tortured, agonized. What could he do? He never considered bringing a force of men from Stockton to deal with the thing, for best of all men he knew the utter futility of such a course. Nor would the story he told have even been listened to in Stockton. Yet the thing must be crushed, and soon. It would be best, perhaps, to give the last two entries in the diary in full. The first reads:

"I came back through the former camp of the brain today and spent some time examining the tentacle-machines there. As I thought, they are intricate mechanisms, capable of receiving an outside command and translating it into action, but that is all. I examined, too, the machine that produces molten metal and discovered the principle of the thing. It sucks up ordinary earth and separates the metallic atoms in that earth from the non-metallic, and pours out a constant stream of metal in this way. It is mostly aluminum, but inexplicably hardened and reinforced, probably by addition of outside elements. The principle of the thing is fairly simple and I am beginning to understand the power used to move the metal giants. I think that it could be applied differently, more effectively."

And a little farther, the very last entry, tremendous in its implications; an entry, Lanier noted, that was dated two weeks before:

"I have just thought, if I were able to control those tentacle-machines, what might be done. And why not? The commands of the metal brain were undoubtedly transmitted to them by some form of radio waves, as is the case also with the cylinder things. And if I could control them in the same manner, would I be able—strike at the center——"

The entry stopped there, abruptly, and though Lanier thumbed the pages he found no more writing in the little book. His brain was whirling, but in it was a wild hope, half doubting, half believing. Could such a thing——?

Very carefully he reread certain passages in the diary, striving to calculate the position of the places mentioned. An hour later he was already a few miles from the house, heading toward the spot where he believed was the new camp of the metal brain. Evening was drifting down on the world like a cloud of gray powder, and soon came the thick, obscuring darkness.

That night he slept within a little group of pines, on a heap of gathered boughs, waking only at dawn. He stretched and yawned, then snapped to alertness as a sound came whispering faintly through the forest, a distant, wailing scream.

It came from the direction in which he was heading, and aroused at once, he plunged ahead at top speed. After he had gone the little glade was very silent, except for that distant cry. The chattering birds and squirrels had ceased their tiny clamor, vaguely frightened by the unfamiliar sound. All the creatures of the wild were silent, fearful, listening ....

Chapter 8

A sound of crashing trees greeted Lanier as he went on, and then, very much louder, the whistling scream he had already heard, near by, clamorous. Aflame with excitement he pushed on, forced through a cruel growth of briars and down a wooded hillside, emerging with a sudden shock into a grassy basin, more than a half-mile across, level and treeless. And in its center was a great circle that flashed brilliantly in the sunlight, shining, magnificent. A circular, gleaming platform, and on it, hanging a few inches above its surface, a dark, egg-shaped object, with two thin, tapering arms. The metal brain!

An electric shock seemed to pass through Lanier at sight of it. The super-intelligence that was destroying the civilization of man, casting him from his lordship of the world! A metal king on its throne of metal! For the first time Lanier realized the soulless nature of the thing, cold, precise, unhuman, unswerving in purpose, terrible.

Standing near the platform was one of the towering metal giants, and it was from this one that there emanated the screaming signal he had heard. And over at the basin's farther side, where the hills beyond sank down to it in a long, wooded slope, stood another of the great fighting-machines, also motionless.

Lanier sensed a quality of waiting, of expectancy, in the attitude of the brain and its minions. Over beyond that wooded slope, the crashing of trees began again and he wondered if the other metal giants were returning from their raid to the north. Louder, even louder, became that snapping and roar of falling timber, and now a shape began to loom up at the top of that long slope, a gigantic shape that was moving rapidly toward the basin.

On it came, until its whole bulk was in view, poised on the ridge, and Lanier jerked with astonishment, for the thing was a mighty

78

wheel, a wheel that must have been at least 50 feet taller than even the immense fighting-machines, whose huge, shining spokes and broad, point-studded rim were of smooth metal, and at the hub of which swung a square, boxlike structure of the same material.

Again the whistling signal of the nearer fighting-machine ripped the silence, and now it was answered from far away, toward the east. Lanier looked and saw, in surprise, four others of the metal giants, very far away, hurrying across the hills toward the basin, with mighty, whirling steps. The four that had been left at Stockton, coming at the summons of the metal brain, for what? Aid, battle— that mighty wheel, a foe of the metal brain—then, who—?

"Detmold!" Lanier's cry was like a trumpet call, a scream of comprehension and gladness and faith. "Detmold!" He had constructed the wheel to crush the metal brain and its minions, had built it up using the tentacle-machines as his own tools, controlling them in the way he had thought, fighting the metal brain with the instruments of its own making.

And now the great wheel was slowly rolling down the slope toward the outer most metal giant. There was no sound to indicate the source of the wheel's motive power, but Lanier little doubted that Detmold had seized and utilized the same secret of atomic power that had been used by the brain for its own creatures. Slowly, almost clumsily, the wheel lumbered down to the basin, until it was but a few hundred feet above the outer fighting-machine. Suddenly the inaction of the latter ended and one long arm flashed out, holding a globe from which the deadly gas spurted toward the hub of the wheel.

With unexpected, lightning rapidity, the larger machine swerved to one side, then, pivoting instantly, rolled with terrific speed and power toward the erect giant, striking it with a deafening crash. The fighting-machine went down, and as the huge wheel rolled over it there was a cracking of metal, and the thing lay broken and harmless.

Over in the east the four approaching fighting-machines were striding toward the basin with utmost speed, screaming their signals, that were answered by the metal giant left functioning in the basin, that stood beside the brain and its platform. And it was toward this remaining enemy that the wheel advanced, slowly, cautiously, edging forward like a snake that can strike with lightening speed. It followed a course that circled with the edge of the basin, and as it passed near Lanier, he saw the tiny figure of a man at the box-structure at the hub, saw Detmold, intent on the control of the giant mechanism; and then the wheel had rolled past him and was moving slowly toward

79

the metal platform and the fighting giant beside it.

On it went, until it was very near the monster machine there, then paused, twisting, hovering, turning. Flash!—and it had struck at the watchful giant, struck and missed. Since the thing had turned in time to avoid the impact. Instantly the wheel turned and struck again, and Lanier cried out to see it crash squarely into the fighting-machine. But the latter was not overturned. It braced itself to stand and wound its mighty arms around the spokes of the wheel in a great effort to hold it back from the platform and the brain. The hurrying metal giants in the east were very near now, striding almost into the basin, racing madly toward this combat of titans. And on the metal circle rested the brain, its lens-eyes turned toward the battle, directing the efforts of its creatures as they battled and hurried in its behalf.

The long arms were still twisting through the spokes of the wheel, that was still striving to reach the near-by platform. Suddenly one of those arms released its hold on a spoke and swept up to the hub, caught the tiny figure of the man there and hurled him toward the edge of the basin, where Lanier saw him strike a tree there. And at the sight, Lanier screamed, ran forward with fists clenched, shouting insane, childish threats, an ant beside the two battling giants. But now, without the controlling hand of its builder, the wheel was whirling, toppling, falling, crashing down onto the circular platform, smashing fighting-machine and metal brain beneath its mighty bulk, crushing both into a twisted heap of metal.

Crash!—and Lanier stood quite still. Over at the eastern edge of the basin the four metal giants had suddenly slumped down and lay motionless, sunken into the heaps of cold, lifeless metal, as also must have done all those other metal giants that were spreading terror at Wheeling, as all the creatures of the metal brain must have done when released from its commands by its shattering. Truly, Detmold had struck at the center, had smashed completely the dreadful menace that was his own creature. In awe and wonder, in swiftly flooding thankfulness and gratitude, Lanier looked about. All around was silence.

Chapter 9

The face of Detmold was very peaceful when Lanier found him, huddled at the foot of a great tree. It was as if, at the very moment of death, he had known his victory and had seen in that victory atonement for the evil done by his creature. With a shattered piece of metal Lanier dug a deep grave beneath the tree, and placed his friend in it, rolling a great stone to its head when he had filled it.

"Good-bye, Detmold," he whispered. "I think—I hope—that you have found some peace, now. Good-bye!"

There was no answer from the cold mound of earth that lay like a brown scar on the bright carpet of grass. But it seemed that the wind was answering, sighing through the trees like a released spirit; that the pines were answering, pointing like lofty, dark-green spears to the blue depths above, where was an infinite freedom, a calm, eternal silence.

Wearily, Lanier walked away, an ache in his heart, a choking tightness in his throat. Very soon he stood again on the hills above the valley, contemplating the ruins of Stockton. The morning sunlight there was brilliant, and over the broken city lay a quietness, a tranquility, that was like a protecting cloak. There was no smoke or sign of life.

But the people would return, Lanier thought. Word of the collapse of the outside metal giants would have spread swiftly, and already the cautious soldiers would be advancing, slowly, doubtfully. And later, others, single, adventuring spirits, small groups, crowds of hundreds. They would drift back to the ruined city and there would be puffing of steam-shovels and clatter of riveters and sawing and hammering and all sounds of building. They would come back ....

Away to the east, far up the valley, there was a crying of bugles.

THE END

The DIAMOND LENS
⊰ By Fitz-James O'Brien ⊱

Chapter 1

The Bending of the Twig

rom a very early period of my life the entire bent of my inclinations had been towards microscopic investigations. When I was not more than ten years old, a distant relative of our family, hoping to astonish my inexperience, constructed a simple microscope for me, by drilling in a disk of copper a small hole, in which a drop of pure water was sustained by capillary attraction. This very primitive apparatus, magnifying some fifty diameters, presented, it is true, only indistinct and imperfect forms, but still sufficiently wonderful to work up my imagination to a preternatural state of excitement.

Seeing me so interested in this rude instrument, my cousin explained to me all that he knew about the principles of the microscope, related to me a few of the wonders which had been accomplished through its agency, and ended by promising to send me one regularly constructed, immediately on his return to the city. I counted the days, the hours, the minutes, that intervened between that promise and his departure.

Meantime I was not idle. Every transparent substance that bore the remotest resemblance to a lens I eagerly seized upon, and employed in vain attempts to realize that instrument, the theory of whose construction I as yet only vaguely comprehended. All panes of glass containing those oblate spheroidal knots familiarly known as "bull's eyes" were ruthlessly destroyed, in the hope of obtaining lenses of marvelous power. I even went so far as to extract the crystaline humor from the eyes of fishes and animals, and endeavored to press it into the microscopic service. I plead guilty to having stolen the glasses from my Aunt Agatha's spectacles, with a dim idea of grinding them into lenses of wonderous magnifying properties,—in which attempt it is scarcely necessary to say that I totally failed.

A Real Microscope at last

At last the promised instrument came. It was of that order known as Field's simple microscope, and had cost perhaps about fifteen dollars. As far as educational purposes went, a better apparatus could not have been selected. Accompanying it was a small treatise on the microscope,—its history, uses and discoveries. I comprehended then for the first time the "Arabian Nights Entertainments." The dull veil of ordinary existence that hung across the world seemed suddenly to roll away, and to lay bare a land of enchantments. I felt towards my companions as the seer might feel towards the ordinary masses of men. I held conversations with nature in a tongue which they could not understand. I was in daily communication with living wonders, such as they never imagined in their wildest visions. I penetrated beyond the external portal of things, and roamed through the sanctuaries: where they beheld only a drop of rain slowly rolling down the window-glass, I saw a universe of beings animated with all the passions common to physical life, and convulsing their minute sphere with struggles as fierce and protracted as those of men. In the common spots of mould, which my mother, good housekeeper that she was, fiercely scooped away from her jam pots, there abode for me, under the name of mildew, enchanted gardens, filled with dells and avenues of the densest foliage and most astonishing verdure, while from the fantastic boughs of these microscopic forests hung strange fruits glittering with green, and silver, and gold.

It was no scientific thirst that at this time filled my mind. It was the pure enjoyment of a poet to whom a world of wonders had been disclosed. I talked of my solitary pleasures to none. Alone with my microscope, I dimmed my sight, day after day and night after night, poring over the marvels which it unfolded to me. I was like one who, having discovered the ancient Eden still existing in all its primitive glory, should resolve to enjoy it in solitude, and never betray to mortal the secret of its locality. The rod of my life was bent at this moment. I destined myself to be a microscopist.

He Imagines Himself a Discoverer

Of course, like every novice, I fancied myself a discoverer. I was ignorant at the time of the thousands of acute intellects engaged in the same pursuit as myself, and with the advantage of instruments a thousand times more powerful than mine. The names of Leeuwenhoek, Williamson, Spencer, Ehrenberg, Schultz, Dujardin, Schact, and Schleiden were then entirely unknown to me, or if known, I was ignorant of their patient and wonderful researches. In every fresh specimen of cryptogamia which I placed beneath my instrument I believed that I discovered wonders of which the world was as yet ignorant. I remember well the thrill of delight and admiration that shot through me the first time that I discovered the common wheel animalcule (*Rotifera vulgaris*) expanding and contracting its flexible spokes, and seemingly rotating through the water. Alas! As I grew older, and obtained some works treating of my favorite study, I found that I was only on the threshold of a science to the investigation of which some of the greatest men of the age were devoting their lives and intellects.

As I grew up, my parents, who saw but little likelihood of anything practical resulting from the examination of bits of moss and drops of water through a brass tube and a piece of glass, were anxious that I should choose a profession. It was their desire that I should enter the counting-house of my uncle, Ethan Blake, a prosperous merchant, who carried on business in New York. This suggestion I decisively combatted. I had no taste for trade; I should only make a failure; in short, I refused to become a merchant.

But it was necessary for me to select some pursuit. My parents were staid New England people, who insisted on the necessity of labor; and therefore, although, thanks to the bequest of my poor Aunt Agatha, I should, on coming of age, inherit a small fortune sufficient to place me above want, it was decided that, instead of waiting for this, I should act the nobler part, and employ the intervening years in rendering myself independent.

Selecting a Profession

After much cogitation I complied with the wishes of my family, and selected a profession. I determined to study medicine at the New York Academy. This disposition of my future suited me. A removal from my relatives would enable me to dispose of my time as I pleased without fear of detection. As long as I paid my Academy fees, I might shirk attending the lectures if I chose; and, as I never had the remotest intention of standing an examination, there was no danger of my being "plucked." Besides, a metropolis was the place for me. There I could obtain excellent instruments, the newest publications, intimacy with men of pursuits kindred with my own,—in short, all things necessary to insure a profitable devotion of my life to my beloved science. I had an abundance of money, few desires that were not bounded by my illuminating mirror on one side and my object-glass on the other; what, therefore, was to prevent my becoming an illustrious investigator of the veiled worlds? It was with the most buoyant hope that I left my New England home and established myself in New York.

CHAPTER II
The Longing of a Man of Science

My first step, of course, was to find suitable apartments. These I obtained, after a couple of days' search, in Fourth Avenue; a very pretty second-floor unfurnished, containing sitting-room, bed-room, and a smaller apartment which I intended to fit up as a laboratory. I furnished my lodgings simply, but rather elegantly, and then devoted all my energies to the adornment of the temple of my worship. I visited Pike, the celebrated optician, and passed in review his splendid collection of microscopes,—Field's Compound, Hingham's, Spencer's, Nachet's Binocular (that founded on the principles of the stereoscope), and at length fixed upon that form known as Spencer's Trunnion Microscope, as combining the greatest number of improvements with an almost perfect freedom from tremor. Along with this I purchased every possible accessory,—draw-tubes, micrometers, a *camera-lucida*, lever-stage, achromatic condensers, white cloud illuminators, prisms, parabolic condensers, polarizing apparatus, forceps, aquatic boxes, fishing-tubes, with a host of other articles, all of which would have been useful in the hands of an experienced microscopist, but, as I afterwards discovered, were not of the slightest present value to me. It takes years of practice to know how to use a complicated microscope. The optician looked suspiciously at me as I made these wholesale purchases. He evidently was uncertain whether to set me down as some scientific celebrity or a madman. I think he inclined to the latter belief. I suppose I was mad. Every great genius is mad upon the subject in which he is greatest. The unsuccessful madman is disgraced and called a lunatic.

At last Some Real Discoveries Are Made

Mad or not, I set myself to work with a zeal which few scientific students have ever equalled. I had everything to learn relative to the delicate study upon which I had embarked,—a study involving the most earnest patience, the most rigid analytic powers, the steadiest hand, the most untiring eye, the most refined and subtle manipulation.

For a long time half my apparatus lay inactively on the shelves of my laboratory, which was now most amply furnished with every possible contrivance for facilitating my investigations. The fact was that I did not know how to use some of my scientific implements,— never having been taught microscopics,—and those whose use I understood theoretically were of little avail, until by practice I could attain the necessary delicacy of handling. Still, such was the fury of my ambition, such the untiring perseverance of my experiments, that, difficult of credit as it may be, in the course of one year I became theoretically and practically an accomplished microscopist.

During this period of my labors, in which I submitted specimens of every substance that came under my observation to the action of my lenses, I became a discoverer,—in a small way, it is true, for I was very young, but still a discoverer. It was I who destroyed Ehrenberg's theory that the *Volvox globator* was an animal, and proved that his "monads" with stomachs and eyes were merely phases of the formation of a vegetable cell, and were, when they reached their mature state, incapable of the act of conjugation, or any true generative act, without which no organism rising to any stage of life higher than vegetable can be said to be complete. It was I who resolved the singular problem of rotation in the cells and hairs of plants into ciliary attraction, in spite of the assertions of Mr. Wenham and others, that my explanation was the result of an optical illusion.

But notwithstanding these discoveries, laboriously and painfully made as they were, I felt horribly dissatisfied. At every step I found myself stopped by the imperfections of my instruments. Like all active microscopists, I gave my imagination full play. Indeed, it is a common complaint against many such, that they supply the defects of their instruments with the creations of their brains. I imagined depths beyond depths in nature which the limited power of my lenses prohibited me from exploring. I lay awake at night constructing imaginary microscopes of immeasurable power, with which I seemed to pierce through all the envelopes of matter down to its original atom. How I cursed those imperfect media which necessity through ignorance compelled me to use! How I longed to discover the secret of some perfect lens, whose magnifying power should be limited only by the resolvability of the object, and which at the same time should be free from spherical and chromatic aberrations, in short from all the obstacles over which the poor microscopist finds himself conditionally stumbling! I felt convinced that the simple microscope, composed of a single lens of such vast yet perfect power was possible of construction. To attempt to bring the compound microscope up to such a pitch would have been commencing at the wrong end; this latter being simply a partially successful endeavor to remedy those very defects of the simple instrument, which, if conquered, would leave nothing to be desired.

Working On the Manufacture of Microscopes

It was in this mood of mind that I became a constructive microscopist. After another year passed in this new pursuit, experimenting on every imaginable substance,—glass, gems, flints, crystals, artificial crystals formed of the alloy of various vitreous materials,—in short, having constructed as many varieties of lenses as Argus had eyes, I found myself precisely where I started, with nothing gained save an extensive knowledge of glassmaking. I was almost dead with despair. My parents were surprised at my apparent want of progress in my medical studies, (I had not attended one lecture since my arrival in the city,) and the expenses of my mad pursuit had been so great as to embarrass me very seriously.

I was in this frame of mind one day, experimenting in my laboratory on a small diamond,—that stone, from its great refracting power, having always occupied my attention more than any other,— when a young Frenchman, who lived on the floor above me, and who was in the habit of occasionally visiting me, entered the room.

In Search of a Diamond Microscope Lens

I think that Jules Simon was a Jew. He had many traits of the Hebrew character: a love of jewelry, of dress, and of good living. There was something mysterious about him. He always had something to sell, and yet went into excellent society. When I say sell, I should perhaps have said peddle; for his operations were generally confined to the disposal of single articles,—a picture, for instance, or a rare carving in ivory, or a pair of duelling pistols, or the dress of a Mexican *caballero*. When I was first furnishing my rooms, he payed me a visit, which ended in my purchasing an antique silver lamp, which he assured me was a Cellini,—it was handsome enough even for that,—and some other knickknacks for my sitting-room. Why Simon should pursue this petty trade I never could imagine. He apparently had plenty of money, and had the *entrée* of the best houses in the city,—taking care, however, I suppose, to drive no bargains within the enchanted circle of the Upper Ten. I came at length to the conclusion that this peddling was but a mask to cover some greater object, and even went so far as to believe my young acquaintance to be implicated in the slave-trade. That, however, was none of my affair.

On the present occasion, Simon entered my room in a state of considerable excitement.

"*Ah! Mon ami!*" he cried, before I could even offer him the ordinary salutation, "it has occurred to me to be the witness of the most astonishing things in the world. I promenade myself to the house of Madame——How does the little animal—*le renard* —name himself in the Latin?"

A Spiritualistic Medium

"Vulpes," I answered.

"Ah! Yes.—Vulpes. I promenade myself to the house of Madame Vulpes."

"The spirit medium?"

"Yes, the great medium. Great heavens! What a woman! I write on a slip of paper many questions concerning affairs the most secret,— affairs that conceal themselves in the abysses of my heart the most profound; and behold! by example! what occurs? This devil of a woman makes me replies the most truthful to all of them. She talks to me of things that I do not love to talk of to myself. What am I to think? I am fixed to the earth!"

"Am I to understand you, M. Simon, that this Mrs. Vulpes replied to questions secretly written by you, which questions related to events known only to yourself?"

"Ah! More than that, more than that," he answered, with an air of some alarm. "She related to me things—But," he added, after a pause, and suddenly changing his manner, "why occupy ourselves with these follies? It was all the biology, without doubt. It goes without saying that it has not my credence.—But why are we here, *mon ami?* It has occurred to me to discover the most beautiful thing as you can imagine,—a vase with green lizards on it, composed by the great Bernard Palissy. It is in my apartment; let us mount. I go to show it to you."

I followed Simon mechanically; but my thoughts were far from Palissy and his enamelled ware, although I, like him, was seeking in the dark a great discovery. This casual mention of the spiritualist, Madame Vulpes, set me on a new track. What if this spiritualism should be really a great fact? What if, through communication with more subtle organisms than my own, I could reach at a single bound the goal, which perhaps a life of agonizing mental toil would never enable me to attain?

While purchasing the Palissy vase from my friend Simon, I was mentally arranging a visit to Madame Vulpes.

CHAPTER III
The Spirit of Leeuwenhoek

Two evenings after this, thanks to an arrangement by letter and the promise of an ample fee, I found Madame Vulpes awaiting me at her residence alone. She was a coarse-featured woman, with keen and rather cruel dark eyes, and an exceedingly sensual expression about her mouth and under jaw. She received me in perfect silence, in an apartment on the ground floor, very sparely furnished. In the centre of the room, close to where Mrs. Vulpes sat, there was a common round mahogany table. If I had come for the purpose of sweeping her chimney, the woman could not have looked more indifferent to my appearance. There was no attempt to inspire the visitor with awe. Everything bore a simple and practical aspect. This intercourse with the spiritual world was evidently as familiar an occupation with Mrs. Vulpes as eating her dinner or riding in an omnibus.

"You come for a communication, Mr. Linley?" said the medium, in a dry, business-like tone of voice.

"By appointment,—yes."

"What sort of communication do you want?—a written one?"

"Yes,—I wish for a written one."

"From any particular spirit?"

"Yes."

"Have you ever known this spirit on this earth?"

"Never. He died long before I was born. I wish merely to obtain from him some information which he ought to be able to give better than any other."

"Will you seat yourself at the table, Mr. Linley," said the medium, "and place your hands upon it?"

I obeyed,—Mrs. Vulpes being seated opposite to me, with her hands also on the table. We remained thus for about a minute and a half, when a violent succession of raps came on the table, on the back of my chair, on the floor immediately under my feet, and even on the window panes. Mrs. Vulpes smiled composedly.

"They are very strong to-night," she remarked. "You are fortunate." She then continued, "Will the spirits communicate with this gentlemen?"

90

Vigorous affirmative.

"Will the particular spirit he desires to speak with communicate?"

A very confused rapping followed this question.

"I know what they mean," said Mrs. Vulpes, addressing herself to me; "they wish you to write down the name of the particular spirit that you desire to converse with. Is that so?" she added, speaking to her invisible guests.

That it was so was evident from the numerous affirmatory responses. While this was going on, I tore a slip from my pocketbook, and scribbled a name, under the table.

"Will this spirit communicate in writing with this gentleman?" asked the medium once more.

After a moment's pause, her hand seemed to be seized with a violent tremor, shaking so forcibly that the table vibrated. She said that a spirit had seized her hand and would write. I handed her some sheets of paper that were on the table, and a pencil. The latter she held loosely in her hand, which presently began to move over the paper with a singular and seemingly involuntary motion. After a few moments had elapsed, she handed me the paper, on which I found written, in a large, uncultivated hand, the words, "He is not here, but has been sent for." A pause of a minute or so now ensued, during which Mrs. Vulpes remained perfectly silent, but the raps continued at regular intervals. When the short period I mention had elapsed, the hand of the medium was again seized with its convulsive tremor, and she wrote, under this strange influence, a few words on the paper, which she handed to me. They were as follows: —

"I am here. Question me.

"LEEUWENHOEK."

I was astounded. The name was identical with that I had written beneath the table, and carefully kept concealed. Neither was it at all probable that an uncultivated woman like Mrs. Vulpes should know even the name of the great father of microscopics. It may have been biology; but this theory was soon doomed to be destroyed. I wrote on my slip—still concealing it from Mrs. Vulpes—a series of questions, which, to avoid tediousness, I shall place with the responses, in the order in which they occurred: —

I.—Can the microscope be brought to perfection?

SPIRIT.—Yes.

I.—Am I destined to accomplish this great task?

SPIRIT.—You are.

I.—I wish to know how to proceed to attain this end. For the love which you bear to science, help me!

SPIRIT.—A diamond of one hundred and forty carats, submitted to

91

electro-magnetic currents for a long period, will experience a rearrangement of its atoms *inter se,* and from that stone you will form the universal lens.

I.—Will great discoveries result from the use of such a lens?

SPIRIT.—So great that all that has gone before is as nothing.

I.—But the refractive power of the diamond is so immense, that the image will be formed within the lens. How is that difficulty to be surmounted?

SPIRIT.—Pierce the lens through its axis, and the difficulty is obviated. The image will be formed in the pierced space, which will itself serve as a tube to look through. Now I am called. Good night.

The Diamond Found

I cannot at all describe the effect that these extraordinary communications had upon me. I felt completely bewildered. No biological theory could account for the *discovery* of the lens. The medium might, by means of biological *rapport* with my mind, have gone so far as to read my questions, and reply to them coherently. But biology could not enable her to discover that magnetic currents would so alter the crystals of the diamond as to remedy its previous defects, and admit of its being polished into a perfect lens. Some such theory may have passed through my head, it is true; but if so, I had forgotten it. In my excited condition of mind there was no course left but to become a convert, and it was in a state of the most painful nervous exaltation that I left the medium's house that evening. She accompanied me to the door, hoping that I was satisfied. The raps followed us as we went through the hall, sounding on the balusters, the flooring, and even the lintels of the door. I hastily expressed my satisfaction, and escaped hurriedly into the cool night air. I walked home with but one thought possessing me,—how to obtain a diamond of the immense size required. My entire means multiplied a hundred times over would have been inadequate to its purchase. Besides, such stones are rare, and become historical. I could find such only in the regalia of Eastern or European monarchs.

CHAPTER IV
The Eye Of Morning

There was a light in Simon's room as I entered my house. A vague impulse urged me to visit him. As I opened the door of his sitting-room unannounced, he was bending, with his back toward me, over a Carcel lamp, apparently engaged in minutely examining some object which he held in his hands. As I entered, he started suddenly, thrust his hand into his breast pocket and turned to me with a face crimson with confusion.

"What!" I cried, "pouring over the miniature of some fair lady? Well, don't blush so much; I won't ask to see it."

Simon laughed awkwardly enough, but made none of the negative protestations usual on such occasions. He asked me to take a seat.

"Simon," said I, "I have just come from Madame Vulpes."

This time Simon turned as white as a sheet, and seemed stupefied, as if a sudden electric shock had smitten him. He babbled some incoherent words, and went hastily to a small closet where he usually kept his liquors. Although astonished at his emotion, I was too preoccupied with my own idea to pay much attention to anything else.

"You say truly when you call Madame Vulpes a devil of a woman," I continued. "Simon, she told me wonderful things to-night, or rather was the means of telling me wonderful things. Ah! if I could only get a diamond that weighed one hundred and forty carats!"

Scarcely had the sigh with which I uttered this desire died upon my lips, when Simon, with the aspect of a wild beast, glared at me savagely, and, rushing to the mantel piece, where some foreign weapons hung on the wall, caught up a Malay creese, and brandished it furiously before him.

"No!" he cried in French, into which he always broke when excited. "No! you shall not have it! You are perfidious! You have consulted with that demon, and desire my treasure! But I shall die first! Me! I am brave! You cannot make me fear!"

The Dealer Is Suspicious

All this, uttered in a loud voice trembling with excitement, astounded me. I saw at a glance that I had accidentally trodden upon the edges of Simon's secret, whatever it was. It was necessary to reassure him.

"My dear Simon," I said, "I am entirely at a loss to know what you mean. I went to Madame Vulpes to consult her on a scientific problem, to the solution of which I discovered that a diamond of the size I just mentioned was necessary. You were never alluded to during the evening, nor, so far as I was concerned, even thought of. What can be the meaning of this outburst? If you happen to have a set of valuable diamonds in your possession, you need fear nothing from me. The diamond which I require you could not possess; or, if you did possess it, you would not be living here."

Something in my tone must have completely reassured him; for his expression immediately changed to a sort of constrained merriment, combined, however, with a certain suspicious attention to my movements. He laughed, and said that I must bear with him; that he was at certain moments subject to a species of vertigo, which betrayed itself in incoherent speeches, and that the attacks passed off as rapidly as they came. He put his weapon aside while making this explanation, and endeavored, with some success, to assume a more cheerful air.

All this did not impose on me in the least. I was too much accustomed to analytical labors to be baffled by so flimsy a veil. I determined to probe the mystery to the bottom.

"Simon," I said gayly, "let us forget all this over a bottle of Burgundy. I have a case of Lausseure's *Clos Vougeot* down-stairs, fragrant with the odors and ruddy with the sunlight of the Côte d'Or. Let us have up a couple of bottles. What say you?"

"With all my heart," answered Simon, smilingly.

I produced the wine and we seated ourselves to drink. It was of a famous vintage, that of 1848, a year when war and wine throve together,—and its pure but powerful juice seemed to impart renewed vitality to the system. By the time we had half finished the second bottle, Simon's head, which I knew was a weak one, had begun to yield, while I remained calm as ever, only that every draught seemed to send a flush of vigor through my limbs. Simon's utterance became more and more indistinct. He took to singing French chansons of a not very moral tendency. I rose suddenly from the table just at the conclusion of one of those incoherent verses, and, fixing my eyes on him with a quiet smile, said: "Simon, I have deceived you. I learned your secret this evening. You may as well be frank with me. Mrs. Vulpes, or rather one of her spirits, told me all."

A Wonderful Rose Diamond

He started with horror. His intoxication seemed for the moment to fade away, and he made a movement towards the weapon that he had a short time before laid down. I stopped him with my hand.

"Monster" he cried, passionately, "I am ruined! What shall I do? You shall never have it! I swear by my mother!"

"I don't want it," I said; "rest secure, but be frank with me. Tell me all about it."

The drunkenness began to return. He protested with maudlin earnestness that I was entirely mistaken,—that I was intoxicated; then asked me to swear eternal secrecy, and promised to disclose the mystery to me. I pledged myself, of course, to all. With an uneasy look in his eyes, and hands unsteady with drink and nervousness, he drew a small case from his breast and opened it. Heavens! How the mild lamp-light was shivered into a thousand prismatic arrows, as it fell upon a vast rose-diamond that glittered in the case! I was no judge of diamonds, but I saw at a glance that this was a gem of rare size and purity. I looked at Simon with wonder, and—must I confess it?—with envy. How could he have obtained this treasure? In reply to my questions, I could just gather from his drunken statements (of which, I fancy, half the incoherence was affected) that he had been superintending a gang of slaves engaged in diamond-washing in Brazil; that he had seen one of them secrete a diamond, but, instead of informing his employers, had quietly watched the negro until he saw him bury his treasure; that he had dug it up and fled with it, but that as yet he was afraid to attempt to dispose of it publicly,—so valuable a gem being almost certain to attract too much attention to its owner's antecedents,—and he had not been able to discover any of those obscure channels by which such matters are conveyed away safely. He added that in accordance with the oriental practice, he had named his diamond with the fanciful title of "The Eye of Morning."

While Simon was relating this to me, I regarded the great diamond attentively. Never had I beheld anything so beautiful. All the glories of light, ever imagined or described, seemed to pulsate in its crystalline chambers. Its weight, as I learned from Simon, was exactly one hundred and forty carats. Here was an amazing coincidence. The hand of destiny seemed in it. On the very evening when the spirit of Leeuwenhoek communicates to me the great secret of the microscope, the priceless means which he directs me to employ start up within my easy reach! I determined, with the most perfect deliberation, to possess myself of Simon's diamond.

He Murders the Dealer

I sat opposite to him while he nodded over his glass, and calmly revolved the whole affair. I did not for an instant contemplate so foolish an act as a common theft, which would of course be discovered, or at least necessitate flight and concealment, all of which must interfere with my scientific plans. There was but one step to be taken,—to kill Simon. After all, what was the life of a little peddling Jew, in comparison with the interests of science? Human beings are taken every day from the condemned prisons to be experimented on by surgeons. This man, Simon, was by his own confession a criminal, a robber, and I believed on my soul a murderer. He deserved death quite as much as any felon condemned by the laws: why should not I, like the government, contrive that his punishment should contribute to the progress of human knowledge?

The means for accomplishing everything I desired lay within my reach. There stood upon the mantlepiece a bottle half full of French laudanum. Simon was so occupied with his diamond, which I had just restored to him, that it was an affair of no difficulty to drug his glass. In a quarter of an hour he was in a profound sleep.

I now opened his waistcoat, took the diamond from the inner pocket in which he had placed it, and removed him to the bed, on which I laid him so that his feet hung down over the edge. I had possessed myself of the Malay creese, which I held in my right hand, while with the other I discovered as accurately as I could by pulsation the exact locality of the heart. It was essential that all the aspects of his death should lead to the surmise of self-murder. I calculated the exact angle at which it was probable that the weapon, if leveled by Simon's own hand, would enter his breast; then with one powerful blow I thrust it up to the hilt in the very spot which I desired to penetrate. A convulsive thrill ran through Simon's limbs. I heard a smothered sound issue from his throat, precisely like the bursting of a large air-bubble, sent up by a diver, when it reaches the surface of the water; he turned half round on his side, and, as if to assist my plans more effectually, his right hand, moved by some mere spasmodic impulse, clasped the handle of the creese, which it remained holding with extraordinary muscular tenacity. Beyond this there was no apparent struggle. The laudanum, I presume, paralyzed the usual nervous action. He must have died instantly.

There was yet something to be done. To make it certain that all suspicion of the act should be diverted from any inhabitant of the house to Simon himself, it was necessary that the door should be found in the morning *locked on the inside*. How to do this, and afterwards escape myself? Not by the window; that was a physical impossibility. Besides, I was determined that the windows *also* should be found bolted. The solution was simple enough. I descended softly to my own room for a peculiar instrument which I had used for holding small slippery substances, such as minute spheres of glass, etc. This instrument was nothing more than a long slender hand-vice, with a very powerful grip, and a considerable leverage, which last was accidentally owing to the shape of the handle. Nothing was simpler than, when the key was in the lock, to seize the end of its stem in this vice, through the keyhole, from the outside, and so lock the door. Previously, however, to doing this, I burned a number of papers on Simon's hearth. Suicides almost always burn papers before they destroy themselves. I also emptied some more laudanum into Simon's glass,—having first removed from it all traces of wine,—cleaned the other wine-glass, and brought the bottles away with me. If traces of two persons drinking had been found in the room, the question naturally would have arisen, Who was the second? Besides, the wine-bottles might have been identified as belonging to me. The laudanum I poured out to account for its presence in his stomach, in case of a *post-mortem examination*. The theory naturally would be, that he first intended to poison himself, but, after swallowing a little of the drug, was either disgusted with its taste, or changed his mind from other motives, and chose the dagger. These arrangements made, I walked out, leaving the gas burning, locked the door with my vice, and went to bed.

A Verdict of Suicide

Simon's death was not discovered until nearly three in the afternoon. The servant, astonished at seeing the gas burning,—the light streaming on the dark landing from under the door,—peeped through the keyhole and saw Simon on the bed. She gave the alarm. The door was burst open, and the neighborhood was in a fever of excitement.

Every one in the house was arrested, myself included. There was an inquest; but no clue to his death beyond that of suicide could be obtained. Curiously enough, he had made several speeches to his friends the preceding week, that seemed to point to self-destruction. One gentleman swore that Simon had said in his presence that "he was tired of life." His landlord affirmed that Simon, when paying him his last month's rent, remarked that "he should not pay him rent much longer." All the other evidence corresponded,—the door locked inside, the position of the corpse, the burnt papers. As I anticipated, no one knew of the possession of the diamond by Simon, so that no motive was suggested for his murder. The jury, after a prolonged examination, brought in the usual verdict, and the neighborhood once more settled down into its accustomed quiet.

CHAPTER V
Animula

The three months succeeding Simon's catastrophe I devoted night and day to my diamond lens. I had constructed a vast galvanic battery, composed of nearly two thousand pairs of plates,—a higher power I dared not use, lest the diamond should be calcined. By means of this enormous engine I was enabled to send a powerful current of electricity continually through my great diamond, which it seemed to me gained in lustre every day. At the expiration of a month I commenced the grinding and polishing of the lens, a work of intense toil and exquisite delicacy. The great density of the stone, and the care required to be taken with the curvatures of the surfaces of the lens, rendered the labor the severest and most harassing that I had yet undergone.

At last the eventful moment came; the lens was completed. I stood trembling on the threshold of new worlds. I had the realization of Alexander's famous wish before me. The lens lay on the table, ready to be placed upon its platform. My hand fairly shook as I enveloped a drop of water with a thin coating of oil of turpentine, preparatory to its examination,—a process necessary in order to prevent the rapid evaporation of the water. I now placed the drop on a thin slip of glass under the lens, and throwing upon it, by the combined aid of a prism and a mirror, a powerful stream of light, I approached my eye to the minute hole drilled through the axis of the lens. For an instant I saw nothing save what seemed to be an illuminated chaos, a vast luminous abyss. A pure white light, cloudless and serene, and seemingly limitless as space itself, was my first impression. Gently, and with the greatest care, I depressed the lens a few hair's-breadths. The wonderous illumination still continued, but as the lens approached the object a scene of indescribable beauty was unfolded to my view.

I seemed to gaze upon a vast space, the limits of which extended far beyond my vision. An atmosphere of magical luminousness permeated the entire field of view. I was amazed to see no trace of animalculous life. Not a living thing, apparently, inhabited that dazzling expanse. I comprehended instantly that, by the wonderous power of my lens, I had penetrated beyond the grosser particles of aqueous matter, beyond the realms of infusoria and protozoa, down to the original gaseous globule, into whose luminous interior I was gazing, as into an almost boundless dome filled with a supernatural radiance.

The First Visions of Beauty

It was, however, no brilliant void into which I looked. On every side I beheld beautiful organic forms, of unknown texture, and colored with the most enchanting hues. These forms presented the appearance of what might be called, for want of a more specific definition, foliated clouds of the highest rarity; that is, they undulated and broke into vegetable formations, and were tinged with splendors compared with which the gilding of our autumn woodlands is as dross compared with gold. Far away into the illimitable distance stretched long avenues of these gaseous forests, dimly transparent, and painted with prismatic hues of unimaginable brilliancy. The pendent branches waved along the fluid glades until every vista seemed to break through half-lucent ranks of many-colored drooping silken pennons. What seemed to be either fruits or flowers, pied with a thousand hues, lustrous and ever varying, bubbled from the crowns of this fairy foliage. No hills, no lakes, no rivers, no forms animate or inanimate, were to be seen, save those vast auroral copses that floated serenely in the luminous stillness, with leaves and fruits and flowers gleaming with unknown fires, unrealizable by mere imagination.

How strange, I thought, that this sphere should be thus condemned to solitude! I had hoped, at least, to discover some new form of animal life,—perhaps of a lower class than any with which we are at present acquainted, but still, some living organism. I found my newly discovered world, if I may so speak, a beautiful chromatic desert.

While I was speculating on the singular arrangements of the internal economy of Nature, with which she so frequently splinters into atoms our most compact theories, I thought I beheld a form moving slowly through the glades of one of the prismatic forests. I looked more attentively, and found that I was not mistaken. Words cannot depict the anxiety with which I awaited the nearer approach of this mysterious object. Was it merely some inanimate substance, held in suspense in the attenuated atmosphere of the globule? Or was it an animal endowed with vitality and motion? It approached, flitting behind the gauzy, colored veils of cloud-foliage, for seconds dimly revealed, then vanishing. At last the violet pennons that trailed nearest to me vibrated; they were gently pushed aside, and the form floated out into the broad light.

99

The Glorious Animula

It was a female human shape. When I say human, I mean it possessed the outlines of humanity,—but there the analogy ends. Its adorable beauty lifted it illimitable heights beyond the loveliest daughter of Adam.

I cannot, I dare not, attempt to inventory the charms of this divine revelation of perfect beauty. Those eyes of mystic violet, dewy and serene, evade my words. Her long, lustrous hair following her glorious head in a golden wake, like the track sown in heaven by a falling star, seems to quench my most burning phrases with its splendors. If all the bees of Hybla nestled upon my lips, they would still sing but hoarsely the wonderous harmonies of outline that enclosed her form.

She swept out from between the rainbow-curtains of the cloud-trees into the broad sea of light that lay beyond. Her motions were those of some graceful naiad, cleaving, by a mere effort of her will, the clear, unruffled waters that fill the chambers of the sea. She floated forth with the serene grace of a frail bubble ascending through the still atmosphere of a June day. The perfect roundness of her limbs formed suave and enchanting curves. It was like listening to the most spiritual symphony of Beethoven the divine, to watch the harmonious flow of lines. This, indeed, was a pleasure cheaply purchased at any price. What cared I, if I had waded to the portal of this wonder through another's blood? I would have given my own to enjoy one such moment of intoxication and delight.

Breathless with gazing on this lovely wonder, and forgetful for an instant of everything save her presence, I withdrew my eye from the microscope eagerly,—alas! As my gaze fell on the thin slide that lay beneath my instrument, the bright light from mirror and from prism sparkled on a colorless drop of water! There, in that tiny bead of dew, this beautiful being was forever imprisoned. The planet Neptune was not more distant from me than she. I hastened once more to apply my eye to the microscope.

Animula (let me now call her by that dear name which I subsequently bestowed on her) had changed her position. She had again approached the wonderous forest, and was gazing earnestly upwards. Presently one of the trees—as I must call them—unfolded a long ciliary process, with which it seized one of the gleaming fruits that glittered on its summit, and, sweeping slowly down, held it within reach of Animula. The sylph took it in her delicate hand and began to eat. My attention was so entirely absorbed by her, that I could not apply myself to the task of determining whether this singular plant was or was not instinct with volition.

More About His Love, Animula

I watched her, with the most profound attention as she made her repast. The suppleness of her motions sent a thrill of delight through my frame; my heart beat madly as she turned her beautiful eyes in the direction of the spot in which I stood. What would I not have given to have had the power to precipitate myself into that luminous ocean, and float with her through those groves of purple and gold! While I was thus breathlessly following her every movement, she suddenly started, seemed to listen for a moment, and then cleaving the brilliant ether in which she was floating, like a flash of light, pierced through the opaline forest, and disappeared.

Instantly a series of the most singular sensations attacked me. It seemed as if I had suddenly gone blind. The luminous sphere was still before me, but my daylight had vanished. What caused this sudden disappearance? Had she a lover or a husband? Yes, that was the solution! Some signal from a happy fellow-being had vibrated through the avenues of the forest, and she had obeyed the summons.

The agony of my sensations, as I arrived at this conclusion, startled me. I tried to reject the conviction that my reason forced upon me. I battled against the fatal conclusion,—but in vain. It was so. I had no escape from it. I loved an animalcule!

It is true that, thanks to the marvelous power of my microscope, she appeared of human proportions. Instead of presenting the revolting aspect of the coarser creatures, that live and struggle and die, in the more easily resolvable portions of the water-drop, she was fair and delicate and of surpassing beauty. But of what account was all that? Every time that my eye was withdrawn from the instrument, it fell on a miserable drop of water, within which, I must be content to know, dwelt all that could make my life lovely.

Could she but see me once! Could I for one moment pierce the mystical walls that so inexorably rose to separate us, and whisper all that filled my soul, I might consent to be satisfied for the rest of my life with the knowledge of her remote sympathy. It would be something to have established even the faintest personal link to bind us together,—to know that at times, when roaming through those enchanted glades, she might think of the wonderful stranger, who had broken the monotony of her life with his presence, and left a gentle memory in her heart!

But it could not be. No invention of which human intellect was capable could break down the barriers that nature had erected. I might feast my soul upon her wondrous beauty, yet she must always remain ignorant of the adoring eyes that day and night gazed upon her, and, even when closed, beheld her in dreams. With a bitter cry of anguish I fled from the room, and, flinging myself on my bed, sobbed myself to sleep like a child.

CHAPTER VI
The Spilling of the Cup

I arose the next morning almost at daybreak, and rushed to my microscope. I trembled as I sought the luminous world in miniature that contained my all. Animula was there. I had left the gas-lamp, surrounded by its moderators, burning, when I went to bed the night before. I found the sylph bathing, as it were, with an expression of pleasure animating her features, in the brilliant light which surrounded her. She tossed her lustrous golden hair over her shoulders with innocent coquetry. She lay at full length in the transparent medium, in which she supported herself with ease, and gambolled with the enchanting grace that the nymph Salamacis might have exhibited when she sought to conquer the modest Hermaphroditus. I tried an experiment to satisfy myself if her powers of reflection were developed. I lessened the lamplight considerably. By the dim light that remained, I could see an expression of pain flitt across her face. She looked upward suddenly, and her brows contracted. I flooded the stage of the microscope again with a full stream of light, and her whole expression changed. She sprang forward like some substance deprived of all weight. Her eyes sparkled and her lips moved. Ah! if science had only the means of conducting and reduplicating sounds, as it does the rays of light, what carols of happiness would then have entranced my ears! what jubilant hymns to Adonis would have thrilled the illumined air!

I now comprehended how it was that the Count de Gabalis peopled his mystic world with sylphs,—beautiful beings whose breath of life was lambent fire, and who sported forever in regions of purest ether and purest light. The Rosicrucian had anticipated the wonder that I had practically realized.

The Passion Grows Stronger

How long this worship of my strange divinity went on thus I scarcely know. I lost all note of time. All day from early dawn, and far into the night, I was to be found peering through that wonderful lens. I saw no one, went nowhere, and scarce allowed myself sufficient time for my meals. My whole life was absorbed in contemplation as rapt as that of any of the Romish saints. Every hour that I gazed upon the divine form strengthened my passion,—a passion that was always overshadowed by the maddening conviction, that, although I could gaze on her at will, she never, never could behold me!

At length, I grew so pale and emaciated, from want of rest, and continual brooding over my insane love and its cruel conditions, that I determined to make some effort to wean myself from it. "Come," I said, "this is at best but a fantasy. Your imagination has bestowed on Animula charms which in reality she does not possess. Seclusion from female society has produced this morbid condition of mind. Compare her with the beautiful women of your own world, and this false enchantment will vanish."

The Dancer On the Stage at Niblo's Garden

I looked over the newspapers by chance. There I beheld the advertisement of a celebrated *danseuse* who appeared nightly at Niblo's*. The Signorina Caradolce had the reputation of being the most beautiful as well as the most graceful woman in the world. I instantly dressed and went to the theatre.

The curtain drew up. The usual semicircle of fairies in white muslin were standing on the right toe around the enamelled flower-bank, of green canvas, on which the belated prince was sleeping. Suddenly a flute is heard. The fairies start. The trees open, the fairies all stand on the left toe, and the queen enters. It was Signorina. She bounded forward amid thunders of applause, and, lighting on one foot, remained poised in air. Heavens! was this the great enchantress that had drawn monarchs at her chariot-wheels? Those heavy muscular limbs, those thick ankles, those cavernous eyes, that stereotyped smile, those crudely painted cheeks! Where were the vermeil blooms, the liquid expressive eyes, the harmonious limbs of Animula?

The Signorina danced. What gross, discordant movements! The play of her limbs was all false and artificial. Her bounds were painful athletic efforts; her poses were angular and distressed the eye. I

*Niblo's Garden was a famous old-time New York theatre.—Ed.

could bear it no longer; with an exclamation of disgust that drew every eye upon me, I rose from my seat in the very middle of Signorina's *pas-de-fascination,* and abruptly quitted the house.

I hastened home to feast my eyes once more on the lovely form of my sylph. I felt that henceforth to combat this passion would be impossible. I applied my eye to the lens. Animula was there,—but what could have happened? Some terrible change seemed to have taken place during my absence. Some secret grief seemed to cloud the lovely features of her I gazed upon. Her face had grown thin and haggard; her limbs trailed heavily; the wondrous lustre of her golden hair had faded. She was ill!—ill, and I could not assist her! I believe at that moment I would have gladly forfeited all claims to my human birthright, if I could only have been dwarfed to the size of an animalcule, and permitted to console her from whom fate had forever divided me.

I racked my brain for the solution of this mystery. What was it that afflicted the sylph? She seemed to suffer intense pain. Her features contracted, and she even writhed, as if with some internal agony. The wondrous forests appeared also to have lost half their beauty. Their hues were dim and in some places faded away altogether. I watched Animula for hours with a breaking heart, and she seemed absolutely to wither away under my very eye. Suddenly I remembered that I had not looked at the water-drop for several days. In fact, I hated to see it; for it reminded me of the natural barrier between Animula and myself. I hurriedly looked down on the stage of the microscope. The slide was still there,—but, great heavens! The water-drop had vanished! The awful truth burst upon me; it had evaporated, until it had become so minute as to be invisible to the naked eye; I had been gazing on its last atom, the one that contained Animula,—and she was dying!

The Disappearance of Animula

I rushed again to the front of the lens, and looked through. Alas! The last agony had seized her. The rainbow-hued forests had all melted away, and Animula lay struggling feebly in what seemed to be a spot of dim light. Ah! The sight was horrible: the limbs once so round and lovely shrivelling up into nothing; the eyes—those eyes that shown like heavens—being quenched into black dust; the lustrous golden hair now lank and discolored. The last throe came. I beheld that final struggle of the blackening form—and I fainted.

When I awoke out of a trance of many hours, I found myself lying amid the wreck of my instrument, myself as shattered in mind and body as it. I crawled feebly to my bed, from which I did not rise for months.

They say now that I am mad; but they are mistaken. I am poor, for I have neither the heart nor the will to work; all my money is spent, and I live on charity. Young men's associations that love a joke invite me to lecture on Optics before them, for which they pay me, and laugh at me while I lecture. "Linley, the mad microscopist," is the name I go by. I suppose that I talk incoherently while I lecture. Who could talk sense when his brain is haunted by such ghastly memories, while ever and anon among the shapes of death I behold the radiant form of my lost Animula!

THE END

The THING from "OUTSIDE"
By George Allen England

**T**hey sat about their camp-fire, that little party of Americans retreating southward from Hudson Bay before the on-coming menace of the great cold. Sat there, stolid under the awe of the North, under the uneasiness that the day's trek had laid upon their souls. The three men smoked. The two women huddled close to each other. Fireglow picked their faces from the gloom of night among the dwarf firs. A splashing murmur told of the Albany River's haste to escape from the wilderness, and reach the Bay.

"I don't see what there was in a mere circular print on a rock-ledge to make our guides desert," said Professor Thorburn. His voice was as dry as his whole personality. "Most extraordinary."

"*They* knew what it was, all right," answered Jandron, geologist of the party. "So do I." He rubbed his cropped mustache. His eyes glinted grayly. I've seen prints like that before. That was on the Labrador. And I've seen things happen, where they were."

"Something surely happened to our guides, before they'd got a mile into the bush," put in the Professor's wife; while Vivian, her sister, gazed into the fire that revealed her as a beauty, not to be spoiled even by a tam and a rough-knit sweater. "Men don't shoot wildly, and scream like that, unless—"

"They're all three dead now, anyhow," put in Jandron. "So *they're* out of harm's way. While we—well, we're two hundred and fifty wicked miles from the C.P.R. rails."

"Forget it, Jandy!" said Marr, the journalist. "We're just suffering from an attack of nerves, that's all. Give me a fill of 'baccy. Thanks. We'll all be better in the morning. Ho-hum! Now, speaking of spooks and such—"

He launched into an account of how he had once exposed a fraudulent spiritualist, thus proving—to his own satisfaction—that nothing existed beyond the scope of mankind's everyday life. But nobody gave him much heed. And silence fell upon the little night-encampment in the wilds; a silence that was ominous.

Pale, cold stars watched down from spaces infinitely far beyond man's trivial world.

Next day, stopping for chow on a ledge miles upstream, Jandron discovered another of the prints. He cautiously summoned the other two men. They examined the print, while the women-folk were busy

107

by the fire. A harmless thing the marking seemed; only a ring about four inches in diameter, a kind of cup-shaped depression with a raised center. A sort of glaze coated it, as if the granite had been fused by heat.

Jandron knelt, a well-knit figure in bright mackinaw and canvas leggings, and with a shaking finger explored the smooth curve of the print in the rock. His brows contracted as he studied it.

"We'd better get along out of this as quick as we can," said he in an unnatural voice, "You've got your wife to protect, Thorburn, and I,—well, I've got Vivian. And—"

"*You* have?" nipped Marr. The light of an evil jealously gleamed in his heavy-lidded look. "What you need is an alienist."

"Really, Jandron," the Professor admonished, "you mustn't let your imagination run away with you."

"I suppose it's imagination that keeps this print cold!" The geologist retorted. His breath made faint, swirling coils of vapor above it.

"Nothing but a pot-hole," judged Thorburn, bending his spare, angular body to examine the print. The Professor's vitality all seemed centered in his big-bulged skull that sheltered a marvelous thinking machine. Now he put his lean hand to the base of his brain, rubbing the back of his head as if it ached. Then, under what seemed some powerful compulsion, he ran his bony finger around the print in the rock.

"By Jove, but it *is* cold!" he admitted. "And looks as if it had been stamped right out of the stone. Extraordinary!"

"Dissolved out, you mean," corrected the geologist. "By cold."

The journalist laughed mockingly.

"Wait till I write this up!" he sneered. "'Noted Geologist Declares Frigid Ghost Dissolves Granite!'"

Jandron ignored him. He fetched a little water from the river and poured it into the print.

"Ice!" ejaculated the Professor. "Solid ice!"

"Frozen in a second," added Jandron, while Marr frankly stared. "And it'll never melt, either. I tell you, I've seen some of these rings before; and every time, horrible things have happened. Incredible things! Something burned this ring out of the stone—burned it out with the cold interstellar space. Something that can import cold as a permanent quality of matter. Something that can kill matter, and totally remove it."

"Of course that's all sheer poppycock," the journalist tried to laugh, but his brain felt numb.

"This something, this Thing," continued Jandron, "is a Thing that

108

can't be killed by bullets. It's what caught our guides on the barrens, as they ran away—poor fools!"

A shadow fell across the print in the rock. Mrs. Thorburn had come up, was standing there. She had overheard a little of what Jandron had been saying. "Nonsense!" she tried to exclaim, but she was shivering so she could hardly speak.

That night, after a long afternoon of paddling and portaging—laboring against inhibitions like those in a nightmare—they camped on shelving rocks that slanted to the river.

"After all," said the Professor, when supper was done, "we mustn't get into a panic. I know extraordinary things are reported from the wilderness, and more than one man has come out, raving. But we, by Jove! With our superior brains—we aren't going to let Nature play us any tricks!"

"And of course," added his wife, her arm about Vivian, "everything in the universe *is* a natural force. There's really no super-natural, at all."

"Admitted," Jandron replied. "But how about things *outside* the universe?"

"And they call you a scientist?" gibed Marr; but the Professor leaned forward, his brows knit.

"Hm!" he grunted. A little silence fell.

"You don't mean, really," asked Vivian, "that you think there's life and intelligence—Outside?"

Jandron looked at the girl. Her beauty, haloed with ruddy gold from the firelight, was a pain to him as he answered:

"Yes, I do. And dangerous life, too. I know what I've seen, in the North Country. I know what I've seen!"

Silence again, save for the crepitation of the flames, the fall of an ember, the murmur of the current. Darkness narrowed the wilderness to just that circle of flickering light ringed by the forest and the river, brooded over by the pale stars.

"Of course you can't expect a scientific man to take you seriously," commented the Professor.

"I know what I've seen! I tell you there's Something entirely outside man's knowledge."

"Poor fellow!" scoffed the journalist; but even as he spoke his hand pressed his forehead.

"There are Things at work," Jandron affirmed, with dogged persistence. He lighted his pipe with a blazing twig. Its flame revealed his face drawn, lined. "Things. Things that reckon with us no more than we do with ants. Less, perhaps."

The flame of the twig died. Night stood closer, watching.

109

"Suppose there are?" the girl asked. "What's that got to do with these prints in the rock?"

"*They,*" answered Jandron, "are marks left by one of those Things. Footprints, maybe. That Thing is near us, here and now!"

Marr's laugh broke a long stillness.

"And you," he exclaimed, "with an A. M. and a B. S. to write after your name."

"If you knew more," retorted Jandron, "you'd know a devilish sight less. It's only ignorance that's cock-sure."

"But," dogmatized the Professor, "no scientist of any standing has ever admitted any outside interference with this planet."

"No, and for thousands of years nobody ever admitted that the world was round, either. What I've seen, I know."

"Well, what *have you seen?*" asked Mrs. Thorburn, shivering.

"*You'll excuse me, please, for not going into that just now.*"

You mean," the Professor demanded, dryly, "*if the—Hm!—this suppositious Thing wants to—?*"

"*It'll do any infernal thing it takes a fancy to, yes! If it happens to want us—* "

"*But what could* Things like that want of us? Why should They come here, at all?"

"Oh, for various reasons. For inanimate objects, at times, and then again for living beings. They've come here lots of times, I tell you," Jandron asserted with a strange irritation, "and got what They wanted, and then gone away to—Somewhere. If one of Them happens to want us, for any reason, It will take us, that's all. If It doesn't want us, It will ignore us, as we'd ignore gorillas in Africa if we were looking for gold. But if it was gorilla-fur we wanted, that would be different for the gorillas, wouldn't it?"

"What in the world," asked Vivian, "could a—well, a Thing from Outside want of *us?*"

"What do men want, say, of guinea-pigs? Men experiment with 'em, of course. Superior beings use inferior, for their own ends. To assume that man is the supreme product of evolution is gross self-conceit. Might not some superior Thing want to experiment with human beings?

"But how?" demanded Marr.

"The human brain is the most highly-organized form of matter known to this planet. Suppose, now—"

"Nonsense!" interrupted the Professor. "All hands to the sleeping-bags, and no more of this. I've got a wretched headache. Let's anchor in Blanket Bay!"

He, and both the women, turned in. Jandron and Marr sat a while longer by the fire. They kept plenty of wood piled on it, too, for an unnatural chill transfixed the night-air. The fire burned strangely blue, with greenish flicks of flame.

At length, after vast acerbities of disagreement, the geologist and the newspaperman sought their sleeping-bags. The fire was a comfort. Not that a fire could avail a pin's weight against a Thing from interstellar space, but subjectively it was a comfort. The instincts of a million years, centering around protection by fire, cannot be obliterated.

After a time—worn out by a day of nerve-strain and of battling with swift currents, of flight from Something invisible, intangible— they all slept.

The depths of space, star-sprinkled, hung above them with vastness immeasurable, cold beyond all understanding of the human mind.

Jandron woke first, in a red dawn.

He blinked at the fire, as he crawled from his sleeping-bag. The fire was dead; and yet it had not burned out. Much wood remained unconsumed, charred over, as if some gigantic extinguisher had in the night been lowered over it.

"*Hmmm!*" growled Jandron. He glanced about him, on the ledge. "Prints, too. I might have known!"

He aroused Marr. Despite all the journalists's mocking hostility, Jandron felt more in common with this man of his own age than with the Professor, who was close on sixty.

"Look here, now!" said he. "*It* has been all around here. See? *It* put out our fire—maybe the fire annoyed *It*, some way—and *It* walked round us, everywhere." His gray eyes smouldered. "I guess, by gad, you've got to admit facts, now!"

The journalist could only shiver and stare.

"Lord, what a head I've got on me, this morning!" he chattered. He rubbed his forehead with a shaking hand, and started for the river. Most of his assurance had vanished. He looked badly done up.

"Well, what say?" Demanded Jandron. "See these fresh prints?"

"Damn the prints!" retorted Marr, and fell to grumbling some unintelligible thing. He washed unsteadily, and remained crouching at the river's lip, inert, numbed.

Jandron, despite a gnawing at the base of his brain, carefully examined the ledge. He found prints scattered everywhere, and some even on the river-bottom near the shore. Wherever water had collected in the prints on the rock, it had frozen hard. Each print in the river-bed, too, was white with ice. Ice that the rushing current could not melt. "Well, by gad!" he exclaimed. He lighted his pipe and tried to think. Horribly afraid—yes, he felt horribly afraid, but determined. Presently, as a little power of concentration came back, he noticed that all the prints were in straight lines, each mark about two feet from the next.

"*It* was observing us while we slept," said Jandron.

"What nonsense are you talking, eh?" demanded Marr. His dark, heavy face sagged. "Fire, now, and grub!"

He got up and shuffled unsteadily away from the river. Then he stopped with a jerk, staring.

"Look! Look a' that axe!" he gulped, pointing.

Jandron picked up the axe, by the handle, taking good care not to touch the steel. The blade was white-furred with frost. And deep into it, punching out part of the edge, one of the prints was stamped.

"This metal," said he, "is clean gone. It's been absorbed. The Thing doesn't recognize any difference in materials. Water and steel and rock are all the same to It."

"You're crazy!" snarled the journalist. "How could a Thing travel on one leg, hopping along, making marks like that?"

"It could roll, if it was disk-shaped. And—"

A cry from the Professor turned them. Thorburn was stumbling toward them, hands out and tremulous.

"My wife—!" he choked.

Vivian was kneeling beside her sister, frightened, dazed.

"Something's happened!" stammered the Professor. "Here—come here—!"

Mrs. Thorburn was beyond any power of theirs, to help. She was still breathing; but her respirations were stertorous, and a complete paralysis had stricken her. Her eyes, half-open and expressionless, showed pupils startlingly dilated. No resources of the party's drug-kit produced the slightest effect on the woman.

The next half-hour was a confused panic, breaking camp, getting Mrs. Thorburn into a canoe, and leaving that accursed place, with a furious energy of terror that could no longer reason. Up-stream, ever up against the swirl of the current the party fought, driven by horror. With no thought of food or drink, paying no heed to landmarks, lashed forward only by the mad desire to be gone, the three men and the girl flung every ounce of their energy into the paddles. Their panting breath mingled with the sound of swirling eddies. A mist-blurred sun brooded over the northern wilds. Unheeded, hosts of black-flies sang high-pitched keenings all about the fugitives. On either hand the forest waited, watched.

Only after two hours of sweating toil had brought exhaustion did they stop, in the shelter of a cove where black waters circled, foam-

112

flecked. There they found the Professor's wife—she was dead.

Nothing remained to do but bury her. At first Thorburn would not hear of it. Like a madman he insisted that through all hazards he would fetch the body out. But no—impossible. So, after a terrible time, he yielded.

In spite of her grief, Vivian was admirable. She understood what must be done. It was her voice that said the prayers; her hand that—lacking flowers—laid the fir boughs on the cairn. The Professor was dazed past doing anything, saying anything.

Toward mid-afternoon, the party landed again, many miles up-river. Necessity forced them to eat. Fire would not burn. Every time they lighted it, it smouldered and went out with a heavy, greasy smoke. The fugitives ate cold food and drank water, then shoved off in two canoes and once more fled.

In the third canoe, hauled to the edge of the forest, lay all the rock-specimens, data and curios, scientific instruments. The party kept only Marr's diary, a compass, supplies, fire-arms and medicine-kit.

"We can find the things we've left—sometime," said Jandron, noting the place well. "Sometime—after *It* has gone."

"And bring the body out," added Thorburn. Tears, for the first time, wet his eyes. Vivian said nothing. Marr tried to light his pipe. He seemed to forget that nothing, not even tobacco, would burn now.

Vivian and Jandron occupied one canoe. The other carried the Professor and Marr. Thus the power of the two canoes was about the same. They kept well together, up-stream.

The fugitives paddles and portaged with a dumb, desperate energy. Toward evening they struck into what they believed to be the Mamattawan. A mile up this, as the blurred sun faded beyond a wilderness of ominous silence, they camped. Here they made determined efforts to kindle fire. Not even alcohol from the drug-kit would start it. Cold, they mumbled a little food; cold, they huddled into their sleeping-bags, there to lie with darkness leaden on their fear. After a long time, up over a world void of all sound save the river-flow, slid an amber moon notched by the ragged tops of the conifers. Even the wail of a timber-wolf would have come as welcome relief; but no wolf howled.

Silence and night enfolded them. And everywhere they felt that *It* was watching.

Foolishly enough, as a man will do foolish things in a crisis, Jandron laid his revolver outside his sleeping-bag, in easy reach. His thought—blurred by a strange, drawing headache—was:

"If *It* touches Vivian, I'll shoot!"

113

He realized the complete absurdity of trying to shoot a visitant from interstellar space; from the Fourth Dimension, maybe. But Jandron's ideas seemed tangled. Nothing would come right. He lay there, absorbed in a kind of waking nightmare. Now and then, rising on an elbow, he hearkened; all in vain. Nothing so much as stirred.

His thought drifted to better days, when all had been health, sanity, optimism; when nothing except jealousy of Marr, as concerned Vivian, had troubled him. Days when the sizzle of the frying-pan over friendly coals had made friendly wilderness music; when the wind and the northern star, the whirr of the reel, the whispering vortex of the paddle in clear water had all been things of joy. Yes, and when a certain happy moment had, through some word or look of the girl, seemed to promise his heart's desire. But now—

"Damn it, I'll save *her,* anyhow!" he swore with savage intensity, knowing all the while that what was to be, would be, unmitigably. Do ants, by any waving of antenna, stay the down-crushing foot of man?

Next morning, and the next, no sign of the Thing appeared. Hope revived that possibly It might have flitted away elsewhere; back, perhaps, to outer space. Many were the miles the urging paddles spurned behind. The fugitives calculated that a week more would bring them to the railroad. Fire burned again. Hot food and drink helped, wonderfully. But where were the fish?

"Most extraordinary," all at once said the Professor, at noonday camp. He had become quite rational again. "Do you realize, Jandron, we've seen no traces of life in some time?"

The geologist nodded. Only too clearly he had noted just that, but he had been keeping still about it.

"That's so, too!" chimed in Marr, enjoying the smoke that some incomprehensible turn of events was letting him have. "Not a muskrat or beaver. Not even a squirrel or bird."

"Not so much as a gnat or black-fly!" the Professor added. Jandron suddenly realized that he would have welcomed even those.

That afternoon, Marr fell into a suddenly vile temper. He mumbled curses against the guides, the current, the portages, everything. The Professor seemed more cheerful. Vivian complained of an oppressive headache. Jandron gave her the last of the aspirin tablets; and as he gave them, took her hand in his.

"I'll see *you* through, anyhow," said he. "I don't count, now. Nobody counts, only you!"

She gave him a long, silent look. He saw the sudden glint of tears in her eyes; felt the pressure of her hand, and knew they two had never been so near each other as in that moment under the shadow of the Unknown.

Next day—or it may have been two days later, for none of them could be quite sure about the passage of time—they came to a deserted lumber-camp. Even more than two days might have passed; because now their bacon was all gone, and only coffee, tobacco, beef-cubes and pilot-bread remained. The lack of fish and game had cut alarmingly into the duffle-bag. That day—whatever day it may have been—all four of them suffered terribly from headache of an odd, ring-shaped kind, as if something circular were being pressed down about their heads. The Professor said it was the sun that made his head ache. Vivian laid it to the wind and the gleam of the swift water, while Marr claimed it was the heat. Jandron wondered at all this, inasmuch as he plainly saw that the river had almost stopped flowing, and the day had become still and overcast.

They dragged their canoes upon a rotting stage of fir-poles and explored the lumber-camp; a mournful place set back in an old "slash," now partly overgrown with scrub poplar, maple and birch. The log buildings, covered with tar-paper partly torn from the pole roofs, were of the usual North Country type. Obviously the place had not been used for years. Even the landings-stage where once logs had been rolled into the stream had sagged to decay.

"I don't quite get the idea of this," Marr exclaimed. "Where did the logs go to? Downstream, of course. But *that* would take 'em to Hudson Bay, and there's no market for spruce timber or pulpwood at Hudson Bay." He pointed down the current.

"You're entirely mistaken," put in the Professor. "Any fool could see this river runs the other way. A log thrown in here would go down toward the St. Lawerence!"

"But then," asked the girl, "why can't we drift back to civilization?" The Professor retorted:

"Just what we *have* been doing, all along! Extraordinary, that I have to explain the obvious!" He walked away in a huff.

"I don't know but he's right, at that," half admitted the journalist. "I've been thinking almost the same thing, myself, the past day or two—that is, ever since the sun shifted."

"What do you mean, shifted?" from Jandron.

"You haven't noticed it?"

"But there's been no sun at all, for at least two days!"

"Hanged if I'll waste time arguing with a lunatic!" Marr growled. He vouchsafed no explanation of what he meant by the sun's having "shifted," but wandered off, grumbling.

"What *are* we going to do?" the girl appealed to Jandron. The sight of her solemn, frightened eyes, of her palm-outward hands and (at last) her very feminine fear, constricted Jandron's heart.

"We're going through, you and I," he answered simply. "We've got to save them from themselves, you and I have."

Their hands met again, and for a moment held. Despite the dead calm, a fir-tip at the edge of the clearing suddenly flicked aside, shrivelled as if frozen. But neither of them saw it.

The fugitives, badly spent, established themselves in the "barroom" or sleeping shack of the camp. They wanted to feel a roof over them again, if only a broken one. The traces of men comforted them: a couple of broken peavies, a pair of snowshoes with the thongs all gnawed off, a cracked bit of mirror, a yellowed almanac dated 1899.

Jandron called the Professor's attention to this almanac, but the Professor thrust it aside.

"What do I want of a Canadian census-report?" he demanded, and fell to counting the bunks, over and over again. His big bulge of his forehead, that housed the massive brain of him, was oozing sweat. Marr cursed what he claimed was sunshine through the holes in the roof, though Jandron could see none; claimed the sunshine made his head ache.

"But it's not a bad place," he added. "We can make a blaze in that fireplace and be comfy. I don't like that window, though."

"What window?" asked Jandron. "Where?"

Marr laughed, and ignored him. Jandron turned to Vivian, who had sunk down on the "Deacon-seat" and was staring at the stove.

"*Is* there a window here?" he demanded.

"Don't ask me," she whispered. "I—I don't know."

With a very thriving fear in his heart, Jandron peered at her a moment. He fell to muttering;

"I'm Wallace Jandron. Wallace Jandron, 37 Ware Street, Cambridge, Massachusetts. I am quite sane. And I'm going to stay so. I'm going to save her! I know perfectly well what I'm doing. And I'm sane. Quite, quite sane!"

After a time of confused and purposeless wrangling, they got a fire going and made coffee. This, and cube bouillon with hardtack, helped considerably. The camp helped, too. A house, even a poor and broken one, is a wonderful barrier against a Thing from—Outside.

Presently darkness folded down. The men smoked, thankful that tobacco still held out. Vivian lay in a bunk that Jandron had piled with spruce boughs for her, and seemed to sleep. The Professor fretted like a child, over the blisters his paddle had made upon his hands. Marr laughed, now and then; though what he might be laughing at was not apparent. Suddenly he broke out:

"After all, what should *It* want of us?"

"Our brains, of course," the Professor answered, sharply.

"That lets Jandron out," the journalist mocked.

"But," added the Professor, "I can't imagine a Thing callously destroying human beings. And yet—"

He stopped short, with surging memories of his dead wife.

"What was it," Jandron asked, "that destroyed all of those people in Valladolid, Spain, that time so many of 'em died in a few minutes after having been touched by an invisible Something that left a slight red mark on each? The newspapers were full of it."

"Piffle!" yawned Marr.

"I tell you," insisted Jandron, "there are forms of life as superior to us as we are to ants. We can't see 'em. No ant ever saw a man. And did any ant ever form the least conception of a man? These Things have left thousands of traces, all over the world. If I had my reference-books—"

"Tell that to the marines!"

"Charles Fort, the greatest authority in the world on unexplained phenomena," persisted Jandron, "gives innumerable cases of happenings that science can't explain, in his 'Book of the Damned.' He claims this earth was once a No-Man's land where all kinds of Things explored and colonized and fought for possession. And he says that now everybody's warned off, except the Owners. I happen to remember a few sentences of his: 'In the past, inhabitants of a host of worlds have dropped here, hopped here, wafted here, sailed, flown, motored, walked here; have come singly, have come in enormous numbers; have visited for hunting, trading, mining. They have been unable to stay here, have made colonies here, have been lost here.'"

"Poor fish, to believe that!" mocked the journalist, while the Professor blinked and rubbed his bulging forehead.

"I *do* believe it!" insisted Jandron. "The world is covered with relics of dead civilizations, that have mysteriously vanished, leaving nothing but their temples and monuments."

"Rubbish!"

"How about Easter Island? How about all the gigantic works there and in a thousand other places—Peru, Yucatan and so on—which certainly no primitive race ever built?"

"That's thousands of years ago," said Marr, "and I'm sleepy. For heaven's sake, can it!"

"Oh, all right. But *how* explain things, then!"

"What the devil could one of those Things want of our brains?" suddenly put in the Professor. "After all, what?"

"Well, what do we want of lower forms of life? Sometimes food. Again, some product or other. Or just information. Maybe It is just experimenting with us, the way we poke an ant-hill. There's always this to remember, that the human brain-tissue is the most highly-organized form of matter in this world."

"Yes," admitted the Professor, "but what—?"

"It might want brain-tissue for food, for experimental purposes, for lubricant—how do I know?"

Jandron fancied he was still explaining things; but all at once he found himself waking up in one of the bunks. He felt terribly cold, stiff, sore. A sift of snow lay here and there on the camp floor, where it had fallen through holes in the roof.

"Vivian!" he croaked hoarsely. "Thorburn! Marr!"

Nobody answered. There was nobody to answer. Jandron crawled with immense pain out of his bunk, and blinked round with bleary eyes. All of a sudden he saw the Professor, and gulped.

The Professor was lying stiff and straight in another bunk, on his back. His waxen face made a mask of horror. The open, starings eyes, with pupils immensely dilated, sent Jandron shuddering back. A livid ring marked the forehead, that now sagged inward as if empty.

"Vivian!" croaked Jandron, staggering away from the body. He fumbled to the bunk where the girl had lain. The bunk was quite deserted.

On the stove, in which lay half-charred wood—wood smothered out of as if by some noxious gas—still stood the coffee-pot. The liquid in it was frozen solid. Of Vivian and the journalist, no trace remained.

Along one of the sagging beams that supported the roof, Jandron's horror-blasted gaze perceived a straight line of frosted prints, ring-shaped, bitten deep.

"Vivian! Vivian!"

No answer.

Shaking, sick, gray, half-blind with a horror not of this world, Jandron peered slowly around. The duffle-bag and supplies were gone. Nothing was left but that coffee-pot and the revolver at Jandron's hip.

Jandron turned, then. A-stare, his skull feeling empty as a burst drum, he crept lamely to the door and out—out into the snow.

Snow. It came slanting down. From a gray sky it steadily filtered. The trees showed no leaf. Birches, poplars, rock-maples all stood naked. Only the conifers drooped sickly-green. In a little shallow across the river snow lay white on thin ice.

118

Ice? Snow? Rapt with terror, Jandron stared. Why, then, he must have been unconscious three or four weeks? But how—?

Suddenly, all along the upper branches of trees that edged the clearing, puffs of snow flicked down. The geologist shuffled after two half-obliterated sets of footprints that wavered toward the landing.

His body was leaden. He wheezed, as he reached the river. The light, dim as it was, hurt his eyes. He blinked in a confusion that could just perceive one canoe was gone. He pressed a hand to his head, where an iron band seemed screwed up tight, tighter.

"Vivian! Marr! Halloooo!"

Not even an echo. Silence clamped the world; silence, and a cold that gnawed. Everything had gone a sinister gray.

After a certain time—though time now possessed neither reality nor duration—Jandron dragged himself back to the camp and stumbled in. Heedless of the staring corpse he crumpled down by the stove and tried to think, but his brain had been emptied of power. Everything blent to a gray blur. Snow kept slithering in through the roof.

"Well, why don't you come and get me, Thing?" suddenly snarled Jandron. "Here I am. Damn you, come and get me!"

Voices. Suddenly he heard voices. Yes, somebody was outside, there. Singularly aggrieved, he got up and limped to the door. He squinted out into the gray; saw two figures down by the landing. With numb indifference he recognized the girl and Marr.

"Why should they bother me again?" he nebulously wondered. Can't they go away and leave me alone?" He felt peevish irritation.

Then, a modicum of reason returning, he sensed that they were arguing. Vivian, beside a canoe freshly dragged from thin ice, was pointing; Marr was gesticulating. All at once Marr snarled, turned from her, plodded with bent back toward the camp.

"But listen!" she called, her rough-knit sweater all powdered with snow. "*That's* the way!" she gestured downstream.

"I'm not going either way!" Marr retorted. "I'm going to stay right here!" He came on, bareheaded. Snow grayed his stubble of beard; but on his head it melted as it fell, as if some fever there had raised the brain-stuff to improbable temperatures. "I'm going to stay right here, all summer." His heavy lids sagged. Puffy and evil, his lips showed a glint of teeth. "Let me alone!"

Vivian lagged after him, kicking up the ash-like snow. With indifference, Jandron watched them. Trivial human creatures!

Suddenly Marr saw him in the doorway and stopped short. He drew his gun; he aimed at Jandron.

"You get out!" he mouthed. "Why in—— can't you stay dead?"

119

"Put that gun down, you idiot!" Jandron managed to retort. The girl stopped and seemed trying to understand. "We can get away yet, if we all stick together."

"Are you going to get out and leave me alone?" demanded the journalist, holding his gun steadily enough.

Jandron, wholly indifferent, watched the muzzle. Vague curiosity possessed him. Just what, he wondered, did it feel like to be shot?

Marr pulled trigger.

Snap!

The cartridge missed fire. Not even powder would burn.

Marr laughed, horribly, and shambled forward. "Serves him right!" he mouthed. "He'd better not come back again!"

Jandron understood that Marr had seen him fall. But still he felt himself standing there, alive. He shuffled away from the door. No matter whether he was alive or dead, there was always Vivian to be saved.

The journalist came to the door, paused, looked down, grunted and passed into the camp. He shut the door. Jandron heard the rotten wooden bar of the latch drop. From within echoed a laugh, monstrous in its brutality.

Then quivering, the geologist felt a touch on his arm.

"Why did you desert us like that?" he heard Vivian's reproach. "Why?"

He turned, hardly able to see her at all.

"Listen," he said, thickly. "I'll admit anything. It's all right. But just forget it, for now. We've got to get out o' here. The Professor is dead, in there, and Marr's gone mad and barricaded himself in there. So there's no use staying. There's a chance for us yet. Come along!"

He took her by the arm and tried to draw her toward the river, but she held back. The hate in her face sickened him. He shook in the grip of a mighty chill.

"Go, with—you?" she demanded.

"Yes, by God!" he retorted, in a swift blaze of anger, "or I'll kill you where you stand. *It* shan't get you, anyhow!"

Swiftly piercing, a greater cold smote to his inner marrows. A long row of the cup-shaped prints had just appeared in the snow beside the camp. And from these marks wafted a faint, bluish vapor of unthinkable cold.

"What are you staring at?" the girl demanded.

"Those prints! In the snow, there—see?" He pointed a shaking finger.

"How can there be snow at this season?"

He could have wept for the pity of her, the love of her. On her

120

red tam, her tangle of rebel hair, her sweater, the snow came
steadily drifting; yet there she stood before him and prated of
summer. Jandron heaved himself out of a very slough of dawn-
dragging lassitudes. He whipped himself into action.

"Summer, winter—no matter!" he flung at her. "You're coming
along with me!" He seized her arm with the brutality of desperation
that must hurt, to save. And murder, too, lay in his soul. He knew
that he would strangle her with his naked hands, if need were,
before he would ever leave her there, for *It* to work Its horrible will
upon.

"You come with me," he mouthed, "or by the Almighty—!"

Marr's scream in the camp, whirled him toward the door. That
scream rose higher, higher, even more and more piercing, just like
the screams of the runaway Indian guides in what now appeared the
infinitely long ago. It seemed to last hours; and always it rose, rose,
as if being wrung out of a human body by some kind of agony not
conceivable in this world. Higher, higher—

Then it stopped.

Jandron hurled himself against the plank door. The bar smashed;
the door shivered inward.

With a cry, Jandron recoiled. He covered his eyes with a hand that
quivered, claw-like.

"Go away, Vivian! Don't come here—don't look—"

He stumbled away, babbling.

Out of the door crept something like a man. A queer, broken, bent
over thing; a thing crippled, shrunken and flabby, that whined.

This thing—yes, it was still Marr—crouched down at one side,
quivering, whimpering. It moved its hands as a crushed ant moves
its antennae, jerkily, without significance.

All at once Jandron no longer felt afraid. He walked quite steadily
to Marr, who was breathing in little gasps. From the camp issued an
odor unlike anything terrestial. A thin, grayish grease covered the
sill.

Jandron caught hold of the crumpling journalist's arm. Marr's eyes
leered, filmed, unseeing. He gave the impression of a creature whose
back has been broken, whose whole essence and energy have been
wrenched asunder, yet in which life somehow clings, palpitant. A
creature vivisected.

Away through the snow Jandron dragged him. Marr made no
resistance; just let himself be led, whining a little, palsied, rickety,
shattered. The girl, her face whitely cold as the snow that fell on it,
came after.

Thus they reached the landing at the river.

121

"Come, now, let's get away!" Jandron made shift to articulate. Marr said nothing. But when Jandron tried to bundle him into a canoe, something in the journalist revived with swift, mad hatefulness. That something lashed him into a spasm of wiry, incredibly venomous resistance. Slavers of blood and foam streaked Marr's lips. He made horrid noises, like an animal. He howled dismally, and bit, clawed, writhed and grovelled! He tried to sink his teeth into Jandron's leg. He fought appallingly, as men must have fought in the inconceivably remote days even before the Stone Age. And Vivian helped him. Her fury was a tiger-cat's.

Between the pair of them, they almost did him in. They almost dragged Jandron down—and themselves, too—into the black river that ran swiftly sucking under the ice. Not till Jandron had quite flung off all vague notions and restraints of gallantry; not until he struck from the shoulder—to kill, if need were—did he best them.

He beat the pair of them unconscious, trussed them hand and foot with the painters of the canoes, rolled them into the larger canoe, and shoved off.

After that, the blankness of a measureless oblivion descended.

Only from what he was told, weeks after, in the Royal Victoria Hospital at Montreal, did Jandron ever learn how and when a field-squad of Dominion Foresters had found them drifting in Lake Moosawamkeag. And that knowledge filtered slowly into his brain during a period inchoate as Iceland fogs.

That Marr was dead and the girl alive—that much, at all events, was solid. He could hold to that; he could climb back, with that, to the real world again.

Jandron climbed back, came back. Time healed him, as it healed the girl. After a long, long while, they had speech together. Cautiously he sounded her wells of memory. He saw that she recalled nothing. So he told her white lies about capsized canoes and the sad death—in realistically-described rapids—of all the party except herself and him.

Vivian believed. Fate, Jandron knew, was being very kind to both of them.

But Vivian could never understand in the least why her husband, not very long after marriage asked her not to wear a wedding-ring or any ring whatever.

"Men are so queer!" covers a multitude of psychic agonies.

Life, for Jandron—life, softened by Vivian—knit itself up into some reasonable semblance of a normal pattern. But when, at lengthening intervals, memories even now awake—memories crawling amid the slime of cosmic mysteries that it is madness to approach—or when at certain times Jandron sees a ring of any sort, his heart chills with a cold that reeks of the horrors of Infinity.

And from the shadows past the boundaries of our universe seem to beckon Things that, God grant, can never till the end of time be known on earth.

THE END

LONG

First Place: **The Mad Planet**   *Murray Leinster*

We recently published a charming tale by the author of this story, entitled "The Runaway Skyscraper." Great as was that story, this one is even greater. The possibility that our planet will some day be dominated by the insect world has been admitted by our greatest entomologists, and the possibility of this is not half so remote as one might think.

Some of our deepest thinkers believe that it is not only possible, but most probable, that this may happen, or possibly has happened in the past. At any rate, Mr. Murray Leinster gives us an insight into the life of our planet under the altered conditions.

It is a story tremendous in its possibilities, and the author has written it with such a facile pen, that you cannot lay the story aside until you have come to its conclusion.
                                                                    Hugo Gernsback—1926

Second Place: **The Moon Metal**   *Garrett P. Serviss*

One of the finest pieces of scientification ever written is THE MOON METAL. This classic, by the well-known Professor Garrett P. Serviss, contains a tremendous amount of excellent science. While this story was written at the close of the 19th century no one in this latter day of transmission of radio over great distances, and the actual accomplishment of transmutation of gases and the like, can find fault or can question that such a scheme, as propounded by the author—that is, of extracting ore or metal from a distant body without intervening physical means—can some day be accomplished.

The story keeps up a tremendous interest, because you are not permitted to know, for quite a long stretch, just how The Moon Metal was extracted from the moon. The illustrious author has long enjoyed a reputation as a popularizer of natural science. Here we see him as a true scientific story teller.   *Hugo Gernsback—1926*

Third Place: **Beyond the Pole**   *A. Hyatt Verrill*

Here is one of the most gripping stories that it has ever been our good fortune to read. At the same time, it is one of the best scientifiction works of the modern school that we have lately seen. It is easily the best scientifiction story of this year.

The author, in choosing a civilization of lobster-like people, should not be accused of sketching an impossiblity. Indeed, it is impossible to say, at this moment, in what form an intelligent reasoning creature might or might not exist. Just because we have never met a reasoning creature different from a human being tells nothing, and we certainly should not be so arrogant as to think that intelligence, as we know it, combined with reasoning, exists solely in the human type.

So far we have not been able to penetrate the secrets of ant life, or of the bee life, despite our so-called "intelligence," so we should not judge too harshly what is and what is not possible, when it comes to reasoning intelligence.

In nature we know that everything is repeated—not only once, but thousands of times. Why should reasoning intelligence be represented only in one species?

At any rate, we know that somehow you will feel that "Beyond the Pole" is a real story, where real facts are given to you for what they are worth. It is an engrossing story that cannot fail to grip you from start to finish.   *Hugo Gernsback—1926*

Incorrect spelling of Verrill on page 241 from original magazine.

The MAD PLANET
By Murray Leinster

CHAPTER I

The World Insane

n all his lifetime of perhaps twenty years, it had never occurred to Burl to wonder what his grandfather had thought about his surroundings. The grandfather had come to an untimely end in a rather unpleasant fashion which Burl remembered vaguely as a succession of screams coming more and more faintly to his ears while he was being carried away at the top speed of which his mother was capable.

Burl had rarely or never thought of the old gentlemen since. Surely he had never wondered in the abstract of what his greatgrandfather thought, and most surely of all, there never entered his head such a purely hypothetical question as the one of what his many-times-great-grandfather—say of the year 1920—would have thought of the scene in which Burl found himself.

He was treading cautiously over a brownish carpet of fungus growth, creeping furtively toward the stream which he knew by the generic title of "water." It was the only water he knew. Towering far above his head, three man-heights high, great toadstools hid the grayish sky from his sight. Clinging to the foot-thick stalks of the toadstools were still other fungi, parasites upon the growths that had once been parasites themselves.

Burl himself was a slender young man wearing a single garment twisted about his waist, made from the wing-fabric of a great moth, the members of his tribe had slain as it emerged from its cocoon. His skin was fair, without a trace of sunburn. In all his lifetime he had never seen the sun, though the sky was rarely hidden from view save by the giant fungi which, with monster cabbages, were the only growing things he knew. Clouds usually spread overhead, and when they did not, the perpetual haze made the sun but an indefinitely brighter part of the sky, never a sharply edged ball of fire. Fantastic mosses, misshapen fungus growths, colossal molds and yeasts, were the essential parts of the landscape through which he moved.

Once as he had dodged through the forest of huge toadstools, his shoulder touched a cream-colored stalk, giving the whole fungus a tiny shock. Instantly, from the umbrella-like mass of pulp overhead, a fine and impalpable powder fell upon him like snow. It was the season when the toadstools sent out their spores, or seeds, and they had been dropped upon him at the first sign of disturbance.

Furtive as he was, he paused to brush them from his head and hair. They were deadly poison, as he knew well.

Burl would have been a curious sight to a man of the twentieth century. His skin was pink like that of a child, and there was but little hair upon his body. Even that on top of his head was soft and downy. His chest was larger than his forefathers' had been, and his ears seemed almost capable of independent movement, to catch threatening sounds from any direction. His eyes, large and blue, possessed pupils which could dilate to extreme size, allowing him to see in almost complete darkness.

He was the result of the thirty thousand years' attempt of the human race to adapt itself to the change that had begun in the latter half of the twentieth century.

At about that time, civilization had been high, and apparently secure. Mankind had reached a permanent agreement within itself, and all men had equal opportunities to education and leisure. Machinery did most of the labor of the world, and men were only required to supervise its operation. All men were well-fed, all men were well-educated, and it seemed that until the end of time the earth would be the abode of a community of comfortable human beings, pursuing their studies and diversions, their illusions and their truths. Peace, quietness, privacy, freedom were universal.

Then, just when men were congratulating themselves that the Golden Age had come again, it was observed that the planet seemed ill at ease. Fissures opened slowly in the crust, and carbonic acid gas—the carbon dioxide of chemists—began to pour out into the atmosphere. That gas had long been known to be present in the air, and was considered necessary to planet life. Most of the plants of the world took the gas and absorbed its carbon into themselves, releasing the oxygen for use again.

Scientists had calculated that a great deal of the earth's increased fertility was due to the larger quantities of carbon dioxide released by the activities of man in burning his coal and petroleum. Because of those views, for some years no great alarm was caused by the continuous exhalation from the world's interior.

Constantly, however, the volume increased. New fissures constantly opened, each one adding a new source of carbon dioxide, and each one pouring into the already laden atmosphere more of the gas—beneficent in small quantities, but as the world learned, deadly in large ones.

The percentage of the heavy, vapor-like gas increased. The whole body of the air became heavier through its admixture. It absorbed more moisture and became more humid. Rainfall increased. Climates grew warmer. Vegetation became more luxuriant—but the air

128

gradually became less exhilarating.

Soon the health of mankind began to be affected. Accustomed through long ages to breath air rich in oxygen and poor in carbon dioxide, men suffered. Only those who lived on high plateaus or on tall mountain-tops remained unaffected. The plants of the earth, though nourished and increasing in size beyond those ever seen before, were unable to dispose of the continually increasing flood of carbon dioxide exhaled by the weary planet.

By the middle of the twenty-first century it was generally recognized that a new carboniferous period was about to come when the earth's atmosphere would be thick and humid, unbreathable by man, when giant grasses and ferns would form the only vegetation.

When the twenty-first century drew to a close the whole human race began to revert to conditions closely approximating savagery. The lowlands were unbearable. Thick jungles of rank growth covered the ground. The air was depressing and enervating. Men could live there, but it was a sickly, feverridden existence. The whole population of the earth desired the high lands, and as the low country became more unbearable, men forgot their two centuries of peace.

They fought destructively, each for a bit of land where he might live and breathe. Then men began to die, men who had persisted in remaining near sea-level. They could not live in the poisonous air. The danger zone crept up as the earth-fissures tirelessly poured out their steady streams of foul gas. Soon men could not live within five hundred feet of sea-level. The lowlands went uncultivated, and became jungles of a thickness comparable only to those of the first carboniferous period.

Then men died of sheer inanition at a thousand feet. The plateaus and mountain-tops were crowded with folk struggling for a foothold and food beyond the invisible menace that crept up, and up—

These things did not take place in one year, or in ten. Not in one generation, but in several. Between the time when the chemists of the International Geophysical Institute announced that the proportion of carbon dioxide in the air had increased from .04 per cent to .1 per cent and the time when at sea-level six per cent of the atmosphere was the deadly gas, more than two hundred years intervened.

Coming gradually, as it did, the poisonous effects of the deadly stuff increased with insidious slowness. First the lassitude, then the heaviness of brain, then the weakness of body. Mankind ceased to grow in numbers. After a long period, the race had fallen to a fraction of its former size. There was room in plenty on the mountain-tops—but the danger-level continued to creep up.

There was but one solution. The human body would have to inure itself to the poison, or it was doomed to extinction. It finally developed a toleration for the gas that had wiped out race after race and nation after nation, but at a terrible cost. Lungs increased in size to secure the oxygen on which life depended, but the poison, inhaled at every breath, left the few survivors sickly and filled with a perpetual weariness. Their minds lacked the energy to cope with new problems or transmit the knowledge they possessed.

And after thirty thousand years, Burl, a direct descendant of the first president of the Universal Republic, crept through a forest of toadstools and fungus growths. He was ignorant of fire, of metals, of the uses of stone and wood. A single garment was worn by him. His language was a scanty group of a few hundred labial sounds, conveying no abstractions and few concrete ideas.

He was ignorant of the uses of wood. There was no wood in the scanty territory furtively inhabited by his tribe. With the increase in heat and humidity the trees had begun to die out. Those of northern climes went first, the oaks, the cedars, the maples. Then the pines— the beeches went early—the cypresses, and finally even the forests of the jungles vanished. Only grasses and reeds, bamboos and their kin, were able to flourish in the new, steaming atmosphere. The thick jungles gave place to dense thickets of grasses and ferns, now become tree-ferns again.

And then the fungi took their place. Flourishing as never before, flourishing on a planet of torrid heat and perpetual miasma, on whose surface the sun never shown directly because of an ever-thickening bank of clouds that hung sullenly overhead, the fungi sprang up. About the dank pools that festered over the surface of the earth, fungus growths began to cluster. Of every imaginable shade and color, of all monstrous forms and malignant purposes, of huge size and flabby volume, they spread over the land.

The grasses and ferns gave place to them. Squat toadstools, flaking molds, evil-smelling yeasts, vast mounds of fungi inextricably mingled as to species, but growing, forever growing and exhaling an odor of dark places.

The strange growths now grouped themselves in forests, horrible travesties on the vegetation they had succeeded. They grew and grew with feverish intensity beneath a clouded or a haze-obscured sky, while above them fluttered gigantic butterflies and huge moths, sipping daintily of their corruption.

The insects alone of all the animal world above water, were able to endure the change. They multiplied exceedingly, and enlarged

130

themselves in the thickened air. The solitary vegetation—as distinct from fungus growths—that had survived was now a degenerate form of the cabbages that had once fed peasants. On those rank, colossal masses of foliage, the stolid grubs and caterpillars ate themselves to maturity, then swung below in strong cocoons to sleep the sleep of metamorphosis from which they emerged to spread their wings and fly.

The tiniest butterflies of former days had increased their span until their gaily colored wings should be described in terms of feet, while the larger emperor moths extended their purple sails to a breadth of yards upon yards. Burl himself would have been dwarfed beneath the overshadowing fabric of their wings.

It was fortunate that they, the largest flying creatures, were harmless or nearly so. Burl's fellow tribesmen sometimes came upon a cocoon just about to open, and waited patiently beside it until the beautiful creature within broke through its matted shell and came out into the sunlight.

Then, before it had gathered energy from the air, and before its wings had swelled to strength and firmness, the tribesmen fell upon it, tearing the filmy delicate wings from its body and the limbs from its carcass. Then, when it lay helpless before them, they carried away the juicy, meat-filled limbs to be eaten, leaving the still living body to stare helplessly at this strange world through its many faceted eyes and become a prey to the voracious ants who would soon clamber upon it, and carry it away in tiny fragments to their underground city.

Not all the insect world was so helpless or so unthreatening. Burl knew of wasps almost the length of his own body who possessed stings that were instantly fatal. To every species of wasp, however, some other insect is predestined prey, and the furtive members of Burl's tribe feared them but little, as they sought only the prey to which their instinct led them.

Bees were similarly aloof. They were hard put to it for existence, those bees. Few flowers bloomed, and they were reduced to expedients once considered signs of degeneracy in their race. They gathered bubbling yeasts and fouler things, occasionally from the nectarless blooms of the rank, giant cabbages. Burl knew the bees. They droned over, nearly as large as he was himself, their bulging eyes gazing at him with abstracted preoccupation. And crickets, and beetles, and spiders—

Burl knew spiders! His grandfather had been the prey of one of the hunting tarantulas, which had leaped with incredible ferocity from his excavated tunnel in the earth. A vertical pit in the ground, two feet in diameter, went down for twenty feet. At the bottom of that lair the black-bellied monster waited for the tiny sounds that would warn him of prey approaching his hiding-place. (*Lycosa fasciata*).

Burl's grandfather had been careless, and the terrible shrieks he uttered as the horrible monster darted from the pit and seized him had lingered vaguely in Burl's mind ever since. Burl had seen, too, the monster webs of another species of spider, and watched from a safe distance as the misshapen body of the huge creature sucked the juices from a three-foot cricket that had become entangled in its trap.

Burl had remembered the strange stripes of yellow and black and silver that crossed upon its abdomen (*Epiera fasciata*). He had been fascinated by the struggles of the imprisoned insect, coiled in a hopeless tangle of sticky, gummy ropes the thickness of Burl's finger, cast about its body before the spider made any attempt to approach.

Burl knew these dangers. They were a part of his life. It was his accustomedness to them, and that of his ancestors, that made his existence possible. He was able to evade them; so he survived. A moment of carelessness, an instant's relaxation of his habitual caution, and he would be one with his forebears, forgotten meals of long-dead, inhuman monsters.

Three days before, Burl had crouched behind a bulky, shapeless fungus growth while he watched a furious duel between two huge horned beetles. Their jaws, gaping wide, clicked and clashed upon each other's impenetrable armor. Their legs crashed like so many cymbals as their polished surfaces ground and struck against each other. They were fighting over some particularly attractive bit of carrion.

Burl had watched with all his eyes until a gaping orifice appeared in the armor of the smaller of the two. It uttered a shrill cry, or seemed to cry out. The noise was actually the tearing of the horny stuff beneath the victorious jaws of the adversary. The wounded beetle struggled more and more feebly. At last it collapsed, and the conqueror placidly began to eat the conquered before life was extinct.

Burl waited until the meal was finished, and then approached the scene with caution. An ant—the forerunner of many—was already inspecting the carcass.

Burl usually ignored the ants. They were stupid, short-sighted insects, and not hunters. Save when attacked, they offered no injury. They were scavengers, on the look-out for the dead and dying, but they would fight viciously if their prey were questioned, and they were dangerous opponents. They were from three inches in length for the tiny black ants to a foot for the large termites.

Burl was hasty when he heard the tiny clickings of their limbs as they approached. He seized the sharp-pointed snout of the victim, detached from the body, and fled from the scene.

Later, he inspected his find with curiosity. The smaller victim had been a Minotaur beetle, with a sharp-pointed horn like that of a rhinoceros to reinforce his offensive armament, already dangerous because of his wide jaws. The jaws of a beetle work from side to side, instead of up and down, and this had made the protection complete in no less than three directions.

Burl inspected the sharp, dagger-like instrument in his hand. He felt its point, and it pricked his finger. He flung it aside as he crept to the hidingplace of his tribe. There were only twenty of them, four or five men, six or seven women, and the rest girls and children.

Burl had been wondering at the strange feelings that came over him when he looked at one of the girls. She was younger than Burl—perhaps eighteen—and fleeter of foot than he. They talked together, sometimes, and once or twice Burl shared with her an especially succulent find of foodstuffs.

The next morning he found the horn where he had thrown it, sticking in the flabby side of a toadstool. He pulled it out, and gradually, far back in his mind, an idea began to take shape. He sat for some time with the thing in his hand, considering it with a far-away look in his eyes. From time to time he stabbed at a toadstool, awkwardly, but with gathering skill. His imagination began to work fitfully. He visualized himself stabbing food with it as the larger beetle had stabbed the former owner of the weapon in his hand.

Burl could not imagine himself coping with one of the fighting insects. He could only picture himself, dimly, stabbing something that was food with this death-dealing thing. It was longer than his arm and though clumsy to the hand, an effective and terribly sharp implement.

He thought. Where was there food, food that lived, that would not fight back? Presently he rose and began to make his way toward the tiny river. Yellow-bellied newts swam in its waters. The swimming larvae of a thousand insects floated about its surface or crawled upon its bottom.

There were deadly things there, too. Giant crayfish snapped their horny claws at the unwary. Mosquitoes of four-inch wing-spread sometimes made their humming way above the river. The last survivors of their race, they were dying out for lack of the plant-juices on which the male of the species lived, but even so they were formidable. Burl had learned to crush them with fragments of fungus.

He crept slowly through the forest of toadstools. Brownish fungus was underfoot. Strange orange, red, and purple molds clustered about the bases of the creamy toadstool stalks. Once Burl paused to run his sharp-pointed weapon through a fleshy stalk and reassure himself that what he planned was practicable.

He made his way furtively through the forest of misshapen growths. Once he heard a tiny clicking, and froze into stillness. It was a troop of four or five ants, each some eight inches long, returning along their habitual pathway to their city. They moved sturdily, heavily laden, along the route marked with the odorous formic acid exuded from the bodies of their comrades. Burl waited until they had passed, then went on.

He came to the bank of the river. Green scum covered a great deal of its surface, scum occasionally broken by a slowly enlarging bubble of some gas released from decomposing matter on the bottom. In the center of the placid stream the current ran a little more swiftly, and the water itself was visible.

Over the shining current water-spiders ran swiftly. They had not shared in the general increase of size that had taken place in the insect world. Depending upon the capillary qualities of the water to support them, an increase in size and weight would have deprived them of the means of locomotion.

From the spot where Burl first peered at the water the green scum spread out for many yards into the stream. He could not see what swam and wriggled and crawled beneath the evil-smelling covering. He peered up and down the banks.

Perhaps a hundred and fifty yards below, the current came near the shore. An out-cropping of rock there made a steep descent to the river, from which yellow shelf-fungi stretched out. Dark-red and orange above, they were light-yellow below, and they formed a series of platforms above the smoothly flowing stream. Burl made his way cautiously toward them.

On his way he saw one of the edible mushrooms that formed so large a part of his diet, and paused to break from the flabby flesh an amount that would feed him for many days. It was too often the custom of his people to find a store of food, carry it to their hiding-place, and then gorge themselves for days, eating, sleeping, and waking only to eat again until the food was gone.

Absorbed as he was in his plan of trying his new weapon, Burl was tempted to return with his booty. He would give Saya of this food, and they would eat together. Saya was the maiden who roused unusual emotions in Burl. He felt strange impulses stirring within him when she was near, a desire to touch her, to caress her. He did not understand.

He went on, after hesitating. If he brought her food, Saya would be pleased, but if he brought her of the things that swam in the stream, she would be still more pleased. Degraded as his tribe had become, Burl was yet a little more intelligent than they. He was an atavism, a throwback to ancestors who had cultivated the earth and subjugated its animals. He had a vague idea of pride, unformed but potent.

No man within memory had hunted or slain for food. They knew of meat, yes, but it had been the fragments left by an insect-hunter, seized and carried away by the men before the perpetually alert ant-colonies had sent their foragers to the scene.

If Burl did what no man before him had done, if he brought a whole carcas to his tribe, they would envy him. They were preoccupied solely with their stomachs, and after that with the preservation of their lives. The perpetuation of the race came third in their consideration.

They were herded together in the leaderless group, coming to the same hiding-place that they might share in the finds of the lucky and gather comfort from their numbers. Of weapons, they had none. They sometimes used stones to crack open the limbs of the huge insects they found partly devoured, cracking them open for the sweet meat to be found inside, but they sought safety from their enemies solely in flight and hiding.

Their enemies were not as numerous as might have been imagined. Most of the meat-eating insects have their allotted prey. The sphex—a hunting wasp-feeds solely upon grasshoppers. Other wasps eat flies only. The pirate-bee eats bumblebees only. Spiders were the principal enemies of man, as they devour with a terrifying impartiality all that falls into their clutches.

Burl reached the spot from which he might gaze down into the water. He lay prostrate, staring into the shallow depths. Once a huge crayfish, as long as Burl's body, moved leisurely across his vision. Small fishes and even the huge newts fled before the voracious creature.

After a long time the tide of underwater life resumed its activity. The wriggling grubs of the dragon-flies reappeared. Little flecks of silver swam into view—a school of tiny fish. A larger fish appeared, moving slowly through the water.

Burl's eyes glistened and his mouth watered. He reached down with his long weapon. It barely touched the water. Disappointment filled him, yet the nearness and the apparent practicability of his scheme spurred him on.

He considered the situation. There were the shelf-fungi below him. He rose and moved to a point just above them, then thrust his spear down. They resisted its point. Burl felt them tentatively with his foot, then dared to thrust his weight to them. They held him firmly. He clambered down and lay flat upon them, peering over the edge as before.

The large fish, as long as Burl's arm, swam slowly to and fro below him. Burl had seen the former owner of his spear strive to thrust it into his opponents, and knew that a thrust was necessary. He had tried his weapon upon toadstools—had practiced with it. When the fish swam below him, he thrust sharply downward. The spear seemed to bend when it entered the water, and missed its mark by inches, to Burl's astonishment. He tried again and again.

He grew angry with the fish below him for eluding his efforts to kill it. Repeated strokes had left it untouched, and it was unwary, and did not even try to run away.

Burl became furious. The big fish came to rest directly beneath his hand. Burl thrust downward with all his strength. This time the spear, entering vertically, did not seem to bend. It went straight down. Its point penetrated the scales of the swimmer below, transfixing that lazy fish completely.

An uproar began. The fish, struggling to escape, and Burl, trying to draw it up to his perch, made a huge commotion. In his excitement Burl did not observe a tiny ripple some distance away. The monster crayfish was attracted by the disturbance and was approaching.

The unequal combat continued. Burl hung on desperately to the end of his spear. Then there was a tremor in Burl's support, it gave way, and fell into the stream with a mighty splash. Burl went under, his eyes open, facing death. And as he sank, his wide-open eyes saw waved before him the gaping claws of the huge crayfish, large enough to severe a limb with a single stroke of its jagged jaws.

CHAPTER II

The Black-Bellied Spider

He opened his mouth to scream, a replica of the terrible screams of his grandfather, seized by a black-bellied tarantula years before, but no sound came forth. Only bubbles floated to the surface of the water. He beat the unresisting fluid with his hands—he did not know how to swim. The colossal creature approached leisurely, while Burl struggled helplessly.

His arms struck a solid object, and grasped it convulsively. A second later he had swung it between himself and the huge crustacean. He felt a shock as the mighty jaws closed upon the cork-like fungus, then felt himself drawn upward as the crayfish released his hold and the shelf-fungus floated to the surface. Having given way beneath him, it had been carried below him in his fall, only to rise within his reach just when most needed.

Burl's head popped above water and he saw a larger bit of the fungus floating near by. Less securely anchored to the rocks of the river-bank than the shelf to which Burl had trusted himself, it had been dislodged when the first shelf gave away. It was larger than the fragment to which Burl clung, and floated higher in the water.

Burl was cool with a terrible self possession. He seized it and struggled to draw himself on top of it. It tilted as his weight came upon it, and nearly overturned, but he paid no heed. With desperate haste, he clawed with hands and feet until he could draw himself clear of the water, of which he would forever retain a slight fear.

As he pulled himself upon the furry, orange-brown upper surface, a sharp blow struck his foot. The crayfish, disgusted at finding only what was to it a tasteless morsel in the shelf-fungus, had made a languid stroke at Burl's wriggling foot in the water. Failing to grasp the fleshy member, the crayfish retreated, disgruntled and annoyed.

And Burl floated down-stream, perched, weaponless and alone, frightened and in constant danger, upon a flimsy raft composed of a degenerate fungus, floating slowly down the stream of a river in whose waters death lurked unseen, upon whose banks was peril, and above whose reaches danger fluttered on golden wings.

It was a long time before he recovered his self-possession, and when he did he looked first for his spear. It was floating in the water, still transfixing the fish whose capture had endangered Burl's life. The fish now floated with its belly upward, all life gone.

So insistent was Burl's instinct for food that his predicament was

137

forgotten when he saw his prey just out of his reach. He gazed at it, and his mouth watered, while his cranky craft went down-stream, spinning slowly in the current. He lay flat on the floating fungoid, and strove to reach out and grasp the end of the spear.

The raft tilted and nearly flung him overboard again. A little later he discovered that it sank more readily on one side than on the other. That was due, of course, to the greater thickness—and consequently greater buoyancy—of the part which had grown next the rocks of the river-bank.

Burl found that if he lay with his head stretching above that side, it did not sink into the water. He wriggled into this new position, then, and waited until the slow revolution of his vessel brought the spear-shaft near him. He stretched his fingers and his arm, and touched, then grasped it.

A moment later he was tearing strips of flesh from the side of the fish and cramming the oily mess into his mouth with great enjoyment. He had lost his edible mushroom. That danced upon the waves several yards away, but Burl ate contentedly of what he possessed. He did not worry about what was before him. That lay in the future, but suddenly he realized that he was being carried farther and farther from Saya, the maiden of his tribe who caused strange bliss to steal over him when he contemplated her.

The thought came to him when he visualized the delight with which she would receive a gift of part of the fish he had caught. He was suddenly stricken with dumb sorrow. He lifted his head and looked longingly at the river banks.

A long, monotonous row of strangely colored fungus growths. No healthy green, but pallid, cream-colored toadstools, some bright orange, lavender, and purple molds, vivid carmine "rusts" and mildews, spreading up the banks from the turgid slime. The sun was not a ball of fire, but merely shown as a bright golden patch in the haze-filled sky, a patch whose limits could not be defined or marked.

In the faintly pinkish light that filtered down through the air a multitude of flying objects could be seen. Now and then a cricket or a grasshopper made its bullet-like flight from one spot to another. Huge butterflies fluttered gayly above the silent seemingly lifeless world. Bees lumbered anxiously about, seeking the cross-shaped flowers of the monster cabbages. Now and then a slender-waisted, yellow-stomached wasp flew alertly through the air.

Burl watched them with a strange indifference. The wasps were as long as himself. The bees, on end, could match his height. The butterflies ranged, from tiny creatures bearly capable of shading his face, to colossal things in the folds of whose wings he could have

138

been lost. And above him fluttered dragon-flies, whose long, spindle-like bodies were three times the length of his own.

Burl ignored them all. Sitting there, an incongruous creature of pink skin and soft brown hair upon an orange fungus floating in midstream, he was filled with despondency because the current carried him forever farther and farther from a certain slender-limbed maiden of his tiny tribe, whose glances caused an odd commotion in his breast.

The day went on. Once, Burl saw upon the blue-green mold that there spread upward from the river, a band of large, red Amazon ants, marching in orderly array, to raid the city of a colony of black ants, and carry away the eggs they would find there. The eggs would be hatched, and the small black creatures made the slaves of the brigands who had stolen them.

The Amazon ants can live only by the labor of their slaves, and for that reason are mighty warriors in their world. Later, etched against the steaming mist that overhung everything as far as the eye could reach, Burl saw strangely shaped, swollen branches rearing themselves from the ground. He knew what they were. A hard-rinded fungus that grew upon itself in peculiar mockery of the vegetation that had vanished from the earth.

And again he saw pear-shaped objects above some of which floated little clouds of smoke. They, too, were fungus growths, puffballs, which when touched emit what seems a puff of vapor. These would have towered above Burl's head, had he stood beside them.

And then, as the day drew to an end, he saw in the distance what seemed a range of purple hills. They were tall hills to Burl, some sixty or seventy feet high, and they seemed to be the agglomeration of a formless growth, multiplying its organisms and forms upon itself until the whole formed an irregular, cone-shaped mound. Burl watched them apathetically.

Presently, he ate again of the oily fish. The taste was pleasant to him, accustomed to feed mostly upon insipid mushrooms. He stuffed himself, though the size of his prey left by far the larger part still un-eaten.

He still held his spear firmly beside him. It had brought him into trouble, but Burl possessed a fund of obstinacy. Unlike most of his tribe, he associated the spear with the food it had secured, rather than with the difficulty into which it had led him. When he had eaten his fill he picked it up and examined it again. The sharpness of its point was unimpaired.

Burl handled it meditatively, debating whether or not to attempt to fish again. The shakiness of his little raft dissuaded him, and he abandoned the idea. Presently he stripped a sinew from the garment about his middle and hung the fish about his neck with it. That would leave him both hands free. Then he sat cross-legged upon the soggily floating fungus, like a pink-skinned Buddha, and watched the shores go by.

Time had passed, and it was drawing near sunset. Burl, never having seen the sun save as a bright spot in the overhanging haze, did not think of the coming of night as "sunset." To him it was the letting down of darkness from the sky.

To-day happened to be an exceptionally bright day, and the haze was not as thick as usual. Far to the west, the thick mist turned to gold, while the thicker clouds above became blurred masses of dull-red. Their shadows seemed like lavender from the contrast of shades. Upon the still surface of the river, all the myriad tints and shadings were reflected with an incredible faithfulness, and the shining tops of the giant mushrooms by the river brim glowed faintly pink.

Dragonflies buzzed over his head in their swift and angular flight, the metallic luster of their bodies glistening in the rosy light. Great yellow butterflies flew lightly above the stream. Here, there, and everywhere upon the water appeared the shell-formed boats of a thousand caddis flies, floating upon the surface while they might.

Burl could have thrust his hand down into their cavities and seized the white worms that inhabited the strange craft. The huge bulk of a tardy bee droned heavily overhead. Burl glanced upward and saw the long proboscis and the hairy hinder legs with their scanty load of pollen. He saw the great, multiple-lensed eyes with their expression of stupid preoccupation, and even the sting that would mean death alike for him and for the giant insect, should it be used.

The crimson radiance grew dim at the edge of the world. The purple hills had long been left behind. Now the slender stalks of ten thousand round-domed mushrooms lined the river-bank, and beneath them spread fungi of all colors, from the rawest red to palest blue, but all now fading slowly to a monochromatic background in the growing dusk.

The buzzing, fluttering, and the flapping of the insects of the day died slowly down, while from a million hiding-places there crept out into the deep night soft and furry bodies of great moths, who preened themselves and smoothed their feathery antennae before taking to the air. The strong-limbed crickets set up their thunderous noise—grown gravely bass with the increasing size of the organs by which the sound was made—and then there began to gather on the water those slender spirals of tenuous mist that would presently

140

blanket the stream in a mantle of thin fog.

Night fell. The clouds above seemed to lower and grow dark. Gradually, now a drop and then a drop, the languid fall of large, warm raindrops that would drip from the moisture-laden skies all through the night began. The edge of the stream became a place where great disks of coolly glowing flame appeared.

The mushrooms that bordered on the river were faintly phosphorescent *(Pleurotus phosphoreus)* and shone coldly upon the "rusts" and flake-fungi beneath their feet. Here and there a ball of lambent flame appeared, drifting idly above the steaming, festering earth.

Thirty thousand years before, men had called them "will-o'-the-wisps," but Burl simply stared at them, accepting them as he accepted all that passed. Only a man attempting to advance in the scale of civilization tries to explain everything that he sees. The savage and the child are most often content to observe without comment, unless the legends told by wise folk who are possessed by the itch of knowledge are repeated to them.

Burl watched for a long time. Great fireflies whose beacons lighted up their surroundings for many yards—fireflies Burl knew to be as long as his spear—great fireflies shed their intermittent glows upon the stream. Softly fluttering wings, in great beats that poured torrents of air upon him, passed above Burl

The air was full of winged creatures. The night was broken by their cries, by the sound of their invisible wings, by their cries of anguish and their mating calls. Above him and on all sides the persistent, intense life of the insect world went on ceaselessly, but Burl rocked back and forth upon his frail mushroom boat and wished to weep because he was being carried from his tribe, and from Saya—Saya of the swift feet and white teeth of the shy smile.

Burl may have been homesick, but his principal thoughts were of Saya. He had dared greatly to bring a gift of fresh meat to her, meat captured as meat had never been known to be taken by a member of the tribe. And now he was being carried from her!

He lay, disconsolate, upon his floating atom on the water for a great part of the night. It was long after midnight when the mushroom raft struck gently and remained grounded upon a shallow in the stream.

When the light came in the morning, Burl gazed about him keenly. He was some twenty yards from the shore, and the greenish scum surrounded his now disintegrating vessel. The river had widened out until the other bank was barely to be seen through the haze above the surface of the river, but the nearer shore seemed firm and no

141

more full of dangers than the territory his tribe inhabited. He felt the depth of the water with his spear, then was struck with the multiple usefulness of that weapon. The water would come but slightly above his ankles.

Shivering a little with fear, Burl stepped down into the water, then made for the bank at the top of his speed. He felt a soft something clinging to one of his bare feet. With an access of terror, he ran faster, and stumbled upon the shore in a panic. He stared down at his foot. A shapeless, flesh-colored pad clung to his heel, and as Burl watched, it began to swell slowly, while the pink of its wringled folds deepened.

It was no more than a leech, sharing in the enlargement nearly all the lower world had undergone, but Burl did not know that. He thrust at it with the side of his spear, then scraped frantically at it, and it fell off, leaving a blotch of blood upon the skin where it came away. It lay, writhing and pulsating upon the ground, and Burl fled from it.

He found himself in one of the toadstool forests with which he was familiar, and finally paused, disconsolatly. He knew the nature of the fungus growth about him, and presently fell to eating. In Burl the sight of food always produced hunger—a wise provision of nature to make up for the instinct to store food, which he lacked.

Burl's heart was small within him. He was far from his tribe, and far from Saya. In the parlance of this day, it is probable that no more than forty miles, separated them, but Burl did not think of distances. He had come down the river. He was in a land he had never known or seen. And he was alone.

All about him was food. All the mushrooms that surrounded him were edible, and formed a store of sustenance Burl's whole tribe could not have eaten in many days, but that very fact brought Saya to his mind more forcibly. He squatted on the ground, wolfing down the insipid mushroom in great gulps, when an idea suddenly came to him with all the force of inspiration.

He would bring Saya here, where there was food, food in great quantities, and she would be pleased. Burl had forgotten the large and oily fish that still hung down his back from the sinew about his neck, but now he rose, and its flapping against him reminded him again.

He took and fingered it all over, getting his hands and himself thoroughly greasey in the process, but he could eat no more. The thought of Saya's pleasure at the sight of that, too, reinforced his determination.

With all the immediacy of a child or a savage he set off at once.

142

He had come along the bank of the stream. He would retrace his steps along the bank of the stream.

Through the awkward aisles of the mushroom forest he made his way, eyes and ears open for possibilities of danger. Several times he heard the omnipresent clicking of ants on their multifarious businesses in the wood, but he could afford to ignore them. They were foragers rather than hunters. He only feared one kind of ant, the army-ant, which sometimes travels in hordes of millions, eating all that it comes upon. In ages past, when they were tiny creatures not an inch long, even the largest animals fled from them. Now that they measured a foot in length, not even the gorged spiders whose distended bellies were a yard in thickness, dared offer them battle.

The mushroom-forest came to an end. A cheerful grasshopper (*Ephigger*) munched delicately at some dainty it had found. Its hind legs were bunched beneath it in perpetual readiness for flight. A monster wasp appeared above—as long as Burl himself—poised an instant, dropped, and seized the luckless feaster.

There was a struggle, then the grasshopper became helpless, and the wasp's flexible abdomen curved delicately. Its sting entered the jointed armor of his prey, just beneath the head. The sting entered with all the deliberate precision of a surgeon's scalpel, and all struggle ceased.

The wasp grasped the paralyzed, not dead, insect and flew away. Burl grunted, and passed on. He had hidden when the wasp darted down from above.

The ground grew rough and Burl's progress became painful. He clambered arduously up steep slopes and made his way cautiously down their farther sides. Once he had to climb through a tangled mass of mushrooms so closely placed, and so small, that he had to break them apart with blows of his spear before he could pass, when they shed upon him torrents of a fiery-red liquid that rolled off his greasy breast and sank into the ground (*Lactarius deliciosus*).

A strange self-confidence now took possession of Burl. He walked less cautiously and more boldly. The mere fact that he had struck something and destroyed it provided him with a curious fictitious courage.

He had climbed slowly to the top of a red-clay cliff, perhaps a hundred feet high, slowly eaten away by the river when it overflowed. Burl could see the river. At some past flood-time it had lapped at the base of the cliff on whose edge he walked, though now it came no nearer than a quarter-mile.

The cliffside was almost covered with shelf-fungi, large and small, white, yellow, orange, and green in indescribable confusion and

143

luxuriance. From a point halfway up the cliff the inch-thick cable of a spider's web stretched down to an anchorage on the ground, and the strangely geometrical pattern of the web glistened evilly.

Somewhere among the fungi of the cliffside the huge creature waited until some unfortunate prey should struggle helplessly in its monster snare. The spider waited in a motionless, implacable patience, invincibly certain of prey, utterly merciless to its victims.

Burl strutted on the edge of the cliff, a silly little pink-skinned creature with an oily fish slung about his neck and a draggled fragment of a moth's wing about his middle. In his hand he bore the long spear of a minotaur beetle. He strutted, and looked scornfully down upon the whitely shining trap below him. He struck mushrooms, and they had fallen before him. He feared nothing. He strode fearlessly along. He would go to Saya and bring her to this land where food grew in abundance.

Sixty paces before him, a shaft sank vertically in the sandy, clayey soil. It was a carefully rounded shaft, and lined with silk. It went down for perhaps thirty feet or more, and there enlarged itself into a chamber where the owner and digger of the shaft might rest. The top of the hole was closed by a trap-door, stained with mud and earth to imitate with precision the surrounding soil. A keen eye would have been needed to perceive the opening. But a keen eye now peered out from a tiny crack, the eye of the engineer of the underground dwelling.

Eight hairy legs surrounded the body of the creature that hung motionless at the top of the silk-lined shaft. A huge misshapen globe formed its body, colored a dirty brown. Two pairs of ferocious mandibles stretched before its fierce mouth parts. Two eyes glittered evilly in the darkness of the burrow. And over the whole body spread a rough, mangy fur.

It was a thing of implacable malignance, of incredible ferocity. It was the brown hunting-spider, the American tarantula (*Mygale Hentzii*). Its body was two feet and more in diameter, and its legs, outstretched, would cover a circle three yards across. It watched Burl, its eyes glistening. Slaver welled up and dropped from its jaws.

And Burl strutted forward on the edge of the cliff, puffed up with a sense of his own importance. The white snare of the spinning spider below him impressed him as amusing. He knew the spider would not leave its web to attack him. He reached down and broke off a bit of fungus growing at his feet. Where he broke it, it was oozing a soupy liquid and was full of tiny maggots in a delirium of feasting. Burl flung it down into the web, and then laughed as the black bulk of the hidden spider swung down from its hiding-place to investigate.

The tarantula, peering from its burrow, quivered with impatience. Burl drew near, and nearer. He was using his spear as a lever, now, and prying off bits of fungus to fall down the cliffside into the colossal web. The spider, below, went leisurely from one place to another, investigating each new missile with its palpi, then leaving them as they appeared lifeless and undesirable prey. Burl laughed again as the particularly large lump of shelf-fungus narrowly missed the black-and-silver figure below. Then—

The trap-door fell into place with a faint click, and Burl whirled about. His laughter turned to a scream. Moving toward him with incredible rapidity, the monster tarantula opened its dripping jaws. Its mandibles gaped wide. The poison fangs were unsheathed. The creature was thirty paces away, twenty paces -ten. It leaped into the air, eyes glittering, all its eight legs extended to seize, fangs bared—

Burl screamed again, and thrust out his arms to ward off the impact of the leap. In his terror, his grasp upon his spear had become agonized. The spear-point shot out and the tarantula fell upon it. Nearly a quarter of the spear entered the body of the ferocious thing.

It stuck upon the spear, writhing horribly, still struggling to reach Burl, who was transfixed with horror. The mandibles clashed, strange sounds came from the beast. Then one of the attenuated hairy legs rasped across Burl's forearm. He gasped in ultimate fear and stepped backward—and the edge of the cliff gave way beneath him.

He hurtled downward, still clutching the spear which held the writhing creature from him. Down through space, his eyes glassy with panic, the two creatures—the man and the giant tarantula— fell together. There was a strangely elastic crash and crackling. They had fallen into the web beneath them.

Burl had reached the end of terror. He could be no more fear-struck. Struggling madly in the gummy coils of an immense web, which ever bound him more tightly, with a wounded creature shuddering in agony not a yard from him—yet a wounded creature that still strove to reach him with its poison fangs—Burl had reached the limit of panic.

He fought like a madman to break the coils about him. His arms and breast were greasy from the oily fish, and the sticky web did not adhere to them, but his legs and body were inextrcably fastened by the elastic threads spread for just such prey as he.

He paused a moment, in exhaustion. Then he saw, five yards away, the silvery and black monster waiting patiently for him to weary himself. It judged the moment propitious. The tarantula and

145

the man were one in its eyes, one struggling thing that had fallen opportunely into its snare. They were moving but feebly now. The spider advanced delicately, swinging its huge bulk nimbly along the web, paying out a cable after it as it came.

Burl's arms were free, because of the greasy coating they had received. He waved them wildly, shrieking at the pitiless monster that approached. The spider paused. Those moving arms suggested mandibles that might wound or slap.

Spiders take few hazards. This spider was no exception to the rule. It drew cautiously near, then stopped. Its spinnerets became busy, and with one of its eight legs, used like an arm, it flung a gummy silk impartially over both the tarantula and the man.

Burl fought against the descending shroud. He strove to thrust it away, but in vain. In a matter of minutes he was completely covered in a silken cloth that hid even the light from his eyes. He and his enemy, the giant tarantula, were beneath the same covering, though the tarantula moved but weakly.

The shower ceased. The web-spider had decided that they were helpless. Then Burl felt the cables of the web give slightly, as the spider approached to sting and suck the sweet juices from its prey.

CHAPTER III

The Army Ants

he web yielded gently as the added weight of the black-bellied spider approached. Burl froze into stillness under his enveloping covering. Beneath the same silken shroud the tarantula writhed in agony upon the point of Burl's spear. It clashed its jaws, shuddering upon the horny barb.

Burl was quiet in an ecstacy of terror. He waited for the poison-fangs to be thrust into him. He knew the process. He had seen the leisurely fashion in which the giant spiders delicately stung their prey, then withdrew to wait without impatience for the poison to do its work.

When their victim had ceased to struggle they drew near again, and sucked the sweet juices from the body, first from one point and then another, until what had so recently been a creature vibrant with life became a shrunken, withered husk—to be flung from the web at nightfall. Most spiders are tidy housekeepers, destroying their snares daily to spin anew.

The bloated, evil creature moved meditatively about the shining sheet of silk it had cast over the man and the giant tarantula when they fell from the cliff above. Now only the tarantula moved feebly. Its body was outlined by a bulge in the concealing shroud, throbbing faintly as it still struggled with the spear in its vitals. The irregularly rounded protuberance offered a point of attack for the web-spider. It moved quickly forward, and stung.

Galvanized into fresh torment by his new agony, the tarantula writhed in a very hell of pain. Its legs, clustered about the spear still fastened into its body, struck out purposelessly, in horrible gestures of delirious suffering. Burl screamed as one of them touched him and struggled himself.

His arms and head were free beneath the silken sheet because of the grease and oil that coated them. He clutched at the threads about him and strove to draw himself away from his deadly neighbor. The threads did not break, but they parted one from another, and a tiny opening appeared. One of the tarantula's attenuated limbs touched him again. With the strength of utter panic he hauled himself away, and the opening enlarged. Another struggle, and Burl's head emerged into the open air, and he stared down for twenty feet upon an open space almost carpeted with the chitinous remains of his present captor's former victims.

Burl's head was free, and his breast and arms. The fish slung over his shoulder had shed its oil upon him impartially. But the lower part of his body was held firm by the gummy snare of the web-spider, a snare far more tenacious than any birdlime ever manufactured by man.

He hung in his tiny window for a moment, despairing. Then he saw, at a little distance, the bulk of the monster spider, waiting patiently for its poison to take effect and the struggling of its prey to be stilled. The tarantula was no more than shuddering now. Soon it would be still, and the black-bellied creature waiting on the web would approach for its meal.

Burl withdrew his head and thrust desperately at the sticky stuff about his loins and legs. The oil upon his hands kept it from clinging to them, and it gave a little. In a flash of inspiration, Burl understood. He reached over his shoulder and grasped the greasy fish; tore it in a dozen places and smeared himself with the now rancid exudation, pushing the sticky threads from his limbs and oiling the surface from which he had thrust it away.

He felt the web tremble. To the spider, its poisen seemed to have failed of effect. Another sting seemed to be necessary. This time it would not insert its fangs into the quiescent tarantula, but would sting where the disturbance was manifest—would send its deadly venom into Burl.

He gasped, and drew himself toward his window. It was as if he would have pulled his legs from his body. His head emerged, his shoulders, half his body was out of the hole.

· The colossal spider surveyed him, and made ready to cast more of its silken sheet upon him. The spinnerets became active and the sticky stuff about Burl's feet gave way! He shot out of the opening and fell sprawling, awkwardly and heavily, upon the earth below, crashing upon the shrunken shell of a flying beetle which had fallen into the snare and had not escaped as he had.

Burl rolled over and over, and then sat up. An angry foot-long ant stood before him, its mandibles extended threateningly, while its antennae waved wildly in the air. A shrill stridulation filled the air.

In ages past, when ants were tiny creatures of lengths to be measured in fractions of an inch, learned scientists debated gravely if their tribe possessed a cry. They believed that certain grooves upon the body of the insects, after the fashion of those upon the great legs of the cricket, might offer the means of uttering an infinitly high-pitched sound too shrill for man's ears to catch.

Burl knew that the stridulation was caused by the doubtful insect before him, though he had never wondered how it was produced.

148

The cry was used to summon others of its city, to help it in its difficulty or good fortune.

Clickings sounded fifty or sixty feet away. Comrades were coming to aid the pioneer. Harmless save when interfered with—all save the army ant, that is—the whole ant tribe was formidable when aroused. Utterly fearless, they could pull down a man and slay him as so many infuriated fox terriers might have done thirty thousand years before.

Burl fled, without debate, and nearly collided with one of the anchoring cables of the web from which he had barely escaped a moment before. He heard the shrill sound behind him suddenly subside. The ant, short-sighted as all ants were, no longer felt itself threatened and went peacefully about the business Burl had interrupted, that of finding among the gruesome relics beneath the spider's web some edible carrion which might feed the inhabitants of its city.

Burl sped on for a few hundred yards, and stopped. It behooved him to move carefully. He was in strange territory, and as even the most familiar territory was full of sudden and implacable dangers, unknown lands were doubly or trebly perilous.

Burl, too, found difficulty in moving. The glutinous stuff from the spider's shroud of silk still stuck to his feet and picked up small objects as he went along. Old ant-gnawed fragments of insect armour pricked him even through his toughened soles.

He looked about cautiously and removed them, took a dozen steps and had to stop again. Burl's brain had been uncommonly stimulated of late. It had gotten him into at least one predicament—due to his invention of a spear—but had no less readily led to his escape from another. But for the reasoning that had led him to use the grease from the fish upon his shoulder in oiling his body when he struggled out of the spider's snare, he would now be furnishing a meal for that monster.

Cautiously, Burl looked all about him. He seemed to be safe. Then, quite deliberately, he sat down to think. It was the first time in his life that he had done such a thing. The people of his tribe were not given to meditation. But an idea had struck Burl with all the force of inspiration—an abstract idea.

When he was in difficulties, something within him seemed to suggest a way out. Would it suggest an inspiration now? He puzzled over the problem. Childlike—and savage-like—the instant the thought came to him he proceeded to test it out. He fixed his gaze upon his foot. The sharp edges of pebbles, of the remains of insect-armour, of a dozen things, hurt his feet when he walked. They had done so

149

even since he had been born, but never before had his feet been sticky so that the irritation continued for more than a single step.

Now he gazed upon his foot, and waited for the thought within him to develop. Meanwhile he slowly removed the sharp-pointed fragments, one by one. Partly coated as they were with the half-liquid gum from his feet, they clung to his fingers as they had to his feet, except upon those portions where the oil was thick as before.

Burl's reasoning, before, was simple and of the primary order. Where oil covered him, the web did not. Therefore he would coat the rest of himself with oil. Had he been placed in the same predicament again, he would have used the same means of escape. But to apply a bit of knowledge gained in one predicament to another difficulty was something he had not yet done.

A dog may be taught that by pulling on the latch-string of a door he may open it, but the same dog coming to a high and close-barred gate with a latch-string attached will never think of pulling on this second latch-string. He associates a latch-string with the opening of the door. The opening of a gate is another matter entirely.

Burl had been stirred to one invention by imminent peril. That is not extraordinary. But to reason in cold blood, as he presently did, that oil on his feet would nullify the glue upon his feet and enable him again to walk in comfort—that was a triumph. The inventions of savages are essentially matters of life and death, of food and safety. Comfort and luxury are only produced by intelligence of a high order.

Burl, in safety, had added to his comfort. That was truly a more important thing in his development than almost any other thing he could have done. He oiled his feet.

It was an almost infinitesimal problem, but Burl's struggles with the mental process of reasoning were actual. Thirty thousand years before him, a wise man had pointed out that education is simply training in thought, in efficient and effective thinking. Burl's tribe had been too much preoccupied with food and mere existence to think, and now Burl, sitting at the base of a squat toadstool that all but concealed him, reexemplified Rodin's "Thinker" for the first time in many generations.

For Burl to reason, that oil upon the soles of his feet would guard him against sharp stones was as much a triumph of intellect as any masterpiece of art in the ages before him. Burl was learning how to think.

He stood up, walked, and crowed in sheer delight, then paused a moment in awe of his own intelligence. Thirty-five miles from his tribe, naked, unarmed, utterly ignorant of fire, of wood, of any

150

weapons save a spear he had experimented with the day before, abysmally uninformed concerning the very existence of any art or science, Burl stopped to assure himself that he was very wonderful.

Pride came to him. He wished to display himself to Saya, these things upon his feet, and his spear. But his spear was gone.

With touching faith in the efficacy of this new pastime, Burl sat promptly down again and knitted his brows. Just as a superstitious person, once convinced that by appeal to a favorite talisman he will be guided aright, will inevitably apply to that talisman on all occasions, so Burl plumped himself down to think.

These questions were easily answered. Burl was naked. He would search out garments for himself. He was weaponless. He would find himself a spear. He was hungry—and would seek food, and he was far from his tribe, so he would go to them. Puerile reasoning, of course, but valuable because it was consciously reasoning, consciously appealing to his mind for guidance in difficulty, deliberate progress from a mental desire to a mental resolution.

Even in the high civilization of ages before, few men had really used their brains. The great majority of people had depended upon machines and their leaders to think for them. Burl's tribe-folk depended on their stomachs. Burl, however, was gradually developing the habit of thinking which makes for leadership and which would be invaluable to his little tribe.

He stood up again and faced up-stream, moving slowly and cautiously, his eyes searching the ground before him keenly and his ears alert for the slightest sound of danger. Gigantic butterflies riotous in coloring, fluttered overhead through the misty haze. Sometimes a grasshopper hurtled through the air like a projectile, its transparent wings beating the air frantically. Now and then a wasp sped by, intent upon its hunting, or a bee droned heavily along, anxious and worried, striving in a nearly flowerless world to gather the pollen that would feed the hive. Here and there Burl saw flies of various sorts, some no larger than his thumb, but others the size of his whole hand. They fed upon the juices that dripped from the maggot-infested mushrooms, when filth more to their liking was not at hand.

Very far away a shrill roaring sounded faintly. It was like a multitude of clickings blended into a single sound, but was so far away that it did not impress itself upon Burl's attention. He had all the strictly localized vision of a child. What was near was important, and what was distant could be ignored. Only the imminent required attention, and Burl was preoccupied.

Had he listened, he would have realized that army ants were

abroad in countless millions, spreading themselves out in a broad array and eating all they came upon far more destructively than so many locusts.

Locusts in past ages had eaten all green things. There were only giant cabbages and a few such tenacious rank growths in the world that Burl knew. The locusts had vanished with civilization and knowledge and the greater part of mankind, but the army ants remained as an invincible enemy to men and insects, and the most of the fungus growths that covered the earth.

Burl did not notice the sound, however. He moved forward, briskly though cautiously, searching with his eyes for garments, food, and weapons. He confidently expected to find all of them within a short distance.

Surely enough, he found a thicket—if one might call it so—of edible fungi no more than half a mile beyond the spot where he had improvised his sandals to protect the soles of his feet.

Without especial elation, Burl tugged at the largest until he had broken off a food supply for several days. He went on, eating as he did so, past a broad plain a mile and more across, being broken into odd little hillocks by gradually ripening and suddenly developing mushrooms with which he was unfamiliar.

The earth seemed to be in process of being pushed aside by rounded protuberances of which only the tips showed. Blood-red hemispheres seemed to be forcing aside the earth so they might reach the outer air.

Burl looked at them curiously, and passed among them without touching them. They were strange, and to Burl most strange things meant danger. In any event, Burl was full of a new purpose now. He wished garments and weapons.

Above the plain a wasp hovered, a heavy object dangling beneath its black belly, ornamented by a single red band. It was a wasp—the hairy sand-wasp—and it was bringing a paralyzed gray caterpiller to its burrow.

Burl watched it drop down with the speed and sureness of an arrow, pull aside a heavy, flat stone, and descend into the ground. It had a vertical shaft dug down for forty feet or more.

It descended, evidently inspected the interior, reappeared, and vanished into the hole again, dragging the gray worm after it. Burl, marching on over the broad plain that seemed stricken with some erupting disease from the number of red pimples making their appearance, did not know what passed below, but observed the wasp emerge again and busily scratch dirt and stones into the shaft until it was full.

The wasp had paralyzed a caterpillar, taken it to the already prepared burrow, laid an egg upon it, and filled up the entrance. In course of time the egg would hatch into a grub barely as long as Burl's forefinger, which would then feed upon the torpid caterpillar until it had waxed large and fat. Then it would weave itself a chrysalis and sleep a long sleep, only to wake as a wasp and dig its way to the open air.

Burl reached the farther side of the plain and found himself threading the aisles of one of the fungus forests in which the growths were hideous, misshapen travesties upon the trees they had supplanted. Bloated, yellow limbs branched off from rounded, swollen trunks. Here and there a pear-shaped puff-ball, Burl's height and half as much again, waited craftily until a chance touch should cause it to shoot upward a curling puff of infinitely fine dust.

Burl went cautiously. There were dangers here, but he moved forward steadily, none the less. A great mass of edible mushroom was slung under one of his arms, and from time to time he broke off a fragment and ate of it, while his large eyes searched this way and that for threats of harm.

Behind him, a high, shrill roaring had grown slightly in volume and nearness, but was still too far away to impress Burl. The army ants were working havoc in the distance. By thousands and millions, myriads upon myriads, they were foraging the country, clambering upon every eminence, descending into every depression, their antennae waving restlessly and their mandibles forever threateningly extended. The ground was black with them, and each was ten inches and more in length.

A single such creature would be formidable to an unarmed and naked man like Burl, whose wisest move would be flight, but in their thousands and millions, they presented a menace from which no escape seemed possible. They were advancing steadily and rapidly, shrill stridulations and a multitude of clickings marking their movements.

The great, helpless caterpillars upon the giant cabbages heard the sound of their coming, but were too stupid to flee. The black multitudes covered the rank vegetables and tiny but voracious jaws began to tear at the flacid masses of flesh.

Each creature had some futile means of struggling. The caterpillars strove to throw off their innumerable assailants by writhings and contortions, wholly ineffective. The bees fought their entrance to the gigantic hives with stings and wingbeats. The moths took to the air in helpless blindness when discovered by the relentless throngs of small black insects which reeked of formic acid and left the ground

153

behind them denuded of every living thing.

Before the oncoming horde was a world of teeming life, where mushrooms and fungi fought with thinning numbers of giant cabbages for foothold. Behind the black multitude was—nothing. Mushrooms, cabbages, bees, wasps, cricket, every creeping and crawling thing that did not get aloft before the black tide reached it was lost, torn to bits by tiny mandibles. Even the hunting spiders and tarantulas fell before the hosts of insects, having killed many in their final struggles, but overwhelmed by sheer numbers. And the wounded and dying army ants made food for their sound comrades.

There is no mercy among insects. Only the web-spiders sat unmoved and immovable in their colossal snares, secure in the knowledge that their gummy webs would discourage attempts at invasion along the slender supporting cables.

Surging onward, flowing like a monstrous, murky tide over the yellow, steaming earth, the army ants advanced. Their vanguard reached the river, and recoiled. Burl was perhaps five miles distant when they changed their course, communicating the altered line of march to those behind them in some mysterious fashion of transmitting intelligence.

Thirty thousand years before, scientists had debated gravely over the means of communication among ants. They had observed that a single ant finding a bit of booty too large for him to handle alone would return to the ant-city and return with others. From that one instance they deduced a language of gesture made with the antennae.

Burl had no wise theories. He merely knew facts, but he knew that the ants had some form of speech or transmission of ideas. Now, however, he was moving cautiously along toward the stamping-grounds of his tribe, in complete ignorance of the black blanket of living creatures creeping over the ground toward him.

A million tragedies marked the progress of the insect army. There was a tiny colony of mining bees—Zebra bees—a single mother, some four feet long, had dug a huge gallery with some ten cells, in which she laid her eggs and fed her grubs with hard-gathered pollen. The grubs had waxed fat and large, became bees and laid eggs in their turn, within the gallery their mother had dug out for them.

Ten such bulky insects now foraged busily for grubs within the ancestral home, while the founder of the colony had grown draggled and wingless with the passing of time. Unable to forage, herself, the old bee became the guardian of the nest or hive, as is the custom among the mining bees. She closed the opening of the hive with her head, making a living barrier within the entrance, and withdrawing

154

to give entrance and exit only to duly authenticated members of the colony.

The ancient and draggled concierge of the underground dwelling was at her post when the wave of army ants swept over her. Tiny, evil-smelling feet trampled upon her. She emerged to fight with mandible and sting for the sanctity of the hive. In a moment she was a shaggy mass of biting ants, rending and tearing at her chitinous armour. The old bee fought madly, viciously, sounding a buzzing alarm to the colonists yet within the hive. They emerged, fighting as they came, for the gallery leading down was a dark flood of small insects.

For a few moments a battle such as would make an epic was in process. Ten huge bees, each four to five feet long, fighting with legs and jaw, wing and mandible, with all the ferocity of as many tigers. The tiny, vicious ants covered them, snapping at their multiple eyes, biting at the tender joints in their armour—sometimes releasing the larger prey to leap upon an injured comrade wounded by the huge creature they battled in common.

The fight, however, could have but one ending. Struggle as the bees might, herculean as their efforts might be, they were powerless against the incredible numbers of their assailants, who tore them into tiny fragments and devoured them. Before the last shred of the hive's defenders had vanished, the hive itself was gutted alike of the grubs it had contained and the food brought to the grubs by such weary effort of the mature bees.

The army ants went on. Only an empty gallery remained, that and a few fragments of tough armour, unappetizing even to the omnivorous ants.

Burl was meditatively inspecting the scene of a recent tragedy, where rent and scraped fragments of a great beetle's shiny casing lay upon the ground. A greater beetle had come upon the first and slain him. Burl was looking upon the remains of the meal.

Three or four minims, little ants barely six inches long, foraged industriously among the bits. A new ant-city was to be formed, and the queen-ant lay hidden a half-mile away. These were the first hatchlings, who would feed the larger ants on whom would fall the great work of the ant-city. Burl ignored them, searching with his eyes for a spear or weapon of some sort.

Behind him the clicking roar, the high-pitched stridulations of the horde of army ants, rose in volume. Burl turned disgustedly away. The best he could find in the way of a weapon was a fiercely toothed hind-leg. He picked it up, and an angry whine rose from the ground.

One of the black minims was working busily to detach a fragment of flesh from the joint of the leg, and Burl had snatched the morsel from him. The little creature was hardly half a foot in length, but it advanced upon Burl, shrilling angrily. He struck it with the leg and crushed it. Two of the other minims appeared, attracted by the noise the first had made. Discovering the crushed body of their fellow, they unceremoniously dismembered it and bore it away in triumph.

Burl went on, swinging the toothed limb in his hand. It made a fair club, and Burl was accustomed to use stones to crush the juicy legs of such giant crickets as his tribe sometimes came upon. He formed a half-defined idea of a club. The sharp teeth of the thing in his hand made him realize that a sidewise blow was better than a spear-like thrust.

The sound behind him had become a distant whispering, high-pitched, and growing nearer. The army ants swept over a mushroom forest, and the yellow, umbrella-like growths swarmed with black creatures devouring the substance on which they found a foot-hold.

A great blue-bottle fly, shining with a metalic luster, reposed in an ecstacy of feasting, sipping through its long proboscis the dark-colored liquid that dripped slowly from a mushroom. Maggots filled the mushroom, and exuded a solvent pepsin that liquefied the white firm "meat."

They fed upon this soup, this gruel, and a surplus dripped to the ground below, where the blue-bottle drank eagerly. Burl drew near, and struck. The fly collapsed into a writhing heap. Burl stood over it for an instant, pondering.

The army ants came nearer, down into a tiny valley, swarming into and through a little brook over which Burl had leaped. Ants can remain under water for a long time without drowning, so the small stream was but a minor obstacle, though the current of the water swept many of them off their feet until they choked the brook-bed and their comrades passed over their struggling bodies dry-shod. They were no more than temporarily annoyed however, and crawled out to resume their march.

About a quarter of a mile to the left of Burl's line of march, and perhaps a mile behind the spot where he stood over the dead blue-bottle fly, there was a stretch of an acre or more where the giant, rank cabbages had so far resisted the encroachments of the ever-present mushrooms. The pale, cross-shaped flowers of the cabbages formed food for many bees, and the leaves fed numberless grubs and worms, and loud-voiced crickets which crouched about on the ground, munching busily at the succulent green stuff. The army ants swept into the green area, ceaselessly devouring all they came upon.

A terrific din arose. The crickets hurtled away in rocket-like flight, in a dark cloud of wildly-beating wings. They shot aimlessly in any direction, with the result that half, or more than half, fell in the midst of the black tide of devouring insects and were seized as they fell. They uttered terrible cries as they were being torn to bits. Horrible inhuman screams reach the Burl's ears.

A single such cry of agony would not have attracted Burl's attention—he lived in the very atmosphere of tragedy—but the chorus of creatures in torment made him look up. This was no minor horror. Wholesale slaughter was going on. He peered anxiously in the direction of the sound.

A stretch of sickly yellow fungus was here and there interspersed with a squat toadstool or a splash of vivid color where one of the many "rusts" had found a foothold. To the left a group of awkward, misshapen fungoids clustered in silent mockery of a forest of trees. There was a mass of faded green, where the giant cabbages stood.

With the true sun never shining upon them save through a blanket of thick haze or heavy clouds, they were pallid things, but they were the only green things Burl had seen. Their nodding white flowers with four petals in the form of a cross glowed against the yellowish-green leaves. But as Burl gazed toward them, the green became slowly black.

From where he stood, Burl could see two or three great grubs in lazy contentment, eating ceaselessly of the cabbages on which they rested. Suddenly first one and then the other began to jerk spasmodically. Burl saw that about each of them a tiny rim of black had clustered. Tiny black motes milled over the green surfaces of the cabbages. The grubs became black, the cabbages became black. Horrible contortions of the writhing grubs told of the agonies they were enduring. Then a black wave appeared at the further edge of the stretch of sickly yellow fungus, a glistening, living wave, that moved forward rapidly with the roar of clickings and a persistent overtone of shrill stridulations.

The hair rose upon Burl's head. He knew what this was! He knew all too well the meaning of that tide of shining bodies. With a gasp of terror, all his intellectual preoccupations forgotten, he turned and fled in ultimate panic. And the tide came slowly on after him.

CHAPTER IV

The Red Death

e flung away the great mass of edible mushroom, but clung to his sharp-toothed club desperately, and darted through the tangled aisles of the little mushroom forest with a heedless disregard of the dangers that might await him there. Flies buzzed about him loudly, huge creatures, glittering with a metallic luster. Once he was struck upon the shoulder by the body of one of them, and his skin was torn by the swiftly vibrating wings of the insect, as long as Burl's hand.

Burl thrust it away and sped on. The oil with which he was partly covered had turned rancid, now, and the odor attracted them, connoisseurs of the fetid. They buzzed over his head, keeping pace even with his head-long flight.

A heavy weight settled upon his head, and in a moment was doubled. Two of the creatures had dropped upon his oily hair, to sip the rancid oil through their disgusting proboscides. Burl shook them off with his hand and ran madly on. His ears were keenly attuned to the sound of the army ants behind him, and it grew but little farther away.

The clicking roar continued, but began to be overshadowed by the buzzing of the flies. In Burl's time the flies had not great heaps of putrid matter in which to lay their eggs. The ants—busy scavengers—carted away the debris of the multitudinous tragedies of the insect world long before it could acquire the gamey flavor beloved by the fly maggots. Only in isolated spots were the flies really numerous, but there they clustered in clouds that darkened the sky.

Such a buzzing, whirling cloud surrounded the madly-running figure of Burl. It seemed as though a miniature whirlwind kept pace with the little pink-skinned man, a whirlwind composed of winged bodies and multi-faceted eyes. He twirled his club before him, and almost every stroke was interrupted by an impact against a thinly-armoured body which collapsed with a spurting of reddish liquid.

An agonizing pain as of a red-hot iron struck upon Burl's back. One of the stinging flies had thrust its sharp-tipped proboscis into Burl's flesh to suck the blood.

Burl uttered a cry and—ran full tilt into the thick stalk of a blackened and draggled toadstool. There was a curious crackling as of wet punk or brittle, rotten wood. The toadstool collapsed upon itself with a strange splashing sound. Many flies had laid their eggs in the fungoid, and it was a teeming mass of corruption and ill-smelling liquid.

With the crash of the toadstool's "head" upon the ground, it fell into a dozen pieces, and the earth for yards around was spattered with a stinking liquid in which tiny, headless maggots twitched convulsively.

The buzzing of the flies took on a note of satisfaction, and they settled by hundreds about the edges of the ill-smelling pools, becoming lost in the ecstacy of feasting while Burl staggered to his feet and darted off again. This time he was but a minor attraction to the flies, and but one or two came near him. From every direction they were hurrying to the toadstool feast, to the banquet of horrible liquefied fungus that lay spread upon the ground.

Burl ran on. He passed beneath the wide-spreading leaves of a giant cabbage. A great grasshopper crouched upon the ground, its tremendous jaws crunching the rank vegetation voraciously. Half a dozen great worms ate steadily from their restingplaces among the leaves. One of them slung itself beneath an over-hanging leaf—which would have thatched a dozen homes for as many men—and was placidly anchoring itself in preparation for the spinning of a cocoon in which to sleep the sleep of metamorphosis.

A mile away, the great black tide of army ants was advancing relentlessly. The great cabbage, the huge grasshopper, and all the stupid caterpillars upon the wide leaves would soon be covered with the tiny, biting insects. The cabbage would be reduced to a chewed and destroyed stump, the colossal, furry grubs would be torn into a myriad mouthfuls and devoured by the black army ants, and the grasshopper would strike out with terrific, unguided strength, crushing its assailants by blows of its powerful hind-legs and bites of its great jaws. But it would die, making terrible sounds of torment as the vicious mandibles of the army ants found crevaces in its armour.

The clicking roar of the ants' advance overshadowed all other sound now. Burl was running madly, his breath coming in great gasps, his eyes wide with panic. Alone of all the world about him, he knew the danger behind. The insects he passed were going about their business with that terrifying efficiency found only in the insect world.

There is something strangely daunting in the actions of an insect. It moves so directly, with such uncanny precision, with such utter indifference to anything but the end in view. Cannabalism is a rule, almost without exception. The paralysis of prey, so it may remain alive and fresh—though in agony—for weeks on end, is a common practice. The eating piecemale of still-living victims is a matter of course.

Absolute mercilessness, utter callousness, incredible inhumanity beyond anything known in the animal world is the natural and commonplace practice of the insects. And these vast cruelties are performed by armoured, machine-like creatures with an abstraction and a routine air that suggests a horrible Nature behind them all.

Burl nearly stumbled upon a tragedy. He passed within a dozen yards of a space where a female dung-beetle was devouring the mate whose honeymoon had begun that same day and ended in that grewsome fashion. Hidden behind a clump of mushrooms, a great yellow-banded spider was coyly threatening a smaller male of her own species. He was discretely ardent, but if he won the favor of the grewsome creature he was wooing, he would furnish an appetizing meal for her some time within twenty-four hours.

Burl's heart was pounding madly. The breath whistled in his nostrils—and behind him, the wave of army ants was drawing nearer. They came upon the feasting flies. Some took to the air and escaped but others were too engrossed in their delicious meal. The twitching little maggots, stranded upon the earth by the scattering of their soupy broth, were torn in pieces. The flies who were seized vanished into little maws. The serried ranks of black insects went on.

The tiny clickings of their limbs, the perpetual challenges and cross-challenges of crossed antennae, the stridulations of the creatures, all combined to make a high-pitched but deafening din. Now and then another sound pierced the noises made by the ants themselves. A cricket, seized by a thousand tiny jaws, uttered cries of agony. The shrill note of the crickets had grown deeply bass with the increase in size of the organs that uttered it.

There was a strange contrast between the ground before the advancing horde and that immediately behind it. Before, a busy world, teeming with life. Butterflies floating overhead on lazy wings, grubs waxing fat and huge upon the giant cabbages, crickets eating, great spiders sitting quietly in their lairs waiting with invincible patience for prey to draw near their trap-doors or fall into their webs, colossal beetles lumbering heavily through the mushroom forests, seeking food, making love in the monstrous, tragic fashion.

And behind the wide belt of army ants—chaos. The edible mushrooms gone. The giant cabbages left as mere stumps of unappetizing pulp, the busy life of the insect world completely wiped out save for the flying creatures that fluttered helplessly over an utterly changed landscape. Here and there little bands of stragglers moved busily over the denuded earth, searching for some fragment of food that might conceivably have been overlooked by the main body.

Burl was putting forth his last ounce of strength. His limbs trembled, his breathing was agony, sweat stood out upon his forehead. He ran, a little, naked man with the disjointed fragment of a huge insect's limb in his hand, running for his insignificant life, running as if his continued existence among the million tragedies of that single day was the purpose for which the universe had been created.

He sped across an open space a hundred yards across. A thicket of beautifully golden mushrooms (*Agaricus coelareus*) barred his way. Beyond the mushrooms a range of strangely colored hills began, purple and green and black and gold, melting into each other, branching off from each other, inextricably tangled.

They rose to a height of perhaps sixty or seventy feet, and above them a little grayish haze had gathered. There seemed to be a layer of tenuous vapor upon their surfaces, which slowly rose and coiled, and gathered into a tiny cloudlet above their tips.

The hills, themselves, were but masses of fungus, mushrooms and rusts, fungoids of every description, yeasts, "musts," and every form of fungus growth which had grown within itself and about itself until this great mass of strangely colored, spongy stuff had gathered in a mass that undulated unevenly across the level earth for miles.

Burl burst through the golden thicket and attacked the ascent. His feet sank into the spongy sides of the hillock. Panting, gasping, staggering from exhaustion, he made his way up the top. He plunged into a little valley on the fartherer side, up another slope. For perhaps 10 minutes he forced himself on, then collapsed. He lay, unable to move further, in a little hollow, his sharp-toothed club still clasped in his hands. Above him, a bright yellow butterfly with a thirty-foot spread of wings fluttered lightly.

He lay motionless, breathing in great gasps, his limbs refusing to lift him.

The sound of the army ants continued to grow near. At last, above the crest of the last hillock he had surmounted, two tiny antennae appeared, then the black, glistening head of an army ant, the forerunner of its horde. It moved deliberately forward, waving its antennae ceaselessly. It made its way toward Burl, tiny clickings coming from the movements of its limbs.

A little wisp of tenuous vapor swirled toward the ant, a wisp of the same vapor that had gathered above the whole range of hills as a thin, low cloud. It enveloped the insect—and the ant seemed to be

161

attacked by a strange convulsion. Its legs moved aimlessly. It threw itself desperately about. If it had been an animal, Burl would have watched with wondering eyes while it coughed and gasped, but it was an insect breathing through air-holes in its abdomen. It writhed upon the spongy fungus growth across which it had been moving.

Burl, lying in an exhausted, panting heap upon the purple mass of fungus, was conscious of a strange sensation. His body felt strangely warm. He knew nothing of fire or the heat of the sun, and the only sensation of warmth he had ever known was that caused when the members of his tribe had huddled together in their hiding place when the damp chill of the night had touched their soft-skinned bodies. Then the heat of their breath and their bodies had kept out the chill.

This heat that Burl now felt was a hotter, fiercer heat. He moved his body with a tremendous effort, and for a moment the fungus was cool and soft beneath him. Then, slowly the sensation of heat began again, increased until Burl's skin was red and inflamed from the irritation.

The thin and tenuous vapor, too, made Burl's lungs smart and his eyes water. He was breathing in great, chokey gasps, but the period of rest—short as it was—had enabled him to rise and stagger on. He crawled painfully to the top of the slope, and looked back.

The hill-crest on which he stood was higher than any of those he had passed in his painful run, and he could see clearly the whole of the purple range. Where he was, he stood near the farther edge of the range, which was here perhaps half a mile wide.

It was a ceaseless, undulating mass of hills and hollows, ridges and spurs, all of them colored, purple and brown and golden-yellow, deepest black and dingy white. And from the tips of most of the pointed hills little wisps of vapor rose up.

A thin, dark cloud had gathered overhead. Burl could look to the right and left to see the hills fading into the distance, growing fainter as the haze above them seemed to grow thicker. He saw, too, the advancing cohorts of the army ants, creeping over the tangled mass of fungus growth. They seemed to be feeding as they went, upon the fungus that had gathered into these incredible monstrosities.

The hills were living. They were not upheavals of the ground, they were festering heaps of insanely growing, festering mushrooms and fungus. Upon most of them a purple mould had spread itself so that they seemed a range of purple hills, but here and there patches of other vivid colors showed, and there was a large hill whose whole side was a brilliant golden hue. Another had tiny bright-red spots of a strange and malignant mushroom whose properties Burl did not know, scattered all over the purple with which it was covered.

Burl leaned heavily upon his club and watched dully. He could run no more. The army ants were spreading everywhere over the mass of fungus. They would reach him soon.

Far to the right the vapor thickened. A column of smoke arose. What Burl did not know and would never know was that far down in the interior of that compressed mass of fungus, slow oxidation had been going on. The temperature of the interior had been raised. In the darkness and the dampness deep down in the hills, spontaneous combustion had begun.

Just as the vast piles of coal the railroad companies of thirty thousand years before had gathered together sometimes began to burn fiercely in their interiors, and just as the farmer's piles of damp straw or hay suddenly burst into fierce flames from no cause, so these huge piles of tinder-like mushrooms had been burning slowly within themselves.

There had been no flames, because the surface remained intact and nearly air-tight. But when the army ants began to tear at the edible surfaces despite the heat they encountered, fresh air found its way to the smoldering masses of fungus. The slow combustion became rapid combustion. The dull heat became fierce flames. The slow trickle of thin smoke became a huge column of thick, choking, acrid stuff that set the army ants that breathed it into spasms of convulsive writhing.

From a dozen points the flames burst out. A dozen or more columns of blinding smoke rose to the heavens. A pall of fume-laden smoke gathered above the range of purple hills, while Burl watched apathetically. And the serried ranks of armyants marched on to the widening furnaces that awaited them.

They had recoiled from the river, because their instinct had warned them. Thirty thousand years without danger from fire, however, had let their racial fear of fire die out. They marched into the blazing orifices they had opened in the hills, snapping with their mandibles at the leaping flames, springing at the glowing tinder.

The blazing areas widened, as the purple surface was undermined and fell in. Burl watched the the phenomenon without comprehension and even without thankfulness. He stood, panting more and more slowly, breathing more and more easily, until the glow from the approaching flames reddened his skin and the acrid smoke made tears flow from his eyes.

Then he retreated slowly, leaning on his club and looking back. The black wave of the army ants was sweeping into the fire, sweeping into the incredible heat of that carbonized material burning with an open flame. At last there were only the little bodies of stragglers from the great ant army, scurrying here and there over the ground their comrades had denuded of all living things. The bodies of the main army had vanished—burnt to crisp ashes in the furnace of the hills.

There had been agony in that flame, dreadful agony such as no man would like to dwell upon. The insane courage of the ants, attacking with their horny jaws the burning masses of fungus, rolling over and over with a flaming missile clutched in their mandibles, sounding their shrill war-cry while cries of agony came from them—blinded, their antennae burnt off, their lidless eyes scorched by the licking flames, yet going madly forward on flaming feet to attack, ever attack this unknown and unknowable enemy.

Burl made his way slowly over the hills. Twice he saw small bodies of the army ants. They had passed between the widening surfaces their comrades had opened, and they were feeding voraciously upon the hills they trod on. Once Burl was spied, and a shrill war-cry was sounded, but he moved on, and the ants were busily eating. A single ant rushed toward him. Burl brought down his club and a writhing body remained, to be eaten later by its comrades when they came upon it.

Again night fell. The sky grew red in the west, though the sun did not shine through the ever-present cloud bank. Darkness spread across the sky. Utter blackness fell over the whole mad world, save where the luminous mushrooms shed their pale light upon the ground and fireflies the length of Burl's arm shed their fitful gleams upon an earth of fungus growths and monstrous insects.

Burl made his way across the range of mushroom hills, picking his path with his large blue eyes whose pupils expanded to great size. Slowly, from the sky, now a drop and then a drop, now a drop and then a drop, the nightly rain that would continue until daybreak began.

Burl found the ground hard beneath his feet. He listened keenly for sounds of danger. Something rustled heavily in a thicket of mushrooms a hundred yards away. There were sounds of preening, and of delicate feet placed lightly here and there upon the ground. Then the throbbing beat of huge wings began suddenly, and a body took to the air.

A fierce, down-coming current of air smote Burl, and he looked upward in time to catch the outline of a huge body—a moth—as it passed above him. He turned to watch the line of its flight, and saw a strange glow in the sky behind him. The mushroom hills were still burning.

He crouched beneath a squat toadstool and waited for the dawn, his club held tightly in his hands, and his ears alert for any sound of danger. The slow-dropping, sodden rain kept on. It fell with irregular, drum-like beats upon the tough top of the toadstool under which he had taken refuge

Slowly, slowly, the sodden rainfall continued. Drop by drop, all the night long, the warm pellets of liquid came from the sky. They boomed upon the hollow heads of the toadstools, and splashed into the steaming pools that lay festering all over the fungus-covered earth.

And all the night long the great fires grew and spread in the mass of already half-carbonized mushroom. The flare at the horizon grew brighter and nearer. Burl, naked and hiding beneath a huge mushroom, wondering, with wide eyes, what this thing was, watched it grow near him. He had never seen a flame before.

The overhanging clouds were brightened by the flames. Over a stretch at least a dozen miles in length and from half a mile to three miles across, seething furnaces sent columns of dense smoke up to the roof of clouds, luminous from the glow below them, and spreading out and forming an intermediate layer below the cloudbanks themselves.

It was like the glow of all the many lights of a vast city thrown against the sky—but the last great city had molded into fungus-covered rubbish thirty thousand years before. Like the flitting of airplanes above the populous city, too, was the flitting of fascinated creatures above the glow.

Moths and great flying beetles, gigantic gnats and midges grown huge with the passing of time, they fluttered and danced the dance of death above the flames. As the fire grew nearer to Burl, he could see them.

Colossal, delicately-formed creatures swooped above the strange blaze. Moths with their riotously-colored wings of thirty-foot spread beat the air with mighty strokes, and their huge eyes glowed like carbuncles as they stared with the frenzied gaze of intoxicated devotees into the glowing flames below them.

Burl saw a great peacock moth soring above the burning mushroom hills. Its wings were all of forty feet across, and fluttered like gigantic sails as the moth gazed down at the flaming furnace below. The separate flames had united, now, and a single sheet of white-hot burning stuff spread across the country for miles, sending up its clouds of smoke, in which and through which the fascinated creatures flew.

Featherly antennae of the finest lace spread out before the head of the peacock moth, and its body was softest, richest velvet. A ring of snow-white down marked where its head began, and the red glow from below smote on the maroon of its body with a strange effect.

For one instant it was outlined clearly. Its eyes glowed more redly than any ruby's fire, and the great delicate wings were poised in flight. Burl caught the flash of the flames upon two great iridescent spots upon the wide-spread wings. Shining purple and vivid red, the glow of opal and the sheen of pearl, all the glory of chalcedony and of chrysoprase formed a single wonder in the red glare of burning fungus. White smoke compassed the great moth all about, dimming the radiance of its gorgeous dress.

Burl saw it dart straight into the thickest and brightest of the licking flames, flying madly, eagerly into the searing, hellish heat as a willing, drunken sacrifice to the god of fire.

Monster flying beetles with their horny wingcases stiffly stretched, blundered above the reeking, smoking pyre. In the red light from before them they shown like burnished metal, and their clumsy bodies with the spurred and fierce-toothed limbs darted like so many grotesque meteors through the luminous haze of ascending smoke.

Burl saw strange collisions and still stranger meetings. Male and female flying creatures circled and spun in the glare, dancing their dance of love and death in the wild raidiance from the funeral pyre of the purple hills. They mounted higher than Burl could see, drunk with the ecstacy of living, then descended to plunge headlong to death in the roaring fires beneath them.

From every side the creatures came. Moths of brightest yellow with soft and furry bodies palpitant with life flew madly into the column of light that reached to the overhanging clouds, then moths of deepest black with grewsome symbols upon their wings came swiftly to dance, like motes in sunlight, above the glow.

And Burl sat crouched beneath an overshadowing toadstool and watched. The perpetual, slow, sodden raindrops fell. A continuual faint hissing penetrated the sound of the fire—the raindrops being turned to steam. The air was alive with flying things. From far away Burl heard a strange, deep bass muttering. He did not know the cause, but there was a vast swamp, of the existence of which he was ignorant, some ten or fifteen miles away, and the chorus of insect-eating giant frogs reached his ears even at that distance.

The night wore on, while the flying creatures above the fire danced and died, their numbers ever recruited by flesh arrivals. Burl sat tensely still, his wide eyes watching everything, his mind groping for an explanation of what he saw. At last the sky grew dimly gray, then brighter, and day came on. The flames of the burning hills grew faint as the fire died down, and after a long time Burl crept from his hiding-place and stood erect.

A hundred yards from where he was, a straight wall of smoke rose from the still smoldering fungus, and Burl could see it stretching for miles in either direction. He turned to continue on his way, and saw the remains of one of the tragedies of the night.

A huge moth had flown into the flames, been horribly scorched and floundered out again. Had it been able to fly, it would have returned to its devouring deity, but now it lay immovable upon the ground, its antennae seared hopelessly, one beautiful, delicate wing burned in gaping holes, its eyes dimmed by flame and its exquisitely tapering limbs broken and crushed by the force with which it had struck the ground. It lay helpless upon the earth, only the stumps of its antennae moving restlessly, and its abdomen pulsating slowly as it drew painracked breaths.

Burl drew near and picked up a stone. He moved on presently, a velvet cloak cast over his shoulders, gleaming with all the colors of the rainbow. A gorgeous mass of soft, blew moth fur was about his middle, and he had bound upon his forehead two yard-long, golden fragments of the moth's magnificent antennae. He strode on slowly, clad as no man had been clad in all the ages.

After a little he secured a spear and took up his journey to Saya, looking like a prince of Ind upon a bridal journey—though no mere prince ever wore such raiment in days of greatest glory.

CHAPTER V

The Conqueror

or many long miles Burl threaded his way through a single forest of thin-stalked toadstools. They towered three man-heights high, and all about their bases were streaks and splashes of the rusts and molds that preyed upon them. Twice Burl came to open glades, wherein open, bubbling pools of green slime festered in corruption, and once he hid himself fearfully as a monster scarabeus beetle lumbered within three yards of him, moving heavily onward with a clanking of limbs as of some mighty machine.

Burl saw the mighty armor and the inward-curving jaws of the creature, and envied him his weapons. The time was not yet come, however, when Burl would smile at the great insect and hunt him for the juicy flesh contained in those armored limbs.

Burl was still a savage, still ignorant, still timid. His principal advance had been that whereas he had fled without reasoning, he now paused to see if he need flee. In his hands he bore a long, sharp-pointed, chitinous spear. It had been the weapon of a huge, unnamed flying insect scorched to death in the burning of the purple hills, which had floundered out of the flames to die. Burl had worked for an hour before being able to detach the weapon he coveted. It was as long and longer than Burl himself.

He was a strange sight, moving slowly and cautiously through the shadowed lanes of the mushroom forest. A cloak of delicate velvet in which all the colors of the rainbow played in iridescent beauty hung from his shoulders. A mass of soft and beautiful moth fur was about his middle, and in the strip of sinew about this waist the fiercely toothed limb of a fighting beetle was thrust carelessly. He had bound to his forehead twin sacks of a great moth's feathery golden antennae.

Against the play of color that came from his borrowed plumage his pink skin showed in odd contrast. He looked like some proud knight walking slowly through the gardens of goblin's castle. But he was still a fearful creature, no more than the monstrous creatures about him save in the possession of latent intelligence. He was weak—and therein lay his greatest promise. A hundred thousand years before him his ancestors had been forced by lack of claws and fangs to develop brains.

Burl was sunk as low as they had been, but he had to combat more horrifying enemies, more inexorable threatenings, and many times more crafty assailants. His ancestors had invented knives and spears and flying missiles. The creatures about Burl had knives and spears a thousand times more deadly than the weapons that had made his ancestors masters of the woods and forests.

Burl was in comparison vastly more weak than his forbears had been, and it was that weakness that in times to come would lead him and those who followd him to heights his ancestors had never known. But now—

He heard a discordant, deep bass bellow, coming from a spot not twenty yards away. In a flash of panic he darted behind a clump of the mushrooms and hid himself, panting in sheer terror. He waited for an instant in frozen feer, motionless and tense. His wide, blue eyes were glassy.

The bellow came again, but this time with a querulous note. Burl heard a crashing and plunging as of some creature caught in a snare. A mushroom fell with a brittle snapping, and a spongy thud as it fell to the ground was followed by a tremendous commotion. Something was fighting desperately against something else, but Burl did not know what creature or creatures might be in combat.

He waited for a long time, and the noise gradually died away. Presently Burl's breath came more slowly, and his courage returned. He stole from his hiding-place, and would have made away, but something held him back. Instead of creeping from the scene, he crept cautiously over toward the source of the noise.

He peered between two cream-colored toadstool stalks and saw the cause of the noise. A wide, funnel-shaped snare of silk was spread out before him, some twenty yards across and as many deep. The individual threads could be plainly seen, but in the mass it seemed a fabric of sheerest, finest texture. Held up by the tall mushrooms, it was anchored to the ground below, and drew away to a tiny point through which a hole gave on some yet unknown recess. And all the space of the wide snare was hung with threads, fine, twisted threads no more than half the thickness of Burl's finger.

This was the trap of a labyrinth spider. Not one of the interlacing threads was strong enough to hold the feeblest of prey, but the threads were there by thousands. A great cricket had become entangled in the maze of sticky lines. Its limbs thrashed out, smashing the snare-lines at every stroke, but at every stroke meeting and becoming entangled with a dozen more. It thrashed about mightily, emitting at intervals the horrible, deep bass cry that the chirping voice of the cricket had become with its increase in size.

Burl breathed more easily, and watched with a fascinated curiosity. Mere death—even tragic death—as among insects held no great

169

interest for him. It was a matter of such common and matter-of-fact occurrence that he was not greatly stirred. But a spider and his prey was another matter.

There were few insects that deliberately sought man. Most insects have their allotted victims, and will touch no others, but spiders have a terrifying impartiality. One great beetle devouring another was a matter of indifference to Burl. A spider devouring some luckless insect was but an example of what might happen to him. He watched alertly, his gaze travelling from the emmeshed cricket to the strange orifice at the rear of the funnel-shaped snare.

The opening darkened. Two shining, glistening eyes had been watching from the rear of the funnel. It drew itself into a tunnel there, in which the spider had been waiting. Now it swung out lightly and came toward the cricket. It was a gray spider (*Agelena labyrinthica*), with twin black ribbons upon his thorax, next the head, and with two stripes of curiously speckled brown and white upon its abdomen. Burl saw, too, two curious appendages like a tail.

It came nimbly out of its tunnel-like hiding-place and approached the cricket. The cricket was struggling only feebly now, and the cries it uttered were but feeble, because of the confining threads that fettered its limbs. Burl saw the spider throw itself upon the cricket and saw the final, convulsive shudder of the insect as the spider's fangs pierced its tough armor. The sting lasted a long time, and finally Burl saw that the spider was really feeding. All the succulent juices of the now dead cricket were being sucked from its body by the spider. It had stung the cricket upon the haunch, and presently it went to the other leg and drained that, too, by means of its powerful internal suction-pump. When the second haunch had been sucked dry, the spider pawed the lifeless creature for a few moments and left it.

Food was plentiful, and the spider could afford to be dainty in its feeding. The two choicest titbits had been consumed. The remainder could be discarded.

A sudden thought came to Burl and quite took his breath away. For a second his knees knocked together in self-induced panic. He watched the gray spider carefully, with growing determination in his eyes. He, Burl, had killed a hunting-spider upon the red-clay cliff. True, the killing had been an accident, and had nearly cost him his own life a few minutes later in the web-spider's snare, but he had killed a spider, and of the most deadly kind.

Now, a great ambition was growing in Burl's heart. His tribe had always feared spiders too much to know much of their habits, but they knew one or two things. The most important was that the snare-

170

spiders never left their lairs to hunt—never! Burl was about to make a daring application of that knowledge.

He drew back from the white and shining snare and crept softly to the rear. The fabric gathered itself into a point and then continued for some twenty feet as a tunnel, in which the spider waited while dreaming of its last meal and waiting for the next victim to become entangled in the labyrinth in front. Burl made his way to a point where the tunnel was no more than ten feet away, and waited.

Presently, through the interstices of the silk, he saw the gray bulk of the spider. It had left the exhausted body of the cricket, and returned to its resting-place. It settled itself carefully upon the soft walls of the tunnel, with its shining eyes fixed upon the tortuous threads of its trap. Burl's hair was standing straight up upon his head from sheer fright, but he was the slave of an idea.

He drew near and poised his spear, his new and sharp spear, taken from the body of an unknown dying creature killed by the burning purple hills. Burl raised the spear and aimed its sharp and deadly point at the thick gray bulk he could see dimly through the threads of the tunnel. He thrust it home with all his strength—and ran away at the top of his speed, glassy-eyed from terror.

A long time later he ventured near again, his heart in his mouth, ready to fleeat the slightest sound. All was still. Burl had missed the horrible convulsions of the wounded spider, had not heard the frightfull gnashings of its fangs as it gnashed at the piercing weapon, had not seen the silken threads of the tunnel ripped and torn as the spider—hurt to death—had struggled with insane strength to free itself.

He came back beneath the overshadowing toadstools, stepping quietly and cautiously, to find a great rent in the silken tunnel, to find the great gray bulk lifeless and still, half-fallen through the opening the spear had first made. A little puddle of evil-smelling liquid lay upon the ground below the body, and from time to time a droplet fell from the spear into the puddle with a curious splash.

Burl looked at what he had done, saw the dead body of the creature he had slain, saw the ferocious mandibles, and the keen and deadly fangs. The dead eyes of the creature still stared at him malignantly, and the hairy legs were still braced as if further to enlarge the gaping hole through which it had partly fallen.

Exultation filled Burl's heart. His tribe had been but furtive vermin for thousands of years, fleeing from the mighty insects, and, hiding from them, if overtaken, but waiting helplessly for death, screaming shrilly in terror.

He, Burl, had turned the tables. He had slain one of the enemies

171

of his tribe. His breast expanded. Always his tribesmen went quietly and fearfully, making no sound. But a sudden exultant yell burst from Burl's lips—the first hunting cry from the lips of a man in a hundred centuries!

The next second his pulse nearly stopped in sheer panic at having made such a noise. He listened fearfully, but there was no sound. He drew near his prey and carefully withdrew his spear. The viscid liquid made it slimy and slippery, and he had to wipe it dry against a leathery toadstool. Then Burl had to conquer his logical fear again before daring to touch the creature he had slain.

He moved off presently, with the belly of the spider upon his back and two of the hairy legs over his shoulders. The other limbs of the monster hung limp, and trailed upon the ground. Burl was now a still more curious sight as a gayly colored object with a cloak shining in iridescent colors, the golden antennae of a great moth rising from his forehead, and the hideous bulk of a gray spider for a burden.

He moved through the thin-stalked mushroom forest, and because of of the thing he carried all creatures fled before him. They did not fear man—their instinct was slow-moving—but during all the millions of years that insects have existed, there have existed spiders to prey upon them. So Burl moved on in solemn state, a brightly clad man bent beneath the weight of a huge and horrible monster.

He came upon a valley full of torn and blackened mushrooms. There was not a single yellow top among them. Every one had been infested with tiny magots which had liquefied the tough meat of the mushroom and caused it to drip to the ground below. And all the liquid had gathered in a golden pool in the center of the small depression. Burl heard a loud humming and buzzing before he topped the rise that opened the valley for his inspection. He stopped a moment and looked down.

A golden-red lake, its center reflecting the hazy sky overhead. All about, blacken mushrooms, seeming to have been charred and burned by a fierce flame. A slow-flowing golden brooklet trickled slowly over a rocky ledge, into the larger pool. And all about the edges of the golden lake, in ranks and rows, by hundreds, thousands, and by millions, were ranged the green-gold, shining bodies of great flies.

They were small as compared with the other insects. They had increased in size but a fraction of the amount that the bees, for example, had increased; but it was due to an imperative necessity of their race.

The flesh-flies laid their eggs by hundreds in decaying carcases. The others layed their eggs by hundreds in the mushrooms. To feed the magots that would hatch, a relatively great quantity of food was needed, therefore the flies must remain comparatively small, or the body of a single grasshopper, say, would furnish food for but two or three grubs instead of the hundreds it must support.

Burl stared down at the golden pool. Bluebottles, greenbottles, and all the flies of metallic luster were gathered at the Lucullan feast of corruption. Their buzzing as they darted above the odorous pool of golden liquid made the sound Burl had heard. Their bodies flashed and glittered as they darted back and forth, seeking a place to alight and join in the orgy.

Those which clustered about the banks of the pool were still as if carved from metal. Their huge, red eyes glowed, and their bodies shown with an obscene fatness. Flies are the most disgusting of all insects. Burl watched them a moment, watched the interlacing streams of light as they buzzed eagerly above the pool, seeking a place at the festive board.

A drumming roar sounded in the air. A golden speck appeared in the sky, a slender, needlelike body with transparent, shining wings and two huge eyes. It grew nearer and became a dragon-fly twenty feet and more in length, its body shimmering, purest gold. It poised itself above the pool and then darted down. Its jaws snapped viciously and repeatedly, and at each snapping the glittering body of a fly vanished.

A second dragon-fly appeared, its body a vivid purple, and a third. They swooped and rushed above the golden pool, snapping in mid air, turning their abrupt, angular turns, creatures of incredible ferocity and beauty. At the moment they were nothing more or less than slaughtering-machines. They darted here and there, their many-faceted eyes burning with blood-lust. In that mass of buzzing flies even the most voracious appetite must be sated, but the dragon-flies kept on. Beautiful, slender, graceful creatures, they dashed here and there above the pond like avenging fiends or the mythical dragons for which they had been named.

And the loud, contented buzzing kept on as before. Their comrades were being slaughtered by hundreds not fifty feet above their heads, but the glittering rows of red-eyed flies gorging themselves upon the golden, evil-smelling liquid kept placidly on with their feasting. The dragon-flies could contain no more, even of their chosen prey, but they continued to swoop madly above the pool, striking down the buzzing flies even though the bodies must perforce drop uneaten. One or two of the dead flies—crushed to a pulp by the angry jaws of a great dragon-fly—dropped among its feasting brothers. They shook themselves.

173

Presently one of them placed its disgusting proboscis upon the mangled form and sipped daintily of the juices exuding from the broken armor. Another joined it, and another. In a little while a cluster of them elbowed and pushed each other for a chance to join in the cannibalistic feast.

Burl turned aside and went on, while the slim forms of the dragon-flies still darted here and there above the pool, still striking down the droning flies with vengeful strokes of their great jaws, while a rain of crushed bodies was falling to the contented, glistening, horde below.

Only a few miles farther on Burl came upon a familiar landmark. He knew it well, but from a safe distance as always. A mass of rock had heaved itself up from the nearly level plain over which he was traveling, and formed a outjutting cliff. At one point the rock overhung a shear drop, making an inverted ledge—a roof over nothingness—which had been prempted by a hairy creature and made into a fairylike dwelling. A white hemisphere clung tenaciously to the rock above, and long cables anchored if firmly.

Burl knew the place as one to be fearfully avoided. A Clotho spider (*Clotho Durandi*), had built itself a nest there, from which it emerged to hunt the unwary. Within that half-globe there was a monster, resting upon a cushion of softest silk. But if one went too near, one of the little inverted arches, seemingly firmly closed by a wall of silk, would open and a creature out of a dream of hell emerge, to run with fiendish agility toward its prey.

Surely, Burl knew the place. Hung upon the outer walls of the silken palace were stones and tiny boulders, discarded fragments of former meals, and the gutted armor from limbs of ancient prey. But what caused Burl to know the place most surely and most terribly was another decoration that dangled from the castle of this insect ogre. This was the shrunken, dessicated figure of a man, all its juices extracted and the life gone.

The death of that man had saved Burl's life two years before. They had been together, seeking a new source of edible mushrooms for food. The Clotho spider was a hunter, not a spinner of snares. It sprang suddenly from behind a great puff-ball, and the two men froze in terror. Then it came swiftly forward and deliberately chose its victim. Burl had escaped when the other man was seized. Now he looked meditatively at the hiding-place of his ancient enemy. Some day—

But now he passed on. He went past the thicket in which the great moths hid during the day, and past the pool—a turgid thing of slime and yeast—in which a monster water-snake lurked. He penetrated the little wood of the shining mushrooms that gave out light at night, and the shadowed place where the truffle-hunting beetles went chirping thunderously during the dark hours.

And then he saw Saya. He caught a flash of pink skin vanishing behind the thick stalk of a squat toadstool, and ran forward, calling her name. She appeared, and saw the figure with the horrible bulk of the spider upon its back. She cried out in horror, and Burl understood. He let his burden fall and went swiftly toward her.

They met. Saya waited timidly until she saw who this man was, and then astonishment went over her face. Gorgeously attired, in an iridescent cloak from the whole wing of a great moth, with a strip of softest fur from a night-flying creature about his middle, with golden, feathery antennae bound upon his forehead, and a fierce spear in his hands—this was not the Burl she had known.

But then he moved slowly toward her, filled with a fierce delight at seeing her again, thrilling with joy at the slender gracefulness of her form and the dark richness of her tangled hair. He held out his hands and touched her shyly. Then, manlike, he began to babble excitedly of the things that happened to him, and dragged her toward his great victim, the gray-bellied spider.

Saya trembled when she saw the furry bulk lying upon the ground, and would have fled when Burl advanced and took it up upon his back. Then something of the pride that filled him came vicariously to her. She smiled a flashing smile, and Burl stopped short in his excited explanation. He was suddenly tongue-tied. His eyes became pleading and soft. He laid the huge spider at her feet and spread out his hands imploringly.

Thirty thousand years of savagery had not lessened the feminity in Saya. She became aware that Burl was her slave, that these wonderful things he wore and had done were as nothing if she did not approve. She drew away—saw the misery in Burl's face—and abruptly ran into his arms and clung to him, laughing happily. And quite suddenly Burl saw with extreme clarity that all these things he had done, even the slaying of a great spider, were of no importance whatever beside this most wonderful thing that had just happened, and told Saya so quite humbly, but holding her very close to him as he did so.

And so Burl came back to his tribe. He had left it nearly naked, with but a wisp of moth-wing twisted about his middle, a timid, fearful trembling creature. He returned in triumph, walking slowly and fearlessly down a broad lane of golden mushrooms toward the hiding place of his people.

Upon his shoulders was draped a great and many-colored cloak

175

made from the whole of a moth's wing. Soft fur was about his middle. A spear was in his hand and a fierce club at his waist. He and Saya bore between them the dead body of a huge spider— aforetime the dread of the pink-skinned, naked men.

But to Burl the most important thing of all was that Saya walked beside him openly, acknowledging him before all the tribe.

THE END

The MOON METAL
By Garrett P. Serviss

Chapter I

South Polar Gold

hen the news came of the discovery of gold at the south pole, nobody suspected that the beginning had been reached of a new era in the world's history. The newsboys cried "Extra!" as they had done a thousand times for murders, battles, fires, and Wall Street panics, but nobody was excited. In fact, the reports at first seemed so exaggerated and improbable that hardly anybody believed a word of them. Who could have been expected to credit a despatch, forwarded by cable from New Zealand, and signed by an unknown name, which contained such a statement as this:

"A seam of gold which can be cut with a knife has been found within ten miles of the south pole."

The discovery of the pole itself had been announced three years before, and several scientific parties were known to be exploring the remarkable continent that surrounds it. But while they had sent home many highly interesting reports, there had been nothing to suggest the possibility of such an amazing discovery as that which was now announced. Accordingly, most sensible people looked upon the New Zealand despatch as a hoax.

But within a week, and from a different source, flashed another despatch which more than confirmed the first. It declared that gold existed near the south pole in practically unlimited quantity. Some geologists said this accounted for the greater depth of the Antarctic Ocean. It had always been noticed that the southern hemisphere appeared to be a little overweighted. People now began to prick up their ears, and many letters of inquiry appeared in the newspapers concerning the wonderful tidings from the south. Some asked for information about the shortest route to the new gold-fields.

In a little while several additional reports came, some *via* New Zealand, others *via* South America, and all confirming in every respect what had been sent before. Then a New York newspaper sent a swift steamer to the Antarctic, and when this enterprising journal published a four-page cable describing the discoveries in detail, all doubt vanished and the rush began.

Gold Loses its Value, and the Markets of the World Are Upset

Some time I may undertake a description of the wild scenes that occurred when, at last, the inhabitants of the northern hemisphere were convinced the boundless stores of gold existed in the unclaimed and uninhabited wastes surrounding the south pole. But at present I have something more wonderful to relate.

Let me briefly depict the situation.

For many years silver had been absent from the coinage of the world. Its increasing abundance rendered it unsuitable for money, especially when contrasted with gold. The "silver craze," which had raged in the closing decade of the nineteenth century, was already a forgotten incident of financial history. The gold standard had become universal, and business all over the earth had adjusted itself to that condition. The wheels of industry ran smoothly, and there seemed to be no possibility of any disturbance or interruption. The common monetary system preveiling in every land fostered trade and facilitated the exchange of products. Travelers never had to bother their heads about the currency of money; any coin that passed in New York would pass for its face value in London, Paris, Berlin, Rome, Madrid, St. Petersburg, Constantinople, Cairo, Khartoum, Jerusalem, Peking, or Yeddo. It was indeed the "Golden Age," and the world had never been so free from financial storms.

Upon this peaceful scene the south polar gold discoveries burst like an unheralded tempest.

I happened to be in the company of a famous bank president when the confirmation of those discoveries suddenly filled the streets with yelling newsboys.

The Gold Standard Eliminated and Disaster Impending

Get me one of those 'extras'!" he said, and an office-boy ran out to obey him. As he perused the sheet his face darkened.

"I'm afraid it's too true," he said, at length. "Yes, there seems to be no getting around it. Gold is going to be as plentiful as iron. If there were not such a flood of it, we might manage, but when they begin to make trousers buttons out of the same metal that is now locked and guarded in steel vaults, where will be our standard of worth? My dear fellow," he continued, impulsively laying his hand on my arm, "I would as willingly face the end of the world as this that's coming?"

"You think it so bad, then?" I asked. "But most people will not agree with you. They will regard it as very good news."

"How can it be good?" he burst out. "What have we got to take

180

the place of gold? Can we go back to the age of barter? Can we substitute cattle-pens and wheat-bins for the strong boxes of the Treasury? Can commerce exist with no common measure of exchange?"

"It does indeed look serious," I assented.

"Serious! I tell you, it is the deluge!"

There at he clapped on his hat and hurried across the street to the office of another celebrated banker.

His premonitions of disaster turned out to be but too well grounded. The deposits of gold at the south pole were richer than the wildest reports had represented them. The shipments of the precious metal to America and Europe soon became enormous—so enormous that the metal was no longer precious. The price of gold dropped like a falling stone, with accelerated velocity, and within a year every money centre in the world had been swept by a panic. Gold was more common than iron. Every government was compelled to demonetize it, for when once gold had fallen into contempt it was less valuable in the eyes of the public than stamped paper. For once the world had thoroughly learned the lesson that too much of a good thing is worse than none of it.

Gold is Brought Into Economic Use

Then somebody found a new use for gold by inventing a process by which it could be hardened and tempered, assuming a wonderful toughness and elasticity without losing its non-corrosive property, and in this form it rapidly took the place of steel.

In the mean time every effort was made to bolster up credit. Endless were the attempts to find a substitute for gold. The chemists sought it in their laboratories and the mineralogists in the mountains and deserts. Platinum might have served, but it, too, had become a drug in the market through the discovery of immense deposits. Out of the twenty odd elements which had been rarer and more valuable than gold, such as uranium, gallium, etc., not one was found to answer the purpose. In short, it was evident that since both gold and silver had become too abundant to serve any longer for a money standard, the planet held no metal suitable to take their place.

The entire monetary system of the world must be readjusted, but in the readjustment it was certain to fall to pieces. In fact, it had already fallen to pieces; the only recourse was to paper money, but whether this was based upon agriculture or mining or manufacture, it gave varying standards, not only among the different nations, but in successive years in the same country. Exports and imports practically ceased. Credit was discredited, commerce perished, and the world, at a bound, seemed to have gone back, financially and industrially to the dark ages.

One final effort was made. A great financial congress was assembled at New York. Representatives of all the nations took part in it. The ablest financiers of Europe and America united the efforts of their genius and the results of their experience to solve the great problem. The various governments all solemnly stipulated to abide by the decision of the congress.

But, after spending months n hard but fruitless labor, that body was no nearer the end of its undertaking than when it first assembled. The entire world awaited its decision with bated breath, and yet the decision was not formed.

At this paralyzing crisis a most unexpected event suddenly opened the way.

CHAPTER II

The Magician of Science

n attendant entered the room where the perplexed financiers were in session and presented a peculiar-looking card to the president, Mr. Boon. The President took the card in his hand and instantly fell into a brown study. So complete was his absorption that Herr Finster, the celebrated Berlin banker, who had been addressing the chair for the last two hours from the opposite end of the long table, got confused, entirely lost track of his verb, and suddenly dropped into his seat, very red in the face and wearing a most injured expression.

But President Boon paid no attention except to the singular card, which he continued to turn over and over, balancing it on his fingers and holding it now at arm's-length and then near his nose, with one eye squinted as if he were trying to look true a hole in the card.

At length this odd conduct of the presiding officer drew all eyes upon the card, and then everybody shared the interest of Mr. Boon. In shape and size the card was not extraordinary, but it was composed of metal. What metal? That question had immediately arisen in Mr. Boon's mind when the card came into his hand, and now it exercised the wits of all the others. Plainly it was not tin, brass, copper, bronze, silver, aluminum—although its lightness might have suggested that metal—nor even base gold.

The President, although a skilled metallurgist, confessed his inability to say what it was. So intent had he become in examining the curious bit of metal that he forgot it was a visitor's card of introduction, and did not even look for the name which it presumably bore.

The Reception of a Visitor's Wonderful Card

As he held the card up to get a better light upon it a stray sunbeam from the window fell across the metal and instantly it bloomed with exquisite colors!

The President's chair being in the darker end of the room, the radiant card suffused the atmosphere about him with a faint rose tint, playing with surprising liveliness into alternate canary color and violet.

The effect upon the company of clear-headed financiers was

extremely remarkable. The unknown metal appeared to exercise a kind of mesmeric influence, its soft hues blending together in a chromatic harmony which captivated the sense of vision as the ears are charmed by a perfectly rendered song. Gradually all gathered in an eager group around the president's chair.

"What can it be?" was repeated from lip to lip.

"Did you ever see anything like it?" asked Mr. Boon for the twentieth time.

None of them had even seen the like of it. A spell fell upon the assemblage. For five minutes no one spoke, while Mr. Boon continued to chase the flickering sunbeam with the wonderful card. Suddenly the silence was broken by a voice which had a touch of awe in it:

"It must be the metal!"

The speaker was an English financier, First Lord of the Treasury, Hon. James Hampton-Jones, K.C.B. Immediately everybody echoed his remark, and the strain being thus relieved, the spell dropped from them and several laughed loudly over their momentary aberration.

The Visitor Himself Enters

President Boon recollected himself, and, coloring slightly, placed the card flat on the table, in order more clearly to see the name. In plain red letters it stood forth with such surprising distinctness that Mr. Boon wondered why he had so long overlooked it.

"DOCTOR MAX SYX"

"Tell the gentleman to come in," said the President, and thereupon the attendant threw open the door.

The owner of the mysterious card fixed every eye as he entered. He was several inches more than six feet in height. His complexion was very dark, his eyes were intensely black, bright, and deep-set, his eyebrows were bushy and up-curled at the ends, his sable hair was close-trimmed, and his ears were narrow, pointed at the top, and prominent. He wore black mustaches, covering only half the width of his lip and drawn into projecting needles on each side, while a spiked black beard adorned the middle of his chin.

He smiled as he stepped confidently forward, with a courtly bow, but it was a very disconcerting smile, because it more than half resembled a sneer. This uncommon person did not wait to be addressed.

"I have come to solve your problem," he said, facing President Boon, who had swung round on his pivoted chair.

"The metal!" exclaimed everybody in a breath, and with a unanimity and excitement which would have astonished them if they had been spectators instead of actors of the scene. The tall stranger bowed and smiled again:

"Just so," he said. "What do you think of it?"

"It is beautiful!"

Again the reply came from every mouth simultaneously, and again if the speakers could have been listeners they would have wondered not only at their earnestness, but at their words, for why should they instantly and unanimously pronounce that beautiful which they had not even seen? But every man knew he had seen it, for instinctively their minds reverted to the card and recognized in it the metal referred to. The mesmeric spell seemed once more to fall upon the assemblage, for the financiers noticed nothing remarkable in the next act of the stranger, which was to take a chair, uninvited, at the table, and the moment he sat down he became the presiding officer as naturally as if he had just been elected to that post. They all waited for him to speak, and when he opened his mouth they listened with breathless attention.

The Visitor's Story

His words were of the best English, but there was some peculiarity, which they had already noticed, either in his voice or his manner of enunciation, which struck all of the listeners as denoting a foreigner. But none of them could satisfactorily place him. Neither the Americans, the Englishmen, the Germans, the Frenchmen, the Russians, the Austrians, the Italians, the Spaniards, the Turks, the Japanese, nor the Chinese at the board could decide to what race or nationality the stranger belonged.

"This metal," he began, taking the card from Mr. Boon's hand, "I have discovered and named. I call it 'artemisium.' I can produce it, in the pure form, abundantly enough to replace gold, giving it the same relative value that gold possessed when it was the universal standard."

As Dr. Syx spoke he snapped the card with his thumb-nail and it fluttered with quivering hues like a humming-bird hovering over a flower. He seemed to await a reply, and President Boon asked:

"What guarantee can you give that the supply would be adequate and continuous?"

185

"I will conduct a committee of this congress to my mine in the Rocky Mountains, where, in anticipation of the event, I have accumulated enough refined artemisium to provide every civilized land with an amount of coin equivalent to that which it formerly held in gold. I can there satisfy you of my ability to maintain the production."

"But how do we know that this metal of yours will answer the purpose?"

"Try it," was the laconic reply.

"There is another difficulty," pursued the president. "People will not accept a new metal in place of gold unless they are convinced that it possesses equal intrinsic value. They must first become familiar with it, and it must be abundant enough and desirable enough to be used sparingly in the arts, just as gold was."

"I have provided for all that," said the stranger, with one of his disconcerting smiles. "I assure you that there will be no trouble with the people. They will be only too eager to get and to use the metal. Let me show you."

He stepped to the door and immediately returned with two black attendants bearing a large tray filled with articles shaped from the same metal as that of which the card was composed. The financiers all jumped to their feet with exclamations of surprise and admiration, and gathered around the tray, whose dazzling contents lighted up the corner of the room where it had been placed as if the moon were shining there.

The New Metal Artemisium

There were elegantly formed vases, adorned with artistic figures, embossed and incised, and glowing with delicate colors which shimmered in tiny waves with the slightest motion of the tray. Cups, pins, finger-rings, earrings, watchchains, combs, studs, lockets, medals, tableware, models of coins—in brief, almost every article in the fabrication of which precious metals have been employed was to be seen there in profusion, and all composed of the strange new metal which everybody on the spot declared was far more spendid than gold.

"Do you think it will answer?" asked Dr. Syx.

"We do," was the unanimous reply.

All then resumed their seats at the table, the tray with its magnificent array having been placed in the centre of the board. This display had a remarkable influence. Confidence awoke in the breasts of the financiers. The dark clouds that had oppressed them rolled off, and the prospect grew decidedly brighter.

"What terms do you demand?" at length asked Mr. Boon, cheerfully rubbing his hands.

"I must have military protection for my mine and reducing works," replied Dr. Syx. "Then I shall ask the return of one per cent on the circulating medium, together with the privilege of disposing of a certain amount of the metal—to be limited by agreement—to the public for use in the arts. Of the proceeds of this sale I will pay ten per cent to the government in consideration of its protection."

"But," exclaimed President Boon, "that will make you the richest man who ever lived!"

"Undoubtedly," was the reply.

"Why," added Mr. Boon, opening his eyes wider as the facts continued to dawn upon him, "you will become the financial dictator of the whole earth!"

"Undoubtedly," again responded Dr. Syx, unmoved. "That is what I purpose to become. My discovery entitles me to no less. But, remember, I place myself under government inspection and restriction. I should not be allowed to flood the market, even if I were disposed to do so. But my own interest would restrain me. It is to my advantage that artemisium, once adopted, shall remain stable in value."

A shadow of doubt suddenly crossed the President's face.

"Suppose your secret is discovered," he said.

"Surely your mine will not remain the only one. If you, in so short a time, have been able to accumulate an immense quantity of the new metal, it must be extremely abundant. Others will discover it, and then where shall we be?"

While Mr. Boon uttered these words, those who were watching Dr. Syx (as the President was not) resembled persons whose startled eyes are fixed upon a wild beast preparing to spring. As Mr. Boon ceased speaking he turned towards the visitor, and instantly his lips fell apart and his face paled.

Dr. Syx, the Visitor, is Imperious

Dr. Syx had drawn himself up to his full stature, and his features were distorted with that peculiar mocking smile which had now returned with a concentrated expression of mingled self-confidence and disdain.

"Will you have relief, or not?" he asked in a dry, hard voice. "What

187

can you do? I alone possess the secret which can restore industry and commerce. If you reject my offer, do you think a second one will come?"

President Boon found voice to reply, stammeringly:

"I did not mean to suggest a rejection of the offer. I only wished to inquire if you thought it probable that there would be no repetition of what occurred after gold was found at the south pole?"

"The earth may be full of my metal," returned Dr. Syx, almost fiercely, "but so long as I alone possess the knowledge how to extract it, is it of any more worth than common dirt? But come," he added, after a pause and softening his manner, "I have other schemes. Will you, as representatives of the leading nations, undertake the introduction of artemisium as a substitute for gold, or will you not?"

"Can we not have time for deliberation?" asked President Boon

"Yes, one hour. Within that time I shall return to learn your decision," replied Dr. Syx, rising and preparing to depart. "I leave these things," pointing to the tray, "in your keeping, and," significantly, "I trust your decision will be a wise one."

His curious smile again curved his lips and shot the ends of his mustache upward, and the influence of that smile remained in the room when he had closed the door behind him. The financiers gazed at one another for several minutes in silence, then they turned towards the coruscating metal that filled the tray.

CHAPTER III

The Teton Mountains

way on the western border of Wyoming, in the all but inaccessible heart of the Rocky Mountains, three mighty brothers, "the Big Tetons," look perpendicularly into the blue eye of Jenny's Lake, lying at the bottom of the profound depression among the mountains called Jackson's Hole. Bracing against one another for support, these remarkable peaks lift their granite spires from 12,000 to nearly 14,000 feet into the blue dome that arches the crest of the continent. Their sides, and especially those of their chief, the Grand Teton, are streaked with glaciers, which shine like silver trappings when the morning sun comes up above the wilderness of mountains stretching away eastward from the hole.

When the first white men penetrated this wonderful region, and one of them bestowed his wife's name upon Jenny's Lake, they were intimidated by the Grand Teton. It made their flesh creep, accustomed though they were to rough scrambling among mountain gorges and on the brows of immense precipices, when they glanced up the face of the peak, where the cliffs fall, one below another, in a series of breathless descents, and imagined themselves clinging for dear life to those skyey battlements.

But when, in 1872, Messrs. Stevenson and Langford finally reached the top of the Grand Teton—the only successful members of the party of nine practiced climbers who had started together from the bottom—they found there a little rectangular enclosure, made by piling up rocks, six or seven feet across and three feet in height, bearing evidences of great age, and indicating that the red Indians had, for some unknown purpose, resorted to the summit of this tremendous peak long before the white men invaded their mountains. Yet neither the Indians nor the whites ever really conquered the Teton, for above the highest point that they attained rises a granite buttress, whose smooth vertical sides seemed to them to defy everything but wings.

Winding across the sage-covered floor of Jackson's Hole runs the Shoshone, or Snake River, which takes its rise from Jackson's Lake at the northern end of the basin, and then, as if shrinking from the threatening brows of the Tetons, whose fall would block its progress, makes a detour of one hundred miles around the buttressed heights of the range before it finds a clear way across Idaho, and so on to the Columbia River and the Pacific Ocean.

A Visit to Syx's Works in the Teton Mountains

On a July morning, about a month after the visit of Dr. Max Syx to the assembled financiers in New York, a party of twenty horsemen, following a mountain-trail, arrived on the eastern margin of Jackson's Hole, and pausing upon a commanding emminence, with exclamations of wonder, glanced across the great depression, where lay the shining coils of the Snake River, at the towering forms of the Tetons, whose ice-striped cliffs flashed lightings in the sunshine. Even the impassive broncos that the party rode lifted their heads inquiringly, and snorted as if in equine astonishment at the magnificent spectacle.

One familiar with the place would have noticed something, which, to his mind, would have seemed more surprising than the pageantry of the mountains in their morning sun-bath. Curling above one of the wild gorges that cut the lower slopes of the Tetons was a thick black smoke, which, when lifted by a passing breeze, obscured the precipices halfway to the summit of the peak.

Had the Grand Teton become a volcano? Certainly no hunting or exploring party could make a smoke like that. But a word from the leader of the party of horsemen explained the mystery.

"There is my mill, and the mine is underneath it."

The speaker was Dr. Syx, and his companions were members of the financial congress. When he quitted their presence in New York, with the promise to return within an hour for their reply, he had no doubt in his own mind what that reply would be. He knew they would accept his proposition, and they did. No time was then lost in communicating with the various governments, and arrangements were quickly perfected whereby, in case the inspection of Dr. Syx's mine and its resources proved satisfactory, America and Europe should unite in adopting the new metal as the basis of their coinage. As soon as this stage in the negotiations was reached, it only remained to send a committee of financiers and metallurgists, in company with Dr. Syx, to the Rocky Mountains. They started under the doctor's guidance, completing the last stage of their journey on horseback.

"An inspection of the records at Washington," Dr. Syx continued, addressing the horsemen, "will show that I have filed a claim covering ten acres of ground around the mouth of my mine. This was done as soon as I had discovered the metal. The filing of the claim and the subsequent proceedings which perfected my ownership

190

attracted no attention, because everybody was thinking of the south pole and its gold-fields,"

Explanation From Dr. Syx

The party gathered closer around Dr. Syx and listened to his words with silent attention, while their horses rubbed noses and jingled their gold-mounted trappings.

"As soon as I had legally protected myself," he continued, "I employed a force of men, transported my machinery and material across the mountains, erected my furnaces, and opened the mine. I was safe from intrusion, and even from idle curiosity, for the reason I have just mentioned. In fact, so exclusive was the attraction of the new gold-fields that I had difficulty in obtaining workmen, and finally I sent to Africa and engaged negroes, whom I placed in charge of trustworthy foremen. Accordingly, with a half a dozen exceptions, you will see only black men at the mine."

"And with their aid you have mined enough metal to supply the mints of the world?" asked President Boon.

"Exactly so," was the reply. "But I no longer employ the large force which I needed at first."

"How much metal have you on hand? I am aware that you have already answered this question during our preliminary negotiations, but I ask it again for the benefit of some members of our party who were not present then."

"I shall show you to-day," said Dr. Syx, with his curious smile, "2500 tons of refined artemisium, stacked in rock-cut vaults under the Grand Teton."

"And you have dared to collect such inconceivable wealth in one place?"

"You forget that it is not wealth until the people have learned to value it, and the governments have put their stamp upon it."

"True, but how did you arrive at the proper moment?"

"Easily. I first ascertained that before the Antarctic discoveries the world contained alltogether about 16,000 tons of gold, valued at $450,000 per ton, or $7,200,000,000 worth all told. Now my metal weighs, bulk for bulk, one-quarter as much as gold. It might be reckoned at the same intrinsic value per ton, but I have considered it preferable to take advantage of the smaller weight of the new metal, which permits us to make coins of the same size as the old ones, but only one-quarter as heavy, by giving to artemisium four times the value per ton that gold had. Thus only 4000 tons of the

191

new metal are required to supply the place of 16,000 tons of gold. The 2500 tons which I already have on hand are more than enough for coinage. The rest I can supply as fast as needed.

The party did not wait for further explanations. They were eager to see the wonderful mine and the store of treasure. Spurs were applied, and they galloped down the steep trail, forded the Snake River, and skirting the shore of Jenny's Lake, soon found themselves gazing up the headlong slopes and dizzy parapets of the Grand Teton. Dr. Syx led them by a steep ascent to the mouth of the canyon, above one of whose walls stood his mill, and where the "Champ! Champ!" of a powerful engine saluted their ears.

The Wealth of the World

An electric light shot its penetrating rays into a gallery cut through virgin rock and running straight towards the heart of the Teton. The centre of the gallery was occupied by a narrow railway, on which a few flat cars, propelled by electric power, passed to and fro. Black-skinned and silent workmen rode on the cars, both when they came laden with broken masses of rock from the farther end of the tunnel and when they returned empty.

Suddenly, to an eye situated a little way within the gallery, appeared at the entrance the dark face of Dr. Syx, wearing its most discomposing smile, and a moment later, the broader countenance of President Boon loomed in the electric glare beside the doctor's black frame-work of eyebrows and mustache. Behind them were grouped the other visiting financiers.

"This tunnel," said Dr. Syx, "leads to the mine head, where the ore-bearing rock is blasted."

As he spoke a hollow roar issued from the depths of the mountain, followed in a short time by a gust of foul air.

"You probably will not care to go in there," said the doctor, "and, in fact, it is very uncomfortable. But we should follow the next car-load to the smelter, and you can witness the reduction of the ore."

Accordingly when another car came rumbling out of the tunnel, with its load of cracked rock, they all accompanied it into an adjoining apartment, where it was cast into a metallic chute, through which, they were informed, it reached the furnace.

"While it is melting," explained Dr. Syx, "certain elements, the nature of which I must beg to keep secret, are mixed with the ore, causing chemical action which results in the extraction of the metal. Now let me show you pure artemisum issuing from the furnace."

The Metal Shown Running from the Furnace

He led the visitors through two apartments into a third, one side of which was walled by the front of a furnace. From this projected two or three small spouts, and iridescent streams of molten metal fell from the spouts into earthen receptacles from which the blazing liquid was led, like flowing iron, into a system of molds, where it was allowed to cool and harden.

The financiers looked on wondering, and their astonishment grew when they were conducted into the rock-cut store-rooms beneath, where they saw metallic ingots glowing like gigantic opals in the light which Dr. Syx turned on. They were piled in rows along the walls as high as a man could reach. A very brief inspection sufficed to convince the visitors that Dr. Syx was able to perform all that he promised. Although they had not penetrated the secret of his process of reducing the ore, yet they had seen the metal flowing from the furnace, and the piles of ingots proved conclusively that he had uttered no vain boast when he said he could give the world a new coinage.

But President Boon, being himself a metallurgist, desired to inspect the mysterious ore a little more closely. Possibly he was thinking that if another mine was destined to be discovered he might as well be the discoverer as anybody. Doctor Syx attempted no concealment, but his smile became more than usually scornful as he stopped a laden car and invited the visitors to help themselves.

"I think," he said, "that I have struck the only load of this ore in the Teton, or possibly in this part of the world, but I don't know for certain. There may be plenty of it only waiting to be found. That, however, doesn't trouble me. The great point is that nobody except myself knows how to extract the metal."

Mr. Boon closely examined the chunk of rock which he had taken from the car. Then he pulled a lense from his pocket, with a depreciatory glance at Dr. Syx.

"Oh, that's all right," said the latter, with a laugh, the first that these gentlemen had ever heard from his lips, and it almost made them shudder; "put it to every test, examine it with the microscope, with fire, with electricity, with the spectroscope—in every way you can think of! I assure you it is worth your while!"

Again Dr. Syx uttered his freezing laugh, passing into the familiar smile, which had now become an undisguised mock.

"Upon my word," said Mr. Boon, taking his eye from the lens, "I

193

see no sign of any metal here!"

"Look at the green specks!" cried the doctor, snatching the specimen from the president's hand. "That's it! That's artemisium! But it's of no use unless you can get it out and purify it, which is my secret?"

Dr. Syx Laughs

For the third time, Dr. Syx laughed, and his merriment affected the visitors so disagreeably that they showed impatience to be gone. Immediately he changed his manner.

"Come into my office," he said, with a return to the graciousness which had characterized him ever since the party started from New York.

When they were all seated, and the doctor had handed round a box of cigars, he resumed the conversation in his most amiable manner.

"You see, gentlemen," he said, turning a piece of ore in his fingers, "'artemisium is like aluminum. It can only be obtained in the metallic form by a special process. While these greenish particles, which you may perhaps mistake for chrysolite, or some similar silicate, really contain the precious metal, they are not entirely composed of it. The process by which I separate out the metallic element while the ore is passing through the furnace is, in truth, quite simple, and its very simplicity guards my secret. Make your minds easy as to over-production. A man is as likely to jump over the moon as to find me out."

"But," he continued, again changing his manner, "we have had business enough for one day; now for a little recreation."

While speaking the doctor pressed a button on his desk, and the room, which was illuminated by electric lamps—for there were no windows in the building—suddenly became dark, except part of one wall, where a broad area of light appeared.

Dr. Syx's voice had become very soothing when next he spoke.

"I am fond of amusing myself with a peculiar form of the magic-lantern, which I invented some years ago, and which I have never exhibited except for the entertainment of my friends. The pictures will appear upon the wall, the apparatus being concealed."

He had hardly ceased speaking when the illuminated space seemed to melt away, leaving a great opening, through which the spectators looked as if into another world on the opposite side of the wall. For a minute or two they could not clearly discern what was presented;

then, gradually, the flitting scenes and figures became more distinct until the lifelikeness of the spectacle absorbed their whole attention.

Before them passed, in panoramic review, a sunny land, filled with brilliant-hued vegetation, and dotted with villages and cities which were bright with light-colored buildings. People appeared moving through the scenes, as in a cinemetograph exhibition, but with infinitely more semblance of reality. In fact, the pictures, blending one into another, seemed to be life itself. Yet it was not an earth-like scene. The colors of the passing landscape were such as no man in the room had ever beheld; and the people, tall, round-limbed, with florid complexion, golden hair, and brilliant eyes and lips, were indescribably beautiful and graceful in all their movements.

Dr. Syx's Movies

From the land the view passed out to sea, and bright blue waves, edged with creaming foam, ran swiftly under the spectator's eyes, and occasionally, driven before light winds, appeared fleets of daintily shaped vessels, which reminded the beholder, by their flashing wings, of the feigned "Ship of Pearl."

After the fairy ships and breezy sea views came a long, curving line of coast, brilliant with coral sands, and indented by frequent bays, along whose enchanting shores lay pleasant towns, the landscapes behind them splendid with groves, meadows, and streams.

Presently the shifting photographic tape, or whatever the mechanism may have been, appeared to have settled upon a chosen scene, and there it rested. A broad champaign reached away to distant sapphire mountains, while the foreground was occupied by a magnificent house, resembling a large country villa, fronted with a garden, shaded by bowers and festoons of huge, brilliant flowers. Birds of radiant plumage flitted among the trees and blossoms, and then appeared a company of gayly attired people, including many young girls, who joined hands and danced in a ring, apparently with shouts of laughter, while a group of musicians standing near thrummed and blew upon curiously shaped instruments.

End of the Movie Show

Suddenly the shadow of a dense cloud flitted across the scene; whereupon the brilliant birds flew away with screams of terror which almost seemed to reach the ears of the onlookers through the wall. An expression of horror came over the faces of the people. The children broke from their merry circle and ran for protection to their elders. The utmost confusing and whelming terror were evidenced for a moment—then the ground split asunder, and the house and the garden, with all their living occupants, were swallowed by an awful chasm which opened just where they had stood. The great rent ran in a widening line across the sunlit landscape until it reached the horizon, when the distant mountains crumbled, clouds poured in from all sides at once, and billows of flame burst through them as they veiled the scene.

But in another instant the commotion was over, and the world whose curious spectacles had been enacted as if on the other side of a window, seemed to retreat swiftly into space, until at last, emerging from a fleacy cloud, it reappeared in the form of the full moon hanging in the sky, but larger than is its wont, with its dry ocean-beds, its keen-spired peaks, its ragged mountain ranges, its gaping chasms, its immense crater rings, and Tycho, the chief of them all, shooting raylike streaks across the scarred face of the abandoned lunar globe.

The show was ended, and Dr. Syx, turning on only a partial illumination in the room, rose slowly to his feet, his tall form appearing strangely magnified in the gloom, and invited his bewildered guests to accompany him to his house, outside the mill, where he said dinner awaited them. As they emerged into daylight they acted like persons just aroused from an opiat dream.

CHAPTER IV

Wonders of the New Metal

ithin a twelvemonth after the visit of President Boon and his fellow-financiers to the mine in the Grand Teton a railway had been constructed from Jackson's Hole, connecting with one of the Pacific lines, and the distribution of the new metal was begun. All of Dr. Syx's terms had been accepted. United States troops occupied a permanent encampment on the upper waters of the Snake River, to afford protection, and as the consignments of precious ingots were hurried east and west on guarded trains, the mints all over the world resumed their activity. Once more a common monetary standard prevailed, and commerce revived as if touched by a magic wand.

Artemisium quickly won its way in popular favor. Its matchless beauty alone was enough. Not only was it gladly accepted in the form of money, but its success was instantaneous in the arts. Dr. Syx and the inspectors representing the various nations found it difficult to limit the output to the agreed-upon amount. The demand was incessant.

Goldsmiths and jewellers continually discovered new excellencies in the wonderful metal. Its properties of translusence and refraction enabled skillful artists to perform marvels. By suitable management a chain of artemisium could be made to resemble a string of vari-colored gems, each separate link having a tint of its own, while, as the wearer moved, delicate complimentary colors chased one another, in rapid undulation, from end to end.

A fresh charm was added by the new metal to the personal adornment of women, and an enhanced spendor to the pageants of society. Gold in its palmiest days had never enjoyed such a vogue. A crowded reception-room or a dinner-party where artemisium abounded possessed an indescribable atmosphere of luxury and richness, refined in quality, yet captivating to every sense. Imaginative persons went so far as to aver that the sight and presence of the metal exercised a strangely soothing and dreamy power over the mind, like the influence of moonlight streaming through the tree-tops on a still, balmly night.

The public curiosity in regard to the origin of artemisium was boundless. The various nations published official bulletins in which the general facts—omitting, of course, such incidents as the singular exhibition seen by the visiting financiers on the wall of Dr. Syx's office—were detailed to gratify the universal desire for information.

President Boon not only submitted the specimens of ore-bearing rock which he had brought from the mine to careful analysis, but also appealed to several of the greatest living chemists and mineralogists to aid him; but they were all equally mistified. The green substance contained in the ore, although differing slightly from ordinary chrysolite, answered all the known tests of that mineral. It was remembered, however, that Dr. Syx had said that they would be likely to mistake the substance for chrysolite, and the result of their experiments justified his prediction. Evidently the doctor had gone a stone's cast beyond the chemistry of the day, and, just as evidently, he did not mean to reveal his discovery for the benefit of science, nor for the benefit of any pockets except his own.

The Extraction of the Metal is an Unsolvable Mystery

Notwithstanding the failure of the chemists to extract anything from Dr. Syx's ore, the public at large never doubted that the secret would be discovered in good time, and thousands of prospectors flocked to the Teton Mountains in search of the ore. And without much difficulty they found it. Evidently the doctor had been mistaken in thinking that his mine might be the only one. The new miners hurried specimens of the green-speckled rock to the chemical laboratories for experimentation, and meanwhile began to lay up stores of the ore in anticipation of the time when the proper way to extract the metal should be discovered.

But, alas! that time did not come. The fresh ore proved to be as refractory as that which had been obtained from Dr. Syx. But in the midst of the universal disappointment there came a new sensation.

One morning the newspapers glared with a despatch from Grand Teton station announcing that the metal itself had been discovered by prospectors on the eastern slope of the main peak.

"It outcrops in many places," ran the despatch, "and many small nuggets have been picked out of crevices in the rocks."

The excitement produced by this news was even greater than when gold was discovered at the south pole. Again a mad rush was made for the Tetons. The heights around Jackson's Hole and the shores of Jackson's and Jenny's lakes were quickly dotted with camps, and the military force had to be doubled to keep off the curious, and occasionally menacing, crowds which gathered in the vicinity and seemed bent on unearthing the great secret locked behind the windowless walls of the mill, where the column of black smoke and the roar of the engine served as reminders of the incredible wealth which the sole possessor of that secret was rolling up.

This time no mistake had been made. It was a fact that the metal, in virgin purity, had been discovered scattered in various places on the ledges of the Grand Teton. In a little while thousands had obtained specimens with their own hands. The quantity was distressingly small, considering the number and the eagerness of the seekers, but that it was genuine artemisium not even Dr. Syx could have denied. He, however, made no attempt to deny it.

"Yes," he said, when questioned, "I find that I have been deceived. At first I thought the metal existed only in the form of the green ore, but of late I have come upon veins of pure artemisium in my mine. I am glad for your sakes, but sorry for my own. Still, it may turn out that there is no great amount of free artemisium after all."

The Mountain is Covered with Prospectors

While the doctor talked in this manner close observers detected a lurking sneer which his acquaintances had not noticed since artemisium was first adopted as the money basis of the world.

The crowd that swarmed upon the mountain quickly exhausted all of the visible supply of the metal. Sometimes they found it in a thin stratum at the bottom of crevices, where it could be detached in opalescent plates and leaves of the thickness of paper. These superficial deposits evidently might have been formed from water holding the metal in solution. Occasionally, deep cracks contained nuggets and wiry masses which looked as if they had run together when molten.

The most promising spots were soon staked out in miners' claims, machinery was procured, stock companies were formed, and borings were begun. The enthusiasm arising from the earlier finds and the flattering surface indications caused everybody to work with feverish haste and energy, and within two months one hundred tunnels were piercing the mountain.

For a long time nobody was willing to admit the truth which gradually forced itself upon the attention of the miners. The deeper they went the scarcer became the indications of artemisium! In fact, such deposits as were found were confined to fissures near the surface. But Dr. Syx continued to report a surprising increase in the amount of free metal in his mine, and this encouraged all who had not exhausted their capital to push on their tunnels in the hope of

199

finally striking a vein. At length, however, the smaller operators gave up in despair, until only one heavily capitalized company remained at work.

CHAPTER V

A Strange Discovery

I t is my belief that doctor Max Syx is a deceiver."

The person who uttered this opinion was a young engineer, Andrew Hall, who had charge of the operations of one of the mining companies which were driving tunnels into the Grand Teton.

"What do you mean by that?" asked President Boon, who was the principal backer of the enterprise.

"I mean," replied Hall, "that there is no free metal in this mountain, and Dr. Syx knows there is none."

"But he is getting it himself from his mine," retorted President Boon.

"So he says, but who has seen it? No one is admitted into the Syx mine, his foremen are forbidden to talk, and his workmen are specially imported negroes who do not understand the English language."

"But," persisted Mr. Boon, "how, then, do you account for the nuggets scattered over the mountain? And, besides, what object could Dr. Syx have in pretending that there is free metal to be had for the digging?"

"He may have salted the mountain, for all I know," said Hall. "As for his object, I confess I am entirely in the dark, but, for all that, I am convinced that we shall find no more metal if we dig ten miles for it."

"Nonsense," said the President; "if we keep on we shall strike it. Did not Dr. Syx himself admit that he found no free artemisium until his tunnel had reached the core of the peak? We must go as deep as he has gone before we give up."

"I fear the depths he attains are beyond most people's reach," was Hall's answer, while a thoughtful look crossed his clear-cut brow, "but since you desire it, of course the work shall go on. I should like, however, to change the direction of the tunnel."

"Certainly," replied Mr. Boon; "bore in whatever direction you think proper, only don't despair."

About a month after this conversation Andrew Hall, with whom a community of tastes in many things had made me intimately acquainted, asked me one morning to accompany him into his tunnel.

"I want to have a trusty friend at my elbow," he said, "for, unless I am a dreamer, something remarkable will happen within the next hour, and two witnesses are better than one."

A Friendly Investigator—Andrew Hall proposes to Solve the Mystery

I knew Hall was not the person to make such a remark carelessly, and my curiosity was intensely excited, but, knowing his peculiarities, I did not press him for an explanation. When we arrived at the head of the tunnel I was surprised at finding no workmen there.

"I stopped blasting some time ago," said Hall, in explanation, "for a reason which, I hope, will become evident to you very soon. Lately I have been boring very slowly, and yesterday I paid off the men and dismissed them with the announcement, which I am confident President Boon will sanction after he hears by reports of this morning's work, that the tunnel is abandoned. You see, I am now using a drill which I can manage without assistance. I believe the work is almost completed, and I want you to witness the end of it."

He then carefully applied the drill, which noiselessly screwed its nose into the rock. When it had sunk to a depth of a few inches he withdrew it, and, taking a hand-drill capable of making a hole not more than an eighth of an inch in diameter, cautiously began boring in the centre of the larger cavity. He had made hardly a hundred turns of the handle when the drill shot through the rock! A gratified smile illuminated his features, and he said in a suppressed voice:

"Don't be alarmed; I'm going to put out the light."

Instantly we were in complete darkness, but being close at Hall's side I could detect his movements. He pulled out the drill, and for half a minute remained motionless as if listening. There was no sound.

"I must enlarge the opening" he whispered, and immediately the faint grating of a sharp tool cutting through the rock informed me of his progress.

"There," at last he said, "I think that will do; now for a look."

I could tell that he had placed his eye at the hole and was gazing with breathless attention. Presently he pulled my sleeve.

"Put your eye here," he whispered, pushing me into the proper position for looking through the hole.

Looking Through a Peep-Hole

At first I could discern nothing except a smoky blue glow. But soon my vision cleared a little, and then I perceived that I was gazing into a narrow tunnel which met ours directly end to end. Glancing along the axis of this gallery I saw, some two hundred yards away, a faint light which evidently indicated the mouth of the tunnel.

At the end where we had met it the mysterious tunnel was considerably widened at one side, as if the excavators had started to change direction and then abandoned the work, and in this elbow I could just see the outlines of two or three flat cars load with broken stone, while a heap of the same material lay near them. Through the centre of the tunnel ran a railway track.

"Do you know what you are looking at?" asked Hall in my ear.

"I begin to suspect," I replied, "that you have accidentally run into Dr. Syx's mine."

"If Dr. Syx had been on his guard this accident wouldn't have happened," replied Hall, with an almost inaudible chuckle.

"I heard you remark a month ago," I said, "that you were changing the direction of your tunnel. Has this been the aims of your labors ever since?"

Discoveries Under Hall's Auspices

"You have hit it," he replied. "Long ago I became convinced that my company was throwing away its money in a vain attempt to strike a load of pure artemisium. But President Boon has great faith in Dr. Syx, and would not give up the work. So I adopted what I regarded as the only practical method of proving the truth of my opinion and saving the company's funds. An electric indicater, of my invention, enabled me to locate the Syx tunnel when I got near it, and I have met it end on, and opened this peep-hole in order to observe the doctor's operations. I feel that such spying is entirely justified in the circumstances. Although I cannot yet explain just how or why I feel sure that Dr. Syx was the cause of the sudden discovery of the surface nuggets, and that he has encouraged the miners for his own ends, until he has brought ruin to thousands who have spent their last cent in driving useless tunnels into this mountain. It is a righteous thing to expose him."

"But," I interposed, "I do not see that you have exposed anything yet except the interior of a tunnel."

"You will see more clearly after a while," was the reply.

Hall now placed his eye again at the aperture, and was unable entirely to repress the exclamation that rose to his lips. He remained staring through the hole for several minutes without uttering a word.

Presently I noticed that the lenses of his eye were illuminated by a ray of light coming through the hole, but he did not stir.

After a long inspection he suddenly applied his ear to the hole and listened intently for at least five minutes. Not a sound was audible to me, but, by an occasional pressure of the hand, Hall signified that some important disclosure was reaching his sense of hearing. At length he removed his ear.

"Pardon me," he whispered, "for keeping you so long in waiting, but what I have just seen and overheard was of a nature to admit of no interruption. He is still talking, and by pressing your ear against the hole you may be able to catch what he says."

"Who is 'he'?"

"Look for yourself."

I placed my eye at the aperture, and almost recoiled with the violence of my surprise. The tunnel before me was brilliantly illuminated, and within three feet of the wall of rock behind which we crouched stood Dr. Syx, his dark profile looking almost satanic in the sharp contrast of light and shadow. He was talking to one of his foremen, and the two were the only visible occupants of the tunnel. Putting my ear to the little opening, I heard his words distinctly:

—"end of their rope. Well, they've spent a pretty lot of money for their experience, and I rather think we shall not be troubled again by artemisium-seekers for some time to come."

Spying On Dr. Syx

The doctor's voice ceased, and instantly I clapped my eye to the hole. He had changed his position so that his black eyes now looked straight at the aperture. My heart was in my mouth, for at first I believed from his expression that he had detected the gleam of my eyeball. But if so, he probably mistook it for a bit of mica in the rock, and paid no further attention. Then his lips moved, and I put my ear again to the hole. He seemed to be replying to a question that the foreman had asked.

"If they do," he said, "they will never guess the real secret."

Thereupon he turned on his heel, kicked a bit of rock off the track, and strode away towards the entrance. The foreman paused long enough to turn out the electric lamp, and then followed the doctor.

"Well," asked Hall, "what have you heard?"

I told him everything.

"It fully corroborates the evidence of my own eyes and ears," he remarked, "and we may count ourselves extremely lucky. It is not likely that Dr. Syx will be heard a second time proclaiming his deception with his own lips. It is plain that he was led to talk as he did to the foreman on account of the latter's having informed him of the sudden discharge of my men this morning. Their presence within ear-shot of our hiding-place during their conversation was, of course, pure accident, and so you can see how kind fortune has been to us. I expected to have to watch and listen and form deductions for a week, at least, before getting the information which five lucky minutes have placed in our hands."

While he was speaking my companion busied himself in carefully plugging up the hole in the rock. When it was closed to his satisfaction he turned on the light in our tunnel.

"Did you observe," he asked, "that there was a second tunnel?"

"What do you say?"

"When the light was on in there I saw the mouth of a small tunnel entering the main one behind the cars on the right. Did you notice it?"

"Oh yes," I replied. "I did observe some kind of a dark hole there, but I paid no attention to it because I was so absorbed in the doctor."

"Well," rejoined Hall, smiling, "it was worth considerably more than a glance. As a subject of thought I find it even more absorbing than Dr. Syx. Did you see the track in it?"

"No," I had to acknowledge, "I did not notice that. But," I continued, a little piqued by his manner, "being a branch of the main tunnel, I don't see anything remarkable in its having a track also."

"It was rather dim in that hole," said Hall, still smiling in a somewhat provoking way, "but the railroad track was there plain enough. And, whether you think it was remarkable or not, I should like to lay you a wager that that track leads to a secret worth a dozen of the one we of have overheard."

"My good friend," I retorted, still smarting a little, "I shall not presume to match my stupidity against your perspicacity. I haven't cat's eyes in the dark."

Hall immediately broke out laughing, and, slapping me good-naturedly on the shoulder, exclaimed:

"Come, come now! If you go to kicking back at a fellow like that, I shall be sorry I ever undertook this adventure."

CHAPTER VI

A Mystery Indeed

hen President Boon had heard our story he promptly approved Halls dismissal of the men. He expressed great surprise that Dr. Syx should have resorted to a deception which had been so disasterous to innocent people, and at first he talked of legal proceedings. But, after thinking the matter over, he concluded that Syx was too powerful to be attacked with success, especially when the only evidence against him was that he had claimed to find artemisium in his mine at a time when, as everybody knew, artemisium actually was found outside the mine. There was no apparent motive for the deception, and no proof of malicious intent. In short, Mr. Boon decided that the best thing for him and his stockholders to do was to keep silent about their losses and await events. And, at Hall's suggestion, he also determined to say nothing to anybody about the discovery he had made.

"It could do no good," said Hall, in making the suggestion, "and it might spoil a plan I have in mind."

"What plan?" asked the President.

"I prefer not to tell just yet," was the reply.

I observed that, in our interview with Mr. Boon, Hall made no reference to the side tunnel to which he had appeared to attach so much importance, and I concluded that he now regarded it as lacking significance. In this I was mistaken.

A few days afterwards I received an invitation from Hall to accompany him once more into the abandoned tunnel.

"I have found out what the side-track means," he said, "and it has plunged me into another mystery so dark and profound that I cannot see my way through it. I must beg you to say no word to any one concerning the thing I am about to show you."

I gave the required promise, and we entered the tunnel, which nobody had visited since our former adventure. Having extinguished our lamp, my companion opened the peep-hole, and a thin ray of light streamed through from the tunnel on the opposite side of the wall. He applied his eye to the hole.

"Yes," he said, quickly stepping back and pushing me into his place, "they are still at it. Look, and tell me what you see."

"I see," I replied, after placing my eye at the aperture, "a gang of men unloading a car which has just come out of the side tunnel, and putting its contents upon another car standing on the track of the main tunnel."

"Yes, and what are they handling?"

"Why, ore, of course."

"And do you see nothing significant in that?"

"To be sure!" I exclaimed. "Why, that ore——"

"Hush! Hush!" admonished Hall, putting his hand over my mouth; "don't talk so loud. Now go on, in a whisper."

"The ore," I resumed, "may have come back from the furnace-room, because the side tunnel turns off so as to run parallel with the other."

"It not only may have come back, it actually has come back," said Hall.

"How can you be sure?"

"Because I have been over the track, and know that it leads to a secret apartment directly under the furnace in which Dr. Syx pretends to melt the ore!"

For a minute after hearing this avowal I was speechless.

"Are you serious?" I asked at length.

Dr. Syx is a Systematic Deceiver

"Perfectly serious. Run your finger along the rock here. Do you perceive a seam? Two days ago, after seeing what you have just witnessed in the Syx tunnel, I carefully cut out a section of the wall, making an aperture large enough to crawl through, and, when I knew the workmen were asleep, I crept in there and examined both tunnels from end to end. But in solving one mystery I have run myself into another infinitely more perplexing."

"How is that?"

"Why does Dr. Syx take such elaborate pains to deceive his visitors, and also the government officers? It is now plain that he conducts no mining operations whatever. This mine of his is a gigantic blind. Whenever inspectors or scientific curiosity seekers visit his mill his mute workmen assume the air of being very busy, the cars laden with his so-called 'ore' rumble out of the tunnel, and their contents are ostentatiously poured into the furnace, or appear to be poured into it, really dropping into a receptacle beneath, to be carried back into the mine again. And then the doctor leads his bulled visitors around to the other side of the furnace and shows them the molten metal coming out in streams. Now what does it all mean? That's what I'd like to find out. What's his game? For, mark you, if he doesn't get artemisium from this pretended ore, he gets

207

it from some other source, and right on this spot, too. There is no doubt about that. The whole world is supplied by Syx's furnace, and Syx feeds his furnace with something that comes from his ten acres of Grand Teton rock. What is that something? How does he get it, and where does he hide it? These are the things I should like to find out."

"Well," I replied, "I fear I can't help you."

"But the difference between you and me," he retorted, "is that you can go to sleep over it, while I shall never get another good night's rest so long as this black mystery remains unsolved."

"What will you do?"

"I don't know exactly what. But I've got a dim idea which may take shape after a while."

Hall was silent for some time; then he suddenly asked:

"Did you ever hear of that queer magic-lantern show with which Dr. Syx entertained Mr. Boon and the members of the financial commission in the early days of the artemisium business?"

"Yes, I've heard the story, but I don't think it was ever made public. The newspapers never got hold of it."

"No, I believe not. Odd thing, wasn't it?"

"Why, yes, very odd, but just like the doctor's eccentric ways, though. He's always doing something to astonish somebody, without any apparent earthly reason. But what put you in mind of that?"

"Free artemisium put me in mind of it," replied Hall, quizically.

"I don't see the connection."

"I'm not sure that I do either, but when you are dealing with Dr. Syx nothing is too improbable to be thought of."

Andrew Hall is Meditating

Hall thereupon fell to musing again, while we returned to the entrance of the tunnel. After he had made everything secure, and slipped the key into his pocket, my companion remarked:

"Don't you think it would be best to keep this latest discovery to ourselves?"

"Certainly."

"Because," he continued, "nobody would be benefitted just now by knowing what we know, and to expose the worthlessness of the 'ore' might cause a panic. The public is a queer animal, and never gets scared at just the thing you expect will alarm it, but always at something else."

We had shaken hands and were separating when Hall stopped me.

"Do you believe in alchemy?" he asked.

"That's an odd question from you," I replied. "I thought alchemy was exploded long ago."

"Well," he said, slowly, "I suppose it has been exploded, but then, you know, an explosion may sometimes be a kind of instantaneous education, breaking up old things but revealing new ones."

CHAPTER VII
The Age of Artemisium

Important business called me East soon after the meeting with Hall described in the foregoing chapter, and before I again saw the Grand Teton very stirring events had taken place.

As the reader is aware, Dr. Syx's agreement with the various governments limited the output of his mine. An international commission, continually in session in New York, adjusted the differences arising among the nations concerning financial affairs, and alloted to each the proper amount of artemisium for coinage. Of course, this amount varied from time to time, but a fair average could easily be maintained. The gradual increase of wealth, in houses, machinery, manufactured and artistic products called for a corresponding increase in the circulating medium; but this, too, was easily provided for. An equally painstaking supervision was exercised over the amount of the precious metal which Dr. Syx was permitted to supply to the markets for use in the arts. On this side, also, the demand gradually increased; but the wonderful Teton mine seemed equal to all calls upon its resources.

After the failure of the mining operations there was a moderate revival of the efforts to reduce the Teton ore, but no success cheered the experimenters. Prospectors also wandered all over the earth looking for pure artemisium, but in vain. The general public, knowing nothing of what Hall had discovered, and still believing Syx's story that he also had found pure artemisium in his mine, accounted for the failure of the tunneling operations on the supposition that the metal, in a free state, was excessively rare, and that Dr. Syx had had the luck to strike the only vein of it that the Grand Teton contained. As if to give countenance to this opinion, Dr. Syx now announced, in the most public manner, that he had been deceived again, and that the vein of free metal he had struck being exhausted, no other had appeared. Accordingly, he said, he must henceforth rely exclusively, as in the beginning, upon reduction of the ore.

Artemisium had proved itself an immense boon to mankind, and the new era of commercial prosperity which it had ushered in already exceeded everything that the world had known in the past. School-children learned that human civilization had taken five great strides, known respectively, beginning at the bottom, as the "age of stone," the "age of bronze," the "age of iron," the "age of gold," and the "age of artemisium."

The Mobs Object to the Restriction of the World's Currencies

Nevertheless, sources of dissatisfaction finally began to appear, and, after the nature of such things, they developed with marvellous rapidity. People began to grumble about "contraction of the currency." In every country there arose a party which demanded "free money." Demagogues pointed to the brief reign of paper money after the demonetization of gold as a happy period, when the people had enjoyed their rights, and the "money barons"—borrowing a term from nineteenth-century history—were kept at bay.

Then came denunciations of the international commission for restricting the coinage. Dr. Syx was described as "a devil-fish sucking the veins of the planet and holding it helpless in the grasp of his tentacular billions." In the United States meetings of agitators passed furious resolutions, denouncing the government, assailing the rich, cursing Dr. Syx, and calling upon "the oppressed" to rise and "take their own." The final outcome was, of course, violence. Mobs had to be suppressed by military force. But the most dramatic scene in the tragedy occurred at the Grand Teton. Excited by inflammatory speeches and printed documents, several thousand armed men assembled in the neighborhood of Jenny's Lake and prepared to attack the Syx mine. For some reason the military guard had been depleted, and the mob, under the leadership of a man named Bings, who showed no little talent as a commander and strategist, surprised the small force of soldiers and locked them up in their own guard-house.

Telegraphic communication having been cut off by the astute Bings, a fierce attack was made on the mine. The assailants swarmed up the sides of the canyon, and attempted to break in through the foundation of the buildings. But the masonry was stronger than they had anticipated, and the attack failed. Sharp-shooters then climbed the neighboring heights, and kept up an incessant peppering of the walls with conical bullets driven at four thousand feet per second.

No reply come from the gloomy structure. The huge column of black smoke rose uninterruptedly into the sky, and the noise of the great engine never ceased for an instant. The mob gathered closer on all sides and redoubled the fire of the rifles, to which was now added the belching of several machine-guns. Ragged holes began to appear in the walls, and at the sight of these the assailants yelled with delight. It was evident that the mill could not long withstand so

211

destructive a bombardment. If the besiegers had possessed artillery they would have knocked the buildings into splinters within twenty minutes. As it was, they would need a whole day to win their victory.

A Riot and An Attack on the Mill of Dr. Syx

Suddenly it became evident that the besieged were about to take a hand in the fight. Thus far they had not shown themselves or fired a shot, but now a movement was perceived on the roof, and the projecting arms of some kind of machinery became visible. Many marksmen concentrated their fire upon the mysterious objects, but apparently with little effect. Bings, mounted on a rock, so as to command a clear view of the field, was on the point of ordering a party to rush forward with axes and beat down the formidable doors, when there came a blinding flash from the roof, something swished through the air, and a gust of heat met the assailants in the face. Bings dropped dead from his perch, and then, as if the scythe of the Destroyer had swung downward, and to the right and left in quick succession, the close-packed mob was leveled, rank after rank, until the few survivors crept behind rocks for refuge.

Instantly the atmospheric broom swept up and down the canyon and across the mountain's flanks, and the marksmen fell in bunches like shaken grapes. Nine-tenths of the besiegers were destroyed within ten minutes after the first movement had been noticed on the roof. Those who survived owed their escape to the rocks which concealed them, and they lost no time in crawling off into neighboring chasms, and, as soon as they were beyond eye-shot from the mill, they fled with panic speed.

Then the towering form of Dr. Syx appeared at the door. Emerging without sign of fear or excitement, he picked his way among his fallen enemies, and, approaching the military guard-house, undid the fastening and set the imprisoned soldiers free.

"I think I am paying rather dear for my whistle," he said, with a characteristic sneer, to Captain Carter, the commander of the troop. "It seems that I must not only defend my own people and property when attacked by mob force, but must also come to the rescue of the soldiers whose pay-rolls are met from my pocket."

The captain made no reply, and Dr. Syx strode back to the works. When the released soldiers saw what had occurred their amazement had no bounds. It was necessary at once to dispose of the dead, and this was no easy undertaking for their small force. However, they accomplished it, and at the beginning of their work made a most surprising discovery.

"How's this, Jim?" said one of the men to his comrade, as they stooped to lift the nearest victim of Dr. Syx's withering fire. "What's this fellow got all over him?"

"Artemisium! 'pon my soul!" responded Jim, staring at the body. "He's all coated over with it."

End of the Riot

Immediately from all sides came similar exclamations. Every man who had fallen was covered with a film of the precious metal, as if he had been dipped into an electrolytic bath. Clothing seemed to have been charred, and the metallic atoms had penetrated the flesh of the victims. The rocks all around the battle-field were similarly veneered.

"It looks to me," said Captain Carter, "as if old Syx had turned one of his spouts of artemisium into a hose-pipe and soaked 'em with it."

"That's it," chimed in a Lieutenant, "that's exactly what he's done."

"Well," returned the captain, "if he can do that, I don't see what use he's got for us here."

"Probably he don't want to waste the stuff," said the Lieutenant. "What do you suppose it cost him to plate this crowd?"

"I guess a month's pay for the whole troop wouldn't cover the expense. It's costly, but then—gracious! Wouldn't I have given something for the doctor's hose when I was a youngster campaigning in the Philippines in '99?"

The story of the marvelous way in which Dr. Syx defended his mill became the sensation of the world for many days. The hose-pipe theory, struck off on the spot by Captain Carter, seized the popular fancy, and was generally accepted without further question. There was an element of the ludicrous which robbed the tragedy of some of its horror. Moreover, no one could deny that Dr. Syx was well within his rights in defending himself by any means when so savagely attacked, and his triumphant success, no less than the ingenuity which was supposed to underlie it, placed him in an heroic light which he had not hitherto enjoyed.

As to the demagogues who were responsible for the outbreak and its terrible consequence, they slunk out of the public eye, and the result of the battle at the mine seemed to have been a clearing up of the atmosphere, such as a thunderstorm effects at the close of a season of foul weather.

But now, little as men guessed it, the beginning of the end was close at hand.

CHAPTER VIII

The Detective of Science

he morning of my arrival at Grand Teton station, on my return from the East, Andrew Hall met me with a warm greeting.

"I have been anxiously expecting you," he said, "for I have made some progress towards solving the great mystery. I have not yet reached a conclusion, but I hope soon to let you into the entire secret. In the meantime you can aid me with your companionship, if in no other way, for, since the defeat of the mob, this place has been mighty lonesome. The Grand Teton is a spot that people who have no particular business out here carefully avoid. I am on speaking terms with Dr. Syx, and occasionally, when there is a party to be shown around, I visit his works, and make the best possible use of my eyes. Captain Carter of the military is a capital fellow, and I like to hear his stories of the war in Luzon forty years ago, but I want somebody to whom I can occasionally confide things, and so you are as welcome as moonlight in harvest-time."

"Tell me something about that wonderful fight with the mob. Did you see it?"

"I did. I had got wind of what Bings intended to do while I was down at Pocotello, and I hurried up here to warn the soldiers, but unfortunately I came too late. Finding the military cooped up in the guard-house and the mob masters of the situation, I kept out of sight on the side of the Teton, and watched the siege with my binocular. I think there was very little of the spectacle that I missed."

"What of the mysterious force that the doctor employed to sweep off the assailants?"

"Of course, Captain Carter's suggestion that Syx turned molten artemisium from his furnace into a hose-pipe and sprayed the enemy with it is ridiculous. But it is much easier to dismiss Carter's theory than to substitute a better one. I saw the doctor on the roof with a gang of black workmen, and I noticed the flash of polished metal turned rapidly this way and that, but there was some intervening obstacle which prevented me from getting a good view of the mechanism employed. It certainly bore no resemblance to a hose-pipe, or anything of that kind. No emanation was visible from the machine, but it was stupifying to see the mob melt down."

"How about the coating of the bodies with artemisium?"

"There you are back on the hose-pipe again," laughed Hall. "But, to tell you the truth, I'd rather be excused from expressing an opinion on that operation in wholesale electro-plating just at present. I've the ghost of an idea what it means, but let me test my theory a little before I formulate it. In the meanwhile, won't you take a stroll with me?"

"Certainly; nothing could please me better," I replied. "Which way shall we go?"

"To the top of the Grand Teton."

"What! are you seized with the mountain-climbing fever?"

"Not exactly, but I have a particular reason for wishing to take a look from that pinnacle."

"I suppose you know the real apex of the peak has never been trodden by man?"

"I do know it, but it is just that apex that I am determined to have under my feet for ten minutes. The failure of others is no argument for us."

"Just as you say," I rejoined. "But I suppose there is no indiscretion in asking whether this little climb has any relation to the mystery?"

"If it didn't have an important relation to the clearing up of that dark thing I wouldn't risk my neck in such an undertaking," was the reply.

Wandering Over the Great Teton Peak

Accordingly, the next morning we set out for the peak. All previous climbers, as we were aware, had attacked it from the west. That seemed the obvious thing to do, because the westward slopes of the mountain, while very steep, are less abrupt than those which face the rising sun. In fact, the eastern side of the Grand Teton appears to be absolutely unclimable. But both Hall and I had had experience with rock climbing in the Alps and the Dolomites, and we knew that what looked like the hardest places sometimes turn out to be next to the easiest. Accordingly we decided—the more particularly because it would save time, but also because we yielded to the common desire to outdo our predecessors—to try to scale the giant right up his face.

We carried a very light but exceedingly strong rope, about five hundred feet long, wore nail-shod shoes, and had each a metal-pointed staff and a small hatchet in lieu of the regular mountaineer's ax. Advancing at first along the broken ridge between two gorges we gradually approached the steeper part of the Teton, where the cliffs

looked so shear and smooth that it seemed no wonder that nobody
had ever tried to scale them. The air was deliciously clear and the
sky wonderfully blue above the mountains, and the moon, a few days
past its last quarter, was visible in the soughtwest, its pale crescent
face slightly blued by the atmosphere, as it always appears when
seen in daylight.

> *"Slow westering, a phantom sail—*
> *The lonely soul of yesterday."*

Behind us, somewhat north of east, lay the Syx works, with their
black smoke rising almost vertically in the still air. Suddenly, as we
stumbled along on the rough surface, something whized past my face
and fell on the rock at my feet. I looked at the strange missile, that
had come like a meteor out of open space, with astonishment.

It was a bird, a beautiful specimen of the scarlet tanagers, which
I remembered the early explorers had found inhabiting the Teton
canyons, their brilliant plummage borrowing spendor from contrast
with the gloomy surroundings. It lay motionless, its outstretched
wings having a curious shriveled aspect, while the flaming color of
the breast was half obliterated with smutty patches. Stooping to pick
it up, I noticed a slight bronzing, which instantly recalled to my mind
the peculiar appearance of the victims of the attack on the mine.

"Look here!" I called to Hall, who was several yards in advance.
He turned, and I held up the bird by a wing.

"Where did you get that?" he asked.

"It fell at my feet a moment ago."

Hall glanced in a startled manner at the sky, and then down the
slope of the mountain.

"Did you notice in what direction it was flying?" he asked.

"No, it dropped so close that it almost grazed my nose. I saw
nothing of it until it made me blink."

Andrew Hall Does Not Tell Everything

"I have been heedless," muttered Hall under his breath. At the
time I did not notice the singularity of his remark, my attention being
absorbed in contemplating the unfortunate tanager.

"Look how its feathers are scorched," I said.

"I know it," Hall replied, without glancing at the bird.

"And it is covered with a film of artemisium," I added, a little
piqued by his abstraction.

"I know that, too."

217

"See here, Hall," I exclaimed, "are you trying to make game of me?"

"Not at all, my dear fellow," he replied, dropping his cogitation. "Pray forgive me. But this is no new phenomenon to me. I have picked up birds in that condition on this mountain before. There is a terrible mystery here, but I am slowly letting light into it, and if we succeed in reaching the top of the peak I have good hope that the illumination will increase."

"Here now," he added a moment later, sitting down upon a rock and thrusting the blade of his penknife into a crevice, "what do you think of this?"

He held up a little nugget of pure artemisium, and then went on:

"You know that all this slope was swept as clean as a Dutch housewife's kitchen floor by the thousands of miners and prospectors who swarmed over it a year or two ago, and do you suppose they would have missed such a tidbit if it had been here then?"

"Dr. Syx must have been salting the mountain again," I suggested.

"Well," replied Hall, with a significant smile, "if the doctor hasn't salted it somebody else has, that's plain enough. But perhaps you would like to know precisely what I expect to find out when we get on the topknot of the Teton."

"I should certainly be delighted to learn the object of our journey," I said. "Of course, I'm only going along for company and for the fun of the thing; but you know you can count on me for substantial aid whenever you need it."

"It is because you are so willing to let me keep my own counsel," he rejoined, "and to wait for things to ripen before compelling me to disclose them, that I like to have you with me at critical times. Now, as to the object of this break-neck expedition, whose risks you understand as fully as I do, I need not assure you that it is of supreme importance to the success of my plans. In a word, I hope to be able to look down into a part of Dr. Syx's mill which, if I am not mistaken, no human eye except his and those of his most trustworthy helpers has even been permitted to see. And if I see there what I fully expect to see, I shall have got a long step nearer to a great fortune."

"Good!" I cried. "*En avant,* then! We are losing time."

CHAPTER IX

The Top of the Grand Teton

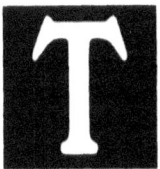

he climbing soon became difficult, until at length we were going up hand over hand, taking advantage of crevices and knobs which an inexperienced eye would have regarded as incapable of affording a grip for the fingers or a support for the toes. Presently we arrived at the foot of a stupendous presipice, which was absolutely insurmountable by an ordinary method of ascent. Parts of it overhung, and everywhere the face of the rock was too free from irregularities to afford any footing, except to a fly.

"Now, to borrow the expression of old Bunyan, we are hard to put to it," I remarked. "If you will go to the left I will take up the right and see if there is any chance of getting up."

"I don't believe we could find any place easier than this," Hall replied, "and so up we go where we are."

"Have you a pair of wings concealed about you?" I asked, laughing at his folly.

"Well, something nearly as good," he responded, unstrapping his napsack. He produced a silken bag, which he unfolded on the rock.

"A balloon!" I exclaimed. "But how are you going to inflate it?"

For reply Hall showed me a receptacle which, he said, contained liquid hydrogen, and which was furnished with a device for retarding the volatilization of the liquid so that it could be carried with little loss.

"You remember I have a small laboratory in the abandoned mine," he explained, "where we used to manufacture liquid air for blasting. This balloon I made for our present purpose. It will just suffice to carry up our rope, and a small but practically unbreakable grapple of hardened gold. I calculate to send the grapple to the top of the precipice with the balloon, and when it has obtained a firm hold in the riven rock there we can ascend, sailor fashion. You see the rope has knots, and I know your muscles are as trustworthy in such work as my own."

There was a slight breeze from the eastward, and the current of air slanting up the face of the peak assisted the balloon in mounting with its burden, and favored us by promptly swinging the little airship, with the grapple swaying beneath it, over the brow of the cliff into the atmospheric eddy above. As soon as we saw that the grapple was well over the edge we pulled upon the rope. The balloon instantly shot into view with the anchor dancing, but, under the

219

influence of the wind, quickly returned to its former position behind the projecting brink. The grapple had failed to take hold.

"'Try, try again' must be our motto now," muttered Hall.

We tried several times with the same result, although each time we slightly shifted our position. At last the grapple caught.

"Now, all together!" cried my companion, and simultaneously we threw our weight upon the slender rope. The anchor apparently did not give an inch.

"Let me go first," said Hall, pushing me aside as I caught the first knot above my head. "It's my device, and it's only fair that I should have the first try."

Climbing Teton Peak and Trying for Its Summit

In a minute he was many feet up the wall, climbing swiftly hand over hand, but occasionally stopping and twisting his leg around the rope while he took breath.

"It's easier than I expected," he called down, when he had ascended about one hundred feet. "Here and there the rock offers a little hold for the knees."

I watched him, breathless with anxiety, and as he got higher, my imagination pictured the little gold grapple, invisible above the brow of the precipice, with perhaps a single thin prong wedged into a crevice, and slowly ploughing its way towards the edge with each impulse of the climber, until but another pull was needed to set it flying! So vivid was my fancy that I tried to banish it by noticing that a certain knot in the rope remained just at the level of my eyes, where it had been from the start. Hall was now fully two hundred feet above the ledge on which I stood, and was rapidly nearing the top of the precipice. In a minute more he would be safe.

Suddenly he shouted, and, glancing up with a leap of the heart, I saw that he was falling! He kept his face to the rock, and came down feet foremost. It would be useless to attempt any description of my feelings; I would not go through that experience again for the price of a battleship. Yet it lasted less than a second. He had dropped not more than ten feet when the fall was arrested.

"All right!" he called, cheerily. "No harm done! It was only a slip."

But what a slip! If the balloon had not carried the anchor several yards back from the edge it would have had no opportunity to catch another hold as it shot forward. And how could we know that the second hold would prove more secure than the first? Hall did not hesitate, however, for one instant. Up he went again. But, in fact, his

220

best chance was in going up, for he was within four yards of the top when the mishap occurred. With a sigh of relief I saw him at last throw his arm over the verge and then wriggle his body upon the ledge. A few seconds later he was lying on his stomach, with his face over the edge, looking down at me. "Come on!" he shouted. "It's all right."

When I had pulled myself over the brink at his side I grasped his hand and pressed it without a word. We understand one another.

"It was pretty close to a miracle," he remarked at last. "Look at this."

The rock over which the grapple had slipped was deeply scored by the unyielding point of the metal, and exactly at the verge of the precipice the prong had wedged itself into a narrow crack, so firmly that we had to chip away the stone in order to release it. If it had slipped a single inch farther before taking hold it would have been all over with my friend.

The Summit Attained by the Two Explorers

Such experiences shake the strongest nerves, and we sat on the shelf we had attained for fully a quarter of an hour before we ventured to attack the next precipice which hung beetling directly above us. It was not as lofty as the one we had just ascended, but it impended to such a degree that we saw we should have to climb our rope while it swung free in the air!

Luckily we had little difficulty in getting a grip for the prongs, and we took every precaution to test the security of the anchorage, not only putting our combined weight repeatedly upon the rope, but flipping and jerking it with all our strength. The grapple resisted every effort to dislodge it, and finally I started up, insisting on my turn as leader.

The height I had to ascend did not exceed one hundred feet, but that is a very great distance to climb on a swinging rope, without a wall within reach to assist by its friction and occasional friendly projections. In a little while my movements, together with the effect of the slight wind, had imparted a most distressing oscilation to the rope. This sometimes carried me with a nerve-shaking bang against a prominent point of the precipice, where I would dislodge loose fragments that kept Hall dodging for his life, and then I would swing out, apparently beyond the brow of the cliff below, so that, as I involuntarily glanced downward, I seemed to be hanging in free space, while the steep mountainside, looking ten times steeper than it really was, resembled the vertical wall of an absolutely bottomless abyss, as if I were suspended over the edge of the world.

I avoided thinking of what the grapple might be about, and in my haste to get through with the awful experience I worked myself fairly out of breath, so that, when at last I reached the rounded brow of the cliff, I had to stop and cling there for fully a minute before I could summon strength enough to lift myself over it.

When I was assured that the grapple was still securely fastened I signalled to Hall and he soon stood at my side, exclaiming, as he wiped the perspiration from his face:

"I think I'll try wings next time!"

But our difficulties had only begun. As we had foreseen, it was a case of Alp above Alp, to the very limit of human strength and patience. However, it would have been impossible to go back. In order to descend the two precipices we had surmounted it would have been necessary to leave our life-lines clinging to the rocks, and we had not rope enough to do that. If we could not reach the top we were lost.

A View from the Summit and Spying on Dr. Syx

Having refreshed ourselves with a bite to eat and a little stimulant, we resumed the climb. After several hours of the most exhausting work I have ever performed we pulled our weary limbs upon the narrow ridge, but a few square yards in area, which constitutes the apex of the Grand Teton. A little below, on the opposite side of a steep-walled gap which divides the top of the mountain into two parts, we saw the singular enclosure of stones which the early white explorers found there, and which they ascribed to the Indians, although nobody has ever known who built it or what purpose it served.

The view was, of course, superb, but while I was admiring it in all its wonderful extent and variety, Hall who had immediately pulled out his binocular, was busy inspecting the Syx works, the top of whose great tufted smoke column was thousands of feet beneath our level. Jackson's Lake, Jenny's Lake, Leigh's Lake, and several lakelets glittered in the sunlight amid the pale grays and greens of Jackson's Hole, while many a bending reach of the Snake River shown amid the wastes of sage-brush and rock.

"There!" suddenly exclaimed Hall, I thought I should find it."

"What?"

"Take a look through my glass at the roof of Syx's mill. Look just in the centre."

"Why, it's open in the middle!" I cried as soon as I had put the glass to my eyes. "There's a big circular hole in the centre of the roof."

"Look inside! Look inside!" repeated Hall, impatiently.

"I see nothing there except something bright."

"Do you call it nothing because it is bright?"

"Well, no," I replied, laughing. "What I mean is that I see nothing that I can make anything of except a shining object, and all I can make of that is that it is bright."

"You've been in the Syx works many times, haven't you?"

"Yes."

"Did you ever see the opening in the roof?"

"Never."

"Then Dr. Syx doesn't show his visitors everything that is to be seen."

"Evidently not since, as we know, he concealed the double tunnel and the room under the furnace."

Dr. Syx An Alchemist

"Dr. Syx has concealed a bigger secret than that," Hall responded, "and the Grand Teton has helped me to a glimpse of it. For several minutes my friend was absorbed in thought. Then he broke out:

"I tell you he's the most wonderful man in the world!"

"Who, Dr. Syx? Well, I've long thought that."

"Yes, but I mean in a different way from what you are thinking of. Do you remember my asking you once if you believed in alchemy?"

"I remember being greatly surprised by your question to that effect."

"Well, now," said Hall, rubbing his hands with a satisfied air, while his eyes glanced keen and bright with the reflection of some passing thought, "Max Syx is greater than any alchemist that ever lived. If those old fellows in the dark ages had accomplished everything they set out to do, they would have been of no more consequence in comparison with our black-browed friend down yonder than—than my head is of consequence in comparison with the moon."

"I fear you flatter the man in the moon," was my laughing reply.

"No, I don't," returned Hall, "and some day you'll admit it."

"Well, what about that something that shines down there? You seem to see more in it than I can."

Dr. Syx is Suspicious About the Climb to the Summit

"But my companion had fallen into a reverie and didn't hear my question. He was gazing abstractedly at the faint image of the wandering moon, now nearing the mountain-top in the distance. Presently his mind seemed to return to the old magnet, and he whirled about and glanced down at the Syx mill. The column of smoke was diminishing in volume, an indication that the engine was about to enjoy one of its periodical rests. The irregularity of these stoppages had always been a subject of remark among practical engineers. The hours of labor were exceedingly erratic, but the engine had never been known to work at night, except on one occasion, and then only for a few minutes, when it was suddenly stopped on account of a fire.

Just as Hall resumed his inspection two huge quarter spheres, which had been resting wide apart on the roof, moved towards one another until their arched sections met over the circular aperture which they covered like the dome of an observatory.

"I expected it," Hall remarked. "But come, it is mid-afternoon, and we shall need all of our time to get safely down before the light fades."

Dr. Syx Speaks to Them

As I have already explained, it would not have been possible for us to return the way we came. We determined to descend the comparatively easy western slopes of the peak, and pass the night on that side of the mountain. Letting ourselves down with the rope into the hollow way that divides the summit of the Teton into two pinnacles, we had no difficulty in descending by the route followed by all previous climbers. The weather was fine, and, having found good shelter among the rocks, we passed the night in comfort. The next day we succeeded in swinging round upon the eastern flank of the Teton, below the more formidable cliffs, and, just at nightfall, we arrived at the station. As we passed the Syx mine the doctor himself confronted us. There was a very displeasing look on his dark countenance, and his sneer was strongly marked.

"So you have been on top of the Teton?" he said.

"Yes," replied Hall, very blandly, "and if you have a taste for that sort of thing I should advise you to go up. The view is immense, as fine as the best in the Alps."

"Pretty ingenious plan, that balloon of yours," continued the doctor, still looking black.

"Thank you," Hall replied, more suavely than ever. "I've been planning that a long time. You probably don't know that mountaineering used to be my chief amusement."

The doctor turned away without pursuing the conversation.

"I could kick myself," Hall muttered as soon as Dr. Syx was out of earshot. "If my absurd wish to outdo others had not blinded me, I should have known that he would see us going up this side of the peak, particularly with the balloon to give us away. However, what's done can't be undone. He may not really suspect the truth, and if he does he can't help himself, even though he is the richest man in the world."

Strange Fate of a Kite

"Are you ready for another tramp?" was Andrew Hall's greeting when we meet early on the morning following our return from the peak.

"Certainly I am. What is your programme for to-day?"

"I wish to test the flying qualities of a kite which I have constructed since our return last night."

"You don't allow the calls of sleep to interfere very much with your activity."

"I haven't much time for sleep just now," replied Hall, without smiling. "The kite test will carry us up the flanks of the Teton, but I am not going to try for the top this time. If you will come along I'll ask you to help me by carrying and operating a light transit. I shall carry another myself. I am desirous to get the elevation that the kite attains and certain other data that will be of use to me. We will make a detour towards the south, for I don't want old Syx's suspicions to be prodded any more."

"What interest can he have in your kite-flying?"

"The same interest that a burglar has in the rap of a policeman's night-stick."

"Then your experiment to-day has some connection with the solution of the great mystery?"

"My dear fellow," said Hall, laying his hand on my shoulder, "until I see the end of that mystery I shall think of nothing else."

In a few hours we were clambering over the broken rocks on the southeastern flank of the Teton at an elevation of about three thousand feet above the level of Jackson's Hole. Finally Hall paused and began to put his kite together. It was a small box-shaped affair, very light in construction, with paper sides.

"In order to diminish the chances of Dr. Syx noticing what we are about," he said, as he worked away, "I have covered the kite with sky-blue paper. This, together with distance, will probably insure us against his notice."

In a few minutes the kite was ready. Having ascertained the direction of the wind with much attention, he stationed me with my transit on a commanding rock, and sought another post for himself at a distance of two hundred yards, which he carefully measured with a gold tape. My instructions were to keep the telescope on the kite as soon as it had attained a considerable height, and to note the angle of elevation and the horizontal angle with the base line joining our points of observation.

"Be particularly careful," was Hall's injunction, "and if anything happens to the kite by all means note the angles at that instant."

As soon as we had fixed our stations Hall began to pay out the string, and the kite rose very swiftly. As it sped away into the blue it was soon practically invisible to the naked eye, although the telescope of the transit enabled me to follow it with ease.

Aerial Trigonomolry—Hall Reticent

Glancing across now and then at my companion, I noticed that he was having considerable difficulty in, at the same time, managing the kite and manipulating his transit. But as the kite continued to rise and steadied in position his task became easier, until at length he ceased to remove his eye from the telescope while holding the string with outstretched hand.

"Don't lose sight of it now for an instant!" he shouted.

For at least half an hour he continued to manipulate the string, sending the kite now high towards the zenith with a sudden pull, and then letting it drift off. It seemed at last to become almost a fixed point. Very slowly the angles changed, when, suddenly, there was a flash, and to my amazement I saw the paper of the kite shrivel and disappear in a momentary flame, and then the bare sticks came tumbling out of the sky.

"Did you get the angles?" yelled Hall, excitedly.

"Yes; the telescope is still pointed on the spot where the kite disappeared."

"Read them off," he called, "and then get your angle with Syx works."

"All right," I replied, doing as he had requested, and noticing at the same time that he was in the act of putting his watch in his pocket. "Is there anything else?" I asked.

"No, that will do, thank you."

Hall came running over, his face beaming, and with the air of a man who has just hooked a particularly cunning old trout.

"Ah!" he exclaimed, "this has been a great success! I could almost dispense with the calculation, but it is best to be sure."

"What are you about, anyhow?" I asked, "and what was it that happened to the kite?"

"Don't interrupt me just now, please," was the only reply I received.

Mr. Hall Decides to Try Alchemy Too

Thereupon my friend sat down on a rock, pulled out a pad of paper, noted the angles which I had read on the transit, and fell to figuring with feverish haste. In the course of his work he consulted a pocket almanac, then glanced up at the sky, muttered approvingly, and finally leaped to his feet with a half-suppressed "Hurrah!" If I had not known him so well I should have thought that he had gone daft.

"Will you kindly tell me," I asked, "how you managed to set the kite afire?"

Hall laughed heartily. "You thought it was a trick, did you?" said he. "Well, it was no trick, but a very beautiful demonstration. You surely haven't forgotten the scarlet tanager that gave you such a surprise the day before yesterday."

"Do you mean," I exclaimed, startled at the suggestion, "that the fate of the bird had any connection with the accident to your kite?"

"Accident isn't precisely the right word," replied Hall. "The two things are as intimately related as own brothers. If you should care to hunt up the kite sticks, you would find that they, too, are now artemisium plated."

"This is getting too deep for me," was all that I could say.

"I am not absolutely confident that I have touched bottom myself," said Hall, "but I'm going to make another dive, and if I don't bring up treasures greater than Vanderdecken found at the bottom of the sea, then Dr. Syx is even a more wonderful human mystery than I have thought him to be."

"What do you propose to do next?"

"To shake the dust of the Grand Teton from my shoes and go to San Francisco, where I have an extensive laboratory."

"So you are going to try a little alchemy yourself, are you?"

"Perhaps; who knows? At any rate, my good friend, I am forever indebted to you for your assistance, and even more for your discretion, and if I succeed you shall be the first person in the world to hear the news."

CHAPTER X

Better Than Alchemy

come now to a part of my narrative which would have been deemed altogether incredible in those closing years of the nineteenth century that witnessed the first steps towards the solution of the deepest mysteries of the ether, although men even then held in their hands, without knowing it, powers which, after they had been mastered and before use had made them familiar, seemed no less than godlike.

For six months after Hall's departure for San Francisco I heard nothing from him. Notwithstanding my intense desire to know what he was doing, I did not seek to disturb him in his retirement. In the meantime things ran on as usual in the world, only a ripple being caused by renewed discoveries of small nuggets of artemisium on the Tetons, a fact which recalled to my mind the remark of my friend when he dislodged a flake of the metal from a crevice during our ascent of the peak. At last one day I received this telegram at my office in New York:

"SAN FRANCISCO, May 16, 1940.
"Come at once. The mystery is solved.

"(Signed) HALL."

As soon as I could pack a grip I was flying westward one hundred miles an hour. On reaching San Francisco, which had made enormous strides since the opening of the twentieth century, owing to the extension of our Oriental possessions, and which already ranked with New York and Chicago among the financial capitals of the world, I hastened to Hall's laboratory. He was there expecting me, and, after a hearty greeting, during which his elation over his success was manifest, he said:

"I am compelled to ask you to make a little journey. I found it impossible to secure the necessary privacy here, and, before opening my experiments, I selected a site for a new laboratory in an unfrequented spot among the mountains this side of Lake Tahoe. You will be the first man, with the exception of my two devoted assistants, to see my apparatus, and you shall share the sensation of the critical experiment."

"Then you have not yet completed your solution of the secret?"

"Yes, I have; for I am as certain of the result as if I had seen it, but I thought you were entitled to be in with me at the death."

A Visit to the Hall Laboratory. Experimenting With a Gold Cathode

From the nearest railway station we took horses to the laboratory, which occupied a secluded but most beautiful site at an elevation of about six thousand feet above sea-level. With considerable surprise I noticed a building surmounted with a dome, recalling what we had seen from the Grand Teton on the roof of Dr. Syx's mill. Hall, observing my look, smiled significantly, but said nothing. The laboratory proper occupied a smaller building adjoining the domed structure. Hall led the way into an apartment having but a single door and illuminated by a skylight.

"This is my sanctum sanctorum," he said, "and you are the first outsider to enter it. Seat yourself comfortably while I proceed to unveil a little corner of the artemisium mystery."

Near one end of the room, which was about thirty feet in length, was a table, on which lay a glass tube about two inches in diameter and thirty inches long. In the farther end of the tube gleamed a lump of yellow metal, which I took to be gold. Hall and I were seated near another table about twenty-five feet distant from the tube, and on this table was an apparatus finished with a concave mirror, whose optical axis was directed towards the tube. It occurred to me at once that this apparatus would be suitable for experimenting with electric waves. Wires ran from it to the floor, and in the cellar beneath was audible the beating of an engine. My companion made an adjustment or two, and then remarked:

"Now, keep your eyes on the lump of gold in the farther end of the tube yonder. The tube is exhausted of air, and I am about to concentrate upon the gold an intense electric influence, which will have the effect of making it a kind of cathode pole. I only use this term for the sake of illustration. You will recall that as long ago as the days of Crookes it was known that a cathode in an exhausted tube would project particles, or atoms, of its substance away in straight lines. Now watch!"

I fixed my attention upon the gold, and presently saw it enveloped in a most beautiful violet light. This grew more intense, until, at times, it was blinding, while, at the same moment, the interior of the tube seemed to have become charged with a luminous vapor of a delicate pinkish hue.

"Watch! Watch!" said Hall. "Look at the nearer end of the tube!"

"Why, it's becoming coated with gold!" I exclaimed.

Continuation of the Experiment

He smiled, but made no reply. Still the strange process continued. The pink vapor became so dense that the lump of gold was no longer visible, although the eye of violet light glared piercingly through the colored fog. Every second the deposit of metal, shining like a mirror, increased, until suddenly there came a curious whistling sound. Hall, who had been adjusting the mirror, jerked away his hand and gave it a flip, as if hot water had spattered it, and then the light in the tube quickly died away, the vapor escaped, filling the room with a peculiar stimulating odor, and I perceived that the end of the glass tube had been melted through, and the molten gold was slowly dripping from it.

"I carried it a little too far," said Hall, ruefully rubbing the back of his hand, "and when the glass gave way under the atomic bombardment a few atoms of gold visited my bones. But there is no harm done. You observed that the instant the air reached the cathode, as I for convenience call the electrified mass of gold, the action ceased."

"But your anode, to continue your simile," I said, "is constantly exposed to the air."

"True," he replied, "but in the first place, of course, this is not really an anode, just as the other is not really a cathode. As science advances we are compelled, for a time, to use old terms in a new sense until a fresh nomenclature can be invented. But we are now dealing with a form of electric action more subtle in its effects than any at present described in the text-books and the transactions of learned societies. I have not yet even attempted to work out the theory of it. I am only concerned with its facts."

"But wonderful as the exhibition you have given is, I do not see," I said, "how it concerns Dr. Syx and his artemisium."

"Listen," replied Hall, settling back in his chair after disconnecting his apparatus. "You no doubt have been told how one night the Syx engine was heard working for a few minutes, the first and only night work it was ever known to have done, and how, hardly had it started up when a fire broke out in the mill, and the engine was instantly stopped. Now there is a very remarkable story connected with that, and it will show you how I got my first clew to the mystery, although it was rather a mere suspicion than a clew, for at first I could make nothing out of it. The alleged fire occurred about a fortnight after our discovery of the double tunnel. My mind was then full of suspicions concerning Syx, because I thought that a man who would fool people with one hand was not likely to deal fairly with the other.

The Suspicious Actions of Dr. Syx Explained

"It was was a glorious night, with a full moon, whose face was so clear in the limpid air that, having found a snug place at the foot of a yellow-pine-tree, where the ground was carpeted with odiferous needles, I lay on my back and renewed my early acquaintance with the romantically named mountains and 'seas' of the Lunar globe. With my binocular I could trace those long white streaks which radiate from the crater ring, called 'Tycho,' and run hundreds of miles in all directions over the moon. As I gazed at these singular objects I recalled the various theories which astronomers, puzzled by their enigmatical aspects, have offered to a more or less confiding public concerning them.

"In the midst of my meditation and moon gazing I was startled by hearing the engine in the Syx works suddenly begin to run. Immediately a queer light, shaped like the beam of a ship's searchlight, but reddish in color, rose high in the moonlit heavens above the mill. It did not last more than a minute or two, for almost instantly the engine was stopped, and with its stoppage the light faded and soon disappeared. The next day Dr. Syx gave it out that on starting up his engine in the night something had caught fire, which compelled him immediately to shut down again. The few who had seen the light, with the exception of your humble servant, accepted the doctor's explanation without a question. But I knew there had been no fire, and Syx's anxiety to spread the lie led me to believe that he had narrowly escaped giving away a vital secret. I said nothing about my suspicions, but upon inquiry I found out that an extra and pressing order for metal had arrived from the Austrian government the very day of the pretended fire, and I drew the inference that Syx, in his haste to fill the order—his supply having been drawn low—had started to work, contrary to his custom, at night, and had immediately found reason to repent his rashness. Of course, I connected the strange light with this sudden change of mind.

"My suspicions having been thus stimulated, and having been directed in a certain way, I began, from that moment to notice closely the hours during which the engine labored. At night it was always quiet, except on that one brief occasion. Sometimes it began early in the morning and stopped about noon. At other times the work was done entirely in the afternoon, beginning sometimes as late as three or four o'clock, and ceasing invariably at sundown. Then again it would start at sunrise and continue the whole day through.

"For a long time I was unable to account for these eccentricities, and the problem was not rendered much clearer, although a startling suggestiveness was added to it, when, at length, I noticed that the periods of activity of the engine had a definite relation to the age of the moon. Then I discovered, with the aid of an almanac, that I could predict the hours when the engine would be busy. At the time of new moon it worked all day; at full moon, it was idle; between full moon and last quarter, it labored in the forenoon, the length of its working hours increasing as the quarter was approached; between last quarter and new moon, the hours of work lengthened, until, as I have said, at new moon they lasted all day; between new moon and first quarter, work began later and later in the forenoon as the quarter was approached, and between first quarter and full moon the laboring hours rapidly shortened, being confined to the latter part of the afternoon, until at full moon complete silence reigned in the mill."

The Moon Is Concerned in Dr. Syx's Mystery

"Well! well!" I broke in, greatly astonished by Hall's singular recital, "you must have thought Dr. Syx was a cross between an alchemist and an astrologer."

"Note this," said Hall, disregarding my interruption, "the hours when the engine worked were invariably the hours during which the moon was above the horizon!"

"What did you infer from that?"

"Of course, I inferred that the moon was directly concerned in the mystery; but how? That bothered me for a long time, but a little light broke into my mind when I picked up, on the mountain-side, a dead bird, whose scorched feathers were bronzed with artemisium, and sometime later another similar victim of a mysterious form of death. Then came the attack on the mine and its tragic finish. I have already told you what I observed on that occasion. But, instead of helping to clear up the mystery, it rather complicated it for a time. At length, however, I reasoned my way partly out of the difficulty. Certain things which I had noticed in the Syx mill convinced me that there was a part of the building whose existence no visitor suspected, and, putting one thing with another, I inferred that the roof must be open above that secret part of the structure, and that if I could get upon a sufficiently elevated place I could see something of what was hidden there.

"At this point in the investigation I proposed to you the trip to the top of the Teton, the result of which you remember. I had calculated the angles with great care, and I felt certain that from the apex of the mountain I should be able to get a view into the concealed chamber, and into just that side of it which I wished particularly to inspect. You remember that I called your attention to a shining object underneath the circular opening in the roof. You could not make out what it was, but I saw enough to convince me that it was a gigantic parabolic mirror. I'll show you a smaller one of the same kind presently.

"Now, at last, I began to perceive the real truth, but it was so wildly incredible, so infinitely remote from all human experience, that I hardly ventured to formulate it, even in my own secret mind. But I was bound to see the thing through to the end. It occurred to me that I could prove the accuracy of my theory with the aid of a kite. You were kind enough to lend your assistance in that experiment, and it gave me irrefragable evidence of the existence of a shaft of flying atoms extending in a direct line between Dr. Syx's pretended mine and the moon!"

"Hall!" I exclaimed, "you are mad!"

My friend smiled good-naturedly, and went on with his story.

Why the Kite Was Burned

The instant the kite shrivelled and disappeared I understood why the works were idle when the moon was not above the horizon, why birds flying across that fatal beam fell dead upon the rocks, and whence the terrible master of that mystery mill derived the power of destruction that could wither an army as the Assyrian host in Byron's poem:

"*Melted like snow in the glance of the Lord.*"

"But how did Dr. Syx turn the flying atoms against his enemies?" I asked.

"In a very simple manner. He had a mirror mounted so that it could be turned in any direction, and would shunt the stream of metallic atoms, heated by their friction with the air, towards any desired point. When the attack came he raised this machine above the level of the roof and swept the mob to a lustrous, if expensive, death."

"And the light at night—"

"Was the shining of the heated atoms, not luminous enough to be visible in broad day, for which reason the engine never worked at night, and the stream of volatized artemisium was never set flowing at full moon, when the lunar globe is above the horizon only during the hours of darkness."

"I see," I said, "whence came the nuggets on the mountain. Some of the atoms, owing to the resistance of the air, fell short and settled in the form of impalpable dust until the winds and rains collected and compacted them in the cracks and crevices of the rocks."

"That was it, of course."

"And now," I added, my amazement at the success of Hall's experiments and the accuracy of his deductions increasing every moment, "do you say that you have also discovered the means employed by Dr. Syx to obtain artemisium from the moon?"

"Not only that," replied my friend, "but within the next few minutes I shall have the pleasure of presenting to you a button of moon metal, fresh from the veins of Artemis herself."

CHAPTER XI

The Looting of the Moon

I shall spare the reader a recital of tireless efforts, continuing through many almost sleepless weeks, whereby Andrew Hall obtained his clew to Dr. Syx's method. It was manifest from the beginning that the agent concerned must be some form of etheric, or so-called electric energy; but how to set it in operation was the problem. Finally he hit upon the apparatus for his initial experiments which I have already described.

"Recurring to what had been done more than half a century ago by Hertz, when he concentrated electric waves upon a focal point by means of a concave mirror," said Hall, "I saw that the key I wanted lay in an extension of these experiments. At last I found that I could transform the energy of an engine into undulations of the ether, which, when they had been concentrated upon a metallic object, like a chunk of gold, imparted to it an intense charge of an apparently electric nature. Upon thus charging a metallic body enclosed in a vacuum, I observed that the energy imparted to it possessed the remarkable power of disrupting its atoms and projecting them off in straight lines, very much as occurs with a cathode in a Crookes's tube. But—and this was of supreme importance—I found that the line of projection was directly towards the apparatus from which the impulse producing the charge had come. In other words, I could produce two poles between which a marvellous interaction occurred. My transformer, with its concentrating mirror, acted as one pole, from which energy was transferred to the other pole, and that other pole immediately flung off atoms of its own substance in the direction of the transformer. But these atoms were stopped by the glass wall of the vacuum tube; and when I tried the experiment with the metal removed from the vacuum, and surrounded with air, it failed utterly.

"This at first completely discouraged me, until I suddenly remembered that the moon is in a vacuum, the great vacuum of interplanetary space, and that it possesses no perceptible atmosphere of its own. At this a great light broke around me, and I shouted 'Eureka!' Without hesitation I constructed a transformer of great power, furnished with a large parabolic mirror to transmit the waves in parallel lines, erected the machinery and buildings here, and when all was ready for the final experiment I telegraphed for you."

Details of Hall's Experiments

Prepared by these explanations I was all on fire to see the thing tried. Hall was no less eager, and, calling in his two faithful assistants to make the final adjustments, he led the way into what he facetiously named "the lunar chamber."

"If we fail," he remarked with a smile that had an element of worriment in it, "it will become the 'lunatic chamber'—but no danger of that. You observe this polished silver knob, supported by a metallic rod curved over at the top like a crane. That constitutes the pole from which I propose to transmit the energy to the moon, and upon which I expect the storm of atoms to be centred by reflection from the mirror at whose focus it is placed."

"One moment," I said. "Am I to understand that you think that the moon is a solid mass of artemisium, and that no matter where your radiant force strikes it a 'cathodic pole' will be formed there from which atoms will be projected to the earth?"

"No," said Hall, "I must carefully choose the point on the lunar surface where to operate. But that will present no difficulty. I made up my mind as soon as I had penetrated Syx's secret that he obtained the metal from those mystic white streaks which radiate from Tycho, and which have puzzled the astronomers ever since the invention of telescopes. I now believe those streaks to be composed of immense veins of the metal that Syx has most appropriately named artemisium, which you, of course, recognize as being derived from the name of the Greek goddess of the moon, Artemis, whom the Romans called Diana. But now to work!"

It was less than a day past the time of new moon, and the earth's satellite was too near the sun to be visible in broad daylight. Accordingly, the mirror had to be directed by means of knowledge of the moon's place in the sky. Driven by accurate clockwork, it could be depended upon to retain the proper direction when once set.

With breathless interest I watched the proceedings of my friend and his assistants. The strain upon the nerves of all of us was such as could not have been borne for many hours at a stretch. When everything had been adjusted to his satisfaction, Hall stepped back, not without betraying his excitement in flushed cheeks and flashing eyes, and pressed a lever. The powerful engine underneath the floor instantly responded. The experiment was begun.

"I have set it upon a point about a hundred miles north of Tycho, where the Yerkes photographs show a great abundance of the white

237

substance," said Hall.

Then he waited. A minute elapsed. A bird, fluttering in the opening above, for a second or two, wrenched our strained nerves. Hall's face turned pale.

"They had better keep away from here," he whispered, with a ghastly smile.

Two minutes! I could hear the beating of my heart. The engine shook the floor.

Three minutes! Hall's face was wet with perspiration. The bird blundered in and startled us again.

Hall Produces Artemisium On a Small Scale

Four minutes! We were like statues, with all eyes fixed on the polished ball of silver, which shown in the brilliant light concentrated upon it by the mirror.

Five minutes! The shining ball had become a confused blue, and I violently winked to clear my vision.

"At last! Thank God! Look! There it is!"

It was Hall who spoke, trembling like an aspen. The silver knob had changed color. What seemed a miniature rainbow surrounded it with consentric circles of blinding brilliance.

Then something dropped flashing into an earthen dish set beneath the ball! Another glittering drop followed, and, at a shorter interval, another!

Almost before a word could be uttered the drops had coalesced and become a tiny stream, which, as it fell, twisted itself into a bright spiral, gleaming with a hundred shifting hues, and forming on the bottom of the dish a glowing, interlacing maze of viscid rings and circlets, which turned and twined about and over one another, until they had blended and settled into a button-shaped mass of hot metallic jelly. Hall snatched the dish away, and placed another in its stead.

"This will be about right for a watch charm when it cools," he said, with a return to his customary self-command. "I promised you the first specimen. I'll catch another for myself."

"But can it be possible that we are not dreaming?" I exclaimed. "Do you really believe that this comes from the moon?"

"Just as surely as rain comes from the clouds," cried Hall, with all his old impatience. "Haven't I just showed you the whole process?"

"Then I congratulate you. You will be as rich as Dr. Syx."

"Perhaps," was the unperturbed reply, "but not until I have

enlarged my apparatus. At present I shall hardly do more than supply mementoes to my friends. But since the principle is established, the rest is mere detail."

Six weeks later the financial centres of the earth were shaken by the news that a new supply of artemisium was being marketed from a mill which had been secretly opened in the Sierras of California. For a time there was almost a panic. If Hall had chosen to do so, he might have precipitated serious trouble. But he immediately entered into negotiations with government representatives, and the inevitable result was that, to preserve the monetary system of the world from upheaval, Dr. Syx had to consent that Hall's mill should share equally with his in the production of artemisium. During the negotiations the doctor paid a visit to Hall's establishment. The meeting between them was most dramatic. Syx tried to blast his rival with a glance, but knowledge is power, and my friend faced his mysterious antagonist, whose deepest secrets he had penetrated, with an unflinching eye. It was remarked that Dr. Syx became a changed man from that moment. His masterful air seemed to have deserted him, and it was with something resembling humility that he assented to the arrangement which required him to share his enormous gains with his conqueror.

The Syx Mill is Blown Up

Of course, Hall's success led to an immediate recrudescence of the efforts to extract artemisium from the Syx ore, and, equally of course, every such attempt failed. Hall, while keeping his own secret, did all he could to discourage the experiments, but they naturally believed that he must have made the very discovery which was the subject of their dreams, and he could not without betraying himself, and upsetting the finances of the planet, directly undeceive them. The consequence was that fortunes were wasted in hopeless experimentation, and, with Hall's achievement dazzling their eyes, the deluded fortune-seekers kept on in the face of endless disappointments and disaster.

And presently there came another tragedy. The Syx mill was blown up! The accident—although many people refused to regard it as an accident, and asserted that the doctor himself, in his chagrin, had applied the match—the explosion, then, occurred about sundown, and its effects were awful. The great works, with everything pertaining to them, and every rail that they contained, were blown to atoms. They disappeared as if they had never existed.

239

Even the twin tunnels were involved in the ruin, a vast cavity being left in the mountainside where Syx's ten acres had been. The force of the explosion was so great that the shattered rock was reduced to dust. To this fact was owing the escape of the troops camped near. While the mountain was shaking to its core, and enormous parapets of living rock were hurled down the precipices of the Teton, no missiles of appreciable size traversed the air, and not a man at the camp was injured.

But Jackson's Hole, filled with red dust, looked for days afterwards like the mouth of a tremendous volcano just after an eruption. Dr. Syx had been seen entering the mill a few minutes before the catastrophy by a sentinel who was stationed about a quarter of a mile away, and who, although he was felled like an ox by the shock, and had his eyes, ears, and nostrils filled with flying dust, miraculously escaped with his life.

After this a new arrangement was made whereby Andrew Hall became the sole producer of artemisium, and his wealth began to mount by leaps of millions toward the starry heights of the billions.

About a year after the explosion of the Syx mill a strange rumor got about. It came first from Budapest, in Hungary, where it was averred several persons of credibility had seen Dr. Max Syx. Millions had been familiar with his face and his personal peculiarities, through actually meeting him, as well as through photographs and descriptions, and, unless there was an intention to deceive, it did not seem possible that a mistake could be made in identification.

There surely never was another man who looked just like Dr. Syx. And, besides, was it not generally known that he must have perished in the awful destruction of his mill?

The Secret of Producing Artemisium Becomes Public Property

Soon after came a report that Dr. Syx had been seen again; this time at Ekaterinburg, in the Urals. Next he was said to have paid a visit to Batang, in the mountainous district of southwestern China, and finally, according to rumor, he was seen in Sicily, at Nicolosi, among the volcanic pimples on the southern slope of Mount Etna.

Next followed something of more curious and even startling interest. A chemist at Budapest, where the first rumors of Syx's reappearance had placed the mysterious doctor, announced that he could produce artemisium, and proved it, although he kept his process secret. Hardly had the sensation caused by this news

240

partially subsided when a similar report arrived from Ekaterinburg; then another from Batang; after that a fourth from Nicolosi!

Nobody could fail to notice the coincidence; wherever the doctor— or was it his ghost?—appeared, there, shortly afterwards, somebody discovered the much-sought secret.

After Syx's apparitions rapidly increased in frequency, followed in each instance by the announcement of another productive artemisium mill. He appeared in Germany, Italy, France, England, and finally at many places in the United States.

"It is the old doctor's revenge," said Hall to me one day, trying to smile, although the matter was too serious to be taken humorously. "Yes, it is his revenge, and I must admit that it is complete. The price of artemisium has fallen one-half within six months. All the efforts we have made to hold back the floor have proved useless. The secret itself is becoming public property. We shall inevitably be overwhelmed with artemisium, just as we were with gold, and the last condition of the financial world will be worse than the first."

My friend's gloomy prognostications came near being fulfilled to the letter. Ten thousand artemisium mills shot their etheric rays upon the moon, and our unfortunate satellite's metal ribs were stripped by atomic force. Some of the great white rays that had been one of the telescopic wonders of the lunar landscapes disappeared, and the face of the moon, which had remained unchanged before the eyes of the children of Adam from the beginning of their race, now looked as if the blast of a furnace had swept it. At night, on the moonward side, the earth was studded with brilliant spikes, all pointed at the heart of its child in the sky.

But the looting of the moon brought disaster to the robber planet. So mad were the efforts to get the precious metal that the surface of our globe was fairly showered with it, productive fields were, in some cases, almost smothered under a metallic coating, the air was filled with shining dust, until finally famine and pestilence joined hands with financial disaster to punish the grasping world.

Then, at last, the various governments took effective measures to protect themselves and their people. Another combined effort resulted in an international agreement whereby the production of the precious moon metal was once more rigidly controlled. But the existence of a monoply, such as Dr. Syx had so long enjoyed, and in the enjoyment of which Andrew Hall had for a brief period succeeded him, was henceforth rendered impossible.

CHAPTER XII

The Last of Dr. Syx

**M**any years after the events last recorded I sat, at the close of a brilliant autumn day, side by side with my old friend Andrew Hall, on a broad, vine-shaded piazza which faced the east, where the full moon was just rising above the rim of the Sierra, and replacing the rosy counter-glow of sunset with its silvery radiance. The sight was calculated to carry the minds of both back to the events of former years. But I noticed that Hall quickly changed the position of his chair, and sat down again with his back to the rising moon. He had managed to save some millions from the wreck of his vast fortune when artemisium started to go to the dogs, and I was now paying him one of my annual visits at his palatial home in California.

"Did I ever tell you of my last trip to the Teton?" he asked, as I continued to gaze contemplatively at the broad lunar disk which slowly detached itself from the horizon and began to swim in the clear evening sky.

"No," I replied, "but I should like to hear about it."

"Or of my last sight of Dr. Syx?"

"Indeed! I did not suppose that you ever saw him, after that conference in your mill, when he had to surrender half of the world to you."

"Once only I saw him again," said Hall, with a peculiar intonation.

"Pray go ahead, and tell me the whole story."

My friend lighted a fresh cigar, tipped his chair into a more comfortable position, and began:

"It was about seven years ago. I had long felt an unconquerable desire to have another look at the Teton and the scenes amid which so many strange events in my life had occurred. I thought of sending for you to go with me, but I knew you were abroad much of your time, and I could not be certain of catching you. Finally I decided to go alone. I travelled on horseback by way of the Snake River canyon, and arrived early one morning in Jackson's Hole. I can tell you it was a gloomy place, as barren and deserted as some of those Arabian wadies that you have been describing to me. The railroad had long ago been abandoned, and the site of the military camp could scarcely be recognized. An immense cavity with ragged walls showed where Dr. Syx's mill used to send up its plume of black smoke.

"As I started up the gaunt form of the Teton, whose beetling precipices had been smashed and split by the great explosion, I was seized with a resistless impulse to climb it. I thought I should like to peer off again from that pinnacle which had once formed so fateful a watch-tower for me. Turning my horse loose to graze in the grassy river bottom, and carrying my rope tether along as a possible aid in climbing, I set out for the ascent. I knew I could not get up the precipices on the eastern side, which we were able to master with the aid of our balloon, and so I bore round, when I reached the steepest cliffs, until I was on the southwestern side of the peak, where the climbing was easier.

The Last Fight of Dr. Syx

"But it took me a long time, and I did not reach the rift in the summit until just before sundown. Knowing that it would be impossible for me to descend at night, I bethought me of the enclosure of rocks, supposed to have been made by Indians, on the western pinnacle, and decided that I could pass the night there.

"The perpendicular buttress forming the easternmost and highest point of the Teton's head would have baffled me but for the fact that I found a long crack, probably an effect of the tremendous explosion, extending from bottom to top of the rock. Driving my toes and fingers into this rift, I managed, with a good deal of trouble, and no little peril, to reach the top. As I lifted myself over the edge and rose to my feet, imagine my amazement at seeing Dr. Syx standing within arm's-length of me!

"My breath seemed pent in my lungs, and I could not even utter the exclamation that rose to my lips. It was like meeting a ghost. Notwithstanding the many reports of his having been seen in various parts of the world, it had always been my conviction that he had perished in the explosion.

"Yet there he stood in the twilight, for the sun was hidden by the time I reached the summit, his tall form erect, and his black eyes gleaming under the heavy brows as he fixed them sternly upon my face. You know I never was given to losing my nerve, but I am afraid I lost it on that occasion. Again and again I strove to speak, but it was impossible to move my tongue. So powerless seemed my lungs that I wondered how I could continue breathing.

"The doctor remained silent, but his curious smile, which, as you know, was a thing of terror to most people, overspread his black-rimmed face and was broad enough to reveal the gleam of his teeth. I felt that he was looking me through and through. The sensation was as if he had transfixed me with an ice-cold blade. There was a gleam of devilish pleasure in his eyes, as though my evident suffering was a delight to him and a gratification of his vengance. At length I succeeded in overcoming the feeling which oppressed me, and, making a step forward, I shouted in a strained voice,

"'You black Satan!'

"I cannot clearly explain the psychological process which led me to utter those words. I had never entertained any enmity towards Dr. Syx, although I had always regarded him as a heartless person, who had purposely led thousands to their ruin for his selfish gain, but I knew that he could not help hating me, and I felt now that, in some inexplicable manner, a struggle, not physical, but spiritual, was taking place between us, and my exclamation, uttered with surprising intensity, produced upon me, and apparently upon him, the effect of a desperate sword thrust which attains its mark.

"Immediately the doctor's form seemed to recede, as if he had passed the verge of the precipice behind him. At the same time it became dim, and then dimmer, until only the dark outlines, and particularly the jet-black eyes, glaring fiercely, remained visible. And still he receded, as though floating in the air, which was now silvered with the evening light, until he appeared to cross the immense atmospheric gulf over Jackson's Hole and paused on the rim of the horizon in the east.

"Then, suddenly, I became aware that the full moon had risen at the very place on the distant mountain-brow where the spectre rested, and as I continued to gaze, as if entranced, the face and figure of the doctor seemed slowly to frame themselves within the lunar disk, until at last he appeared to have quitted the air and the earth and to be frowning at me from the circle of the moon."

While Hall was pronouncing his closing words I had begun to stare at the moon with swiftly increasing interest, until, as his voice stopped, I exclaimed,

"Why, there he is now! Funny I never noticed it before. There's Dr. Syx's face in the moon, as plain as day."

"Yes," replied Hall, without turning round, "and I never like to look at it."

THE END

BEYOND the POLE
~ By A. Hyatt Verill ~

Introductory Note

By Dr. Abbott E. Lyman

Before giving this really marvelous tale to the world, I feel that it is important to offer a few lines of explanation, as well as a brief sketch or synopsis of the events that led to my discovery of the manuscript relating the incredible adventures of this writer.

As a naturalist specializing in ornithology, I had long been attracted to the regions of the little known Antarctic as a rich field for my studies. Very largely, perhaps, my interest in Antarctic ornithology was due to the fact that I resided in New Bedford, a town famous in former years for the number of its whaling vessels, many of which sailed annually for the southern oceans in search of sea-elephant oil. From the officers of these vessels I obtained many specimens of birds' skins and eggs brought back by the obliging whalemen. Such specimens were, however, more or less unsatisfactory for scientific study, and I at last made up my mind to visit the Antarctic in person in order to observe and study that avifauna in its own habitat.

It thus happened that I secured passage upon a whaleship bound for the South Atlantic and South Indian oceans, and, after an uneventful voyage of several months, I found myself gazing from the bark's deck at the frowning mountain peaks of Kerguelen, or as it is also called, Desolation Island.

Here, in company with some ten of the bark's crew, I was landed, and, having been amply supplied with provisions, tools and implements of the whalemen's trade, we saw the vessel sail away for South Georgia, there to land other parties, which, like our own, would remain upon the barren bits of land until the bark's return the following year.

I need not enter into a description of the wonderful fauna and flora of the island, nor need I dilate upon the rare and interesting specimens which rewarded my daily tramps over the bare basaltic hills or through the thick scrub and rank grass of the valleys, although to me those days were filled with fascination and all the naturalist's enthusiasm at treading new fields of study.

Suffice it to state that on one misty morning, having penetrated far into the interior of the island in search of a new rookery of albatross, I was attracted by the strange behavior of one of these great birds.

He appeared unable to rise from the ground, although he repeatedly spread his immense wings and flapped upward for a few inches. But each time he fell back and struggled awkwardly about upon the earth.

My nearer approach disclosed the fact that the bird's legs was entangled in some object among the rocks, and, walking to within a few yards of the albatross, I was surprised to find that a cord or line was attached to the bird's leg, while the other extremity of the cord was fastened to an object that glittered curiously in the light.

Consumed with curiosity, for I knew that no human beings had recently visited the spot, I cautiously approached the albatross, and, throwing my coat over its head, I stooped and endeavored to disengage the line from the bird's leg. I found however, that the cord, which was of a most unusual metallic lustre, was spliced or woven about the leg.

I therefore drew my sailor's sheath knife and strove to cut the line which was scarcely larger than twine. Imagine if you can my surprise when the keen-edged blade slipped uselessly along the cord as though the knife had been of wood and the line of steel!

Judging that the affair was some form of wire rope, I then placed it across a small rock and hammered it with another stone, but without avail. Bending it rapidly back and forth was equally futile, and I therefore turned my attention to the object to which the cord was attached, and which appeared to be a thin glass cylinder some two inches in diameter and approximately six inches in length. Through the crystal I could discern a roll of some material resembling paper, and, feeling sure that this was a message of some sort, I struck the bottle-like receptacle a smart blow with a bit of rock. I remember that, even as I did so, I was mentally wondering how such a fragile receptacle had escaped annihilation during the rough usage to which it must have been subjected by its winged carrier, but even this vague thought did not prepare me for the result of my blow. Indeed, I cannot adequately transcribe my utter amazement as the stone rebounded from the glass container without leaving so much as a scratch or a crack upon the surface!

I was in fact, absolutely dumfounded. Eagerly I stooped, and examined the strange object more closely and minutely. I discovered a small catch or button near one end of the cylinder, and as I pressed upon this, the cord was suddenly released.

With the cylinder now in my possession I gave no further heed to the albatross, which immediately flew off, a most regrettable incident as he carried with him the remarkable ligature which, had I secured it, would have proved of inestimable scientific value. But my attention was focused completely upon the container which I found was remarkably light, about the weight of aluminum, I judged. But, despite its apparently fragile character I could not succeed in either breaking or denting the remarkable material, try as I might.

My curiosity was now at fever heat, for I knew of a certainty that no such material was known to civilized man, and that any message or communication enclosed within it must be of the utmost importance and interest. In order to examine it more closely I opened my pocket lens and commenced most carefully and painstakingly to go over the smooth surface of the astonishing receptacle.

In so doing I advertently brought a point of light to a focus upon the cylinder. All that had gone before was as nothing to the astounding result of this accidental procedure. Instantly the material commenced to melt and run like wax! In a few brief moments I had melted a space completely encircling the cylinder, and, from the aperture thus made I drew forth the roll of manuscript—for such the contents proved to be, and, spreading the pages commenced to read the incredible story written thereon. Certain passages, names and references assured me that the story was no fiction nor the work of a disordered mind, for many of the incidents mentioned as well as names referred to, were familiar to me. I clearly remembered the departure of the bark *Endeavor*, her failure to return, and the various newspaper accounts of her disappearance, with the published lists of her personnel. These facts, as I have stated, would alone have convinced me, even had I not felt assured, from the character of the receptacle chosen to hold the manuscript, that the tale was true, for the material could not have been obtained or prepared in any known country or by any known race of men.

Deeply have I regretted, since that time, the fact that my engrossment with the manuscript swept all thoughts of the cylinder from my mind. I had carelessly dropped it as I secured the contents, and when, having read and reread the astounding tale from beginning to end, I looked for the receptacle, and it could not be found. My closest and most painstaking search failed to reveal it. Whether it had rolled into some crevice or hole in the volcanic rock or whether some curious albatross, attracted by the glitter of the cylinder, had surreptitiously approached and swallowed it, I shall never know.

But even without the cylinder and its attendant cord as corroborative evidence as to the truth of the story I so strangely obtained, the tale itself is so manifestly fact, and is of such incalculable value to the world that I have not the slightest hesitation in publishing it.

The manuscript, quite unaltered, is reproduced in the following pages, and my readers may judge for themselves as to the veracity of the author and the importance of its revelations which are now made public for the first time. The narrative, written legibly in some dark colored medium upon a peculiar parchment-like and exceedingly tough though light material, covered many sheets, and was as follows:

Chapter 1

o whosoever finds this message:—I entreat that you will read, and after reading will either notify the relatives and friends of myself and my comrades of the crew of the bark *Endeavor* of New Bedford, in the State of Massachusetts, U.S.A., of the fate of that vessel and her men, or failing in this, will give this writing to some reliable newspaper in order that it may be published for the benefit and peace of mind of all who have an interest in the fate of the bark which set sail from New Bedford on the fourteenth day of August, 1917.

My name is Franklin Bishop and I was born and resided at Fairhaven, Mass., across the harbor from New Bedford. For many years I followed the sea as a whaleman, until in 1917 I shipped as first mate on the bark *Endeavor*, Captain Ranklin, bound for the South Shetland Islands in search of sea-elephant oil, the price of oil having greatly increased owing to the war. The bark carried a crew of sixteen men, six of whom were Portuguese boat-steerers shipped at Funchal.

I cannot now recall the names or homes of the crew, if indeed I ever knew them, for a large number were greenies—human derelicts, and were known aboardship only by their Christian or their nicknames. The skipper was George Rankin of New London, Ct. The second mate was Jacob Marten of Noank, Ct. The cooper was Nicholas Chester of Mystic, Ct., and the carpenter was a huge, raw boned Scandinavian named Olaf Johnson. But the names matter little, for I have no doubt that even after six years the bark's owners or the New Bedford shipping lists of 1917 can supply the names of all hands with the exception of the Portuguese, and I mention the above merely to prove the truth of my tale and to induce whoever finds it to make known the fate of the bark and of her crew."*

(Foot note by Dr. Lyman)

The following is a clipping from the New Bedford "Mercury" of August 14th, 1917; "Sailed: Bark "Endeavor", Rankin, for Gough, South Georgia and South Shetland Islands via Funchal. It is with pleasure that we note the sailing of the old Whaleship "Endeavor". This is the first of New Bedford's once great fleet of whalers to set sail for the South Atlantic in many years, and we trust that it signifies an awakening of the long dormant industry which once made the name of New Bedford familiar in every corner of the world. It is a direct outcome of the Great War and the consequent advance in the price of oil, and while the latter may be and no doubt is only temporary, our still serviceable old ships may yet reap golden harvests while high

Our voyage, after leaving Funchal, was pleasant and with favorable winds and good weather we made a quick run until south of Tristan da Cunha when we ran into heavy weather with a northeast gale that forced us to shorten sail to almost bare poles. Even then the old bark wallowed heavily and made such bad weather of the sharp irregular seas that we at last were forced to heave to and even to use oil over the bows. This made the ship ride easier but our drift was tremendous and when, on the fifth day, we managed to take sights we found ourselves far off our course and in latitude about 45^0 south and longitude 11^0 west. The exact figures I do not remember.

We had scarcely made sail and gotten our course when another and even harder gale bore down upon us from the northwest, and under bare poles we scudded before it for sixty hours, when, by the hardest work, we managed to set a patch of sail and heaved the bark to.

Hour after hour the storm howled through the rigging, while with aching backs and straining arms we toiled at the pumps day and night.

Gradually the wind died down and intense cold followed, with murky, leaden skies and occasional squalls of snow, while between these puffs the wind fell flat and we drifted helplessly about at the will of the strong and unknown currents of the region. For five long, weary days we drifted, the sky becoming more and more sullen, and with no gleam of sunlight to enable us to make an observation.

On the sixth day, long, oily rollers came running in from the west with a weight that told of wind to follow, and sails were close reefed in readiness for the expected blow. At last, upon the horizon, we saw a streak of white, gleaming against the inky murk, and hardly had we grasped rails and rigging when the hurricane and blinding sleet and snow struck us. Over the old bark went until it seemed as if her yards would trip in the mountainous seas that rushed past her bulwarks. Then gradually she righted, and bearing off before the wind, tore through the huge seas like a mad thing. For ten hours the gale screeched and howled with undiminished fury and every effort to bring the bark into the wind was useless. Moreover the hail and snow was so thick that we could see barely a cable's length from the ship, while rigging and spars were loaded with tons of ice and to

prices continue. The "Endeavor's" officers are well known and experienced men and we wish them and the owners every success and a 'greasy v'yage'. The "Endeavor's" officers are as follows: Captain, George Rankin of New London. First mate, Frank Bishop, Fairhaven. Second, Jacob Marten, Noank. Cooper, Nicholas Chester, Mystic. Carpenter, and blacksmith, Olaf Johnson, Christiana, Sweden. Cook, Wm. Outerbridge, Hamilton, Bermuda. Boatsteerers, Jake Hildebrand, Nantucket. Henry Fogarty, Marthas Vineyard. Michael Mendoza, Cape Verde Island."—A. E. L.

handle ropes was like hauling on steel bars. Then, suddenly from aloft, came the piercing cry "Ice ahead! Port your helm! For God's sake, hard a port!"

Springing to the wheel I threw all my weight upon it, but even with the two men already there, we were unable to swing the bark half a point and a second later, with a grinding crash, we struck the berg.

So great was the shock that all hands were thrown flat upon the deck, and with a splintering roar, the fore- and mainmasts went over the side, dragging the port bulwarks with them and staving a gaping hole in the bark's side as the jagged butts lurched up on the next sea.

Instantly all was confusion. The Portuguese rushed to the boats, only to find that all but two were staved in, and tried to cut away the falls. Luckily the ropes were so sheathed in ice that for a moment they could not lower the boats and in this brief space of time the captain and myself, with the other officers, managed to drive the crazed fellows from the boats and to restore some sort of order.

Provisions and water were thrown into the boats, but the bark was settling so rapidly that before the craft were half provisioned Captain Rankin decided it would be certain death to wait longer. Accordingly the boats were lowered away at once, but as I looked at the huge seas and felt the sweep of the icy gale I turned back and chose to risk going down with the ship rather than add my weight to the overburdened boats that I judged would scarcely live an hour in the terrific welter of sea and wind.

In this decision I was joined by Olaf, the carpenter, and standing upon the rapidly sinking hulk we saw the two tiny whaleboats shove off and disappear in the sleet and snow to leeward. We momentarily expected the bark to sink beneath us and our only hope was that we might have time to build some sort of makeshift raft before the vessel went down. With this idea we at once commenced to gather what materials we could. But long before we had secured even a small part of what we required the bark had settled until the deck was only a few inches above the water. Then suddenly she lurched to port, rolled over on her beam ends and with a slight shudder remained motionless except for a slight rising and falling on the waves. For a moment we were amazed and puzzled and could not understand the matter, for I knew hundreds of fathoms of water lay under our keel. Presently, however, we came to grasp the situation. Evidently the berg on which we struck projected far under water, like a huge shelf, and our ship, passing over this before she struck, had now settled until she rested on the submerged ice shelf. For the time we were safe and although the bark rested in such a slanting position

253

that we were obliged to crawl rather than walk the decks, yet we thanked God that we were there, instead of tossing about in small boats at the mercy of the tempest.

As nothing was to be gained by remaining on deck we entered the cabin and secured food and drink and succeeded in belaying the cabin stove so that we could light a fire, which proved most grateful to our chilled and numbed bodies. Here we sat and smoked for uncounted hours, while dimly the sound of storm and waves came to us or the grating of the bark's keel upon the ice beneath gave us momentary frights. Gradually the storm waned and the waves broke less heavily against our crippled ship. Towards daybreak we both fell asleep and did not awaken until aroused by the cold which became terrific as the fire died down. We kindled a new fire, and wrapping ourselves in heavy coats and oilskins, went on deck. The sun was shining brightly close to the horizon, but as far as I could see there was nothing but gleaming ice floes broken by narrow, open lanes of dark water and lofty bergs. By watching certain spots we soon found that we were drifting rapidly southward and I went below to secure my sextant and take an observation. To my chagrin I found that the captain had taken the instruments with him and we were without means to learn our position except by guess-work. By careful calculation of our drift, and assuming that we had been drifting at the same speed and in the same direction since striking the ice, and allowing for our progress since taking the last observation. I decided that our latitude and longitude must be about 70^0 south and 10^0 east. The cold was now so intense that we descended to the cabin, only occasionally venturing on deck to meet with the same weary, drifting, broken ice. Our case seemed hopeless indeed, for we well knew that we were far beyond the tracks of any ships and that unless some miracle occurred we were doomed to spend the rest of our days upon the helpless wreck, to perish miserably of starvation. With such thoughts we turned in at night and for six days our existence was but a repetition of the first.

On the morning of the seventh day we were startled by a roaring, grinding noise and the sudden violent lurching of the bark. Rushing on deck and fearing the worst, we were thunderstruck to behold—barely a cable's length away—a rocky, ice-capped shore, behind which rose lofty mountains with their summits hidden in clouds. Much to our surprise also we found that the weather had greatly moderated and several big mollymokes were wheeling about the ship while seals and sea-leopards basked on the rocks above the surf. Our ice cradle prevented the bark taking the ground, but in the course of a few moments we managed to scramble over the intervening broken ice and soon stepped upon the shingle. Then, with ropes and hawsers, we succeeded in making our wreck fast to the shore. We were now reasonably sure that the ship would not go adrift, and even if a storm came up and forced us to desert our quarters on board, we could no doubt salvage enough from the wreck to build some manner of craft in which to make our escape from this forbidding and uncharted land.

During the next two or three weeks we busied ourselves carrying ashore fuel and provisions and in constructing a little hut or shelter in which to store the goods or to seek refuge in case of disaster to the bark.

There was no lack of fresh meat, for penguins, albatross, mollymokes and Cape pigeons were thick. Also, we laid in a fine supply of seal skins and oil in preparation for the long and dreary winter which we knew we should be forced to face, for we had no intentions of trusting ourselves to any frail craft we might be able to build until all chances of whaleships reaching us had passed with the summer. Although this work kept us busy and left us little time to think of our plight, yet often, during meals or when done with the day's work, we talked over the probable fates of our comrades and were grateful at our own salvation, even in such an inhospitable land.*

(Foot note by Dr. Lyman)

"Evidently Mr. Bishop did not consider the possibility of any member of the bark's crew having reached land or safety. The following is a clipping from the "New Bedford Mercury" of July 2d, 1919:

"The schooner Petrel, Archibald, arrived yesterday with 600 bbls. of sea-elephant oil; 300 seal skins; 200 bbls. sperm oil; 15 casks spermaceti and 16 lbs. amber gris from the South Atlantic and South Indian oceans. Captain Archibald brought with him the survivors of the ill fated bark "Endeavor" of this port which sailed for the Antarctic on August 14th, 1917. The "Endeavor" struck a berg and foundered near the Bouvets Islands after being driven far off her course by a series of gales. The survivors who have both our heartiest sympathies and our most sincere congratulations, are as follows: Jacob Marten, Noank. Nicholas Chester, Mystic. Michael Mendoza, Cape Verde Island. Henry Fogarty, Marthas Vineyard. Jose Rodriguez, Funchal. Mr. Marten, the second mate of the "Endeavor," states that only two boats were lowered, the others having been stove by falling spars. The other boat contained Captain Rankin and eight men and was lost to sight a few moments after leaving the bark's side. Franklin Bishop, the first mate, and Olaf Johnson, the carpenter, refused to leave the vessel and trust to the boats. After terrible hardships Mr. Marten's boat reached the Bouvets and after three months on those desolate rocks the men were picked up by the Petrel. There can be little doubt that those in the captain's boat, as well as Mr. Bishop and the carpenter, perished."—A. E. L.

CHAPTER 2

s winter approached, however, Olaf became very sullen and morose, often talking to himself and wandering about the rocks, gesticulating and acting strangely.

I became afraid that the poor fellow would lose his mind completely, and, as on many occasions he turned upon me savagely, I was constantly on the alert to protect myself. He had been a wonderful help, for his skill with tools had enabled us to build a comfortable house and without him I would have fared badly indeed.

It was several months after landing that in one of his fits of wandering he fell among slippery rocks and broke his thigh. I did not find him until several hours after the accident, and twixt loss of blood and the pain and the piercing cold, he was past all human help and quite unconscious.

I carried him to the hut and did all in my power for my suffering shipmate, but it was useless. Early the following morning he died, and with heavy heart at the loss of my only companion, I carried his body to a crevice in the hillside and covered it well with stones and gravel, and over it placed a small wooden cross on which I carved his name and the date of his death.

I now became most despondent, for I knew that alone I could never hope to complete the boat we had been working on, and that even if that were possible I would be powerless to handle or navigate it. I could see nothing but the endless winter and utter loneliness before me, with ultimate death through accident or madness, unless by some remote chance a sail hove in sight.

In my calmer moments I held to this slender hope and tried to conjure up all the tales I had heard of castaways living for years alone and yet being rescued in the end. I had little fear of meeting with an accident as long as I kept my mind, and I realized that my greatest danger lay in going mad as Olaf had done. To avoid this as much as possible and to prevent my thoughts from dwelling on my plight, I commenced taking long trips across the hills in search of game, carrying a supply of ammunition and a haversack filled with biscuit or dried meat. On one of these tramps I had wandered several miles from the hut and had reached the summit of a good sized hill, from which I had a wide view of the sea. Far down the shore I noticed some object about which great flocks of sea fowl were gathering, and thinking it a stranded whale or sea elephant, I turned my steps towards the spot. As I rounded a point of rocks and came within plain sight of the object, I almost dropped in my tracks from sheer amazement. Upon the beach before me was a ship's boat!

I broke into a run, and panting, reached the craft from which hundreds of mollymokes and other birds rose screaming. Gaining the boat's side I peered within and recoiled in horror. Stretched upon the thwarts and bottom were the bodies of six men, their faces torn and mutilated by the sea birds. But even in their ghastly state I knew them for Captain Rankin and my former shipmates of the *Endeavor*. I reeled away, for the sight was sickening and stunning, and seized with insane and unreasoning fright, I dropped my gun and dashed off across the rocks and hills, striving with might and main to get as far from the gruesome boat as possible.

At last I dropped from sheer exhaustion among the rocks, but even then the shock was so great that I hid my face and screamed and raved like a madman until consciousness left me.

How long I remained in that condition I cannot say, for when at last I awoke to a knowledge of my surroundings, I found myself wandering about amid thick and thorny scrub on a steep hillside I had never seen before. I was ravenously hungry and thrust my hand into my haversack in search of food, only to find it empty save for a few crumbs of ship's bread. Seating myself on a nearby rock I munched these eagerly and tried to collect my thoughts and reason. I soon came to the conclusion that I had been delirious for a long time, and during my period of temporary madness, had wandered far, for my haversack had been full when I first sighted the boat and was now empty, and I reasoned that I must have devoured my food during my unconscious wanderings. My watch had stopped, but this mattered little, as for months I had been able merely to guess at the time. A search of my pockets failed to reveal my compass but I felt this was no great loss at the time, for I had no doubt that, by climbing a neighboring hill, I could make out the sea and so find my way back to the hut, although I confess that the mere thought of again approaching the ghastly remains of my shipmates filled me with most awful dread and caused me to shudder violently.

My tongue and throat were parched and dry and the hard crumbs of biscuit added to my thirst, so I at once commenced to push my way up the hillside through the shrubbery. As I reached the top and looked about, no gleaming bit of sea greeted my eyes. On every side stretched rolling, round-topped hills, each and all clothed in dull, brownish-gray scrub, save just behind me where, the more distant landscape was hidden from view by a higher range of small mountains. Although my thirst was now unbearable yet I knew that my one hope of finding my way was to ascend the higher hill, and

257

with sinking heart and lagging footsteps I started for them. Slowly and painfully I climbed their rough and rocky slopes, stopping often to rest and regain my failing breath, but at last I stood upon their crest and gazed anxiously about the horizon. For a moment my head swam and a mist floated before my eyes. Then my vision cleared and I saw before me a long, sloping hillside covered with scattered shrubs, while below and stretching far towards the horizon, was a green and pleasant valley on whose farther edge rose high and rugged mountains misty with distance. But though no water gladened my eyes, yet near at hand I saw a number of great birds resembling penguins, and towards these I rapidly made my way. They were stupid and fearless and in a moment I had killed the first one I reached and greedily drank its rich warm blood. This refreshed me greatly, but feeling still hungry, I gathered a quantity of eggs, which I ate raw, and feeling drowsy made my way to a sheltered nook among the rocks and fell into a deep and dreamless sleep.

I awoke feeling strong but half famished, and at once fell to on the helpless birds and their eggs. I now considered my next step and as there evidently was nothing to be gained by retracing my way I decided to travel towards the valley where I judged perhaps water might be found, for although the blood and raw eggs had somewhat quenched my thirst, yet the desire for water was overpowering. As I did not know if I would find more birds farther on, I laid in a good supply of flesh and eggs, and as I noticed that my shoes were almost worn out, I wrapped birds' skins about my feet, binding them in place with strips of the skin.

I now noticed that these birds were not penguins, as I had at first thought, nor in fact anything like any birds I had even before seen. I judged therefore that I was far from the coast, but I was wholly without means of ascertaining the direction of the sea or my position, for I had seen nothing of the sun since finding the boat, although the days were bright enough. As I thought on this its strangeness came to me and I also marveled that I was not suffering from the cold. The more I thought of these matters the more I wondered, for now that I came to think of it, the weather was quite warm and I had seen no snow or ice, even among the crevices of the rocks. But I had other things to occupy my attention, for my thirst for water and my desire to escape from my surroundings filled my head to the exclusion of all less pressing matters, as for hour after hour I tramped on across the valley. From the hilltop it had appeared clothed in soft grass, but when I reached it I found to my sorrow that the vegetation was thorny, pointed-leaf shrubs whose tangled branches formed an almost impenetrable jungle which made my progress painful and slow beyond belief. I soon lost all sense of time or direction, but toiled on towards the distant mountains, eating the birds' flesh and eggs when hungry and at last sinking down to sleep when my tired and torn flesh refused to carry me farther on my way. Only by looking at the hills behind me could I see that I had made any progress towards the mountains, which seemed as distant as ever. But gradually the hills grew dim in the distance, while ahead, the mountains became more distinct and great seams and patches of vegetation appeared upon their slopes. It was well for me that I had laid in a supply of meat and eggs, for I saw no sign of life on the dreary plain, except one great beast that appeared like a gigantic lizard or iguana. In fact, so monstrous was the creature, that I feared my brain had gone adrift again and that it was but a vision of delirium. The beast appeared more afraid of me than I of him, however, and so little interest did I have in anything save the desire for water and to reach the farther side of the valley that I doubt if I would have turned aside or would have fled even though the devil himself had confronted me. Certain it is that the presence of this huge creature—I would say he was forty feet in length—did not prevent me from dropping off to sleep as usual that night.

At last my provisions became perilously low and when finally I reached the bases of the mountains I was reduced to two eggs, while my makeshift boots were gone entirely and my garments were merely a few dirty rags and shreds. To climb those rugged mountains seemed utterly beyond my power, but I noticed a sort of cut or ravine a half mile or so distant, and thinking this might be a pass through the mountains, I dragged myself toward it. It was a deep fissure and extended far up the mountain side and while it made the climb a bit easier I soon found that the task was far greater than I had expected, and only by the utmost efforts could I force my way upward. But some unknown force or instinct seemed to drag me on, and even when my last egg had been devoured I did not despair, but struggled and found my way, foot by foot, over the rocks and boulders and through patches of low scrub, until almost fainting from hunger and thirst, I came to another colony of the strange birds. On these I feasted until satisfied, and while resting and tying more of the bird-skins on my bruised and swollen feet, I found time to give some thought to my surroundings.

I had often heard of the theory of a vast Antarctic continent, and although I of course knew that Shackleton had found the South Pole, still I was now convinced that I had passed the pole and was on this unknown land.

But the fact that the weather was warm puzzled me immensely, while quite beyond my understanding was the fact that I had seen no glimpse of the sun on my long tramp across the plain. No theory, however wild and impossible, would account for this, for it was not dark but as bright as any Antarctic day, and neither could I understand how, especially without the sun, I could feel comfortably warm. At last, giving up the puzzle in despair, I gathered up my load of birds and eggs and once more started on.

And here it may be well to explain why I was able to think upon such matters, which are usually beyond the mind of a sailor, and how, as will be seen later, I happened to have a knowledge of many matters, such as science, mechanics and similar things of which the sailor or whaleman, as a rule, knows nothing. For several years I had been an officer on one of the ships of the United States Fish Commission, and from the scientists engaged in deep sea research I had learned a great deal about natural history which interested me always, and learning for the first time that specimens of animal life, minerals and plants had a cash value, I secured a commission from one of the museums to collect specimens on my whaling voyages to distant parts of the world. This led me to study works on science, and through long Arctic nights, I filled my brain with all manner of knowledge relating to geology, zoology, botany and other similar matters.

Also, I had always been fond of mechanics, and as the whaling industry waned and the demand for sailors decreased in the merchant service, I bent my energies to acquiring a knowledge of machinery so that I might secure a berth on some steam or motor-propelled craft. In doing this I became absorbed in the matter and found vast interest in reading all manner of books and magazines treating of the latest inventions and discoveries in the mechanical world. Of course I had little practical knowledge of these things, but the theories were fixed in my mind, and as it proved later, were of great value to me.

But to resume my narrative. Long and weary as my tramp across the plain had been, tenfold worse was the never ending upward climb towards the cloud-piercing summits of the mountains. My days were measured only by my waking moments, for the light never ceased, and my labor was only marked by long periods of panting, heartbreaking toil and periods of deep sleep, and while, to keep some sort of track of the hours, I had started my watch, yet this gave me no real time, but merely served to let me know how long I slept and how long I toiled upwards. Five days of this labor had again worn my makeshift footgear to pieces and had reduced my provisions to my last egg, when I reached the summit of the mountains, and falling exhausted upon the bare and wind-swept rocks, looked down upon the farther side.

At my first glance my heart gave a great throb of joy and I thanked heaven that I had been led on to the summit. Spreading from the base of the mountains was a wide level plain covered with rich and verdant green, while far away, gleaming like silver in the bright light, stretched a vast expanse of water.

Forgetting my sore, torn feet and my utter exhaustion, I rose and dashed forward down the slope. Stumbling over boulders, tripped by vines and shrubs, falling, sliding and scrambling, I reached the bottom in a few hours and dashed into the luxuriant grass that rose higher than my head. Here my strength failed me, and falling upon the earth, I felt utterly unable to rise again.

Presently I heard a slight rustling sound in the grass near me, and glancing up, beheld a strange animal staring at me in wonder, but evidently without the least fear. Thinking only to secure something to eat I managed to stagger to my feet and started towards the animal. I had no weapon except my knife, but the beast stood his ground until I was within a few feet when, by a sudden spring, I reached his side, and driving my knife into his throat, brought him down. In my famished state his blood and raw, warm meat were as welcome as the daintiest food, and having satisfied myself, I fell asleep beside his partially devoured carcass.

Several hours later I awoke, feeling much stronger, and looked more closely at the beast whose fortunate appearance had saved my life. I found him to be a sort of huge rat or mouse—although I had at first mistaken him for a small deer—and my stomach turned a bit at the thought that I had actually eaten his flesh. I now became conscious of a peculiar quality in the air that I had not noticed before. At first I was puzzled to account for it, but gradually I realized that the light had become intensely blue instead of white or yellow. It was like looking through a blue-tinted glass, and for the first time I noticed that my hands and knife and even the face of my watch, appeared bluish and strange. My longing for water, however, was too great to allow me to give much thought to the matter and turning from the dead animal—for hungry as I was I could not force myself to eat more of him—I started on in the direction of the water I had seen from the mountain top. The grass grew close and was very dry and gave off a dusty, choking material or pollen which filled my eyes, nose and mouth and each moment increased my thirst and dried and blistered my aching, parched throat. But gradually the grass became thinner and now and then I caught glimpses of small creatures and birds that fled before me, while the ground under my feet became

261

less dry and parched, until presently, the damp, sweet smell of water reached me. A moment later I burst through the last of the grass and saw before me a sandy beach lapped by tiny waves whose sound was the most welcome thing I had ever heard. Rushing across the beach, I through myself face down at the water's edge with a sickening fear that the water might be salt. But my first taste reassured me, and burying my face and hands in the waves, I drank until I felt sick and nauseated, when, crawling up the beach on all fours, I drew myself into the shelter of the grass and lost consciousness.

CHAPTER 3

Slowly I opened my eyes and as I did so I screamed aloud with terror and wonder. Standing over me was a fearsome, terrible creature. That he was not a man I knew at my first glance, and yet, there was something that resembled a man about him, but so terribly monstrous, weird and incredible, so utterly inhuman, that I felt sure I must be dreaming or out of my senses. He or it was fully eight feet in height, standing on two legs like a man, and seemingly clad from head to foot in some soft, downy material that glistened with a thousand colors, like the throat of a humming bird or the tints on a soap bubble. Above the shoulders was a large, elongated, pointed head with a wide mouth and a long, pointed snout. From the forehead projected long stalks or horns and on the tip of each of these was an unwinking, gleaming eye like the eyes of a crab. In place of eyebrows two long, slender, jointed, fleshy tentacles drooped down over the creature's shoulders, while the ears were long, soft and pendulous like those of a hound. There was no hair upon the head, but instead, a number of brilliant, shining scales or plates, lapping one over the other from the forehead to the nape of the neck.

No wonder I was horrified and startled at this apparition and as I gazed upon the thing and saw that it possessed three pairs of long, many-jointed arms, I shrieked again at the monstrosity of it. At my cry and my terrified actions, the creature raised one hand in a reassuring gesture and I was further horrified to see that in place of fingers the arm ended in a mass of delicate various-shaped appendages of several sizes, that reminded me of the soft legs on the belly of a crawfish or shrimp. I shrank away as far as possible, but the being seemed to smile, his stalked eyes drew back into his head and he uttered some strange sounds in a low, soft tone which I judge were words of greeting or reassurance, although to my ears they meant nothing.

Finding I did not respond—for I was still too dazed and frightened to utter a sound—the thing stooped and extended a small object towards me. It resembled a ship's bisquit in form and size and as I hesitated to take it the creature pointed to his own mouth and nodded, evidently meaning I was to eat it. I had no difficulty in grasping this meaning and famished as I was, rather hesitatingly took the object and greedily devoured it. In taste it was slightly sweet with a rather pleasant aromatic flavor and I at once signed my desire

263

for more. My weird friend, for I now knew that despite his fearful appearance the creature was well disposed towards me, handed me two more of the biscuits and as he did so I had a chance to look more closely at his hands. They were truly remarkable. Each of the dozen or more finger-like digits was of a distinct form and size. Some were large, strong and blunt; others slender and pointed; others with pincer-like tips, while still others were divided at the extremities into several filaments almost as fine as hairs. Marvelous and repulsive as they seemed, yet I could not help realizing even then what wonderful work such hands might accomplish if they were controlled by intelligence and muscles as perfect as man's, and yet my wildest ideas of such things fell far short of the reality.

Seating himself, or I might say, sprawling himself, beside me, the thing watched me munch the biscuit, and I in turn gazed at him with the utmost curiosity, as I had now partially overcome my dread. I now saw that what I had mistaken for clothing was in reality a growth upon the skin, a material something like wool and yet something like feathers. The feet, too, I found were as strange as the rest of the body or the hands, for in place of toes, they bore round-tipped digits covered with saucer-shaped suckers like those upon the tentacles of an octopus or squid.

Undoubted I was as great a marvel to him as he was to me, for I could see that his surprise at my appearance was tremendous. His long flexible feelers rose and fell about me—though not touching me for which I was thankful—his eyes turned and moved up and down as he looked me over from head to foot, and presently, realizing I no longer feared him, he extended one hand and very gently passed it over my clothing. I shuddered at the first touch, but as one of the appendages or fingers touched my flesh and I found it soft and warm and not cold or clammy as I had expected, my revulsion became less. Still the sensation of being handled or touched by the horribly formed thing was creepy and I had to use all my will to avoid drawing back. Evidently he was greatly surprised at the result of his examination and gazed at me more intently than ever, meanwhile uttering low, strange words or sounds that reminded me of the purring of a cat with a little of the rasping, metallic sound of a cricket.

Presently, seeing I had eaten the last of the biscuits, the creature rose to his two hind feet, folded two other pairs of limbs under his body, and beckoning with the fourth pair, or as I might call them, his arms, made me understand that I was to follow him. Filled with curiosity to know what wonders lay before me, and feeling sure the creature was friendly and peaceable, I also rose and to my amazement found that all my health and strength had returned in a most miraculous manner. I was as refreshed, light hearted and free from aches, soreness or pain as ever in my life and as I walked with springy, buoyant steps after the weird being my mind was filled with wonder. Surely, I thought, the three small biscuits could not have stayed my ravenous appetite and given me such strength, and yet there was no other way to account for it. But whatever the reason, my troubles were over for the present. I had water in plenty before me, the creature leading the way across the beach could provide food, and whatever the future might hold or wherever I might be, I would not die of thirst or starvation, while the incredible giant was friendly and apparently wished to help me.

I had no doubt that he was leading me to some house or settlement, and I was filled with curiosity to see what manner of creatures dwelt in this strange land. That they would be most interesting I felt sure, for I knew that, hitherto, the Antarctic had been thought uninhabited by man, and I wondered if they would resemble Eskimos, Indians or South Sea Islanders. That they should have domesticated such strangely weird creatures as the being who was guiding me, proved not only that they were intelligent, but that I might expect other and perhaps even greater surprises, while the fact that this monstrosity was so kindly and well disposed assured me that his masters would treat me with consideration. It was all very dream-like, and had it not been for my ragged garments, my thorn-torn and bruised flesh and my sore feet I should have felt sure that it was all a figment of my over-wrought brain, for it was almost too incredible to be true. I had set out from the desolate, forbidding shores of the Antarctic within a few degrees of the South Pole, and here I was in a land as mild and pleasant as New England in June; the sea—or what I took to be the sea—was fresh pure water; the brilliant sunshine, which should not have existed at all in this spot, was pale blue instead of white; and before me strode a creature such as no mortal man had ever seen save in some nightmare or the delirium of fever or drink; while to me, at the time, the most incredible thing of all was the fact that after eating three small, dry bisquits I had regained all my strength and felt as fresh—with the exception of my blistered feet—as ever in my life.

We had walked along the beach for some time, and I was beginning to wonder how much farther we must travel, when we rounded a bend and I saw a peculiar object resting on the sand a few yards ahead of us. It was about fifty feet in length, about ten feet in diameter, cylindrical and with pointed ends, resembling in a way a gigantic cigar. In the bluish light it shown with the brilliant lustre of metal, but with a peculiar purplish sheen that was unlike any metal I had ever seen. As we approached this object, I halted in my tracks with gaping mouth and staring, incredulous eyes. A door had opened in the affair, and from the aperture, two more of the weirdly horrible looking creatures had appeared. In every detail they were exactly like my guide, except that one was much smaller and was covered with a pale, pinkish coat of down or feathers, or whatever the material might be called. Instantly, I was aware of a peculiar, vibrating, humming sound and noticed that my companion's feelers or antennae had risen erect above his head and were moving slowly, gracefully back and forth, as were the feelers of the two other creatures; but no word or sound that could be thought speech issued from any of the three.

A moment later we were beside the great, cylindrical object and the two beings who had been within it were gazing at me with the greatest wonder and interest. Their stalked eyes were moving this way and that, studying me from head to foot; their feelers were vibrating with excitement; their lopears were waving like the ears of an elephant, and presently, with queer, low sounds from their lips, they stretched out their jointed limbs and rather hesitatingly and cautiously touched my garments with their many digited hands or feet, whichever they might be called.

I was, I admit, most uneasy and not a little frightened and had a peculiar sense of repulsion as the creatures approached close to me and their tentacles played about my face and their soft finger-like extremities caressed my tattered clothing. But I knew that for the present at least I had no real cause for alarm, for they seemed really gentle creatures. But if my readers—provided this manuscript ever finds a reader—can imagine standing beside three immense crayfish larger than any giant of a dime museum, they can perhaps, in a measure, realize the sensations that went over me.

Even so I found myself wondering if the huge cylinder before me was the dwelling of these weird things, if it was a sort of shell-like house, and if the three were the only denizens of this unknown land, or if there were more of their kind. But I instantly dismissed the thought. They were merely strangely developed, remarkably intelligent beasts and it was inconceivable that they should have constructed the metallic affair from which they had emerged. In fact, the presence of this convinced me that there were human beings not far distant and that the creatures beside me were merely guarding the metallic object and awaiting their master's return. Moreover, the fact that this huge, metal, cigar-like thing was there proved beyond doubt that the men who dwelt in the land were no primitive savages, but intelligent and civilized, although what the purpose of the thing was was quite beyond me. Possibly, I thought, it was some sort of boat—for it looked much like one of the floats to a metal life raft—perhaps a submarine; but there were no signs of rudders, fins, propellers or other external fittings on its smooth surface, and aside from the door or port from which the two creatures had emerged, no opening or aperture in the metal as far as I could see.

But, I had little time for thought on such matters. Their first curiosity satisfied, my guide gestured for me to follow, and entered the big cylinder with the other two following in my footsteps. Scarcely knowing what to expect, I passed through the door and glanced about. I was in a long room or hallway illuminated by a strange luminous glow and an exclamation of the utmost amazement escaped my lips as I discovered that the walls of the cylinder were as transparent as glass. Standing there, I could see the beach, the stretch of water, the green fringe of grass and bushes, as clearly as though I were in the open air and yet from without, the interior of the contrivance had been utterly invisible.

This was astounding enough, but before I could fully appreciate the wonder of it, there were more bewildering matters to fill my brain. The interior held no machinery, the only fittings in sight being couch-like benches, rugs or carpets and an affair at one end which at first glance I took to be a buffet or bar, for it bore a number of shining metallic and glass-like utensils. Above and behind it was a panel or rectangle covered with strange dials and instruments, and as we entered and the door closed behind us with a slight metallic clink, the creature who had first found me approached this buffet-like arrangement. Reaching out his arms, he moved certain things upon the panel, with his other limbs he touched the utensils on the piece of furniture before him. Instantly, there was a strange musical humming which rose swiftly to a whirring sound, liked the muffled noise of machinery and glancing through the transparent sides of the cylinder, I was dumbfounded to see the beach and the water swiftly dropping from beneath us. For a moment I could not understand and then, with a shock at the discovery, I realized that we were mounting upward with incredible speed. Within the space of a few seconds we were several hundred feet above the beach and the next instant my bewildered senses grasped the fact that we were hurtling through the air like a bullet from a rifle.

Almost before I knew it the beach and the grassy plain beyond it were dim in the distance, the faintly outlined waves upon the water seemed to rush backward and yet there was not the least movement appreciable within the transparent cylinder, and although I could see the entire interior from where I stood, there was no sign of machinery, no hint of engines, of whirring wheels or shafts. It was absolutely impossible and incredible. Within a cigar-shaped cylinder, which even if made of aluminum would have weighed tons, I was being hurled through space by invisible means controlled by the indescribably strange creatures beside me.

I peered ahead, for I knew that we must be bound for some definite goal, and saw land rising rapidly into view upon the horizon. Each second it became clearer, a low shore backed by hills deliciously green and bathed in the blue light that flooded everything. And as the land grew rapidly more distinct, bright, shining dots appeared among the greenery and presently, above the water's edge, an immense town or city lay spread. At the speed at which we were traveling we would be there within fifteen minutes, and as I glanced to right and left, I saw a score of craft similar to the one I was in, all rushing through the air like monstrous, gleaming cannon shells. Like streaks of light they crossed our path above or below us; to right and left they passed. Some were tiny things scarcely 10 feet in length; others gigantic affairs several hundred feet in length, but all moving noiselessly, with incredible speed, driven by some unseen, incomprehensible, terrific power. Below us, now, the water was dotted with the strange vessels, their shimmering hulls, if such I may call them, resting on the surface or skittering along slowly and leaving foamy wakes across the little waves. Then we were dropping, descending as lightly as a bit of thistle down, and almost under my feet I saw the outlying buildings of the town. So rapidly did we drop that at the time I had no chance to note the form or details of the buildings, except to see that they were of strange design and color, but even in our swift fall, in that space of a few seconds, I saw that the inhabitants, the beings who thronged the streets, were no humans, but one and all the same grotesque, monstrous creatures as those beside me.

Chapter 4

Shocked as I was at this discovery I saw that our arrival had been noticed, and that from every side, hurrying down the streets, swarming out of buildings, the creatures were rushing in a close packed mass towards a clear, open space like a broad level field which I judged was our landing place. The next moment our strange airship was at rest, and filled with unreasoning dread, trembling at thought of facing that horde of monsters, I followed my guides or captors, which ever they were, through the door and stepped upon the firm earth once more. All about the borders of the field, which I now saw was covered with cradle like structures like the one in which our craft rested, the stalk-eyed, misshappen beings had gathered, a maze of swaying, undulating antennae, of tall, pointed, scale-covered heads and irridescent bodies; but not one attempted to approach or to pass within the boundaries of the landing place.

Hardly had I noticed this, and wondered at it, when from one side a group of the monsters stepped out. At first glance they seemed no different from the others, but as they drew close I saw that they were of a totally different color, being a peculiar violet-blue, and that two pairs of their limbs or arms ended in enormous, vicious-looking claws or nippers like those of a lobster. Even as I noticed this they reached us and I shuddered as I thought of how easily the creatures could crush and tear me to bits with those fearful pincers with their serrated teeth.

But for the present the claws were at rest and closed and their owners made no hostile movement. Forming on either side of my guides and myself, they marched beside us, and before them the crowd fell back, leaving an open lane through which we passed.

Before us were buildings, and for the first time, I obtained a clear view of the structures and gaped, almost as astonished at their appearance as I had been at the monstrous forms of their owners. From high in air they had seemed low, massive structures with nothing particularly remarkable about them, but now, close at hand I saw that they were unlike anything I had ever seen, although in a vague way they reminded me of gigantic iglooes. Windowless they rose like domes of dull-gray above the earth, the only apertures in their walls, dark, yawning, arched doorways towards one of which my guards were marching. As we entered the portal my passing glance showed me that the affairs were not of mud or clay as I had thought at first, but were constructed of small stones and pebbles cemented together with some hard tenacious material giving them the effect of being hewn from coarse pudding stone, or as I believe geologists call it, conglomerate rock.

The next instant we were within the entrance and were descending a steep incline. So sharp was the slope that the skin coverings on my feet slipped, my feet shot out from under me and with a startled cry I went sliding and rolling through the semi-darkness like a bale of cargo down a chute. How far I might have gone or where I might have brought up I cannot say, for with incredible agility, two of the monsters overtook me and with their weird limbs—which made me shudder as they touched me—brought me to a halt and helped me to my feet.

Despite the confusion and my predicament I had noticed that the creatures, when in a hurry, ran along on all fours, or rather I might say on all eights, and I realized that the sucker-like disks on their feet enabled them to navigate the steep passage without the least danger of slipping.

No doubt my mishap seemed very amusing to the strange beings, but no sounds of merriment came from them and to this moment I have never heard anything that remotely resembled a laugh or chuckle issue from the mouths of the creatures.

The whole affair, yes, everything that had occurred since I had seen the castaway boat with the corpses of my dead shipmates, was so dreamlike, so nightmarish that, try as I might, I could not convince myself that I was awake and that the strange events were actually taking place and that the beings,—intelligent, reasoning, possessing powers and mechanical devices beyond anything dreamed of by man, and yet mere beasts or creatures of a lower order,—really existed and were not the creations of a disordered or wandering mind. But my fall was very real and as the creatures aided me to rise and I ruefully rubbed my bruised and barked limbs I knew that the tumble at least was no delirium. Indeed, I think that my mishap was the most convincing thing that had occurred. It is really strange how little, unimportant, every day matters are often of so much greater importance in our lives than great events, and all that I had undergone had failed to impress me as much, or too bring so vividly to my mind, the marvelous situation in which I found myself as that tumble on the steep incline leading through the darkness to the interior of some subterranean chamber.

At the time, however, I had little opportunity to give much thought to such matters. Before me a dull light shown, and a moment later, we emerged from the passage and entered a huge, round chamber. Although, at my first sight of the place, I did not take in the details, it may be as well to describe it at this point of my narrative. The floor was smooth, white and seemed made of some luminous material; the walls glowed with dull light, and the high, domed ceiling appeared as if of glass with brilliant bluish light streaming through it.

About the walls was a low bench or shelf-like arrangement covered with what appeared to be cushions; scattered about were curiously shaped chairs or stools, and in the centre, was a sort of raised dais or platform on which were several more seats and a desk-like arrangement covered with dials and instruments, much like the affair I had already seen in the airship and by means of which the creatures handled the craft. Upon the bench about the walls, and seated on the other stools, were several dozen of the beings to whom I was now becoming accustomed. In a general way they were precisely like my guards and the creature I had first met upon the distant beach, but in details they were different. In fact, no two were exactly alike, although it was not until long afterward that I learned to distinguish the various differences, some of which were very minute. They were of all colors, from white to nearly black, although all had the same peculiar metallic sheen I had already noted, and all likewise possessed eight limbs, the long-stalked eyes and the antennae. Already I had been impressed with the striking resemblance the creatures bore to giant crawfish, but now, as I gazed about the huge chamber, I had the feeling that I was surrounded by huge crustaceans possessed of intelligent, reasoning brains. Possibly I cannot convey to my readers—if by will of God this narrative ever reaches human beings—the weirdly impossible, dreamlike and in a way, horrible sensations that swept over me as I stared at the scaly heads, the slowly moving stalked eyes, the waving, undulating antennae and the eight jointed limbs of these beings and realized that here in this strange land beyond the South Pole evolution had proceeded in a very amazing and very different manner to that which had taken place in the world of men. Years before I had read, among my other books, a work by Darwin on evolution and the survival of the fittest. Although I had never fully accepted the idea that mankind had descended or ascended from some monkey-like ancestor, still I could understand how it might be possible, and I had been convinced that man, as well as other members of the animal kingdom, had developed from other more primitive forms. And now, as I stood within the illuminated chamber, it suddenly dawned upon my mind that the creatures among whom my lot had been cast actually proved Darwin's theory. Here before me and all about me were beings no whit less intelligent than human beings; creatures who had conquered space and time with incredible aircraft; beings who could converse without words and who, I later

271

found, were far in advance of man, and yet who bore not the remotest resemblance to humans. To put the matter in a few words; just as men resemble highly developed and advanced apes, so these beings resembled crustaceans. If the human race had been evolved from some ape-like creature, then beyond the shadow of a doubt, these creatures had been evolved from some lobster-like ancestor. The discovery came to me as a shock. So accustomed are we to think that intelligent, reasoning, civilized beings must be moulded in human form that it rather dazed me to find that the mere form of body and limbs had nothing to do with it; that the mere chance that man's ancestors had been apes or ape-like had led to the physical appearance of human beings, and that, had some other form of life been the fittest to survive and had gone through ages of evolution, our world might have been peopled by insects, reptiles or any other creatures as progressive, intelligent and highly civilized as ourselves.

Here before me was the proof of this. Here evolution had proceeded from cold-blooded, spineless crustaceans, and the result was these shrimp-like giants, possessing powers beyond my own or those of mankind. Of course, at the time, the full significance of the matter did not come to me, but as time passed and I learned how immeasurably beyond man these creatures had advanced I became more and more convinced that the accident of the origin of the human race had been an unfortunate rather than a fortune thing for the world and that, had we been evolved from ants, say, we would have been much farther along the road to highest attainments.

But I am digressing. At the time I was really more impressed by the curious discoveries I made than by thoughts on evolution. One of the first things I noticed, and which oddly enough had quite escaped me hitherto, was the fact that the creatures possessed tails. These were broad, flat affairs composed of overlapping plates or scales and which usually remained folded like fans. This no doubt was the reason they had escaped my notice, for being of the same color and texture as the rest of the bodies, I had taken them for ornamental pendant affairs, portions of the garments which I had thought the things wore, for I had not yet discovered that the feather-like covering of their bodies was a natural growth.

Now, however, I saw that when seated the tails stuck stiffly out behind the creatures, or in some cases were curled around to one side, and that they moved to and fro, opening and shutting in a most fascinating manner. Some I noted also, were far larger than others, and, later, I learned to distinguish the males and females by the form and size of their tails.

Of course all this which has taken so much time to write down occupied but a few instants and my eyes, having swept about the chamber, turned to the dais in the center and the creatures who were seated upon it.

These were taller, more slender and more brilliant in color than the others. Their heads were higher, broader and rounder; their antennae were longer and their eyes, borne on long stalks like the others; seemed to me to have a more intelligent expression, if indeed, such hard, cold, unwinking orbs were capable of expression of any sort.

By intuition I knew that they were leaders or rulers and that I was being brought before them, and somehow this almost human procedure of being led by armed guards before a tribunal surrounded by a curious crowd struck me as both ludicrous and amazing.

That I was in danger never occurred to me. Possibly it was because I had been through so much that I was callous of danger, or perhaps it was because man instinctively looks down upon inferior races or creatures; but whatever the reason, although I was fully aware that I was at their mercy, I felt no fear but rather was filled with interest and curiosity as to what would occur. Indeed, I felt precisely as I have felt when, in dreams, I have been dragged before a court to be tried for my life on some ridiculous charge, and knowing I might be condemned to death, yet I felt no dread of the results, owing to a peculiar subconscious conviction that I would escape harm and would awaken before the actual execution took place.

Also, I was filled with a curiosity as to how the hearing was to be conducted, for while there was no doubt that the creatures could converse readily among themselves, their words, or whatever means they used, were inaudible to me, and when they uttered sounds, as they did at times, the almost metallic noises were utterly unintelligible.

But I had far underestimated the uncanny, incredible powers of the creatures. Suddenly I was aware, as one becomes aware of some unseen person gazing at one in a crowd, that I was being questioned. I cannot describe the sensation, cannot make it clear. There was no sound, nothing to tell me that my ears were receiving any message, and as a matter of fact they were not.

And yet my brains, or some unknown sense, was receiving a message, questions which, could they be put into word, might have been expressed as "Who are you? Whence do you come? What is your purpose?"

Was I dreaming, losing my senses, going mad from my past hardships and my amazing adventures? And then, almost unconsciously, I found myself replying to the inaudible queries. I was trying to explain how I had been shipwrecked, how I had wandered across the mountains and had come to this land, and that my only

273

purpose was, if possible, to return to my own country.

And as I thus responded to the uncanny question entering my brain without audible sounds, I knew from the actions of the strange beings that my replies had been understood. Their antennae waved and trembled excitedly. They turned their stalked eyes and gazed at one another and at myself, and they even uttered the queer metallic sounds which always denoted great excitement.

It had been astounding enough to discover that the creatures could make themselves understood by some occult, uncanny power; but to find that I could make my thoughts clear to them was almost beyond reason. How had it been accomplished? How was it possible for me, a totally different being from another world, to understand these strange creatures? And what was still more astonishing, more inexplicable yet, how had I been able to transfer my thoughts to their brains? Was it some weird, undreamed-of method of mental telepathy, hypnotism or what? Even if they possessed some power, some unknown means of making me understand them, I certainly had no such power. And yet I was convinced that I had made myself clear to them, or at my rate had managed to reply in some fashion to their queries.

And the next instant my belief was confirmed. Once more, in my brain, questions were being registered, questions as intelligible as though I had heard the words spoken in English. I was being asked about "my world," questioned as to details of my journey, as to whether there were more beings like myself and various other matters.

Almost before I realized it, I was replying and, as I could see by the manner of my strange hosts, my words were heard and understood. It is of no use to describe at length the entire interview that followed or to repeat it word for word. It is enough for my purpose to state that my story was as unbelievable and as impossible to them as they and their powers seemed to me. I had appeared from nowhere, a strange, and to them misshapen being, a creature unlike anything they had ever imagined, and I found myself trying to explain, floundering about, trying to make clear matters which to me were most everyday and ordinary things, but to them were so far beyond their comprehension that they were utterly incapable of grasping them.

It was like trying to explain trigonometry or navigation to a small child or to make clear the principles and operation of some complicated machine to a savage. And yet this comparison is not the right one, for strange as it may seem, the creatures were quite capable of understanding the most intricate mechanical devices and scientific matters, although the fact that there were other intelligent beings in the world, or that for that matter there was any world except their own country, was utterly beyond them.

Of course I did not learn this and did not attempt to converse with them on such matters at this first interview. Our talk, for regardless of the fact that they did not speak I must call it a talk, was confined to the most simple matters. But as the weeks, months and years passed and I remained, as I still remain, among them, I tried to tell them of human life and the world I had known and of all manner of things which differed from their own strange ways and existence.

Gradually, too, I became adept at conversing with them by their uncanny means, which, I found later, was nothing supernatural, magical nor so very mysterious after all. It was accomplished in fact by vibrating waves sent through the air, something after the manner in which sound waves are sent, and which were produced by one pair of the creatures' antennae and were caught and heard by another pair.*

(Note by Dr. Lyman).

"Mr. Bishop had of course never heard of radio-telephony. I am of the opinion that the beings among whom he found himself had discovered and perfected some form of radio waves by means of which intelligible messages could be transmitted from mind to mind without audible sounds. In other words, the unspoken thoughts could be transmitted on high frequency waves or on some form of waves akin to electro-magnetic waves. As is well known today, scientists have reason to believe that the lower animals possess a somewhat similar power and can receive and understand certain waves of which we have no knowledge—perhaps the missing waves that in length lie between heat waves and radio waves. It is also believed by many scientists that it is by some such means that pigeons, dogs, cats and even toads find their way home across unknown spaces and for immense distances, and that migratory birds fly unerringly from place to place. Recent investigations have also led to the conclusion that insects and crustaceans converse or at least communicate with one another, by means of waves produced by and received by their antennae. If this be so, then the highly developed and specialized crustaceans who inhabit the strange land described by Mr. Bishop might well have possessed a similar power carried to the nth degree.

Assuming this were so, then there would have been no mystery as to how they understood him or he them, for while spoken words vary with language the thoughts or brain impressions that words express must be identical regardless of spoken dialects or racial differences. Indeed, as will be seen later, Mr. Bishop's discoveries, as he relates them, bear out this logical conclusion. It is also highly probable that all the mechanism of the airships and other contrivances of these strange beings were actuated by waves similar to our electro-magnetic waves"—A. E. L.

Chapter 5

t was soon evident to me that even if the weird creatures could not fully grasp or understand the tale I related, still they believed it, or at least considered that it explained my presence in their land. Possibly they thought me a harmless lunatic, or again they may have decided I was a supernatural being, or maybe I was such a curiousity or monstrosity in their eyes that I was regarded as a valuable specimen. At any rate, whatever the reason, they decided I was not to be harmed, and in fact was to be well treated, for my armed guards were dispersed and I was given to understand,—I would say told but for the fact that no words were spoken—that the being who had first found me on the sand was to be my companion and that he would attend to all my wants. My first and most pressing want was food, for I was once more ravenously hungry and the council or court and onlookers having left the chamber, though lingering and gazing at me most curiously, I expressed my wishes to my strange companion. Immediately he led me through dark passageways to a smaller room and there left me for a moment, returning with a bowl-like vessel containing some liquid and a beautifully devised casket or box filled with the biscuits such as he had given me upon the beach.

I devoured three of these and was about to eat the fourth when the creature, who had been watching me intently, called a halt and by the same strange brain message method warned me that I must be satisfied and that to partake of more might lead to grave results. I confess I was greatly tempted to disregard his warning, for there seemed no more sustenance in the stuff than in a dry cracker, but I remembered what a miraculous effect those I had eaten on the beach had had, and reluctantly replacing the wafer I drank a deep draught of the liquid. It was as clear and colorless as water, for which I had taken it, but as it passed my lips I almost dropped the bowl in surprise, for the beverage was the most delightful and refreshing thing I had ever tasted. It was neither sweet nor sour, but had a taste absolutely impossible to describe. Indeed, there are many things in this strange land which I am at a loss to describe in such a way that those who have not seen or experienced them can understand my meaning. Colors existed which were quite different from anything I had ever seen; there were sounds totally new to my ears and tastes that no words can describe.

Scarcely had the beverage passed my lips when I felt rejuvenated. No wine or liquor could have had such a remarkable effect. Not that it was heady or exhilarating like liquor, for my head remained perfectly clear, but I felt years younger. I seemed as strong and fresh as a youth of twenty and felt ready for anything. Then a delightful drowsiness came over me, and throwing myself on the couch, I instantly dropped off to a dreamless slumber.

I was aroused by the being who had me in charge as he entered the chamber bearing food and drink. As I munched the wafer-like biscuits, which were of a different character from those I had eaten the previous day, I tried my best to communicate with him. Or rather, I might say, to carry on a conversation, for he very evidently understood all that I said. Moreover, as on the preceding day, I was able to understand him. But the difficulty was that we had so little in common that it was almost impossible to converse at any length. However, he made it known that I was free to go and come as I pleased and that I was considered an honored guest from some other sphere, and I was vastly amused when he wished to know if I had dropped from the sky. Evidently the creatures knew nothing of a country beyond the mountain barrier, and in vain I endeavored to explain how I had come over the mountains and to tell of the world on the other side. To him such a thing was incredible, as unbelievable as his land would have been to me before I had seen it. Then, after much trouble, he told me—if I can use the word "told" when no sounds issued from him,—that no inhabitant of this country had ever passed those mountains, that beyond was nothingness and that his country comprised the entire world. This was most astounding to me, for I had come over the mountains without excessive difficulty, and with their marvelous airships I could see no reason why they should not have soared above the peaks. But when I questioned the fellow, and later talked with others, I learned to my amazement that the creatures perished miserably if they rose more than a few hundred feet above the earth. Their airships never attained a height of more than two hundred feet and I was informed that too-venturesome members of the community, who had attempted to traverse the mountains, had gasped and died long before they reached the summits. To them, strange as it may seem, an altitude of five hundred feet was as fatal as a dozen miles in air to human beings. Whether this was due to their physical peculiarities or to some peculiarity in their atmosphere I have never determined. I am of the opinion, however, that it is a little of both. Their air I am sure is far more rarefied than ours and thus of course would be unfit to sustain life even at moderate heights, while being evolved from crustaceans—as I am positive they are—and with modified gills instead of lungs, they are naturally less adaptable to changes in the density of air than are human beings. Indeed, later, when I on one occasion tried to scale the mountains, I discovered that it was with the utmost difficulty that I could breathe, even when half way to the summits.

But this was not the reason why I was forced to remain in this land even to the present time as I shall explain later.

But to resume my narrative of my experiences. As soon as I had finished my breakfast I started out to see the sights. It was, however, some time before I reached the outer air, for I found many most astounding and interesting things to attract me in the underground residences of these strange creatures.

The means of lighting the place was a puzzle, for as I have said, the illumination was a sort of glow that appeared to issue from the walls, floors and ceilings, as if in fact they were made of transluscent material with lights behind them. I examined the material carefully and found it was formed of one continuous unbroken surface, as if moulded or cast in place, as I found later it was. Also, I discovered that it was the same material of which the airships were made. Indeed, later on I found that it was the sole material these beings possessed for constructing anything—that is, aside from wood which was seldom used and was rather a curiosity than otherwise, and a tough grass which they considered of little value, but from which a thin, light and excellent parchment-like material is made,—the material in fact upon which this manuscript is written. But the amazing part of it is that the metalic-like substance so widely used can be so altered or modified that it is adaptable for every purpose.

It can be made opaque, transparent or transluscent; as hard as steel or as soft and plastic as putty; as brittle as glass or as flexible as rubber. It can be beaten or hammered like gold or copper; it can be moulded by hand or machine and then hardened, or it can be melted and cast. Moreover, it can be colored or tinted at will; it can be woven like thread and it can be cut, bored or worked like timber. By certain processes, too, it can be made to emit light indefinitely, while the light may yet be turned off or on at will by means of some electrical or similar power. This same mysterious force serves these creatures in place of steam, heat and all other forms of power.

It was of course a long time before I learned all this, and I was still longer in learning the source of the remarkable substance. Then, to my utter amazement I found it was sulphur! This statement may seem incredible, for sulphur is so well known and its properties so well understood that my fellow men will no doubt accuse me of telling a palpable falsehood. But the secret lies in the fact that these beings have discovered a property of sulphur of which humans are wholly ignorant. This is that sulphur is really a metal, the form known to us being only a salt or oxide, and it is the metallic sulphur which these weird creatures use for such a multitude of purposes.*

It was, as I have said, a great surprise to me to discover this, and I could not help thinking what marvelous accomplishments might be ours if we possessed the knowledge of obtaining this metal. I had never dreamed that a metallic material could be obtained from sulphur, and at first it seemed unbelievable. But as I thought upon the matter, I realized that, after all, it was no more astonishing than that aluminum metal could be secured from the soft rock called bauxite, many cargoes of which had been carried in ships on which I had served. Later, too, I spent much time at the vast deposits of sulphur which seem to underlie the whole country. Although it has been used for countless ages, yet these beings have never had to do any mining, for there are hills and plains composed entirely of the yellow stuff. Indeed, I was not long in deciding that the whole place is nothing more than the interior of a huge volcano, or a series of volcanic craters, which might partly account for the warmth of the climate, for no doubt there is still volcanic activity and heat below the surface of the earth. The processes used for refining the sulphur and transforming it into metal were most interesting, but I am no chemist and the technicalities are far beyond my powers to describe. There are huge works that cover many square miles, and the workers are, I found, all of different types, forms and appearances from the other inhabitants. In fact each art, profession, trade, and class, of the beings is, I soon found, distinct and has been evolved or developed in such a way as to give the greatest efficiency and best results along the lines of endeavor to which each is bound for life. I have mentioned the huge pincer-like claws of the soldiers, or rather police. In the same way, diggers have limbs adapted to their labors; chemists possess appendages as delicate as the most accurately devised instruments, and so on.

(Note by Dr. Lyplan).
"Mr. Bishop was probably unaware that several chemists have declared their belief that the element sulphur is derived from a metallic base. Although no one has yet produced metallic sulphur, yet that does not prove the incorrectness of such an hypothesis. Soda, potash and many other common chemicals, which bear no resemblance to metals are merely salts or oxides of metals, although their metallic bases were formerly unknown. Modern chemistry, however, has, as is well known, produced metallic sodium, potassium, calcium, magnesium, etc."—A. E. L.

279

But to return to the sulphur and its uses. Among other things that interested me greatly was the source of the marvelous power the creatures use. This was, I found, derived from a peculiar blackish and very heavy material which exists in vast quantities near the sulphur deposits. Of itself it is of little value, although it is slightly luminous and will cause sores like burns upon human skin as I discovered to my sorrow. But when combined with the metallic sulphur, or with certain by-products obtained in the manufacture of the latter, it produces most astonishing results. By varying the combinations and the proportions of materials it can be made to emit blinding light which goes on continuously forever without in the least diminishing, or it can be made to explodewith a force greater than dynamite, while by still other methods it may be made to produce invisible power which can be harnessed as readily as steam and yet can be transmitted to great distances through the air, like electricity, but without the use of wires. About one hundred miles from the chief city is an immense power house, if such it may be called, and from this, power or energy is sent broadcast over the whole country. Thus, by having machines adapted to the purpose, this source of power may be tapped and used for any purpose, such as driving airships, industrial work, turning on or off lights etc. But the remarkable part of it, to me, is the fact that no machines, as we know such things, are used. I have visited the plant several times and yet have never found a single wheel, shaft or crank in it. There are merely immense chambers or vats into which the various substance are run, and grid-like mazes of bars and sheets of metal. These are suspended over the vats and a ceaseless play of many-colored and strangely tinted lights and intense heat seems to rush upward from the tanks and to be absorbed by the odd apparatus overhead. From these it is led into a labyrinth of receptacles and a mystifying, to me, network of conduits, cables and huge wires and up-standing rods. These scintillate with flashing lights and emit a cracking sound and send the power in all directions. The strangest thing about it, to my mind, is the fact that the creatures are not injured by this power, even when close to it and while it is passing through their bodies. At first I was deathly afraid of it, for it seemed like terrific discharges of electricity; but I found that even I could stand beside the generators, or whatever they may be called, and that with the colored flashes all about me and enveloping my body, I felt no ill effects. Rather, it gave me a pleasant tingling sensation which left me exhilarated for several days thereafter.*

Also, aside from the metal and the power, many other most valuable things are obtained from the sulphur and the black rock. A vast number of by-products result, and from these all or nearly all the wants of the inhabitants are obtained. Even the strange beverage I have mentioned was manufactured from a by-product, as are coloring materials, certain foods and many other things. Also, as I have said, wood is regarded as a curiosity. This is due to the fact that strangely enough there are practically no real trees in this strange land. By this I do not mean that trees do not exist, for there are great parks or gardens filled with them, but there are no wild trees, if I may use the expression. Ages ago, I understand, there were many, but these were all utilized and exhausted and fearing that trees would become extinct they were preserved in parks as curiosities.

Only when they die is the wood available and the creatures prize this highly and treasure it as though it were a most precious substance, using it as we might use gold or silver. Most of the country is covered with a coarse, sedgy grass, but there are many forms of shrubs and plants and immense areas of bare land which at first puzzled me.

I had seen no cultivated plants or gardens—except park-like places like botanical gardens—and I imagined that the bare areas were fields being prepared for cultivation, as I saw many of the beings working in them. Imagine my wonder when I found that these bare patches of earth provided the inhabitants with their food. Countless years ago, I was informed, the beings had abandoned raising food plants. The plants, so they discovered, merely drew sustenance from the air and soil and transformed this to food fit to eat. And the creatures, reasoning that this process of nature was a round-about method of making food, devised means of obtaining their provisions from the air and earth direct, doing away with the plants entirely.

From the edible materials thus obtained they make the wafer-like biscuit I have referred to and these, with their liquors and little pellets, form their entire diet. Each class or variety of wafer, I learned, contained different food values of a vegetable nature, while

(Note by Dr. Lyman).

"Probably the material described by Mr. Bishop is a very rich radioactive mineral akin to or identical with pitch-blende, and by combining this with derivatives of sulphur the marvelous powers of radium were harnessed. Just how the strange power was produced we cannot say, for Mr. Bishop was of course ignorant of technicalities, as he states. I should imagine, however, that the power was generated by breaking down atoms by means of radio activity and thus releasing the stupendous forces contained in them. This has long been a dream of scientists, for it is well known that a single atom of matter contains incalculable power or energy and that, if it were possible to break or explode atoms undreamed of forces would be at man's disposal. Unquestionably the power described by Mr. Bishop was transmitted by means of electro-magnetic or similar waves."—A. E. L.

the pellets supplies the animal matter, and by choosing these any taste or need could be satisfied. Also, just as they secure provisions of a vegetable nature from the soil itself without the time and trouble involved in raising crops, so they manufacture the foods of an animal nature from the vegetable products. Animals, they say, merely transform the herbage they devour into meat, and such things, so why raise living creatures with great trouble and care and then slaughter them, when the same materials, or at least material containing the same nourishment and the same chemicals, can be made direct?

And a word in regard to the animal life of this strange country may be of interest to any humans who find this document. At certain seasons, vast numbers of birds visit the great lakes or seas, which are all of fresh water, and I have found a great deal of pleasure in watching these, for the albatrosses, mollymokes, gulls and other familiar birds come over the mountains from the world I once knew, and seem to me a bit like visitors and old friends from my home. It was, in fact, these periodical visits of the sea fowl that gave me the idea of sending out my manuscript, in the hope that some man might find it. But to return to the animals that dwell here. There are a number of the giant rat-like creatures, as large as kids, such as the one I killed and devoured when I first gained the base of the mountains, and there are many small birds, but aside from these, no living creatures exist in a wild state. In zoos or museums are many most wonderful creatures, some of which bear a resemblance to those on the other side of the world, but most of which are wholly different and many of which are so astoundingly weird, gigantic or grotesque as to be horrifying, or to make me think I am dreaming or delirious when I look at them.

Some of these are gigantic reptiles with immense scaly bodies and with heads covered with great bony plates and armed with huge horns. They are ferocious looking creatures nearly fifty feet in length, but quite docile and harmless and very stupid. Others resemble giant seals, but instead of being covered with fur, their bodies are smooth and slimy, like eels. There are also creatures with enormously long snake-like necks and great round bodies. These are water animals and should they be seen at sea they would be veritable sea-serpents. There are several great beasts too, which appear to be some sort of elephants, though vastly bigger than any I have ever seen, and there are a few rhinoceros-like animals, besides numbers of smaller things, such as deer, goats, beasts somewhat like ponies, and giant turtles. Of carnivorous beasts there are none and I find nothing that at all resembles an ox or sheep. All these I understand once roamed the country wild, but were destroyed by the strange inhabitants until only those in captivity remained. But perhaps the weirdest of all these creatures in the parks or zoos are the insects. There are butterflies whose wings spread a yard across, flies as big as turkeys, caterpillars with a girth greater than my body and immense spiders with six-foot, hairy legs and immense, staring, fiery red eyes. These always give me a feeling of dread and nausea as I look at them, and many a time I have awakened, screaming, from a nightmare wherein I thought myself being attacked by one of these horrible creatures. The natives, however, seem to have no fear of them and I have often seen the younger ones, or if I may so call them the children, feeding the monstrous spiders through the bars of their cages. These bars by the way are made of the transparent form of the sulphur metal, and looking at the creatures, the bars are all but invisible—as are the cages—so that one seems to see a horrible beast unconfined and ready to spring at one. But of all the insects, those which interest me most are the giant-ants. These are as large as good-sized dogs and are kept in a vast pit-like enclosure. Here they hurry about, and labor ceaselessly, building huge mounds and digging tunnels, only to tear them down and start over again. They are the most ferocious of all the animals also, and if one of their number is injured or sick, the others, after carefully examining him, tear him to bits and devour his still moving body. On one occasion a great lizard-like beast died and his carcass was thrown into the ant pit and I fairly shook with terror as I watched the creatures, gnawing him to bits and with incredible strength dragging the immense body here and there. Often, too, the ants seem to be drilling and they seem to possess intelligences almost human. Often I think what terible havoc they would play should they escape from their den, but I am assured that this is impossible, as the frail looking fence that borders the pit is made of a material that is certain death to any ant that touches it. Indeed, I heard, if I may use that term, the story of these ants. It seems that ages ago,—these beings have no means of recording time by the way,—the ants roamed at large and destroyed the inhabitants everywhere. A constant war was waged between the two races and bloody battles were fought. In a way it was much like the Indian warfare at home, though far more merciless and cruel, for each side made slaves of their captives and gave no quarter.

Then the crustaceon-like beings made a discovery. They found vast numbers of dead ants where an invading army had moved across a great pile of waste material from the sulphur works, and by testing this on captive ants they found that it was instant death to the creatures. This enabled them to exterminate their hereditary enemies, for the material was made in stupendous quantities and placed in a great wall or pile about the advancing host of the

283

inhabitants. Thus guarded, the ants were powerless to harm them, and gradually all but a few of the ants were utterly destroyed. These few survivors were made prisoners and confined and it is the descendants of these that are in the pit today.

Since then, so I understand, there have been no wars or battles in the entire land and the soldiers or police are being done away with, as there is really no need for them. No more soldiers are bred and in a few years none of the old ones will remain alive.

CHAPTER 6

Of the inhabitants of this country, which I now feel sure is a continent or an immense island in the unexplored area beyond the South Pole, I might write many pages. But this manuscript must not be too long, for even written as it is on this wonderfully thin and light material, yet I must have a care that it is not too heavy for the winged messenger to whom I intend to entrust it.

I have already described, to the best of my ability, the personal or physical appearance of the strange beings among whom, I fear, I am destined to remain for the rest of my life. Also, I have spoken of their means of communicating with one another and with myself, and here and there I have given short accounts of their habits and occupations and of their wonderful inventions and accomplishments. But as yet, I have said nothing of their social or family life, their thoughts, laws, codes, public institutions and many other matters which have proved vastly interesting to me, and may perhaps interest my fellow men if Fate wills that this manuscript ever reaches them.

There is so much to write that is strange, incredible and difficult to describe, that I hardly know where to begin. Many long months passed before I could carry on a thought conversation clearly enough to get an insight into many matters; but now that I have been here for over a year, as nearly as I can figure it out, I am able to make myself understood and to understand them as readily as if we spoke a common language.

First perhaps, I should mention that these creatures are comparatively short lived. They seldom reach an age which in my world would be forty years, but as they mature in an incredibly short time their lives are proportionately as long as our own. That is, these creatures become fully grown and with fully developed powers, both mentally and physically, in only a few weeks after emerging from their eggs, so that their life of full mental and physical power is about fourty years, whereas human beings who require from twenty to thirty years to reach full mental and physical power, would have to live to sixty or seventy years in order to equal these beings. Moreover, their mental and physical powers remain unimpaired until death, and age, as we know it, does not exist. Thus their full span of life is made available for their utmost endeavors. I have spoken of them as hatching from eggs and this was to me a most astounding thing when I discovered it. But after all it should not have surprised me, for being crustacean-like, there is no reason why they should not have crustacean-like traits of development and life. The eggs are deposited in places provided for the purposes and are there carefully watched over by beings whose lives are devoted to the purpose, and the young, when they emerge from the eggs, are separated into groups, each group or collection being destined for training, or I might say development, for special purposes. Thus one group will be destined for miners, another for chemists, others for artizans and so on. And the number of young selected for each group is decided by the demands for the specific trades or professions for which they are destined. Thus, if there are a normal number of healthy and able bodied miners and no necessity for more, none of the young of that particular time will be destined for that trade, whereas, if there are say two thousand artizans needed that many young will be set apart for development as artizans. Also, if the number of eggs exceeds the number which the rulers deem necessary, the surplus are destroyed before the young emerge. This is a matter determined by calculations as to the number of beings who are expected to die during the year, and the number of inhabitants who can be safely permitted to exist without danger of want or improper accommodations. As a result, there is no poverty, no want, no idleness and no suffering in the entire country and no surplus or lack of any trade or profession. To me it seemed a most barbarous and inhuman practice at first, but after all they are not human. And in many ways it is a most admirable idea and I cannot help comparing the extraordinary well-being and universal content of these creatures with the dissatisfaction, poverty and suffering of the human race. Moreover, there is no sickness or illness among them. Any member injured or ill is at once done away with, for, so they argue, to cure a sick or injured being necessitates the services of one or more others, even if the ill or injured creature survives and recovers, whereas, should he or she remain a cripple or unfit for duty, he or she is an impediment and may require the constant services of others, as well as the sustenance and support which might be better devoted to healthy, perfect individuals. It may seem a merciless system, but these beings have no sentiment, affection or love as we know them.

Their entire lives are devoted to the well being of the whole community and to performing the duties alloted them. But I do not mean by that they are lacking in pleasures or recreations or are ceaseless workers like the ants. They realize that ceaseless labor drains their powers and that change is a necessity, and their hours of work and recreation are regulated. But their recreations are to me most strange. They consist largely of frolicking in the water, like genuine water creatures, or of racing madly about in a sort of dance until utterly exhausted. Also, they have queer games and athletic contests, and in these they are often so seriously injured as to result in their being done away with. Not that the loss of a limb or of several limbs amounts to much for these creatures can lose nearly all their exterior organs and be none the worse after a few weeks, for like lobsters and crabs, they grow new limbs or appendages readily, and after shedding their skins or shells, appear as whole as ever. This shedding process was of course an astounding thing to me at first, though quite natural, but it was, I am told, one of the greatest drawbacks to their development and well-being and in years long past was a terrific problem to solve. In those days thousands of the creatures shed their old skins at the same time, and for days thereafter, were soft, tender, almost helpless and unfit for duty, and thus the entire nation was at a standstill and was exposed to the attacks of their enemies,—the giant ants and other creatures. Gradually, however, by changing diet and regulating the development of eggs and young, the creatures managed to produce a race whose members did not shed all at once, but cast off their shells at various seasons, so that only a portion of their numbers were helpless at one time. Moreover, they found that garments or coverings could be devised to protect their tender bodies and permit them to perform certain duties.

Of course, though it was amazing to me at first, there are no real family ties and no such things as love or marriage. The males and females perform equal work and are on perfect equality and merely mate at the call of nature for the purpose of propagating the race. At one time, I understand, the beings mated for life and reared their own eggs and young, but the females gradually rebelled at being forced to take no part in the industries and being compelled to devote their time to domestic duties, and the rulers, finding that the race was dying out through neglect of eggs and young; and that countless numbers of the dissatisfied females produced no offspring, were compelled to accede to the females' demands and take over all eggs and young as government wards. This soon led to the females refusing to mate for any considerable length of time, and gradually all family relations were done away with. Also, this led to the necessity of the government predetermining the life and occupation of each young individual, and of destroying thousands of eggs each season. In the old days the young of an artizan or a miner became miners or artizans and inherited many of their parents' traits, while the fact that the females were obliged to rear their own young resulted in limited numbers of progeny. But with the new order of things it was impossible to say who were the parents of the accumulated eggs, and released from all care the females produced far greater numbers of eggs than could be raised without overcrowding the country.

Also, I am told, the females in former times were quite distinct from the males both in physical and mental characters. They were smaller, weaker and more delicate and were quiet, docile and somewhat affectionate. But now I find that it is with the utmost difficulty that the two sexes can be distinguished and that if anything, the females are the larger, stronger and more hardy of the two. Indeed, I was amazed to find that most of the soldiers or police, as well as many of the miners and laborers were females, and, so I was told, whatever troubles or dissentions had arisen were always caused by the aggressive females.

Indeed, I was informed confidentially that the rulers had decided to limit the number of females and were surreptitiously destroying all female young not absolutely necessary for the propagation of the race. This was a most difficult matter, for several members of the government were females and they were anxious to increase the numbers of their sex until all power should be in female hands. To destroy a young creature after it had emerged from the egg unless it is malformed, is a most serious crime and hitherto no one had been able to distinguish a male from a female egg. But, so I was told, one of the greatest chemists or scientists had discovered a means of determining the egg sex and fortunately this scientist was a male. The secret had been assiduously kept from reaching the females and so when eggs were to be destroyed the males could select the female eggs for destruction.

Another rather astounding trait that I discovered was that these creatures are stone deaf when their skins are first shed and that their ears are quite useless until they have placed small pebbles within them.

Whether the presence of these stones enables them to communicate with one another, and with me, without sounds, I cannot say, but it is such a remarkable habit that I feel sure it must have some bearing on the matter. (See footnote by Dr. Lyman).[1]

This habit and their habit of shedding led to a most amusing incident soon after my arrival in this place. Feeling in need of a bath I made my way to the lake, and disrobing, plunged into the water. As I emerged I found a group of the creatures gathered about my ragged clothing and examining the garments with the greatest interest and evident excitement. Then they insisted upon feeling of my naked body and expressed the greatest amazement that I had changed so greatly in appearance. But they were still more amazed when I again put on my clothes. Then one of the beings brought several pebbles which he—with kindly intentions no doubt—tried to insert in my ears. It was with the greatest difficulty that I prevented this and when the creatures found that I could hear without the bits of stone they were absolutely dumbfounded. Neither could they understand—and cannot to this day—why I should not be able to remain under water for hours and crawl about on the bottom as they do.

But to return to their lives and habits. The government, as I have called it, is not like anything on our part of the earth. There are to be sure certain members of the race to whom I have referred as rulers, but they are not rulers in the ordinary sense. The government, if such it may be called, consists of a great number of individuals chosen by the inhabitants to perform certain duties.

Thus one lot had charge of the eggs, another regulates the production of metal, another looks after the food supplies, another has charge of the buildings and so on. Each community appoints a certain number of the members of each of these groups, and those appointed cannot do anything nor make any rules or decisions without the knowledge and consent of the communities from which they are appointed.

Moreover, as these regulators or committeemen, as I may call them, are reared from the eggs with the sole purpose of fulfilling such duties, they have no other objects or purposes in life and carry out their duties honestly and to the best of their abilities.

(Foot note by Dr. Lyman)

It is apparent that Mr. Bishop's studies along the lines of science and zoology had not brought to his attention the well known fact that many if not all crustaceans possess this same habit. Indeed, our common decapods—lobsters and crabs—are almost helpless and appear to lack the sense of direction and the power of definite movements and hearing until tiny grains of sand had been inserted in their ears.

Possibly, in the super-developed crustacean-like creatures Mr. Bishop describes, the pebbles in the ears have some bearing upon their strange means of inter-communication, acting possibly as sensitive detectors to vibratory waves or as sound amplifiers to make the waves audible. Mr. Bishop also forgot, or was not aware, that the higher vertebrates and even human beings possess small bones or bony objects in the ears. The exact use of these has never been definitely ascertained, although it is known that they control the sense of balance, but it is not impossible that they also serve to pick up inaudible waves and thus give human beings and other mammals a sense of direction or the "sixth sense" so much more developed in some individuals than others. It is even within the bounds of possibility that the inexplicable feats of mental telepathy and mind reading may depend upon the development or sensitiveness of these ear bones. —A.E.L.

Each one is delegated to his post for life, and if he or she fails to carry out his or her duties, or in any way disobeys the orders of the community, dire punishment results.

In former times this was death, but the beings, though so heartless and cold blooded in many ways, have done away with the death penalty now and have hit upon a far more sensible plan which would be a credit to human beings. To destroy life, they argue, is, if the being is healthy and uninjured, a loss to the community and necessitates a vast amount of time and trouble in fitting another to take the place of the individual destroyed. So, instead of killing offenders, the violator of law or customs is sent to a far distant part of the country which is devoted entirely to such offenders, and there is forced to rely upon his or her own resources to live and succeed. It is in this way that all the communities are first established. These convict colonies, as I might call them, are under the supervision of the chief settlement and each year are inspected.

If all is going well a certain number of the young of both sexes and different professions is alloted to them, while if matters are not being carried out satisfactorily the colony is broken up and the members divided among other new colonies in still more isolated parts of the land.

Moreover, any disturbances or troubles which may arise or any rebellions against the authorities, are quickly quelled without loss of life or bloodshed. This is done by simply turning off the power in the community where the trouble occurs, and, without the power from the great central station, the beings are utterly helpless. They cannot have light, cannot prepare food, cannot use their airships and cannot exist for any length of time.

I have spoken of the soldiers or police, and have said that as there is no further need for them they are being given up, and that no new members of the force are being raised. Wars among themselves are things of the distant past and the only use for the police today is to regulate sanitary and other rules and to act as escorts or guards and to prevent injuries in crowds or through accidents. But such things are now so rare and the beings are so well trained and so careful to follow out all rules and regulations, which they make themselves, that the police have little to do. Indeed, I was told that the occasion of my arival was the first time that this body had been called out in more than twenty years.

I have so often spoken of things occurring in years past or of happenings ages ago that a word of explanation is necessary. There is, I found, a group of the creatures whose sole duty is to keep the history and records of the country and its denizens. These records are never written, but are retained in the minds of the historians. And, incredible as it may appear, so long have these beings been trained to this one duty that their power to remember the most minute details is simply amazing. They know nothing else to be sure, and are almost too helpless even to move or feed themselves, for every sense is devoted to storing away facts for future reference. Of course one would think that there must come a time when the historical facts would become so numerous that no brain could hold them, but this is overcome in a very clever manner.

No one member of the historian group is expected to remember more than a certain number of facts, or more than a certain number of different facts. Each member retains facts of his own particular class which cover a certain period so that these beings are like a number of volumes. Each year the number of historians in each class is increased by two, or, as I might say, the living volumes of the nation's history are added to annually, one of the new members of each class absorbing and memorizing all the data of the oldest historian in his class, while the other new member of each class memorizes every event in his line which occurs during the year following his appointment. Thus the material known to the older members is always duplicated in a young new member and cannot be lost if the former dies or meets with an accident, while new events are recorded on fresh brains without adding to the burden on the older ones. At the present time there are approximately twenty-thousand of these living volumes of history and by means of calculations—which I found far more involved than working out a ship's position by stars—I found that the history thus available covers a period of about thirty-two thousand years, for in earlier days the new members were not appointed annually. Of course it is a rather difficult matter to look up any certain fact with such a mental history to refer to, but the fact that each class or line of incidents is in the mental charge of separate beings renders it more easy. Thus there are beings who know nothing of history with the exception of industrial events, others know only those occurrences related to politics, others to inventions, others to wars and still others whose minds are filled with facts and data regarding scientific matters.

But as I have said before there is no such time as years as we know them, all time being divided or calculated from generation to generation, but as the new broods of the creatures arrive very nearly a year apart—as nearly as I can figure it out—their computation of time corresponds roughly with our years. And now, while I think of it, let me mention a most remarkable thing which attracted my attention from the first, but which remained a mystery to me for a

291

long time. I mentioned that when I first reached the land I noted an intense blue quality to the light, and after my first amazement at the strange inhabitants and my confusion at my surroundings had passed, I noticed that there was no night. At first I thought that I was mistaken in this and that I had merely slept the twenty-four hours through, but I soon discovered that darkness never descended on this land, and that bright light streamed steadily from the sky. I had thought this was most amazing and that the sun always shown. But I soon found that this was not the case, and that there were streamers of light like the aurora which, however, remained steadfast and like great bands of blinding flame constantly shedding their light upon the place. Moreover, these bands gave, as I have said, a blue or rather violet light, but whether this was the actual color of the light itself or was due to some peculiarity in the atmosphere I have never learned.

I feel sure, however, that this ceaseless daylight and the fact that the warm and balmy climate never varies ten degrees, was the cause of all animal life growing to huge proportions, and also aided the strange crustacean-like beings to reach such a high state of development. It also accounted for their dwelling being underground, while the blue quality of the light was, I found, an important factor in many things. Later, as I shall explain, I discovered that without it many remarkable things were impossible. But I am digressing and must return to the subject of inhabitants, although it was the fact that the light had a great influence on them that caused me to make a note of the double suns and the light at this point of my narrative.

I stated that each class of the inhabitants was distinct, and that the appendages of a miner, artizan, chemist, etc., were adapted to the duties of each, and yet I soon found that the newly hatched young were all identical. Moreover, they bore no slightest resemblance to the adults. They were, in fact, pulpy, soft, misshapen things with immense goggle eyes, spiny heads, and with slender, worm-like, naked bodies bearing ten little flipper-like appendages. A few hours after hatching out they shed their skins and altered in appearance, and every day or two thereafter, their shells were cast, and with each sheding they became more and more like the full grown creatures. But during this period between hatching and full development, they could be incredibly altered or changed by being fed with certain foods or chemicals and by being exposed to certain forces, or I might say rays, produced by combinations of the black mineral and sulphur compounds. Thus, if a batch of young is selected to be chemists they are specially treated as soon as hatched, and each time their skins are cast their appendages become more and

292

more like those of the chemists, until when fully developed, they are perfectly adapted to their predestined trade.

I must not forget, too, to call attention to the fact that there are no rich or well-to-do members of the community, that is, in the way that we understand riches. Some of the beings have more luxurious homes than others, some seem more brilliantly garbed, and some possess air ships while others do not. But anyone may if he or she desires, have as much as any of the others. It is all a matter of wishes and personal tastes, for the resources of the entire country are equally at the disposal of all. Not that any inhabitant can demand a luxurious home, magnificently colored garments and a huge airship. Whatever is allowed the being is his or her just dues as a pro-rata share of all and if a taste runs to airships rather than luxuries at home, the individual can follow his or her taste in the matter. All power, light and sustenance are however equally divided and there is no such thing as money or trade. Services are the only values here, and as each trade or profession is predetermined, all services are accounted of equal value and there are no social cliques or lines and no aristocracy. A miner or laborer is equal in every way to one of the rulers or the guardians of the community, and is entitled to an equal share in everything needed.

But the large ships, such as the one in which I had traveled across the sea to the city, were I found community craft. They are, so to speak, government airships and constantly patrol the entire country, or are used in carrying workers to far distant places and distributing necessities and supplies among the inhabitants. They are the only means of transportation and I was amazed that these beings should have invented such marvelous craft and yet know nothing of railways, motor cars, or in fact any form of wheeled vehicle. But I discovered, a short time ago, why this is so, and my discovery was, in many ways, far more astonishing than anything I had learned since reaching this remarkable land.

CHAPTER 7

find, that for some reason, I have become greatly changed since reaching this strange country. I have become philosophical, or perhaps I might better say pessimistic, and I have spent many hours pondering on matters to which, hitherto, I gave no thought. I have wondered why these beings exist, why they toil and labor and progress, and what part they play in the scheme of this universe. When I have asked what object they had in view, why they strove, I have been told that it was for the good of the race, for the benefit of the nation, for the future of their kind. Exactly the same answers that I have heard to similar queries from humans. But what I have wondered, is that good, that benefit, that future? Meaningless words, I think. Here are these creatures, laboring that they may live, living that they may labor,—in an endless circle. To be sure they have advanced in some ways far beyond my fellow men, and no doubt will advance still more, but of what avail? They are but giant crustaceans after all, and they hatch from eggs, toil through life at the tasks to which they are trained, and come to their death and are forgotten after their brief span of life has been spent, and the world knows not even that they exist. And on the other side of the world, in the land of men, human beings are born, labor and die utterly unknown to these beings. What does it all mean; what place has it all in the scheme of the Universe, I wonder? And when I think on such matters I feel that after all my life is of little moment, that though I am here and my lot is cast among such weird beings, it makes no difference to the world or to the future, for I am but an atom of the whole, one of countless millions of cogs in the gigantic wheel of nature. And while I cannot fathom the riddle of life yet I feel that I must have my place in the whole, that Fate has seen fit to place me here and that, even if all the puny efforts of men and of these creatures seem to lead nowhere, yet must each one of us, and of them, be as essential to the machinery of the Universe as any cog in a real wheel, and without which the whole vast mechanism would jar and jolt and go wrong. So, instead of brooding upon my lot and spending my time vainly wishing to regain my fellow men, I have become resigned.

But I can find no affection, no liking, no fellow feeling for these beings. They have treated me kindly, my every want is provided for, and I occupy a far more important place than ever I could have filled in my world. And in brains, in attainments and in many other ways these beings are even more human than human beings. Yet so strongly influenced are we by physical appearances that to me these creatures are still but beasts and I feel apart from them and with little in common. It is perhaps akin to the feeling that one race of human beings has for another, the same feeling that prevents the white and black races from thorough sympathy and understanding, and that creates prejudices and ill feelings in the nations of the world I knew.

And another thing. These beings, though so intelligent, so industrious, so far advanced, are such brainless, silly creatures! Though they toil and work feverishly and seem to have no idle moments to spare, yet they will cease all, will drop everything and gather in crowds for the most trivial reasons. Yes, even without a reason. Let one of the scurrying, hurrying workers stop and gaze about and instantly a crowd collects, all gazing in the same direction, though there is nothing unusual to be seen, and quite forgetting the tasks on which they were sent. And they are childish to a degree. The simplest, most nonsensical things will fascinate them to such an extent that everything is at a standstill.

Wishing to find exercise and recreation I devised a set of ninepins and a ball, and at sight of these, the throngs grew wildly excited. They gathered about, waving their antennae, turning their long-stalked eyes about, dropping everything, and for an entire day practically all work was abandoned while the beings amused themselves with my crude toys. Tossing a ball and catching it, spinning a top, and a score of other simple amusements, proved equally exciting and interesting to the beings, and the rulers begged me to confine my activities at such things to recreation hours for fear a great calamity might result.

But after all in such matters they are much like men and I wonder if the planets are inhabited and if their denizens also possess similar characteristics and peculiarities.

All this, however, is leading me from the course of my narrative. I have mentioned that I discovered why the beings had no vehicles, save airships, and why, though they were so far in advance of human science, they apparently knew nothing of many of our most useful and important every day matters and inventions.

It came about in this way.

I was seated upon the shores of the lake and gazing across its broad and tranquil surface towards the dim and distant mountain ranges. Sailor-like my mind turned to boats. What a pleasure it would be, I thought, to have some good craft in which to sail those waters, to go where I willed and to explore the shores. I had traveled much

295

in the beings' airships, but I could not handle the contraptions and I longed for the feel of a keel under my feet. And why shouldn't my desires be satisfied? To be sure, I knew that to secure wood to build a boat was out of the question; but there was the metal sulphur. This could be made in thin sheets and a metal boat could be constructed. But then, I thought, how would I manage to make the creatures understand what I wanted? And even if I did could they bend and form and rivet the plates? Then a brilliant idea came to me. Why shouldn't the boat be fashioned of one single piece, moulded or cast into form? It could be. And thus made it would be stronger and better in every way than if built up of plates. Strange that I had not thought of it sooner. The airships' hulls were thus formed and I had only to make a model of the craft I wished in order to have the creatures turn out a seamless metal boat of incredible lightness and strength. For a time, however, even the simple matter of the model puzzled me until it occurred to me to make this from a very thin sheet of metal which, after considerable trouble, I pounded and bent into the desired shape.

The result of my work, and my efforts to make the artizans grasp my ideas, was a boat about eighteen feet in length and five feet beam drawing about three feet aft. I cannot say the lines of the craft were beautiful and I had no expectation of finding her speedy, but she was staunch and buoyant and I thoroughly enjoyed fitting her up. Metal tubes were used for mast and spars, twisted fibre or yarns of the same material as the beings used for their textiles formed ropes and lines, and the sails were made of the same fabric. All the time I was working the creatures regarded my labors with intense interest, though at an entire loss to know what I was about. But of all things the tackle and blocks seemed to fascinate them the most. And when at last my craft was ready and I hoisted sails, and grasping the tiller, trimmed the sheets and sped off with a fresh breeze, the creatures went almost mad with excitement. Here, indeed, was a strange condition of affairs. Beings who had gone far beyond man's dreams in accomplishments, who had conquered the air and yet knew nothing of boats or of sails and had never even seen blocks and tackle.

Of my cruises in the craft I need say little. In her I navigated the chain of great lakes or inland seas, visiting out of the way spots and landing on the very place where I had first thrown myself upon the beach to drink the water after my terrible journey. Here I again attempted to scale the mountains as have already mentioned. But either the climate or the air had affected me, for before I had ascended half way to the summits of the ridge I was utterly spent and was forced to retrace my steps. This was a great blow to me for I had hoped that sooner or later I would be able to make my way back over the mountains to the Antarctic and that I thus might rejoin my fellow men. The perils I knew were terrible and there was not one chance in a million of my succeeding, but even this slim chance was I felt better than to remain forever among the weird beings. Even when I found it impossible I was not utterly discouraged. Possibly, I thought, there might be lower spots in the mountain range, but in the the end I found that the country was completely girded by towering mountains and that the spot where I had crossed was the only point where such a crossing had been possible. But all this is apart from what I was about to set down. On my explorations, however, I found that which had a direct bearing upon my discovery as to why most simple mechanical devices were unknown to the creatures. In one spot I discovered a vast deposit of coal, in another quantities of copper, and I also found iron, silver, gold and many other metals and minerals. Oddly enough, too, the ores seemed to have been mined, for there were yawning openings filled with debris which appeared to be old shafts and tunnels, and yet I knew the beings used none of the metals nor coal. But the discovery of the latter started a new train of thought in my mind. Could I not equip my craft with power and thus be able to cruise about more rapidly and without being dependent upon the wind? Of course I might have induced the creatures to supply me with the strange invisible power they utilized, but somehow, I longed for familiar things, for devices with which I was acquainted, and I cannot hope to express the great comfort and happiness I found in my little boat. Moreover, I felt the necessity of keeping hands and mind busy and so I at once decided to try my mechanical skill at designing and building a small steam engine. Of course my knowledge of machinery was limited, but I knew the principles of steam and steam engines, and after weeks of weary work and innumerable disappointments I managed to turn out a crude sort of affair which actually worked. To be sure it was far too cumbersome and heavy, not to mention its small power, for my craft, but once having mastered the affair I felt that a second attempt would prove far easier and more satisfactory than the first.

But the creatures, who had watched every step of the work, showed indescribable excitement as the smoke rose from the funnel and the steam hissed and the fly wheel revolved. From far and near they flocked, more excited than I had ever seen them, and I realized how Watt or Fulton or other great inventors must have felt when at last they proved that their theories were right and had demonstrated to a wondering multitude that steam could be harnessed and made to serve man.

And then came an astounding discovery. The rulers wished to take possession of my crude engine; not to operate it, but to place it in a special building, a sort of museum as I might say, as a prized treasure. This was, I considered, not unnatural, but when one of the historians—he who held the most ancient records of the race,— explained that in the dim history of the past the beings had made and used such things, I was absolutely dumbfounded. No one, he informed me, had ever seen the machines; they were merely tradition and were considered fabulous, and all unwittingly I had materialized something which by them was regarded very much as we regarded relics of the Pharaohs or of our prehistoric ancestors. Then the living volume of the nation's history went on to explain that legendary lore had it that the creatures' ancient forebearers had possessed many other strange and unknown devices and I was asked if I could not also make some of these as fellow exhibits in the historiorical museum.

Here then I found myself suddenly transformed from a great inventor, proud of exhibiting my superior knowledge and mechanical ability, to a primitive being, a being out of the dim past, a member of a race whose greatest achievements had been known, used and discarded by these super-crustaceans so long ago that even history held no actual records of them. It was a great shock to my pride, but I was quite willing to busy myself at any work that would keep me occupied, even if it went only to prove how far behind the times I was, and soon I became vastly interested in the work and, by my efforts, reconstructing the forgotten past for the strange beings.

Among the first things that I built was a cart, and this amazed the creatures even more than the engine. To them wheels were most marvelous things, akin, I should say from their actions, to magic or witchcraft, and I racked my brains to puzzle out how it was that the wheel, which I had always considered man's most important mechanical invention, should have been discarded and forgotten by the lobster-like beings. Man cannot get on without the wheel. It is the foundation, the basis, of all industry, all machinery, all our most wonderful accomplishments. And yet, here was a nation of highly intelligent creatures, a race which had advanced immeasurably beyond humans in annihilating space and time, beings who had tapped the very source of nature's storehouse of power and who had made marvelous discoveries and never used a wheel in any form. To them the wheel was as obsolete and as useless as a stone axe or a flint knife to us, but instantly, as they saw wheels, they became fascinated with their uses and possibilities. Not that they were of any real benefit in their lives or occupations, but merely because they were strange, antique curiosities which afforded the beings new amusements and sports. Soon, carts or wagons were everywhere, and being most adaptable creatures, the inhabitants were not long in fitting the vehicles with power receivers and were rattling and bumping about in crude motor cars, or rather motor wagons, as pleased as a lot of kids with new toys.

I could not help thinking how this same power applied to modern automobiles would revolutionize motor cars in our world, and I fell to work with a will striving to construct some sort of car which would be an improvement over the solid wheeled, uncomfortable things the creatures were using. I cannot say that the result of my labors and inventive powers would have been a worthy rival even of a tin Lizzie, but it had a greater vogue among the beings than even Ford's famous product had among humans, and motoring became the favorite sport of the entire country. Incredibly swift airships were abandoned, save for utility and business, and just as we human beings—or a large number of us—prefer sail boats or rowing, or even the primitive savage canoe, to the steam or power boat when it comes to recreation, or choose a slow-going horse and carriage rather than a railway train or a motor car for pleasure, so they preferred the crude vehicles bumping over the earth to the silent, smooth sailing, meteor-like airships. I cannot describe, cannot hope to give a picture of the ridiculous, grotesque appearance the creatures presented in their new toys. And accidents were innumerable. Indeed, I believe it is the danger, the risk in using land vehicles, that appeals most strongly to the creatures. They seem to delight in collisions, in broken limbs, and are reckless beyond words. No doubt the dangers are a relief, for their airships are so constructed that accidents are next to impossible and collisions cannot occur, for there are devices which operate in such a way that if two ships come dangerously close the mechanisms automatically operate to repel each other.

Few fatalities have, however, resulted from the use of wheeled vehicles, but beings lacking one or more appendages or even antennae are seen everywhere. And they are marvelously expert in avoiding mishaps by a hair's breadth. Never have I seen such mad driving and the worst traffic jams of New York's thoroughfares are nothing compared with the congestion here in this metropolis of this strange land. And the wheels are used for many other amusements too. There are contraptions for which I am responsible which might be called bicycles, and hoop-rolling is a sport over which the beings grow as excited and become as interested as human beings over golf or tennis.

And of course, having seen the wonderful results of my efforts and my, to them, prehistoric knowledge, I tried my hand at a thousand

and one other matters. Bows and arrows were most astounding
things to these beings, and you can imagine my amazement when,
not content with using a single bow, these weird creatures armed
themselves with three bows at once and discharged a perfect hail of
arrows at the targets. What warriors they would make, I thought.
What unconquerable foes, with their ten appendages or limbs, eight
of which could be used for handling weapons. Each in fact would
equal eight men in one, and for the first time it dawned upon me
that herein was largely the secret of their great achievements, that
they had been able to accomplish eight times as much work as
humans, and I wondered what the results would have been had
Edison, Ford, Marconi or any of our great inventors and geniuses
been equipped by nature to do eight times the work they have done.

Their aptitude with such primitive weapons as bows and arrows
aroused my interest as to what they would do with firearms, and I
bent my energies and inventive powers to the task of making such
things. There was an abundance of sulphur, of course, saltpeter was
to be had and charcoal was not an impossibility, but it was a long
time before I succeeded in making a mixture that would do more
than sputter and burn. But at last I had an apology for gunpowder
and the rest was simple. I had a small cannon made, and having
loaded it and placed a sheet metal target before it, I touched it off.
My powder was poor, slow burning stuff, but it served to throw the
ball and made a respectable detonation, but I was greatly
disappointed at the effect upon the assembled creatures who had
gathered to watch the demonstration. The noise and smoke did not
surprise them in the least, but I might have foreseen this as they
possessed an explosive far more powerful than powder or even
dynamite. In fact it was all together too powerful for use in firearms,
as I discovered with almost fatal results to myself long before I tried
my hand at powder making. They examined the ragged hole torn by
the missile in the metal target and they showed some interest in this,
but their greatest wonder appeared to be that an explosive capable
of doing so much should have been confined in the metal barrel of
the gun. Aside from this, however, the whole experiment failed to
appeal to them. They had no use for such things as guns and
powder, no need of offensive or defensive weapons, and their own
explosive was a thousand times more valuable than powder for their
purposes.

And scores of other things which I made, after endless failures and
by dint of hardest work, were as useless to them as the cannon. And
then at last it came to me that in this strange place man's greatest
inventions, human beings' most marvelous labor-saving devices and
our most prized luxuries and conveniences had no place. That here

was a race or nation of beings where there was no struggle for supremacy, no real industry for personal gain, no riches, no poverty, no competition; that conditions, life, everything, were totally unlike those of my world and that these creatures, ages before my arrival, had passed the stage of human civilization and that to them our customs, habits and mode of life would appear as barbarous and primitive as those of the prehistoric cave dwellers to us.

There is no agriculture, so no demand for agricultural machinery. No vast transportation of foodstuffs and raw materials, for with power whenever required and food and all things needed—with the exception of sulphur—available anywhere, there is little to be carried and airships are all that are required. All resources are equally at the disposal of every member of the community and hence there is no struggle for existence or for wealth, and as every member of the nation is developed, trained and predestined, from the day of hatching, for some definite place in life, there is no ambition, no desire for advancement. In short these beings are mere automatons, machines endowed with life, intelligence and minds, and nothing more. They only differ from insensate mechanisms inasmuch as they have their times for rest and recreation, and I daily thank God that human beings have not yet come to such a pass.

Often, when among my fellow men, I have heard arguments and have read articles in favor of a communistic or socialistic life and government, and picturing the ideal Utopia that the earth would be if men could all be equal, if all wealth could be equally divided and there could be no class distinctions, no struggle for supremacy. Often, too, I have in the past felt that such a state would be desirable, and many a time, when fortune frowned upon me and I compared my lot as a sailor with the ease and luxury of wealthy passengers upon my ships, or with the rich ship owners, I have felt bitterness that some should be so favored and others forced to struggle through life in poverty. But now I realize what dire results would follow were these socialists' ideas fulfilled. Now I realize that there could be no ambition, no desire for betterment, no real happiness in life and no pride if such conditions prevailed. No, a thousand times no. Better dire poverty, unending toil, the abuses and vices, the wars and strife, all the wrongs and woes of mankind and civilization than to become the heartless, impersonal beings that such conditions would lead to. What would the world of men be without love, sentiment, art, music, affection, ambition? What would it be if the human race had no ideals beyond existence and the propagation of the species? What would it be if there was nothing to spur men on, to send them to sleep weary with the day's work but filled with dreams and visions of accomplishments on the morrow; to awaken

301

them filled with determination to succeed, to force their way to the top? What would life amount to if men had no aims, no ideals in life, no necessity to exert themselves, to prove superiority to their fellows, to force their individuality upon the world and to choose their path in life and to be independent, free, leading their own lives as they see fit and with no limit, save their own intelligences and their labors, to what they may accomplish?

It is this, this supposed idealistic sort of life of these beings that made me so heartily sick of my existence among them. Would that those who have found such fault with our civilization, who have endeavored to revolutionize human life and human ways, and to upset conditions that the Almighty in His infinite wisdom has established, might be here with me. Would that those socialistic agitators might be forced to exist here among these creatures.

Anything rather than this state of affairs. At times it seems as if I should go mad, and I find myself longing for something, anything, to upset this machine-like monotonous life about me. Anger, strife, battle—aye, even a war with all its horrors would be welcome.

Chapter 8

long time has passed since I penned my lines. And now I know that beyond question I am doomed to spend all my days among these weird beings. Over and over again I have attempted to find a way out, to discover a means of scaling the mountains, for desperation drove me, and death upon the ice-covered wastes of the polar regions seemed preferrable to life here. But though strong, healthy and as able-bodied as ever, yet, for some strange reason, I could not climb those cliffs. Perhaps it is the food or drink that has robbed me of the power to ascend even to moderate heights, perchance dwelling in this air with its unending blue light has had its effect, and like the creatures who dwell here, I cannot live where once I felt no ill effects. But whatever the reason, the fact remains that each time I have reached a height of a few hundred feet, my muscles have failed me, my strength has given out, and I have been forced to give up. I am as hopelessly caged here as though in a prison and yet the birds come and go at will and I envy them beyond words to express, as I watch the broad-winged albatrosses and great white molly-mokes and screeching gulls and know on their pinions they can rise above the surrounding mountains and leave this side of the world for the other that I shall never see again; that no doubt they gaze upon my fellow men, upon the wide blue sea, and upon white sailed ships and great palatial steamships with the same expressionless eyes they turn upon me and upon the beings dwelling here in this undreamed-of land.

To one of these free winged creatures, these friends of old who come over the edge of the world each year, I shall soon entrust this narrative. Perchance it may never reach a human being. The bird may meet with disaster or it may never look on a civilized man. Or again, even though scores, hundreds, of my fellow men see the creatures, yet it may pass unnoticed and the message may not be read. But there is a chance that, with the metal cylinder, in which I shall place my story, dangling from its leg, the albatross will attract the attention of some one. Perhaps its nesting ground may be near some party of whalemen, or even near a settlement, and it is this chance I cling to. I have no fear that the cylinder will become detached or even broken, despite the rough treatment it will no doubt receive, and even if the bird is not found or the cylinder discovered for years, it and its contents will be intact. I have selected the toughest and hardest of the many varieties of metal for the cylinder, a metal which is far harder than steel and which can be opened or broken only by tremendous force or by a heat greater than fire, and I have used a transparent grade of the metal in order that any one finding it may see that it contains a manuscript, for I well know how curious human beings are to read any scrap of writing that is picked up in a floating or stranded bottle. The cylinder being air tight will preserve the manuscript, and the writing is done with a fluid I found among the waste or by-products of the sulphur factory. It is indelible and will not fade, while the cord by which I shall attach the cylinder to my bird messenger is of the toughest woven metal and cannot be severed by any ordinary means.

And what if my narrative is found and read? Will any mortal man believe it? Will the finder, if finder there be, credit such a story as will be disclosed? No, I suppose not. It is too incredible, too ridiculous to pass as anything more than fiction or the ramblings of a disordered mind. They will think the writer crazy, a madman who has been set down the delusions of his brain, or will think some one is trying to perpetrate a gigantic hoax.

But again, perhaps, if God wills, my narrative may fall into the hands of some person who will be attracted by the strangeness of its container. The transparent metal cylinder will perhaps arouse curiosity, the material on which it is written may give credence to my tale. And if so, then will it be known beyond a doubt that it is no wild fancy, no product of a crazy man; for nowhere in the world of men are such materials known. Often I smile to myself to think what a sensation will be created when the newspapers print accounts of the discovery of the strange manuscript in a still more remarkable container. No doubt, in that case, my story will be read by thousands, perhaps millions of my fellow men. And yet, the cylinder in which I send it may prove of greater interest and value to the world than my story. I can picture the scientists' excitement as they analyze the metal and discussions grow hot as to its origin, while inventors strive to produce the same material for the benefit of mankind.

Such thoughts are a diversion and a comfort to me, and many hours I spend trying to picture in my mind the results of my story and its effect upon the world in case it ever reaches civilized men.

But I must cut short my imaginings, my hopes and fears, for it is all aside from my tale and I must confine myself to the story of my life here on this unknown, mountain-walled continent among these weird beings.

* * *

Since I last took up my manuscript to write, many events have occurred, but that which is of greatest importance, though the creatures here make little of it, is the escape of the captive ants from the zoo wherein they were confined.

To me there is something threatening in this, and I cannot rid myself of a feeling of a dire calamity impending. Always I had been fascinated by the gigantic insects, and hours after hours I have spent, watching them as they labored and rushed about, drilling, carrying on strange evolutions, marching and countermarching, seemingly aimlessly, within their fenced enclosure.

That they could escape, no one dreamed; for as I have said, they were hedged in by network of material fatal to them. But escape they did, and not an ant remains within the pen nor was there a dead ant to tell of the insects having touched the death dealing netting. No, they had been far too intelligent for that, and their apparently aimless labors had been but a clever ruse, a means of concealing their true purpose of tunneling to great depths and, by means of an unsuspected subterranean passage, vanishing, no one knows where. And I feel sure that their constant drilling, their military-like actions, were no more purposeless than their work. To be sure they are few— not more than two hundred at most—and the inhabitants have no fears. They assure me that the ants will soon be recaptured, that in airships these beings can locate the fugitives and either take or destroy them, and that, even if such means fail, the ants may be destroyed by scattering the deadly compound about their haunts and by preventing them from securing food.

Moreover, they point out, the ants are few and are no menace unless in vast numbers, and that long before they can increase enough to be dangerous they will again be under control.

But I cannot put aside my fears, my premonitions. Who can say where the ants have gone? Who can say what their numbers may be? For all anyone knows they may have been increasing by thousands beneath the earth, may have been waiting for months or years until they had reared a horde of their kind in the dark, unseen passages underground. And their strength, activity and tirelessness, are prodigious. One of the great insects has the strength of a score of men or the muscular powers of several giant lobster-like beings. And they multiply with amazing rapidity. Even now they may number countless thousands, may be biding their time in some hidden subterranean lair, storing food, making plans, drilling; only waiting for the time when they will be ready and prepared to overwhelm the country with their armies. And the strangest part of it is that such thoughts should trouble me. Why should it matter to me whether these lobster-like beings or the giant ants are in supremacy. Why should I care what takes place in this country in which I have no interest and which I have grown to hate and detest? It is not fear of personal injuries or death, but I shudder at the thought of being made captive or being destroyed by the ants, for death I feel, might prove better than a life among these creatures. I have tried to analyze my feelings, to fathom the cause of my worries and, though it sounds ridiculous, though even to me it seems impossible, yet I feel sure that it is due to a sense of patriotism.

Patriotism for a land that is my prison, for a race of beings with whom I have nothing in common! And yet it is so. Although I chafe at my enforced life here, although I long to be away from the country and its denizens, although their life, ways and personalities are all repugnant to me, yet such a strange thing is the human mind that I feel as greatly concerned over the impending danger as if these beings were of my own race and it was my own country.

Yes, and if it comes to battle, to a war between the ants and these supercrustaceans, I know in my heart that I shall find myself battling against the ants, using my every effort to aid these monstrous beings in overthrowing their hereditary enemies.

Little did I dream, when I wrote, months ago, that even war would be welcome, how soon my words were to be borne out, for war, bloody, merciless, relentless and horrible beyond words to express is, I feel sure, near at hand.

* * *

A month or more has passed since last I wrote, and, during that interval events have moved rapidly. The ants have been discovered. Scouts have found them, and my worst fears have been more than fulfilled. In incalculable thousands they are swarming on a vast uninhabited area in the north, drilling, gathering vast stores and evidently preparing for a campaign. And yet these beings are not disturbed, have no fears and have made little effort to repel or destroy their enemies. From airships quantities of the death dealing chemicals were dropped upon the ants but with little result. A few were killed but instantly the alarm was given and the ants vanished like magic, seeking safe refuge in subterranean burrows. I have urged these creatures to set forth and attack, to take the offensive against the ants, to drop explosives from airships and thus shatter the burrows and destroy the occupants. And I have sought to induce them to surround themselves with barriers of the ant poison. But my words have been unheeded so far. So long have these creatures lived in peace, so long have they been in complete control, and so many years have passed since they battled with the ants that they have forgotten the terrible power and resources of their enemies and underrate them. Too late, I feel, will they awaken.

But I have not been idle. With the aid of a few who have given ear to my advice I have taken what steps we can to protect the city. We have laid mines about it which can be exploded, and in two airships we have attempted to destroy the ants' retreats with explosive, but our puny efforts have been of little avail. Moreover, in our last assault, one of the airships was disabled by a premature explosion and fell to earth, and I shudder as I write when I think of the awful scene I witnessed when the ants rushed upon the occupants of the airship and with ravenous jaws tore them in pieces while still alive.

And if the ants are victorious that will be the fate of all, yes even of myself. But I have no mind to meet with such a fearful death. I have provisioned my boat and if worst comes to worst I shall flee in her. Across the water the ants cannot follow and miles distant I know of a large island where I shall seek safety—there to pass the remaining days of my life alone.

A week since I wrote those last lines. The ants are advancing now. Already they have overwhelmed two outlying towns and against them the poison and even the explosives seem useless. Slowly but inexorably they come, making their way by underground passages, scurrying to safe retreats far under the earth at first sight of an airship. It is terrible, nightmarish, this invisible, silent advance of the vast hordes of terrible creatures, and the inhabitants are now terror stricken.

Barriers of the poison have been passed by the ants tunneling beneath them; hundreds of the inhabitants of the countryside have fallen victims to the relentless insects, and each day their numbers increase and they draw nearer to this metropolis.

They are within a few miles of the power plant and at any moment may take possession of the sulphur mines. And then the doom of the beings will be sealed. Without resources, without power, all will be helpless, doomed to perish miserably or become prisoners of the ants. And there is no retreat. The insects have overrun the land, have thrown out great encircling armies and our scouts report them on every side.

And now a new and more terrible thing has occurred. The ants are swarming. Their queens, winged and capable of flight, are filling the air, darkening the skies and dropping here, there, everywhere to establish new colonies. Hundreds of them have even dropped within the city and although they have been destroyed yet their numbers seem undiminished. Unseen, they drop at night, hurrying to hidden spots they deposit their eggs, and ere their presence is suspected the warriors have emerged and fall upon the surprised inhabitants and tear them to bits. In their extremity the creatures have besought me to equip them with bows and arrows, guns, anything in the form of weapons. And these have helped. With their arrows, with the bullets from the crude firearms, they have managed to keep the ant army in check, for these are things new to the ants and they have no means of resisting them. Desperate as our case is, yet I have smiled to think how history repeats itself, how these beings have been forced to resort to prehistoric, primitive means to preserve their homes and lives, just as the armies of Europe, despite modern weapons, high explosives, poisonous gases and every latest scientific device, were forced to resort to armor, grenades, medieaval weapons and methods to combat the Germans.

And even the wagons, the motor vehicles, have been brought into play against the ants, for the airships are next to useless. Let an airship rise aloft and the swarming queen ants light upon it by hundreds and bear it to earth with their weight, but the wheeled vehicles, protected, transformed to miniature forts of metal and filled with armed beings, carry terror and destruction among the ants, crushing them beneath the wheels while arrows and bullets strike them down.

But despite all I feel that we are losing, that our efforts have been made too late and that at any moment the horde of insects will overwhelm the power plant and we will be incapable of making food, of producing light, of manufacturing anything, even of operating our vehicles. Long have I foreseen this and in preparation for the calamity I have had steam engines built, but these are all too few to serve all our wants. Would that these beings had but given heed to my words long ago and then all might have been well. Too long they waited and then panic stricken turned to me begging me to take charge, beseeching me to save them. The fate of the country, of the inhabitants depends upon me but I feel that no human efforts, nothing that these beings under my directions can accomplish, will do more than delay the end.

* * *

What I dreaded most has befallen. The ants are in possession of the power plant. Everything is at a standstill. Only the barest necessities of life can be produced with the puny, limited power of my machines, the ancient antiquated mechanisms discarded ages ago by these beings, but what now, when all their marvelous inventions have failed them, are proving their salvation, their one hope.

And it is but a forlorn hope. We are besieged encompassed, surrounded, and each day the encircling cordon is drawing irresistibly nearer.

I fear even to wait longer to entrust this manuscript to a bird. If I wait it may be too late, so tomorrow I shall enclose it in a metal cylinder and shall lash it to the leg of a great albatross I have captured.

And I am ready to flee, to take to my boat. Each day, each hour, the inhabitants are deserting the city. They are taking to the water, are reverting to the habits of their long forgotten ancestors, are becoming crustaceans once more, and forgetting all their great works, all their civilization, all their evolved mentalities, are seeking the depths of the lake and reverting to a submarine life. Perchance ere the city falls all the beings will have forsaken the life they have led for generations, and in the water and the slime beneath it, will have found safety and there will forget all and will degenerate to the lobsters from which they rose. 'Tis a strange, a bizarre thought, but man, in time of dire extremity, when overwhelmed and destroyed, has more than once reverted to savagery and every great nation has fallen, so perhaps 'tis but the law of nature, the working out of God's plan——.

I am about to close, to seal my manuscript to send it out to the world, and I must make haste. Scarcely a dozen of the inhabitants are left. All but these have deserted. Within the hour the ants will overwhelm the city. I must hurry to my boat and escape ere it is too late.

Yes, even now they are coming. They are in the outskirts. Their hordes will cut off my retreat if I do not close at once. It is the end. My narrative must be sealed and entrusted to the albatross which for many weeks I have held captive and awaiting this time. God grant that it may reach the hand of some fellow man."

THE END

www.ingramcontent.com/pod-product-compliance
Lightning Source LLC
Chambersburg PA
CBHW031200020726
47499CB00002B/432